"Will you leave it ⬛⬛⬛⬛⬛⬛

The sharpness in his voice made her jump.

"I'm simply—"

He whipped around. "I said drop it!"

Suddenly Zoe understood. There, in the confines of his pickup, she saw what he hid beneath the layers of inapproachability.

Pain.

Not physical pain, like his hip. No, this kind of pain ran deeper and stronger. It was the kind of pain medicine couldn't help. The kind that ripped a man's insides apart.

Zoe's own insides hurt for him. "I'm sorry," she replied, meaning far more than her earlier intrusion.

She watched as he dragged a shaky hand across the back of his neck. Maybe it was her tone, or the fact that she'd apologized, but some of the edge left his voice. "I don't want to talk about it, okay?"

"Okay." She'd do what he wanted and let the subject drop. For now.

Dear Reader,

You won't find the tiny island of Naushatucket on any map. When my heroine decided to escape the world, she did so to an imaginary representation based on several local islands. However, while her home base might be a product of her imagination, the breathtaking views she sees from her rooftop aren't. In my opinion, Cape Cod and its islands have some of the most gorgeous ocean views in the world. Then again, being a lifelong Massachusetts resident, I might be a tad biased.

This book was a really hard book to write, mainly because I felt it so very important to portray Jake Meyers's experiences with dignity and realism. Hopefully I did him justice.

The more I got to know Jake, the more I also wanted to give him the happy ending he deserved. Enter Zoe Hamilton. She's not looking for love any more than Jake is. Who better to help a broken man heal than a woman who's dedicated herself to helping others? Of course, Zoe's got her own baggage— baggage she hopes to escape with a summer at the shore. And even though neither of them is looking for a relationship, they're about to find out fate thinks otherwise.

Finally, there's dear sweet Reynaldo. Zoe's beloved pet has trials of his own. I think reality was inspiring me. Turns out I have an even bigger soft spot for animals and sob stories than Zoe. I wrote this novel while nursing our own sick cat back from a brain infection.

I hope you enjoy Jake and Zoe's story. Please drop me a line at Barbara@barbarawallace.com and let me know. I love hearing your feedback.

Regards,

Barbara Wallace

BARBARA WALLACE
The Heart of a Hero

Harlequin®

TORONTO NEW YORK LONDON
AMSTERDAM PARIS SYDNEY HAMBURG
STOCKHOLM ATHENS TOKYO MILAN MADRID
PRAGUE WARSAW BUDAPEST AUCKLAND

Recycling programs
for this product may
not exist in your area.

ISBN-13: 978-0-373-17756-1

THE HEART OF A HERO

First North American Publication 2011

Barbara Wallace has been a lifelong romantic and daydreamer, so it's not surprising she decided to become a writer at age eight. However, it wasn't until a coworker handed her a romance novel that she knew where her stories belonged. For years she limited her dreams to nights, weekends and commuter train trips, while working as a communications specialist, PR freelancer and full-time mom. At the urging of her family, she finally chucked the day job to pursue writing full-time, and she couldn't be happier.

Barbara lives in Massachusetts with her husband, their teenage son and two very spoiled, self-centered cats (as if there could be any other kind). Readers can visit her at www.barbarawallace.com, and find her on Facebook. She'd love to hear from you.

To my editors—for being so patient while I worked to get this story just right

To the gals at the Medway Starbucks— for keeping me caffeinated at all hours of the day and night

And as always, to my boys Pete and Andrew— you're my heroes.

CHAPTER ONE

JAKE MEYERS woke with a start, the smell of blood and sulfur still in his nostrils, his eyes searching the shadows for enemies who minutes before had been crystal clear. Kicking off his sweat-soaked covers, he focused on his heart slamming against his ribs. He willed his breathing to slow like they showed him in the hospital. Slow and easy. In. Out. Until the steady intake of air filling his lungs erased the sounds of screams.

Damn. After three and a half weeks without a nightmare, he'd thought they were behind him. No such luck.

With a ragged breath, he looked at the clock on his nightstand, ignoring the shudder triggered by the crimson glow. Five-fifteen. Well, at least this time it was close to dawn. His hip throbbed. The pain always flared more following a nightmare. If he were inclined to examine the reasons, he was sure he'd find some psychosomatic component, but in fact the reasons didn't really matter to him. Pain was pain. He grabbed the bottle of prescription painkillers off the nightstand and knocked over the photograph propped against the lamp as he did so. Reverently he put it back in place. The darkness obscured the image, but he didn't need light to see. He had the faces memorized. Every last one had been etched in his brain for eternity.

Hobbling into the kitchen, he saw a half pot of yesterday's coffee remained. Too tired and still too hazy from his dreams to make a fresh pot, he poured himself a cup and, as the liquid reheated in the microwave, stared out his back window. Outside, the island hung on the edge of morning, silent and gray, the world still except for the occasional screech of a gull diving toward the waves across the street.

And, of course, his thoughts. His thoughts were never silent.

The microwave beeped. Jake grabbed his coffee and stepped onto the back step, letting the overcast dampen his skin as he breathed in the silence. Dew dripped from the pine trees dotting his backyard, their green needles sparkling. A chipmunk poked its head out from beneath a root.

His purgatory shouldn't be so serene, he thought, not for the first time. As far as he was concerned, the world was wasting its early morning splendor on a dead man.

Give yourself time. That's what the doctors at the

VA hospital had told him. *Some wounds don't heal overnight.*

They were wrong, he thought, as he raised the cup to his lips. Some wounds don't heal at all.

"This hideaway of yours, does it have internet access?"

From behind her blue-rimmed glasses, Zoe Hamilton rolled her eyes. "Naushatucket's off the coast of Massachusetts, Caroline, not off the grid."

"If I can't read the label on a map, it might as well be." There was the muffled sound of a register on the other end of the phone. Caroline was out getting her midday latte. "Couldn't you hide out on one of the bigger islands, like Martha's Vineyard or Nantucket?"

"My family didn't own a rental property on Martha's Vineyard or Nantucket. Besides, isn't *remote* a hideout requirement?"

Judging from the extended sigh on the other end, her assistant disagreed. Zoe half listened to the noise while scanning the air around her. Caroline's check-in, though welcome, came at a bad time. "If you're worried about my column getting in on time, I have everything I need to work from here."

"I hope so. 'Ask Zoe's' readers will be distraught if they don't get regular posts from their favorite answer lady."

Answer fraud, more like. "Don't worry. They'll get their responses." Poor trusting saps.

A flash of black caught the corner of her eye; she spun around, eyes following the trajectory.

Success. Her target had landed. The rest of the phone call would have to wait. "I hate to hang up on you, Caroline, but unless there's anything else, I was in the middle of something when you called."

"Fine," Caroline replied with another dramatic sigh. "I know a brush-off when I hear one. Just promise me you won't spend all your time on that island crying your eyes out. That bastard isn't worth the effort."

"I won't." On that point, they both agreed. Thinking of Paul churned up a lot of responses these days, but tears weren't one of them. At least, not anymore.

After making a few additional promises, including assuring Caroline she wouldn't become a complete hermit, Zoe said goodbye and clicked off the phone. "Okay, Birdy, now it's your turn."

From its perch above the open sliding glass door, a swallow, her nemesis for the past half hour, stared back unflinchingly. The creature had been circling the room through her entire phone call, steadfastly ignoring the escape route Zoe had provided. Finally, the bird stopped to rest, giving Zoe her chance.

"I really don't know why you're being so stubborn."

She slipped off the silk scarf she'd been using to hold back her thick dark hair. Immediately a shock of bangs flapped over her glasses. She blew them out of her field of vision and took a step closer, careful not to move too quickly.

"The door is open. All you have to do is fly out and you'll be free."

Her plan was to wave the scarf, using the color and motion to steer the bird off the molding and out the patio door. The swallow, however, had a different plan and, as soon as Zoe lunged forward, decided to dart straight for her. Letting out a screech, Zoe ducked. The bird flew overhead, careening off a ceiling beam before knocking into the mantel and flying up the chimney.

Zoe rolled her eyes. "You've got to be kidding."

When she had first decided to hide out for the summer, buying her parents' Naushatucket property sounded exciting, romantic even. What better place to heal a broken heart than an isolated cottage by the sea? Visions of long reflective walks along the shore and cozy nights by campfires came to mind. Instead, she discovered that her mother had let the property deteriorate since remarrying. Her childhood vacation paradise had become a sorely neglected Cape house with dusty furniture and sand-crusted windows. Screenless windows, she might add, a fact she had discovered when she tried to clear the house of stale air. Enter Birdy, who apparently had been lying in wait for someone to open one of them.

Pushing her glasses back on the bridge of her nose, she knelt down on the hearth and readied herself for round two.

"It's not that I don't appreciate the company and all," she called up, "but Reynaldo and I weren't planning on sharing the house with a bird, and I'm guessing you're not keen on sharing with us. So what do you say you fly out the nice wide door I opened for you?"

Her answer was a panicked flutter of wings against brick.

"Fine. Don't listen to reason." Moving on to Plan B—or C as the case might be—she grabbed the poker from the fireplace set. A loud noise ought to do the trick. Reaching up into the flue, she rattled the poker back and forth. The commotion set off more fluttering, followed by a rustling sound. Zoe looked up.

A shower of creosote, dust and feathers rained down.

Soot covered her from head to toe, clinging to her sweaty skin like iron filings on a magnet. Dust filled her nose. Her mouth tasted like the inside of an ashtray. Coughing, she backed away into the fresh air. Meanwhile, the swallow continued flapping inside the chimney.

Great. This was what she got for trying to help. Hot, sweaty and soot-on. You'd think she'd learn.

"This isn't over, Birdy," she muttered. She reached for the abandoned scarf to clean off her glasses.

"Excuse me."

Zoe jumped. Either Birdy had some serious testosterone issues or she had a guest. A blur in the doorway told her the latter. Slipping her glasses back on, she saw a man standing in the doorway. Tall and lean, with ruddy, weathered skin, he wore the standard island old-timer uniform—faded jeans and an equally faded long-sleeve T-shirt.

He lifted a guilty-looking dachshund to eye level.

Zoe recognized the dog immediately. "Reynaldo! You're supposed to be sleeping in the kitchen."

"I found him digging around my backyard." From the look on his face, he wasn't happy about it, either.

"Sorry about that. He normally isn't a wanderer. Must be the new location." She moved to retrieve the squirming pooch from the stranger's grip before something else happened. "I'm Zoe Brodsk—I mean, Hamilton." She had to stop using her married name. "I just bought the place. I'd shake your hand, but as you can see…"

No need finishing the explanation; the soot spoke for itself. He didn't look like he wanted to shake her hand anyway.

Now that she had a closer view, she realized her neighbor was younger than her initial impression implied. Hair she'd mistaken for silver was really sun-bleached blond. And what she thought was aged ruddiness was really a series of pale scars, several small ones running across the bridge of his nose and one along the curve of his cheekbone. The most prominent was a deep mark that cut from his left temple to the center of his left brow, stopping just above a pair of hard, emerald eyes. Eyes whose intense gaze currently had her rooted to the spot.

Reynaldo squirmed in her arms, sniffing and trying to lick at her ash-covered cheeks. Since adding dog drool to her already filthy face wasn't on her to-do list, Zoe set him down. In a flash, the dachshund ran to the fireplace and began barking. His dancing around reminded her how she'd gotten soot-covered to begin with.

Turning back to her neighbor, she asked, "You don't know anything about capturing birds, do you?"

"Why, you got one of those that escaped while you weren't watching, too?"

"No." For the sake of neighborliness, she decided to ignore the comment. "I've got one stuck in my fireplace that needs rescuing."

He shoved his hands into his jeans pockets, a posture that accentuated a pair of long muscular arms. "How do you know?"

"That I have a bird in the chimney? I saw it fly up there." No need to add that she was the reason why.

"No, I mean how do you know it needs rescuing?"

"Because he's *stuck*. I can hear his wings flapping against the brick."

"Doesn't mean he wants your help."

Was this guy serious? "How else is he going to get free?"

"How about on his own?"

"You're assuming he's capable of freeing himself."

"You're assuming he isn't."

Zoe brushed at her bangs, more to prevent herself rolling her eyes than anything. Who cared what she was assuming? The poor bird needed her help. She wasn't getting into some pointless argument with a man who couldn't be bothered to introduce himself.

"Either way, I need to help this bird out," she said, dismissing the man. Hey, she was from the city; she could be as abrupt and unsocial as the next person. "Thank you for bringing Reynaldo home. I'll make sure he stays out of your backyard."

"Good."

Good. Not *thank you,* but *good.* Somebody needed to work on his people skills. Her "neighbor's" dearth of social graces, however, would have to wait. She had more important tasks to focus on. Assuming their conversation had ended, she returned her attention to the fireplace.

"Leave the room."

"Excuse me?" She frowned at the man from over her shoulder.

"Noise will keep the bird riled up," he replied. "Especially the barking. The two of you should leave. Once the room settles down, the bird will come out."

"What if it doesn't?" From the way the bird was flapping, it might beat itself to death before calming down. "What then?"

"Then I guess you'll find out the first time you light a fire."

Zoe's mouth dropped open. She whirled around to protest, but the stranger had already slipped out the door. So much for the friendly neighborhood welcome wagon. First time you light a fire, indeed.

"No way I'm waiting until the thing burns up in a fire to know if he escaped," she told Reynaldo. "He needs our help now."

With that, she grabbed the poker and readied for another round. "Time to come out, Birdy!" She clanged the poker around the chimney a second time. Then a third.

A loud rustling sound replied, followed by several high-pitched whistles. There was a rush of noise and the swallow came bombing out.

"Ha!" Triumphant, she wiped away the fresh

batch of soot with the back of her hand. The bird *had* needed her help. She watched as it circled the room once, then twice, before heading for the open patio door.

Where it promptly landed on the door-frame molding. In the exact place this rescue mission had begun.

Jake stomped across the yard, up his steps and straight to his refrigerator for a cold beer. Who cared if it was before noon? The day was already shaping up to be a damn lousy one, and that was before he found the dachshund digging around his yard.

He'd come to Naushatucket for solitude. Which was why living next to a rental property suited him just fine. Temporary vacationers seldom offered more than a wave and a nod, too busy cramming their visits with summer fun to attempt conversation. He didn't need a neighbor moving in with her pet and her cheery smile. Hopefully, she'd only stay the summer.

The letter he'd been reading was on the counter where he'd dropped it, the opening paragraph still visible.

Dear Captain Meyers,
As you may have read in the local paper, the Flag Day Committee is honoring our area heroes....

He crumpled the paper in his fist. Heroes, huh? Then they didn't need him.

Dear Zoe,
I'm in love with a man I work with. He's wonderful. Handsome, funny, smart. Problem is, no matter what I do, I can't get him to see me as anything more than the woman in the next office. I know if I can just get his attention, he'll see what a terrific match we would make. He's not dating anyone. In fact, I've overheard him complaining he can't find the right woman. What can I do to make him see the right woman is me?
Invisible

Dear Invisible,
What can I say? Guys are blind idiots. They can't see a good woman even if she's under their noses. And when they do meet the right girl, they'll treat her like dirt and dump her for the first blonde with big breasts that crosses the fairway. Might as well learn this now and save yourself the heartache. If you want love, get a pet.
Zoe

Zoe stared at the answer she just typed. Probably not the answer Invisible wanted to hear. After all, she was

Zoe of 'Ask Zoe,' the woman with all the answers on love and life. If only they knew. What was that old saying? Those who can't, write advice columns? She pressed Delete, erasing her bitter words from the screen if not from her heart.

Normally she didn't have a problem coming up with the kind of advice her readers wanted to hear, but tonight the answers wouldn't come.

Who was she kidding? The answers hadn't come for weeks. Not since Paul made a mockery out of every answer she ever gave.

Reynaldo barked. Zoe gave a smile and scooped him onto the sofa. "Good old Reynaldo. You'll always want me, right? We'll muddle through, you, me and the occasional stray bird."

It had taken thirty minutes, but the swallow finally flew the coop, disappearing while she was busy relocating Reynaldo to an upstairs bedroom. She swore the creature timed its exit specifically to spite her.

Now clean and tired, she lay wrapped in a fleece throw trying to keep the evening chill at bay. She'd forgotten how chilly island nights could be during the late spring. Come next month, heat and humidity would make the sea breeze a welcome visitor, but tonight the chill clung to the last of the crisp air with typical New England stubbornness. There was a fireplacc, but her neighbor's comment had left her reluctant to build one. Bad enough she'd imagined his "told you so" when the bird flew away. She didn't need to prove him right with a chimney fire, too. Until she had the chimney cleaned, the fleece and Reynaldo would have to do. She pulled the blanket a little higher.

Meanwhile her secondary heating source was having trouble settling down, insisting instead on walking up and down the length of her body like a stubby-legged cat. The restlessness meant one of two things—either food or a bathroom break—and since he'd emptied his food dish twenty minutes ago…

She groaned. "All right, let's go."

Outside, the night was gray but for the porch light next door. Zoe stood under her own burnt-out light and watched the moths flitting toward the beam. Despite being the only source of light, there was a somberness to her neighbor's house. Maybe it was the lack of color on its gray, weathered shingles or the memory of its owner's unsmiling face. The memory of bright emerald eyes came floating back.

At the bottom of the steps, Reynaldo sniffed the grass uninterestedly before trotting to the fence dividing the properties.

"That's far enough," she said, calling the dachshund back. After three years together, she liked to believe her little rescue dog would respond to her voice. Wishful thinking, but she liked deluding herself. Why not? She excelled at it, didn't she?

"We said we'd stay in our own yard, remember? How about we try and keep our promise?"

Suddenly the sound of a back door opening breached the quiet. Zoe's insides stilled. Through a gap in the posts, she spied a crop of sun-bleached hair and a somber profile. Funny, only a moment before she'd been thinking his yard dark. Illuminated by the white cone of his porch light, he looked brighter than bright in the gray. Zoe swore she could see the flash of his green eyes as he stared out into the night. In his hand, he held an amber bottle.

Curious, Zoe watched as he drank his beer and studied whatever it was he saw in his backyard. Or was he searching? Though really too far away for her to truly see, he seemed to be focused on a point far past his property line.

After a minute, he raised the bottle one last time and turned back inside. With the flick of a switch, the light disappeared, leaving Zoe and Reynaldo alone in the darkness.

She definitely had to clean the chimney. Waking up to a foggy, gray morning, it took Zoe less than a second to make the decision. Granted, she'd probably only need the fireplace for a week or so, until the summer heat arrived, but that was one week too long to do without. Shivering under the covers in flannel pj's and a sweatshirt was not how she wanted to spend her nights. Especially since Reynaldo insisted on making a predawn bathroom trip every morning.

"I swear, you have a bladder the size of a pea," she said to him.

Palming her coffee mug, she returned to her list. Charles and her mother weren't kidding when they said they'd ignored the property the past couple years. Since Rey had her awake, she decided to make a list of home repairs she needed to tackle. Clearly, Rey needed a dog run, if for no other reason than to keep him out of their green-eyed neighbor's yard. The memory of his laser-sharp gaze sent a tremor down her spine, where it pooled in uncomfortable warmth at the base.

Definitely, a dog run. And a new light for the back door so she wouldn't have to stand in the dark while Rey relieved himself. Those repairs she could do herself. But the chimney… Sadly, chimney sweeping was out of her purview.

"Guess that means I need to find a handyman, Rey. Think this island has one?" Pitcher's Hole was more a fishing hole than a town, though she had noticed a small hardware store near where the ferry docked. "I imagine that's as good a place as any to start asking around. If nothing else, maybe we can find a portable heater for the bedroom." If the dated electrical system could handle the extra voltage.

Getting dressed had never been a big production for her. Less so now that she had no one to impress. A quick brush of her hair, a splash of water on her face and she was done. As she adjusted her glasses, she stared at the reflection in the mirror. Unimpressive blue eyes and hair badly needing a trim stared back. No wonder Paul had only wanted her money. Maybe if she'd spent a little more time, worn a little lipstick…

Zoe shook the thought from her head. She could play what-if 'til the cows came home—Paul would still be out of her life.

Besides, this summer was supposed to be about healing, not bemoaning her new—and no doubt permanent—single status. Better to focus on tasks at hand.

The kitchen was conspicuously empty when she came downstairs. "Rey?"

Barking sounded from outside. Looking to the screen door, she saw the latch had failed to catch. Another item for the to-do list, along with the dog run.

"The size of a pea," she said, stepping outside. "I swear, Rey, the size of a pea."

Reynaldo didn't respond. In fact, much to her dismay, he was nowhere in sight.

Oh, please let him be sniffing around the side bushes and not exploring next door. It was way too early in the morning to face those laser beam eyes.

"You again!"

Zoe groaned. No such luck.

* * *

There wasn't a trace of a smile on her neighbor's face as he held up a very contrite Reynaldo.

Zoe was pretty sure her own face mirrored the dog's. "Sorry. He snuck out while I was in the other room."

"Seems to happen a lot."

Twice. It had happened twice. "He doesn't usually wander far from home. For some reason he has an affinity to your backyard." She forced a smile. "Must be something over there he finds appealing."

Though for the life of her, she didn't know what.

Without so much as cracking a glimmer of a smile, her neighbor—whose name she still didn't know— thrust Reynaldo in her direction. "There's an invention called a leash. I suggest you buy one."

I suggest you buy one. Zoe fought the urge to smirk. At least one of them should try to act civilly. "I'm installing a dog run today."

If he appreciated the gesture, it didn't show on his face. He simply grunted what sounded like an acknowledgment before turning away.

Distracted by the bird and other things yesterday, she'd missed it, but her neighbor had a limp. He clearly favored his right leg. Between this and the scars... Whatever had happened to him, was it the reason for the prickliness? she wondered. Because so far the man had been a six-foot roll of barbed wire, sharp and impossible to approach. With any luck, once she installed the dog run and had Reynaldo back in check, she wouldn't have to cross his thorny path again.

CHAPTER TWO

NAUSHATUCKET ISLAND wasn't a major Cape Cod island. That title belonged to its larger sisters, Nantucket and Martha's Vineyard. Only a handful of its population lived there year-round. Most were like Zoe: transient residents who wanted a summer at the islands but without the big island crowds. As a little girl, Zoe had spent a summer here with her parents when her father was in remission. Back then Pitcher's Hole consisted of a fish market, an ice-cream shop and the ferry station. It didn't consist of much more now, though there were a few additional stores, including the hardware store she had seen yesterday. She headed there first, hoping the staff might know of someone on the island who did repair work. If not, she'd have to bring in someone from New Bedford or one of the other big islands, a cost she wasn't keen on absorbing.

Turned out Pitcher's Hole Hardware was more a marine supply shop than an actual hardware store. Brass fittings and anchor line seemed to be the order of the day. It was also, to Zoe's chagrin, smaller than small, with rows so narrow only one person at a time could navigate them.

Of course, the claustrophobic space might have been tolerable had her neighbor not limped in shortly after her. By merely walking in, the man absorbed all the surrounding air, as if his six-foot frame were twice that size. Zoe, who'd been perusing the rope section, ducked deeper into the aisle. She didn't know why, but his appearance unnerved her. She blamed the barbed-wire layers, layers she could feel from her hiding place as he approached the front counter.

"Morning, Jake," the manager greeted. *So that was his name. Jake.* She'd pictured something far more intimidating. *Jake* was a dependable, solid name, a name you could count on.

In a way, she was surprised the manager and he were on a first-name basis. There was such a solitary air about him, she could easily imagine him never speaking to anyone.

"You called about the clamp connector?"

Case in point, thought Zoe.

The manager took his abruptness in stride. "Your order came over on the boat yesterday. Let me get it."

He disappeared into the back room, leaving Jake alone at the counter. Leaving the two of them alone in the store. Why she found this fact unsettling Zoe didn't know, but she was determined to ignore both the man and her reaction to his proximity. She returned her gaze to the rope display, attempting to calculate the length she would need for Rey's run, but trapped in the cramped space of the store, her neighbor's presence pulled her attention back. Try as she might she found herself stealing glances in his direction. He had, she realized, the most perfect posture she'd ever seen. No wonder he loomed large. Shoulders straight, head high—he commanded attention even in a faded flannel shirt and jeans. She supposed that explained her fascination. Curmudgeon though he might be, he was a compelling one.

The manager returned carrying a pair of packages containing items Zoe couldn't identify. "Here you go. Already on your account so you're all set. By the way, did Kent Mifflin contact you about the Flag Day dedication?"

"Yeah, he did."

"Great, so…"

"Thanks for the clamp connectors."

Zoe watched as Jake gathered his packages and limped out the door. If he noticed the store manager's disappointed expression, his actions didn't show it.

"You looking for something special, miss?"

The question caused her to start. So engrossed had she been in observing her neighbor walk across the street, she'd missed the manager coming to join her. Recovering, she pointed to the rope. "I need ten feet," she said, "and a couple of swivel clips."

"Sure thing." Grabbing a pair of cutters, he began measuring out the length. "You moored at the dock?"

"Setting up a dog run." *So I don't annoy the man who just left here.* "I'm spending the summer on the island."

"You picked a great place. Naushatucket's a great place to unwind."

"I know. My parents used to come summers a long time ago. I just bought their place."

Bringing her to the other reason for her hardware store visit. "Place is a little run-down, though. I'm hoping to make some repairs while I'm here. You wouldn't be able to recommend a handyman, would you?"

"Sure can," the manager replied, coiling the rope between his hand and his elbow. "Best on the island. You can tell him Ira sent you. That way he'll know you're a resident."

"Terrific. Do you know if he sweeps chimneys?"

"Oh, I'm sure he does. He handles just about everything else."

The mere thought of using her fireplace warmed Zoe's inside. With any luck she could get her chimney swept and be basking in warmth in a few days.

"Too bad I didn't talk to you sooner," Ira continued. "I could have introduced you before he left."

"Left?" The warmth inside her began to fade,

replaced by a prickling sensation on the back of her neck. She had a bad feeling Ira was about to say something she didn't want to hear.

"Yeah, he was just here. Name's Jake Meyers." He handed her the coiled length of rope. "You won't find a better contractor on the islands."

Zoe forced a smile. Her neighbor was the handyman.

Oh, yay.

It was a simple business transaction. He had a service; she needed that service. Nothing to get worked up about.

So why was she?

Crossing the line from her front yard to Jake's, Zoe had to forcibly calm herself down. Which was absurd, really. So what if their last two encounters had involved more glaring than conversation? The man was a contractor, and she was a potential customer. She had every right to knock on his front door. There was absolutely no reason for her pulse to be beating so quickly.

In the daylight, the house was far less intimidating. Trimmed green grass and flowering shrubs made the gray seem less bleak, as did the farmer's porch. The building still wasn't bright and cheery by any stretch of the imagination, but the potential was there lurking beneath the surface. More important, the house was well maintained, which boded well for Mr. Meyers's

skills. All she needed to do was swallow her unchar-
acteristic bout of nerves and hire him.

The door swung open before her fist could greet
the wood. "If you're looking for your dog, he's not
here."

His glare burned straight through her and singed
her resolve. Was it too late to back away?

"Reynaldo's locked in the house," she managed
to squeak out. Using her glasses as a stall tactic, she
repositioned the frames while she searched for her
voice. "I figured he was better off staying out of your
way."

"You figured right."

He propped himself against the door frame. For
some reason, Zoe's eyes went to the hands pressed
against the molding. As a means of assessing his
skill, she told herself. His long fingers curved around
the lip of the molding, elegant despite the windburn
and scarring. They looked like very capable hands.

Strong hands.

Quickly she looked back to his face only to find
herself trapped by his hard stare. "Still trying to 'save'
your bird? Or is today a new rescue mission?"

"Neither." Zoe could already feel herself chafing
under his scrutiny. It was as if he were trying to push
her out of his yard with his eyes. "My chimney needs
sweeping."

"That so?"

"At least I think so. The house has been kind of neglected the past couple years...."

"I hadn't noticed."

She flashed a smirk. "Anyway, since the nights are still a little cool, I'd like to use the fireplace and I thought it wise to have the chimney cleaned out before I do. I was at the hardware store this morning—"

"I know."

Meaning he'd noticed her. Had he seen her staring, too? Her stomach did a weird kind of somersault. Swift and sudden, the reaction left her flustered. Once again, she hid behind adjusting her glasses. "Anyway, I asked at the store about a handyman and the manager suggested you. Said you were the best on the island. I was hoping I could hire you."

Jake drew his lips into a tight line. "Hmm."

Not exactly the most enthusiastic response in the world. Either he didn't need the business or—she hated the pebble of insecurity that accompanied her next thought—he didn't want hers. "Are you available? If it's a problem, I'll make sure Reynaldo stays out of your way."

"Because you've done such a bang-up job of that so far."

"He's a little worked up because it's a new location. I assure you, I'm capable of keeping my dachshund under control." The last comment came out sharper than necessary, but she couldn't help it. She didn't appreciate his tone. In fact, now that she thought about it, she didn't appreciate his entire attitude.

"On second thought, never mind." Screw his skills and sexy, capable-looking hands. She didn't need the hassle. "I'll ask the manager to recommend someone else."

"He won't."

"That so?" she replied, quoting him.

"There's a reason Ira said I was the best contractor on the island."

"Really? And what's that?"

"I'm also the only one."

In a flash, Zoe's bravado disappeared. "The only one?"

Jake shrugged. "You might find one or two more in a couple weeks, when the summer population shows up, if you can get one of them to take a break from their vacation."

"In a couple weeks I won't need fires to warm the house."

"No, you probably won't."

Zoe sighed. She was stuck with Mr. Attitude whether she liked it or not. That is, if he took the job. She might have snapped away her opportunity. She offered her best contrite smile. "I don't suppose I can get a do-over?"

"I don't believe in do-overs."

"Oh." So much for that.

"But I will sweep your chimney. Gonna have to go to the Vineyard for supplies, though."

"Oh, that's fine." Relief made her far more agreeable than she should be. "Buy whatever you need."

"I take cash or check. No credit."

"No problem. Give me a working fireplace and I'll pay you in solid gold bars if that's what you want." In the back of her mind she knew she should be getting more information before agreeing to his terms. Like how much he charged, for example. But the promise of a warm bed trumped good business. Besides, if he were the only handyman on the island, which was entirely possible, given the lack of full-time population, then she didn't have a whole lot of negotiation room anyway. "Anything to avoid shivering through the night."

His eyes swept the length of her and Zoe found herself wondering just how she would define the term *anything*. It had been a long time since a man looked at her like she was a woman. At least not without a hidden agenda.

"Cash or check will suffice."

So much for being looked at like a woman. "Right." The deflated sensation in the pit of her stomach was *not* disappointment. Not that kind anyway.

Unsure what to do next, especially with the embarrassment creeping along her skin, she toed the welcome mat and brushed the bangs off her frames. "Well then," she said, clearing her throat. "I'll set up things when you're done." A graceful exit, this was not.

Worse, he continued to stare at her. Hot and hard. Like he was trying to read under her skin. It made her insides all jumpy.

"I'll…" Her voice caught *again*. "I'll let you get back to what you were doing…"

"Where are you going?"

The question came abruptly, sounding more like a command, and froze her just as she was about to step off the porch. "Um, home?" she offered.

"Not if you want your chimney cleaned. Told you, we have to go to the Vineyard for supplies."

"We?" How on earth did she factor in?

"I don't carry a line of credit at the Vineyard store."

"So?" She still wasn't sure what that had to do with her going to the Vineyard or anywhere else with him.

"So," he said, pushing away from the door, "someone's got to pay for your supplies."

Which was why, a half hour later, Zoe found herself ducking the spray as they cruised across the sound in Jake's powerboat. On a good day, the ride took forty-five minutes. It might as well have lasted for eternity since her companion was a stone-faced statue. For the first few minutes, she tried to engage him in conversation, but after the third consecutive one-word answer, she gave up, settling instead for stealing glances at his silent profile.

She had to admit the man knew how to handle a boat. Yet again, she found her attention drawn to his hands and to the way the wheel glided effortlessly under his fingers. He was less steering the boat than commanding it to do his bidding.

Commanding. At the hardware store, she'd thought of him compelling. Now she had a second word to describe him.

There was something else about him, too. A quality she couldn't name. Originally, she'd have said *prickly,* but studying him now, the word didn't quite fit. Oh, he was prickly—okay, he was unfriendly— but her gut told her something about the prickliness didn't ring true. Why she thought that she couldn't say, but her gut said there was more to Jake Meyers than met the eye.

And we all know how well your gut works, right, Zoe? She cringed, remembering how certain she'd been about Paul. The way she'd defended him to everybody. *You don't know him like I do. He needs me.* Paul had needed her all right. Needed her money.

Across the water, Zoe spied the shores of Martha's Vineyard closing in. Come three weeks from now, part-time residents and vacationers would jam both the waterways and the tiny island's streets. At the moment, however, the island belonged to the year-round residents, leaving the bay quiet and half-full.

Jake steered his boat around West Chop and toward Vineyard Haven. About ten yards out, he slowed the engine, engulfing the day in even greater silence as they glided toward an empty slip.

Finally, a chance to do something besides sit with her thoughts. Scrambling forward, she grabbed the rope, and soon as they were close enough, stepped onto the dock. It'd been a while since she'd done any kind of boating, but the lessons came back quickly enough as she deftly tied them off. She then moved starboard, and repeated the task. When finished, she looked up to see Jake studying her handiwork. The glasses obscured part of his expression but she could see he was surprised. The knowledge caused a bubble of pride in her chest. She waited while Jake secured the rest of the boat, thinking, as he moved around, that for a man with a bad leg he carried himself with a great deal of grace. Then again, was she really surprised?

"Store's about a mile up, on Main Street," he said, when he joined her on the pier.

Zoe looked across the parking lot to the tree-lined street. A handful of cars drove by, turning right and disappearing. "I take it we're walking," she said, glad she had thought to wear comfortable shoes today.

"Unless you've got a better idea."

Unfortunately, she didn't.

Jake had already taken off through the parking lot and she had to scramble to catch up. A difficult task, given he had a foot of height on her and she had to take two steps to match one of his.

"Hey!" she called out. "How about we slow it down a bit?" If she had to walk, fine, but she wasn't going to sprint the entire way.

He stopped and if she were a betting woman, she'd say the sag in his shoulders was caused by frustration. There went any points she might have scored back at the dock. "Some of us have shorter legs," she pointed out, in case he'd missed the obvious.

They fell back into step, albeit at a slightly slower pace. Zoe entertained herself by studying the clapboard houses and brick sidewalk. About a hundred yards in, she lost interest and decided to give conversation another shot. "I've never been to this section of the Vineyard. Do you make the trip often?"

"Often enough."

"Downside of island living, I suppose. I should have thought about that before moving to one." She'd only been thinking of getting away. "On the other hand, now I know why my mother didn't make repairs. Too much trouble getting building supplies."

"Most people manage."

"Most people aren't sequestered in an Atlanta townhome. My mother hasn't come north since she remarried. The house was always more my father's anyway. He was the one who planned on using it every summer. At least he did, before he got sick. I forgot about the place myself until my divorce. Then I bought the place from her and—"

Dear God, she was babbling. Worse than babbling, she was oversharing. "Have you lived on the island long?"

"Long enough."

Not surprisingly, Jake did the opposite and *under*shared. She plowed on, not willing to return to silence. "Growing up, my dad called Naushatucket an undiscovered paradise. Of course, I only cared about the beach, but now I can see what he meant. A person can really escape from it all there, can't he?"

"Used to, anyway."

A pointed hint. They stepped off the curb and out of the corner of her eye, she saw Jake grimace. "Leg bothering you?" The question came out before she could stop herself.

"No."

A lie if ever she heard one. It was obvious from the way his mouth pulled in a tight line every time he stepped off his right foot. She stared at him, silently calling him on it, until he could no longer ignore her.

"Hip," he said. "And it always bothers me."

"I'm sorry."

"Why? It's not your hip."

No, but he was in obvious pain, and that made her feel bad. "Look, you don't need to do the chimney today if…"

Wrong thing to say. Sunglasses or no sunglasses, she could feel the heat of his stare bearing down on her. "You asked me to clean your chimney today—I'll clean the damn thing today."

With that, he picked up his pace as if proving a point. "I'll live with the pain."

Jake's hip throbbed so much he had to clench his jaw from the pain. A doctor would probably tell him he was being a stubborn fool. That he was making himself suffer needlessly. Of course, Jake would debate that last word. *Needlessly.* He was pretty damn certain his suffering was justified. Though he did feel a little bad for dragging the Bird Whisperer along.

Speaking of which… He felt her cast another look in his direction, setting his nerves on edge. Since his discharge he'd gotten all kinds of looks. The discreet. The openly gaping. The disgustingly compassionate. All of them with some sort of awe, as if he were a freaking hero.

Little Miss Bird-Whisperer's looks, though… God, but he could feel her pale blue eyes scanning his profile. His skin prickled with the awareness. Without turning, he could picture them wide and curious. Like she was trying to see inside him or something. It irritated the hell out of him. What had made him say yes to her job offer in the first place?

He had bills to pay, that was what. And hanging around the house did nothing but make his thoughts loud, and they were loud enough this morning as it was. A project was exactly what he needed to drown them out for a little while.

The morning overcast had finally burned off, allowing the sun to take hold and warm the air. Jake felt the sweat starting to trickle down the back of his neck. Zoe had peeled off her grey sweatshirt. Jake tried not to notice her bright orange T-shirt or how it fit a little too snugly over her breasts. He was trying not to pay attention to her at all—a desire she seemed intent on disrupting at every opportunity.

"How much farther 'til we get to the store?" she asked.

"Couple blocks." Normally the walk didn't take that long; this morning it was taking forever. He blamed his impossible-to-ignore companion.

"Mind if we stop at that coffee shop on the corner first? I don't know about you, but I could use a cold drink. I'll even pa—"

The words were barely out of her mouth when she stumbled over a dip in the sidewalk. Jake reacted automatically, reaching out with a hand to grab her arm, and caught her as she fell forward. It was a mistake. Catching her meant looking in her direction. Suddenly he had an up-close view of what he'd been trying to ignore. He saw freckles kissing the bridge of a windblown nose and strands of black hair wisping over surprised eyes. A long-dormant awareness, unbidden and unwanted, began stirring somewhere deep inside him.

Quickly, he let go. "You can get your drink if you want. I'll meet you at the hardware store," he said, shoving his hands in his jeans pockets.

To hell with his no-credit policy. Next time he'd make this trip alone and bill her.

Unlike the store in Pitcher's Hole, this particular store was large and well-stocked. Jake used the place whenever he had a large or unusual job. He liked it because they left him alone and he could therefore avoid small talk, something his companion apparently thrived on. As soon as they walked in the door, she'd sought out a clerk and was currently engrossed in a conversation about outdoor lighting. At least it was supposed to be about lighting. He hadn't thought that a terribly amusing topic, and they seemed to be chuckling a little too heartily. Somewhere in between laughs, he caught the word *dachshund*.

"I was telling Javier how Reynaldo seems determined to hang out in your yard," Zoe said when he approached. "He thinks Rey's chasing chipmunks."

"My cousin had a dachshund," the clerk said. "They're big hunters."

"What's wrong with the chipmunks in his yard?" Jake grumbled.

The young man shrugged. "Where's the fun in that?"

Not in his yard, that's where. "Got what I need," he said to Zoe.

The look she gave the clerk was apologetic, as if *he* were the one holding up the process. "Thanks for the suggestion," she said, smiling. "But I'll go with the single spotlight. Javier recommended I get a double one to better keep an eye on Reynaldo, but that might shine a little too brightly into your backyard."

She turned her smile on him, and Jake could practically see the sarcasm behind her expression.

Suddenly they were interrupted by a pair of men in maintenance uniforms. Jake was about to tell them to find another clerk when he realized they weren't there for hardware supplies. Their faces were pale and somber. *"É Ernesto,"* they said. *"Está morto."*

Morto. Dead. His body began to shake. There were more words. *Accident. Car.* Bits and pieces of an explanation that drifted to him from far away, like words whispered in a tunnel. Black closed in him, eating away reality.

Get out. Take cover.

No, no, that wasn't right. *Get to fresh air.* He needed fresh air.

Miles away he saw a doorway. And light. Light meant safety. *There. Go there.* His thoughts were thick and muddled as he staggered toward it, faintly aware of a bell ringing as he lunged toward the parking lot. The sea breeze burnt his lungs as he gulped one ragged breath after another. He made his way across the parking lot, toward the Dumpster across the street. He gripped the front bar, squeezing as tightly as his hands would allow. Stutteringly, his mind began listing his surroundings. Garbage. Blue Dumpster. Gray gravel. He tried to remind himself he wasn't in that place anymore.

"Jake? Jake?"

A voice, soft and gentle, beckoned from the side of the confusion. He squeezed the Dumpster bar tighter, breathing in the stench of garbage, letting the pungency bring him back.

"Jake?" Suddenly the voice was closer and he felt a hand on his shoulder. The touch was tender, soothing. It promised comfort. Peace.

Somehow he managed to turn his head in the voice's direction.

"Are you all right? Did something happen?" Zoe was asking.

The sympathy in her pale blue eyes did more than any grounding technique. Reality crashed back, reminding him where he was and why.

Humiliation swept over him. "I'm fine," he said, pushing off both from the bar and her touch. "I needed some fresh air is all."

"In front of a garbage Dumpster?" She forced herself back into his line of vision. "Was it those two guys? I don't speak Spanish, but…"

"Portuguese. They were speaking Portuguese, not Spanish."

"All right, I don't speak Portuguese, either. Still, I could tell the news wasn't good. The look on Javier's face didn't look good."

"A car accident killed their friend."

Her hand flew to her lips. "My God. That's terrible. Did you know—?"

"No." His skin was clammy and cold. No, he didn't know the man, but he knew the loss. God, but he knew the loss. I just needed air," he lied again. "Stomach's bothering me."

"Are you sure?"

"I'm sure." His reply was rougher than necessary, but he didn't care. He could still feel the memory of Zoe's hand on his shoulder. That the sensation remained made his heart race, and not in a good way. He didn't deserve to feel anything, least of all comfort. "Let's just go back and ring up the supplies."

"The manager already is. He's going to load up his truck and drive us back to the dock."

Good. The sooner they got back, the sooner he could lose himself in work, which meant the sooner he could bury his thoughts.

Along with the sensation of Zoe's touch, still lingering on his skin.

What on earth had she witnessed?

One moment they were buying supplies, the next Jake was bolting for the door. Common sense told her to leave well enough alone. She had enough on her plate putting the pieces of her life back together without getting involved in someone else's problems. Only she'd never been very good at leaving anything alone. Not when someone might need her.

Besides, Jake hadn't said a word since they'd left the hardware store and the continual silence ate at her.

"Do you want to talk about it?" she asked when they'd finished transferring the supplies from Jake's boat to the back of his truck.

"Talk about what?"

"What happened back on the Vineyard? In the parking lot?"

"I told you—I needed fresh air."

"Right, and I'm tall enough to play professional basketball." She didn't buy his excuse for a second. Something had upset him—terrified him, nearly—and she was pretty sure it had to do with the conversation they'd overheard. "Were you in a car accident?"

The laugh he gave her was part amused, part mocking. "No," he replied, climbing into the driver's seat.

But he had been in some kind of accident. Those scars and that limp didn't appear by magic. Taking a page from his book, she stared straight ahead, pretending to watch the road rise over the bluff. "I only ask because sometimes hearing bad news can trigger—"

"Will you leave it alone?" The sharpness in his voice made her jump. "I wanted some air so I went outside. End of story. Now, for God's sake, would you let the subject drop?"

"I'm simply—"

He whipped around. "I said drop it!"

Suddenly Zoe understood. There, in the confines of his pickup, she saw what he hid beneath the layers of inapproachability.

Pain.

Not physical pain, like his hip. No, this kind of pain ran deeper and stronger. It was the kind of pain medicine couldn't help. The kind that ripped a man's insides apart.

Zoe's own insides hurt for him. "I'm sorry," she replied, meaning far more than her earlier intrusion.

She watched as he dragged a shaky hand across the back of his neck. Maybe it was her tone, or the fact that she'd apologized, but some of the edge left his voice. "I don't want to talk about it, okay?"

"Okay." She'd do what he wanted and let the subject drop. For now.

CHAPTER THREE

INSTALLING a dog run was harder than it sounded. For starters, pine trees didn't come with predrilled holes, meaning she had to figure out a way to attach the rope to the trunk. The easiest solution was to simply tie the rope around the trunk, but she couldn't get the knot tight enough. Her efforts kept sliding down to the ground, leaving her no choice but to screw a hook directly into the wood. Hopefully doing so wouldn't hurt the tree.

Jake would know whether it did or not, but she didn't want to ask. As it was, she felt amazingly self-conscious while she was working, convinced he was watching her miscues, and thinking her a royal idiot. No need to compound the situation with silly questions.

Her eyes strayed to the roof, where the handyman was busy attacking her chimney. Lovable chimney sweep from the children's movies he was not. He jammed the hard-bristled brush up and down with such fury, the creosote didn't stand a chance. Working out the pain from before, maybe? What was his story anyhow?

Beads of sweat had formed on the bridge of her nose, causing her glasses to slide. Taking them off, she wiped her damp skin with her sleeve. Man, but it was hot. She wasn't used to physical labor in the heat. If installing a doggy run counted as labor, that was. Still, she was hot and sticky. Jake had to be even stickier. He was working three times as hard and had yet to take a break.

"I'm grabbing a cold drink," she called up to him. "Do you want one?"

He shook his head and, after pausing briefly to wipe the sweat from his face, continued working.

"Talk about stubborn," Zoe said to Reynaldo. The dachshund was laid out dozing on the concrete step. "He wouldn't accept my offer of a drink while we were on the Vineyard, he wouldn't take one after his 'fresh air break,' and now he's still refusing. Either the man's impervious to heat or he wants to be hot and miserable." After today's events, she was leaning toward the latter.

"Well, I don't care how often he refused, he *has* to be thirsty. I am."

She grabbed two bottles of ice water from the kitchen fridge and made her way to the ladder propped on the side of the house.

When she reached the roof, she saw Jake had finished his chimney assault. He stood with his back to her, breathing hard. Sweat and soot had turned his light gray T-shirt dark and heavy. The material stuck to his upper back like a dirty second skin. Zoe couldn't help noticing the muscles underneath. She was close enough that she could see the way they rippled like water every time he breathed deep. A wave of female awareness coiled through her. Even standing still, he moved with grace. Her fingers twitched a little as she wondered what the view might look like beneath the cotton. Was it as hard and taut as the rest of him?

Flushing, she cleared her thoughts and her throat. "I decided to bring you a drink anyway."

His spine stiffened, and she could tell, despite making noise, she'd startled him, making her feel all the more like a voyeur for her earlier thoughts. "Sorry. I didn't realize you were deep in thought. Here."

"Do you always do what you want regardless of what people tell you?"

Talk about a loaded comment. Thoughts of Paul came to mind. "Unfortunately, yes. See, it's kind of my job to know best. Ever hear of 'Ask Zoe'?"

"No."

She wasn't surprised. He didn't strike her as the type to peruse the arts and lifestyle section. "It's a nationally syndicated advice column. People write in and ask me what they should do."

"And you tell them."

"That's the point of asking me, isn't it?"

"What if you're wrong?"

What if, indeed. "Anyway," she said, changing the subject, "as far as bringing you water, I prefer to use the term *executive overruling.* I don't need you getting light-headed from dehydration and falling off my roof."

Jake slipped the water from her hand. "Afraid of a lawsuit?"

"One big payout a year is enough, thank you."

As soon as the words left her mouth, she winced. Once again, she'd said too much. From the way Jake knit his brow, he must have caught her reaction as well. Shoot. Now she felt compelled to explain. "Expensive divorce. And before you say anything, yes, I'm aware of how ironic my situation sounds."

"Ironic?"

"A divorced advice columnist." She tried for a self-deprecating smile. "Guess I *can* be wrong sometimes."

She was grateful that Jake didn't reply; he was too busy draining his unwanted water bottle. Zoe tried not to notice the way his Adam's apple bobbed up and down with each swallow or how his biceps bulged from one simple bend of his arm.

Instead, she turned her attention to the shore across the street. There weren't many places where you could get a better bird's-eye view of the island.

Below them, Naushatucket spread out in beige, navy and green glory.

She scrambled up the last couple of rungs to get a better look, realizing only when she reached her destination how steeply pitched the Cape Cod-style roof was. Standing was awkward at best.

Pressing a hand to the chimney for support, she sat down. Across the street, the beach was mostly empty. The waves rolled gently toward them, their swells dark curves on the water's surface.

To her surprise, Jake lowered himself next to her. She could feel him looking at her. Zoe continued watching the waves. He'd spent the better part of the day ignoring her existence; she could do the same.

Except she hadn't counted on his attention making her skin twitch. Did the man always stare so intently? Even now, his gaze felt like it was looking inside her rather than at her.

"What?" she asked finally.

"Chimney's done," he replied. "You can use it tonight."

"Yay!" she cheered, although sitting in this heat, it was hard to remember why she'd needed a working fireplace to begin with.

She returned to studying the waves, the view turning her thoughtful. It didn't take long for those thoughts to become words. "There's something very centering about the islands, don't you think?"

"If you say so."

"Seriously. The idea of land, solid and strong, while surrounded by water. Can't get much more centered than that." Thoughts of her failures bubbled to the surface. "It's why I bought this place, you know. I was hoping some of that balance would rub off on me."

"How metaphysical of you."

"I take it you disagree with my theory."

Jake shrugged. "You can have any theory you want."

"From your tone, though, you don't believe a place can rub off on you."

"Rub off on you? Sure. But what you're talking about is a sense of peace." He raised the bottle to his mouth. "Big difference," he muttered over the rim. "Helluva big difference."

Zoe wondered if he meant for his sigh to be so long or so sad. She waited for him to go on, hoping for more explanation, but he simply tossed his empty water bottle over the edge of the roof. "Flashing around your chimney needs replacing," he said. "And you've got some loose shingles. Maybe even some soft spots in the wood."

Once again changing the subject. They were both, it appeared, quite adept at doing so. "That your way of telling me I need a new roof?"

"Depends," he replied with a shrug. "How badly do you want water leaking in?"

Short answer? She didn't. Neither did she relish

spending a lot of money on home repairs, which it looked like she was about to do. Damn her mother and Charles for not paying attention to this place.

It was her turn to sigh. "I don't suppose you know how to repair roofs."

"I've fixed one or two."

"Think you can fix this one?"

"Maybe."

Not the answer she wanted to hear. Why bring the darn repairs up, if he wasn't looking for the work?

Jake had pushed himself to his feet. Zoe immediately scrambled after him, except she lacked his innate grace and immediately began wobbling on the pitched slope. For the second time that day, a strong hand wrapped around her forearm, steadying her.

"Thank you," she murmured. Awareness had pooled at the spot where Jake's skin met hers. In the back of her mind, she noted that for a firm grip, his touch was surprisingly light and gentle. "Guess I won't be dancing on rooftops anytime soon," she said, attempting a smile.

The attempt wasn't returned. "You've got droppings," he said.

"What?"

"On the chimney. Probably bats."

Did he say bats? A shiver ran through her, and not the good kind of shiver, either. "Like in get-in-your-hair carry-rabies bats?" As if there were any other kind.

This time there was an attempted smile, or at least he quirked the corner of his mouth. "Afraid you'll have to mount another rescue mission?"

"Try attack. Are you sure there are bats?"

"Don't usually get guano otherwise."

And here she'd thought the swallow was her only pest problem. Bats? The very idea they could be living in her crawl spaces would keep her up all night. Turning her face to his, she mustered her best desperate expression. Not all that hard to do, seeing as she was desperate.

"Can you help me?" she asked him. "Please?"

The sigh Jake gave this time held an additional note. One that she swore sounded a lot like defeat. Zoe watched as he opened his mouth to speak, stopped and then looked down to where he still held her arm. The awareness flared anew. When he finally spoke, his voice was flat.

"I'll have to let you know."

She was waiting for a better answer; Jake could tell. But he was purposely ignoring the flash of orange perched on his ladder. If he looked, he would only find himself staring. It'd been happening all day. As long as she was near his line of sight, his eyes would find her. It was driving him mad. And the way his skin felt whenever he touched her, like it was alive... Well, he didn't like that, either.

So instead of looking, he forced his attention onto

the chimney. What he should have done was go home after that debacle in the store, but home would have only made his mood worse. When working he could bury the thoughts for a little while, 'til he collapsed in a heap of numbness and exhaustion. At least he used to be able to, before bright orange T-shirts and bouncy ponytails got in the way.

Why did he have to bring up the bats? Or the fact he was the only handyman on the island for that matter? Now, he was stuck. Only a coldhearted bastard could look at her face, with that quivering lower lip of hers, and say no. He had no choice but to help her now.

From below he could hear that damn dachshund yipping, followed by Zoe's admonishment to be patient. Sounded like the dog needed centering, too. Imagine thinking you could find peace by staying here on Naushatucket. If only it were that simple. Someone needed to tell her the truth: once you step on the wrong path, no amount of "balance" or redirection will make up for the distance you've already traveled. You can't go back. To use her word from this morning: life didn't come with do-overs.

Surprisingly, it wasn't the potential bat infestation dominating Zoe's thoughts the rest of the day, but the man sweeping her chimney.

On second thought, maybe it wasn't so surprising. After all, he'd been stuck in her head before the bat news; why wouldn't he stay there? Especially after hearing that long, sad sigh. The sound was now permanently merged with the memory of his expression outside the hardware store. So much pain and so many impenetrable layers. She wondered if anyone could ever get through them all to help.

"He's definitely a puzzle begging to be solved," she remarked to Reynaldo as they snuggled on the sofa later that night.

You're doing it again, the voice chimed. *Getting sucked in.* She couldn't resist a challenge any more than she could a sad story. Maybe if she could, she'd have seen the truth about Paul a lot sooner.

The fire in her newly cleaned fireplace crackled merrily, the flame painting the living room a soft orange. Yawning, Zoe tugged the comforter from off the back of the sofa and draped it over her and Reynaldo. A day of exertion in the sun had left her drowsy and more than a little stiff. She wondered how Jake's hip was doing. He'd been limping pretty badly when she saw him finally drag that ladder across the backyard.

Don't start, Zoe.

Her subconscious had a point. She had hundreds of readers looking for her advice. If she was desperate to solve other people's problems, she should focus on them, not the neighbor who had quite clearly told her to butt out.

Still, seeing the pain in those green eyes...

At some point she must have drifted off because before she realized it the pillow beneath her cheek was buzzing. Her cell phone, she realized drowsily. Probably Caroline, calling to nag her about this week's column. She never balked at calling at weird hours and the column was overdue.

"I'm working on it, Caroline," she barked into the transmitter. "No need to check in daily."

"You work too hard, babe."

Paul. Zoe nearly dropped the phone. She hadn't heard his voice in months. Not since she walked out. Hearing it now made her stomach drop.

Balling her free hand into a fist, she took a deep breath, willing her insides to still. "What do you want?" she managed to ask.

"Since when does a guy need an excuse to call his wife?"

"Ex-wife." Now she was over the shock, clarity was setting in. Thankfully. "I distinctly remember sending you papers. We're no longer married."

"I'll always think of us as married in my heart."

Didn't he mean wallet? "So much so you haven't tried to contact me since February."

"I wanted to give you your space."

"My space." He'd certainly given her that, and then some.

"Because I knew I screwed up." There was a pause. She imagined him chewing his thumb; he always did when nervous or deep in thought. "Truth is, I wasn't sure you'd talk to me."

"What makes you think I'm willing to talk with you now?"

He chuckled. "You answered the phone, didn't you?"

"Because I thought you were Caroline. I can still hang up, and I will, unless you tell me why you're calling."

"I miss you."

"I've been gone for months, Paul." He'd been gone even longer, but she doubted he'd understand what she meant.

Meanwhile, he ignored her comment. "I'm playing Savannah this weekend. Remember last year? The tenth hole? The water hazard?"

"I remember." She also remembered him sweet-talking her into ponying up for lessons with Lars Anderson afterward.

"We were good together, Zo."

"Were we?"

"Of course, we were. We were Team Brodsky."

Team Brodsky. She'd coined the silly moniker the night she proposed. At the time, Paul had been on the brink of making the tour. "Make me your partner," she'd said. "We can do great things together. Team Brodsky, all the way to number one." Her backing, his talent. That'd been the plan anyway.

"Ancient history," she said.

"Doesn't have to be." His voice dropped a notch, turning all honeyed and soft.

Once upon a time, that tone of voice would have sent her heart fluttering. Today it brought nothing but regret and bitterness.

"You were—you are—my lucky charm, babe. Always have been."

Not to mention his bankroll. She read the sports pages. He'd missed the cut in the last tournament. His short game was slipping without the expensive coach she'd been paying for.

On the other end of the line, there was another pause. More thumb-biting, she presumed. Finally he spoke again, clearly taking her silence as a willingness to listen. "What do you say? Can we at least talk? That's all I'm asking for. A chance to see you. I need you, Zoe."

And there it was, her Achilles' heel. *Need*. Forget sob stories and challenges. Never had there been a more powerful four-letter word, at least for her, and Paul knew it. Already she could feel the guilt building in her chest. Squeezing the phone, her nails bending against the plastic casing, she fought the emotion's grip. "I have to go."

"One meeting, Zoe. One."

"Goodbye, Paul."

She hung up before he could muster another argument, then quickly blocked his number from her phone before he could call again. And he would call again. Paul never liked rejection.

Dammit! She tossed the phone to the other end of the sofa, where it fell into the cushions. Why'd she have to answer the phone in the first place? Why didn't she take the time to look at the call screen?

It wasn't that she loved Paul. On the contrary, she was angry she had let herself be blinded by infatuation for as long as she did. Zoe Hamilton, Advice Columnist and Patsy. Tell her you need her, and you can walk all over her. Well, no more. Just like Team Brodsky, her days of becoming personally involved were history.

All of a sudden, her warm, cozy living room felt hot and stifling. To quote her neighbor, she needed some fresh air. Outside was still light enough that she could take a good brisk walk on the beach and clear her head.

"Come on, Rey." She nudged the sleeping dog. "Let's get out of here."

Grabbing the dachshund's leash, she headed out the patio door. Halfway through, she collided with a wall of muscle and bay rum.

"There a problem?" she heard Jake ask.

She had a problem all right. Her life. "I was taking Reynaldo for a walk."

Since leaving her, he'd showered and changed. His bangs hung wet against his forehead, and she noticed droplet stains on the collar of his work shirt. The top three buttons were undone, revealing an expanse of tanned skin and blond chest hair. To her mounting annoyance, he looked way too good.

He held up a flashlight and what looked like a fisherman's net. "I thought you wanted to tackle your bat problem."

Right, the bats. Dealing with her pest of an ex-husband had made her forget her house was potentially infested with rabid winged creatures. "And I thought you had to think about it?" she snapped back. Uncalled for? Yes. But he was staring at her in that intense way of his again, and she wasn't in the mood. She wasn't in the mood for anything right now except Reynaldo and a long walk on the beach.

If her neighbor noticed her sharpness, he was ignoring it. In fact, he matched her, edge for edge. "If you want to find where they're nesting, now's the time to look."

"So go look."

He thrust an industrial-size flashlight in her direction. "It's a two-person job."

Oh, great. Just what she wanted to do after a call from her ex. Go hunting for pests. Worse, she doubted her "handyman" would let her decline.

She snatched the flashlight from his hand. "Lead the way," she snapped. "Though, if I get rabies, I'm not paying you."

"They don't usually bite people. You're more likely to get rabies from a skunk than a bat."

"Well, aren't you the bat expert."

"Not an expert. Read up on them, is all."

Zoe blushed. The phone call had left her feeling churlish, and she was taking the feelings out on Jake instead of her ex-husband, which wasn't fair. Curmudgeon or not, he deserved better behavior from her.

She followed him around to the front of the house. "Up there's the area where I found the droppings," he explained. "Flashing's rippled on this side of the chimney, too. I'm guessing that's the point of entry."

In the dusk, Zoe could barely make out where he was talking about, despite the flashlight beam. The "ripple" he mentioned was barely big enough for a bee's nest. The netting, he explained, was to allow the bats to exit but not reenter. Then, after a week or so, they could plug the holes permanently.

Sounded good to Zoe. "What made you read up on bats in the first place?" she asked. Having been put in her place, she was trying to make amends. Plus, the comment had her curious.

"Spent a lot of time in caves. Figured knowing more about them would come in handy."

"Back where you grew up?"

"Afghanistan. Look, there she is." He pointed to a black dot zigzagging across the sky.

Zoe followed his finger, but her mind was more on his last answer than on her winged invader. It all made sense. The scars, the injury, the extreme reaction in the hardware store… How could she not have realized? Jake hadn't been in an accident. He'd been in battle.

"How long were you there?"

"Second one," he replied, ignoring the question. "Definitely coming out from the flashing. I'll have to check for sure, but it's early enough in the season that I don't think they've gotten through to inside the house."

"Good to know." Though she'd prefer to hear more about his military experience. "What am I out here for?"

"You're doing it. Keep the flashlight trained on the roof so I can see what I'm doing. Unless—" he glanced over his shoulder "—you'd rather wait 'til morning."

"Oh, no, tonight is fine. Sooner they're out of my hair…that is, my house," she corrected, "the better." Stepping closer to the ladder, she aimed the flashlight beam toward the roof. "Bright enough?"

"It'll do."

They worked in spotted silence. As clear as it was that Jake was in charge, he had a way about him that inspired her to obey his directions. Maybe it was the confidence of his commands or the surety of his movement. Or the way he told her what to do without pretense or a false front. Either way, they worked together so easily it took Zoe by surprise. She hadn't expected them to be such a good team.

Like Team Brodsky?

Giving herself a mental kick, she focused on shining her flashlight.

"Is that it?" she asked when he came down the ladder. "You're finished?"

"Doesn't take very long to plug a hole. By the way, I think they're all out of the nest, so you can sleep soundly."

"Thank goodness," she said with a sigh. "A warm, bat-free house." Sounded fantastic. "You, Jake Meyers, are my hero."

She couldn't have picked a worse thing to say. In the white glare of her flashlight, Zoe watched as his expression became a haunted, bitter mask.

"Don't ever use that word around me." He ground out the words through clenched teeth. "A hero is the last thing I am."

CHAPTER FOUR

OF ALL the terms Zoe could have used, why'd she have to pick the word *hero*? He could still see her face when she said it, too. Lit up like a kid at Christmas, her smile bright in the dark. The minute she grinned, he got a swell of male pride smack in the middle of his chest.

Jake slammed his beer on the TV tray that doubled as an end table. What right did he have to feel proud about anything, let alone be called a hero? Heroes sacrificed their lives, they saved lives.

Pushing himself from the sofa, he hobbled to his side window. Next door Zoe's house was dark, except for one lone window on the second floor. Her bedroom perhaps? Awareness shot to his groin, causing him to groan. He didn't want to feel this pull of attraction any more than he wanted to feel pride. Mere arousal he could deal with. After all, a man couldn't always help his physical reaction when an attractive woman crossed his path and he'd be kidding himself if he didn't admit Zoe was an attractive woman, in her spunky, wet-kitten kind of way.

This pull, though… All day long, his skin twitched, while his chest felt tight and empty at the same time. He didn't like the feeling. Didn't want the feeling. Hell, he didn't want to *feel,* period.

A cramp ran down the back of his leg. Climbing around all day had him stiff and achy. God, but it had been a long day. Between the nightmare and the flashback, not to mention all the physical labor, he should be ready to drop, and if it were any other night, he would. No such luck tonight. If anything, he was more restless than ever.

Looked like another long night of bad television. Relinquishing himself to his fate, he headed to the sofa, but not before taking one last look at the house next door. Zoe's window had gone dark.

He attributed the strange knot in his chest to beer and exhaustion.

It seemed like Zoe had just fallen asleep when her phone rang. With a groan, she reached over Reynaldo's sleeping body and grabbed the nightstand clock. Five-thirty. Good God.

"Good. You're awake." Caroline's voice was laced with coffee and cigarettes.

"No one's awake at this hour," she muttered. Closing her eyes, she burrowed back into her cave of blankets. "What do you want?"

"Your column."

Naturally. Zoe groaned again. "You know, I'm pretty sure your job title reads 'assistant.' As in assist, not browbeat."

"You hired me to keep you efficient. Which means making sure your column gets in on time. Which means browbeating. And since you've moved yourself to East God-knows-where—"

"Naushatucket."

"Whatever. You leaving the city means I have to start my browbeating extra early."

"Relax, Brunhilda, I still have two days."

"No, you have nine hours. Today's Wednesday, remember?"

"Crap." Panic replaced sleepiness and Zoe sat up straight.

"You forgot, didn't you?" Caroline said.

"I was busy with some house problems. I got distracted."

"House problems? Told you moving to nowhere was a mistake."

"You know, people in cities have house problems, too," Zoe replied. "It's what happens when you buy a house. Regardless, it's no big deal. I hired a handyman." A handyman whose extreme reactions and anguished expression had distracted her far more than anything else last night. Including Paul, she realized with a frown.

Don't ever use that word to describe me. The ache

in her heart that kept her up half the night started up again.

Meanwhile, on the other end of the phone, she could practically hear Caroline smirking over her latte. "Still upset I called so early?"

"Sadly, no." Truth was, for all her browbeating, Caroline was worth her weight in gold. During the worst days of her separation, when she was finding out more and more about Paul's infidelities, Caroline had also been her rock, patiently listening while she ranted and raved about the evils of falling in love with the people you're trying to help. "I'm glad one of us is on top of things."

"Okay, that doesn't sound good. What happened? I thought hiding out was supposed to get you back on your game."

"So did I." Zoe sighed.

"Give yourself time. It's only been a couple of days. Bet you're not even unpacked yet, are you?"

"Almost. I ran into a few home repair issues." Briefly she explained, ending with the story about the bats. "Now I've got these bat nets or whatever they are hanging off my roof. Jake said he'll check them for critters this morning."

"Jake?"

"The handyman I hired."

"Oh, right. I didn't realize you were on a first-name basis."

"This is a small island. Everyone's on a first-name basis."

"Uh-huh."

Again, Zoe could hear the smirk, this time accompanied by a healthy dose of innuendo. "For crying out loud, the ink's barely dry on my divorce. Last thing I'm interested in is another relationship. Besides, this guy's not exactly 'relatable,' if you know what I mean."

"He doesn't like girls?"

"He doesn't like people in general, I don't think." Saying the words brought a lump of sadness to her stomach. "He's got baggage." Too much baggage for one man to carry, she suspected.

"Uh-oh. Sounds like somebody's found a new project."

If only. "He's not looking for help, Caroline. In fact, the exact opposite," she added in a low voice. "I can't explain it, but I almost think he wants to suffer." *Don't ever use that word to describe me.* "He's punishing himself for something, only I don't know what."

"Let me guess. You're the only person who can understand him." More than a little sarcasm laced Caroline's voice. Zoe'd used that very line dozens of times when defending Paul.

"It's nothing like that," she replied. "And remember, friend or not, you can still be fired."

"No, I can't—your career would fall apart without me."

True, though she didn't need to sound so smug.

"Getting back to this handyman," Caroline continued. "Is he cute?"

"I'm not sure *cute* is the right word." She thought about how easily he moved around the roof. "More like very masculine."

"Nice. Break a pipe, then send me a photo of him in a wet T-shirt."

"Very funny. Seriously, this guy has some major issues. It's hard not to wonder what caused them."

"Well, while you're speculating, make sure you focus on getting that column done. Syndicators get very cranky when the content arrives late."

"Yes, boss. Anything else?"

"Yeah, keep your distance. I know you love a good sob story and all…"

Caroline wouldn't say that if she'd seen Jake's eyes. Still, Zoe reassured her. "I have absolutely no intention of repeating past mistakes. My bank account can't afford it."

After going over a few more business details, Zoe hung up and headed downstairs. Thanks to Caroline, going back to sleep was impossible.

Reynaldo came trotting into the kitchen behind her, yawning. Even half asleep, Zoe had to giggle. If dogs could have bedhead, he definitely qualified.

"What do you say we take that walk on the beach we never got to last night?"

Sensing potential freedom, the dachshund perked up with a bark.

This time of morning, the two-mile strip of sand was close to empty. The sun had barely breached the horizon, a large orange-pink half circle that promised another warm day once the pockets of fog burned away. The air smelled of water and salt. Taking a deep breath, Zoe allowed the aroma to wash over her. Yes, she thought, time on the beach was exactly what she needed.

How on earth had her life gotten to this place? Eight months ago she'd been on top of the world. Now here she was, paying support to a philandering husband and living next door to an enigmatic handyman she couldn't get out of her head.

Ever the nudge, Reynaldo whined and pulled on his leash. "Chill, Reynaldo. I don't care how wide open the space is, you need to stay on the leash."

The dachshund whined again. There were birds about and he clearly wanted to chase them. Sighing, she looked up and down the deserted beach. The only people that she could see were two die-hard fishermen casting into the surf.

"You're a spoiled brat, you know that, don't you?"

He took off the second she unhooked his leash.

Free from the confines of his harness, he embarked on a quest to rid the beach of seagulls.

"At least he's not chasing chipmunks."

Hearing Jake's voice, she started. Her neighbor was making his way along the shoreline. He must have come from around the rocks behind her because she hadn't seen him earlier.

Based on the foam cup he held in his hand, she guessed he'd walked to the diner in town. He was wearing a pair of snug, torn jeans and a gray sweatshirt dotted with paint. An equally ragged Boston baseball cap topped his head, and his shoes were covered with sand.

He looked sexy as all get out.

Suddenly Zoe regretted her decision to walk in her flannel pajamas. Combing her hair into something more than a sloppy ponytail would have been nice, too. She quickly undid the tie from her hair and refastened it, hoping she looked nonchalant as she did so.

"Give him time," she quipped. "The day's still early."

His face didn't react to the joke.

She continued, "I didn't know anyone else would be up this early. The sunrise is gorgeous, isn't it?"

In the last minute the sun had risen another inch above the water, bringing its color to more of the sky. "There's something about the light breaking through the gray that makes me feel inspired to tackle the day."

"Makes me think it's early. And that I should be asleep."

Yet he wasn't. In fact, had he slept at all? Given his dark circles and haggard appearance, she wondered.

As soon as Reynaldo realized she had a companion, he took a break from his bird-chasing duties and ran up to them. Rather, he ran up to Jake. Jumping up and down, he barked incessantly as though greeting a long-lost friend.

Jake scowled. "What is with this dog?"

"Apparently he likes you."

"Lucky me."

"Either that or he thinks you've got food. Rey's two biggest motivators are his appetite and his bladder."

"Glad to see he's got the important things down."

Oh, Lord, was that an attempt at humor she heard tripping off his lips? Zoe felt the corners of her mouth tug upward. "No one can accuse him of not having his priorities in order, that's for certain," she said.

Proving her point, Rey turned his attention away from Jake, and promptly trotted to a nearby scrub of beach grass, where he relieved himself. "My assistant, Caroline, calls him my substitute child because I cater to him so much," she remarked.

"She might have a point," Jake replied.

Adjusting her glasses as camouflage, she took a look at her companion. He was sipping his coffee, his green eyes focused on the frolicking dachshund. Again, she was struck by the fatigue and sadness hovering around him. Even standing here with her and Reynaldo, he looked alone. Alone and far away.

"I'd wanted a pet forever." She hoped that sharing might draw him out. "When I was a kid, we couldn't have a pet—my dad had breathing issues—so as soon as I got a place of my own I headed straight for the pound. Believe it or not." She chuckled. "I'd planned on getting a retriever."

"And instead you got the tube of terror."

"Tube of terror?"

"Couldn't think of a *T* word that means annoying," he replied with a shrug.

Zoe laughed. "Reynaldo, tube of terror. Suits him."

Jake's mouth quirked upward, the closest he'd come to a smile since she met him. Seeing it brought more warmth than the rising sun. "So, from retriever to dachshund. How'd that happen?"

"Couldn't help myself. Every time I walked past the cage, he would whimper and look at me with his sad brown eyes. Then the woman at the shelter told me he'd been found abandoned and left tied up behind a drugstore. Soon as I heard that, I was hooked. I've always been a sucker for a good sob story."

"Either that or Reynaldo is a master manipulator."

"You might be right." She was a sucker for those, too. "Anyway, I couldn't stand the idea of the little guy not having a home."

"I'm surprised you were so keen on outing the bats then. Seeing as how you've blocked them from their nests."

"That's different. That was self-preservation. Although…" She frowned. "I didn't think about the fact I was rendering them homeless. Do you think they sell bat houses at the hardware store?"

His head tilted like a questioning puppy, Jake studied her. "You really would buy one, wouldn't you?"

"I booted them from their nest. Shouldn't I help to fix their problem?"

"Do you always feel compelled to solve problems?"

"Sure," Zoe replied, undoing and fixing her ponytail again. She was painfully aware of his eyes sweeping her length, his evaluation spreading through her limbs like honey. She shrugged, affecting nonchalance. "See a problem, try to help. Advice columnist, remember?"

"I remember." He took a long drink from his coffee, silence swirling around him like the ocean breeze. "What if you can't help?"

Was he talking about himself? They sure weren't

talking about bats anymore. There was such resignation in his voice as he spoke, it hurt.

"Not every problem can be fixed," he continued.

"I don't believe that," she countered. "Every problem can be fixed, with time."

"Well, that's why you're the advice columnist and I'm not." Before she could reply, he started walking toward the street. Whatever crack he'd allowed in his armor was sealed once more. "I'll go check your roof to see if any bats got left behind last night. Good luck getting that dog back on a leash."

"If I can't, I'll simply wave a doggy biscuit. Never underestimate the lure of food."

He shot her another half smile, and went on his way.

How long she stood watching the waves, Zoe didn't know. Could have been an hour or a few minutes. The inner peace she'd hoped to find never materialized. She felt off-kilter. Out of sorts. More so than before, if possible. The sadness that laced Jake's voice continued to hang in the air, thick and unrepentant.

What was it about the man that his presence surrounded her even after his departure? Why couldn't she stop thinking about him?

Suddenly her thoughts were cut by the sound of a horn blasting in the morning air. Zoe heard the screech of tires followed by a high-pitched yelp.

Reynaldo. Her eyes searched the dunes looking for him, only to have her stomach sink with dread.

The dachshund was nowhere in sight.

No, no, no. Sand spraying behind her, she took off for the street. *Please, no. Not Reynaldo.* Why had she let him off the leash? Why hadn't she paid closer attention? Stupid, stupid daydreaming. She scrambled over the top ridge onto the street.

A gray sedan was pulled to the side of the road and a pair of elderly fishermen were standing next to it. When they saw her, one of them came rushing over.

"We didn't see him 'til he was in front of the car. Ran right out in the street, he did."

Oh, God, no. Not Rey. She pushed past the man, dreading what she was about to see, only to stop dead in her tracks.

There, legs sprawled in the gravel, sat Jake, his arms wrapped around a very much unscathed Reynaldo.

"We were headed down to the point when the dog darted into the street. If this guy hadn't grabbed him, we would have hit the little guy for sure."

Gratitude—along with a healthy dose of admiration—swelled in Zoe's chest. She wanted to speak, but the words, along with her heart, seemed stuck in her throat, so she settled for kneeling down beside him. Reynaldo squirmed in Jake's grip. Whether out of excitement or from knowing he'd narrowly escaped injury, the dog was bent on licking his savior's chin, a gesture Jake was receiving rather unenthusiastically.

"Calm down, Rey." She'd finally found her voice, albeit it was not much more than a whisper. Gently, her hands shaking, she slipped the dog from Jake's grip. "Are you all right?" she asked Jake.

"Are you talking to me or the dog?"

"You." His gruffness made her smile. "Are you hurt?"

"I'm fine."

"Thank God," one of the fishermen said. Zoe could tell from his tone he'd feared otherwise and was grasping at Jake's answer like a life preserver. "You went down pretty hard when my fender clipped you."

The car struck him? Zoe's eyes shot up to meet Jake's, only to find his expression shuttered.

"I said I'm fine." He moved to push himself up, only to grimace with pain and sit back down.

"You're not all right at all," Zoe said. She shifted Reynaldo to her hip, and reached for him with her now free hand. "Your hip—"

"Zoe, I don't want your help! Just go take care of your damn dog and leave me alone."

Her insides recoiled, but not from Jake's verbal slap. Though harsh, his words were nowhere near as painful as watching him struggle to hide his embarrassment while he accepted a hand up from the fishermen. It took all her effort not to reach out and reassure him when he reached his feet. She stood in silence, arms wrapped around Reynaldo as he nodded a curt thank-you to the men and limped toward his front yard.

"What about your leg?" one of the men called out, only to be waved off.

The driver turned to Zoe. "I honestly didn't see either of them."

"It's not your fault," Zoe replied. "I should have been paying closer attention myself but I got distracted." *Distracted by thoughts of Reynaldo's savior.*

Thoughts that filled her mind with even greater ferocity as she watched him disappear through his front door.

CHAPTER FIVE

Dear Zoe

My boyfriend of three years refuses to talk about marriage. Whenever I bring up the topic, he laughs and says he hasn't "made up his mind yet." My friends tell me I should break up with him, but I'm afraid I won't meet anyone else... I'm overweight and not very pretty.

Ugly in New York

Dear Ugly

If your boyfriend hasn't "made up his mind" in three years, I'm not sure he ever will. More importantly, however, why are you so certain he's your only shot at happiness? Don't be so down on yourself! I'm willing to bet you have far more to offer than you give yourself credit for. My advice: dump the loser and find someone who appreciates you.

Zoe

OKAY, "dump the loser" was probably over the top. She'd end with "give yourself credit for."

Hmm. Reminded her of someone else who didn't give himself enough credit. Lord, but her stomach still churned thinking of how close she had come to losing her precious Reynaldo. If not for Jake...

And he didn't want to be called a hero.

Following Rey's rescue, she'd tried to discourage her handyman from working. As far as she was concerned, her loose shingles could wait a day or two. His hip had to be killing him. But no sooner did she make the suggestion than he'd snapped back, "I said I'd start your roof today so I'm doing it," and hobbled up the ladder.

She could hear him up there now, scraping off shingles. He'd draped a plastic blue tarp around the entire house. It blocked her view and filled every room with dark blue shadows and every five minutes or so, debris would rattle down the plastic like heavy rain. Six and a half hours and he'd yet to take a break, at least not one she'd heard. Like yesterday, he seemed intent on working 'til he dropped. Zoe could picture him up there, muscles straining, sweat dampening his shirt. His face contorting every time he moved...

Well, she decided, pushing the laptop aside, the very least she could do was make sure the man who saved Reynaldo took a lunch break. She still couldn't believe he'd jumped in front of that car. Without him her sweet little dog would be…

Lump sticking in her throat, she paused to pet the dachshund sleeping next to the sofa.

Yeah, she thought, lunch was the least she could do.

Since getting Jake to come down and join her was unlikely, she decided to bring the food to him. Fortunately she'd brought a small beach cooler with her when she moved. She filled it with turkey sandwiches, fruit and cold drinks. As an afterthought, she included a bottle of ibuprofen, and stepped outside.

To her surprise, the sky was far from sunny when she stepped out of her blue-shaded cave. While she'd been inside, her bright cheery sun had been replaced by a collection of gray clouds. Even so, the air felt warm and thick when she reached the top of the ladder. Jake was leaning against his shovel, eyes closed. She'd been right about the sweat. His T-shirt was soaked. The cotton molded across his shoulders and broad chest before falling loose over his flat abdomen.

Zoe's throat ran dry.

"Knock, knock," she said hoarsely.

He started and briefly, when his eyes widened, she worried he might lose his balance. A silly concern, she realized soon enough as he quickly steadied himself. His lips drew into a tight line. He wasn't happy to see her.

Zoe held up her minicooler. "Greetings. I come bearing food. It's lunchtime, in case you haven't noticed."

An unreadable expression crossed his features. "You don't have to feed me."

"Of course I do. Reynaldo would never forgive me, seeing as how food is his life and you saved his life. Which reminds me…" She set the cooler down and eased herself onto the peak, careful not to slip on the exposed wood. "In case I didn't say it before, thank you."

Jake shrugged. "Dog ran into the street—I grabbed him."

"It's a little bigger deal than that," Zoe said. If she didn't think he'd balk at the word, she'd call him a hero again. "I would have lost my best friend today if it weren't for you." She offered up a grateful smile, which he didn't return.

He did, however, meet her eyes. "I'm glad you didn't. No one should have to lose a friend."

Had he? Something about his voice, hollow and sad, made her shiver.

A heavy silence settled between them. Zoe forced herself to look away. "Hope you like turkey on white. One of those women who can whip up a gourmet meal at the drop of a hat, I'm not. Takeout is more my forte. You have no idea how thrilled I was to learn they opened a restaurant near the ticket office."

Jake rubbed the back of his neck. "Not sure I'd

call the 'Tucket a restaurant. More like a glorified greasy spoon."

"Hey, it serves food I don't have to cook—that makes it a five-star restaurant in my book. Now, come sit down and eat your lunch."

Jake was staring at the sandwich she'd thrust in his direction.

"Don't worry, it's edible. I promise."

Carefully, he lowered himself down next to her, his grimace a reminder of how much a personal toll Rey's rescue had taken on him. Reaching into the cooler, Zoe pulled out the bottle of ibuprofen. "Thought you might want this, too."

Jake shook his head. "Won't help."

"Not even a little?"

"Nothing does."

Nothing?

"I've got some prescription stuff at home, but that more dulls it than anything."

His matter-of-factness amazed her. She couldn't imagine living with continual pain, and that fact made what he'd done this morning even more impressive. She wanted to say so but the edge in his voice made her hold back. She settled for a soft murmur of sympathy.

"Stuff happens when you catch a mortar shell," he replied with his typical shrug. As if people caught mortar shells every day.

Dear Lord. "You're lucky you weren't killed."

Jake stared at his sandwich. "So they tell me."

Again, his hollow voice made her shiver.

They continued eating their sandwiches in silence. Part of Zoe wanted to fill the quiet with idle chitchat, but another, more sensible part made her bite her tongue and study the seascape. A line of weather was working its way across the water. To the right, on the edge of shingling, a piece of white string caught her eye. The netting from last night.

"How goes the bat hunting?" she asked. "Find any more winged creatures of the night?"

"No." Was that a half smile teasing his cheek? Tentative as it was, the sight raised Zoe's spirits. "Not so far anyway. The valves were empty—"

"Valves?" she interrupted.

"The netting we installed last night. It was empty and I haven't seen any additional signs of damage. I'll check the attic to make certain, but I'd say you lucked out. You still serious about getting a bat house?"

"Absolutely." Seemed only right. "Bats are people, too, right?"

For whatever reason, the answer met with his approval, because he nodded. "I admire your conscientiousness."

Really? "You do?"

"You sound surprised."

"To be honest, I am," she told him. "I got the impression you think I'm a bit of a flake."

He regarded her. "Not flaky. Hyper-helpful, but not flaky."

"Thank you. I guess." A bit backhanded, perhaps, but he clearly meant it as a compliment. The warmth flooding her cheeks suggested she certainly took it as one.

Goodness, but she didn't get this man. Gruff one minute, reluctantly nice the next—although she suspected he would insist niceness had nothing to do with anything. She could hear Caroline scoffing now, but how could a woman—that is, a person—not meet Jake and be intrigued?

Before she could dwell too long, her thoughts were interrupted by a splash of water landing on her cheek. Then another, followed by another. Looking out to the ocean, she saw the rain line had drawn closer.

"So much for a picnic. Looks like we'll have to finish inside." Without waiting for a response, she plucked Jake's half-eaten sandwich out of his hand. He looked about to protest when the drops started to fall faster. Together they scrambled to pick up the tools and food before the rain moved in.

They didn't make it. In fact, Zoe had barely stepped off the bottom ladder rung when the sky opened up and what had been isolated drops became a steady downpour.

No sooner did they fight their way through a gap in the blue tarp and enter the living room than Reynaldo, annoyed at being left behind, began yelping and dancing circles. Just as he had this morning on the beach, he lavished most of his attention on Jake.

"Reynaldo, heel!" Like the command would do any good. Tongue out, tail wagging, the little dog was practically doing back flips trying to get Jake to notice him.

A giggle bubbled up in Zoe's chest. She didn't know which was more amusing: Reynaldo's desperate ploy or the exaggerated scowl on Jake's face.

"Looks like someone likes you," she said.

"Well, tell him to stop."

"Too late, I'm afraid. Once Rey makes up his mind about a person, nothing will shake him. Like a dog with a bone."

"Ha, ha."

"Seriously. He hated my ex-husband on sight. Used to growl at him. We had to keep him downstairs the nights Paul was home." You'd think she'd have picked up on the hint.

"Anyway—" she shook off the thought "—you might as well get used to having Reynaldo as your new best friend."

"I don't want friends, canine or other."

With that, Jake moved toward a large leather Barcalounger that used to be her father's favorite chair, and propped himself on the arm. "I'll take my sandwich back."

Zoe reached into the cooler and handed it to him.

"You say you don't want friends, and yet you saved mine."

"Told you, right place, right time, is all."

No, he'd told her no one should have to lose a friend. Strange thing to say for a man who didn't want any himself.

The blue-shaded room cast a different kind of shadow over his features, turning his face almost as gray as the weather outside. The lines marking his face were especially apparent today. Without meaning to, she let her gaze follow the longest one down his forehead to his brow. As prominent as these marks on his skin were, she had a feeling the scars below the surface were deeper and far more brutal.

He must have felt her stare because he turned to face her. "What?"

Aw, hell. In for a penny, in for a pound, right? "Was he a good friend?"

"Was who?"

Feigned ignorance wasn't his strong suit, but Zoe played along. "The friend you lost. On the roof, you said no one should lose a friend. That was obviously from personal experience. Were the two of you close?"

His expression remained passive. On the surface, it would look like he didn't react to what she said, but Zoe had been watching. She saw the subtle clench of his jaw as he swallowed his emotions. That said it all.

"I can only imagine what you must have felt," she continued.

Still no reply. He was wrapping himself up the way he'd wrapped the house. "If you ever want to talk…" she began.

"No." Finally he spoke. The word burst out of him like a shot, contorting his face with a distress so stark Zoe's heart hurt.

Right. That's why his eyes had darkened and unspoken words hung in the air around him. She crossed the room to sit on the chair next to him. "Look—" her fingers rested on the curve of his wrist "—I'm no therapist, but keeping things inside isn't healthy for anyone."

"Spare me the platitudes—I'm not one of your readers looking for advice."

Ouch. "You're right. You're not."

"And I don't want your help."

"I know that, too."

Yet she couldn't seem to help herself. His torment called out for help. She could hear it. Feel it. Why else would her heart be twisting in her chest?

"My question is, what do you want?"

"I—" Their eyes locked and his words faded away. The air, which had already felt thick and portentous, shifted. To Zoe, it felt like the warmth had seeped inside her. A heady, intoxicating feeling, it was the kind that gave birth to dangerous notions. But she couldn't pull away. Jake's eyes held her. And when he dropped his gaze to her mouth…

Then suddenly, the sensation disappeared, erased by the electronic sounds of jazz. As Jake fished his cell phone from his pocket, Zoe turned away, putting the distance back between them.

Behind her, Jake swore, the curse mild in volume only.

"Bad news?" She looked at her fingers. They were trembling.

"It's nothing." She didn't have to see his face to know the answer was a lie, and a bad one to boot, but she let it slide.

A couple beats passed. She imagined him studying the call screen on his phone. "You asked what I wanted," he said finally.

She turned back around. "Yes, I did."

"What I want is to be left alone."

Of course he did.

"What's so funny?"

Funny? Zoe realized she was chuckling aloud at the predictability. "Nothing." Her turn to lie poorly. "I couldn't help but wonder if that's your polite way of saying, stop asking questions."

"Nothing polite about it. Look," he asserted, pre-empting her when she opened her mouth to respond, "it's not personal. I don't… Relationships are no longer on my radar."

"I understand." Another poor lie. In truth, a

man like Jake shutting himself off didn't feel right. Especially when instinct told her that hadn't always been the case.

Still, now was not the time to push the point.

"Tell you what," she said. "From now on we're strictly handyman and home owner. No more personal questions."

Emotion flickered in the depths of his eyes. He was surprised that she agreed so easily, no doubt. "Thank you."

"No problem. For what it's worth, I recently made a similar vow myself."

"That so?" Now he definitely looked surprised.

"Surely you didn't think you'd cornered the market on wanting solitude, did you?"

"No." He regarded her for a moment. "Your divorce was more than expensive."

More of a statement than a question, Jake's comment brought with it a surprising feeling of understanding.

"It came with a lot of costs," she said.

"Doesn't everything?"

They looked at each other with nothing but the pitter-patter of rain on the tarp filling the room. Zoe tried to read his expression, but failed. Whatever thoughts were running through that handsome head, they remained hidden from the world.

"Do you want a second sandwich?" she asked at

last. He hadn't finished the first, but Zoe couldn't think of another excuse to speak.

"No, but thank you." Pushing himself to his feet, he stumbled slightly and fell forward, catching his footing a few inches from where she stood. The aroma of bay rum and masculinity wrapped itself around her body. Hooded eyes looked down at her, finding her mouth again.

"I—I should be going," he said. "Thank you for the sandwich."

She waited until he'd slipped around the blue tarp before letting out the long breath she didn't realize she'd been holding. "You're welcome."

The rain moved in for the rest of the day.

For a long time after Jake's departure, Zoe stood in the living room staring at the doorway, as if he might walk back in. He didn't.

Eventually she returned to the work waiting for her. While she still didn't feel like she had answers, her looming deadline left her little choice but to write something. Hopefully her readers would find her advice passable even if she didn't.

Outside, the blue tarp waved and buckled. Heading into the kitchen, she saw Jake pulling the plastic sheeting away from her windows. His hair and clothes were wet. Every so often he'd wipe the rain from his face.

Surely he didn't have to remove the plastic right

now. She could live with a shrouded house. Her eyes traveled to the coffeemaker.

No, he was out there because he wanted to be. She'd already trotted out once today with that silly picnic. She was not going to act like some smitten groupie or beg for his attention. If Jake wanted to be left alone, she would honor his request.

Instead, she poured a cup of coffee, returned to her laptop and focused her attention on the people who wanted it.

The plastic sheet rippled in the wind, making maneuvering difficult, but Jake eventually wrangled it under control. He didn't have to pull the tarp back; tomorrow he would only have to put it back into place. Through the living room window he saw Zoe on the sofa, typing away on her laptop. Her hair hung around her face. Every so often she'd comb it back from her eyes. His eyes traveled to the Barcalounger, his mind harkening back to her body swaying close to his. She'd smelled like lemons. Would her skin taste like them, too? The therapist at the VA used to suggest sucking on lemons to anchor himself during a flashback. *What do you want, Jake?*

No. He wouldn't go there. He'd meant what he said, about wanting to be left alone. He didn't want Zoe bopping up his ladder with sandwiches. He didn't want to "talk" with her or think of her as anything but the woman who hired him.

So instead he stood in the rain and wrestled with the plastic tarp, letting the rain cool his overheated skin.

The next morning, Zoe found herself still decidedly not thinking about her neighbor as she made her way to the hardware store to order a bat house.

"Take a couple days," Ira told her. "We don't stock 'em in the store. You mind?"

Zoe shook her head.

"Good to know. Some people aren't so patient about waiting." He grabbed an order pad from underneath the counter. "By the way, you find that handyman of yours?"

He's not mine, Zoe thought. *He's not anybody's.* Then she realized what the manager meant. "If you're talking about Jake, he's at my house scraping shingles off the roof as we speak."

His dark figure had appeared on her roof just after dawn. Zoe had *not* studied him through her rearview mirror as she drove away. "In fact, he's the reason for the bat house. He found some droppings."

"Good man. Does good work. I've hired him myself more than once."

Zoe couldn't help herself. "You know Jake well?"

"As well as anyone on the island I suppose. He's pretty private. Keeps to himself." He cast an eye at her over his order pad. "Why do you ask?"

"Curious, is all," she replied. Seemed like too vague a word, but she couldn't think of a better one.

"Well, like I said, he's a pretty private person. I'm sure he's got a good reason."

Meaning she'd get no more information from him. "Yes, I'm sure he does."

To be honest, she understood the reticence. The small year-round community naturally would be protective of one another, especially when it came to newcomers like her. Then again, it was possible, given Jake's barriers, Ira knew as little about her handyman as she did.

Her handyman. Second time today the phrase crossed her brain. Like before, she immediately issued a correction. Jake didn't belong to anyone. Especially her. Not that she wanted him to belong to her anyway.

There was no silhouette on the rooftop when she pulled into her drive, only tar paper and bare wood. She parked the car and headed toward the backyard, where she swore she could hear Reynaldo barking. Rounding the corner, she saw Jake attaching the dachshund to his dog run. Her stomach fluttered at the sight.

Because he was being nice to Reynaldo, not because she was relieved he hadn't left.

Rey was doing his usual circling and pirouetting around Jake's legs. "Hold your horses," he was saying. "Let me get you clipped up. There. Go bother the chipmunks for a little while instead of me." With a sharp bark, Rey trotted off toward the back end of the yard.

"See he's got you trained, too," she said, announcing her arrival.

He turned, causing the sunlight to hit his face just right, and light up his eyes like emeralds. Brilliant beyond belief, they somehow managed to look sad and wary at the same time. The effect shot straight through to her heart, and she felt a tiny lurch. He might not want friends, but she was looking at the eyes of a man who needed them.

"Deliveryman came and he started barking his head off," he said. "Wouldn't stop 'til I took him outside."

"He hates being left out of the action. Don't you, you spoiled brat?"

Too involved with sniffing tree roots, the dachshund didn't reply. "Of course," she continued, "now that he's out here with us, he'll ignore us."

"Proof things aren't always what they seem."

What was that odd statement supposed to mean? Cocking her head, she gave him a long, questioning look, hoping for an answer, but his face remained, like always, a sphinxlike mask.

Suddenly, something he said hit her. "Did you say I got a delivery?" Couldn't be the bat house. Probably a package from Caroline. Some item her assistant deemed vital to quality living no doubt, like an espresso maker or a big fat sign emblazoned with her deadline dates.

Jake answered without intonation. "On the back step."

Zoe looked. Then looked again to make sure she saw correctly. Sure enough, a floral arrangement in shades of pink sat by the back door. She'd been so focused on Jake and Reynaldo, she hadn't noticed.

A pretty amazing feat given the arrangement's size. The thing was huge. An over-the-top array of roses, calla lilies and delphinium, the kind of bouquet you'd send when trying to impress. Zoe knew only one person who would make such a grand-scale gesture. She slipped the card from its small white envelope.

Need you forever. Love, Paul

"I didn't know the island had a florist," she murmured. The lame comment was all she could muster. How had he known where to find her? Certainly not from Caroline.

"Doesn't. Came over on the ferry from the mainland."

Paul certainly had outdone himself. She'd never seen such an amazing arrangement. The roses were as big as her fist. Her finger traced a pale pink petal. Such a beautiful, delicate flower.

Too bad he wasted his money.

Picking up the arrangement, she walked over to the side of her garage.

And dropped the bouquet in the trash.

CHAPTER SIX

HER scalp tingled. Jake stood behind her, staring down. She waited for his comment, his question, whatever. After all, not every day did you get to see a woman trash a three-hundred-dollar floral arrangement.

He said nothing.

"I'm going for a walk," she announced, turning abruptly. She needed fresh air to clear away the scent of roses.

Unlike the early morning when only a handful of people dotted the shore, the beach at this time of day was full. Or as full as it could be prior to tourist season. At the public end of the strip, the morning's fishermen had been replaced by a line of multicolored umbrellas and beach towels. Mothers watched toddlers build sand castles. The sound of radios drifted on the wind.

Zoe headed to her left, where the rocks from the jetty formed a tiered tower. Part way up, they flattened, creating a large overhang. It was here she settled, leaning back and letting her legs over the edge. Beneath her feet, the waves crashed over smaller rocks, white foam bubbling into tide pools.

"Hey."

Looking up, she saw Jake approaching, a mug of coffee in his hands. "Took a coffee break," he said.

With impressive agility, he ascended the rocks and joined her. Handing her the mug, he settled himself on the rock next to her. When he was settled, she attempted to hand the cup back, only to have him shake his head.

"Thought you said you took a coffee break."

"I did. Didn't feel like drinking coffee is all."

But he'd brought her one. Gratitude, and something else—something stronger—built inside her. She took a sip, hoping it would push away the thickness in her throat. "Funny, I remember these rocks being much taller when I was little," she said.

"Things always look different when we're kids."

"True." She stared into her mug. "Aren't you going to ask?"

"Ask what?"

"Why I threw away the flowers."

"Figured you didn't like pink."

If he meant the remark to cheer her up, it worked; she smiled. Of course he wouldn't ask. She should have realized.

"They were from my ex-husband," she told him anyway. Since they'd met, she'd overshared. Why stop now? "He must have gotten my address from my mother. Lord knows how, since she never liked him. Said his teeth were too white."

Jake's brow knit in confusion.

"He's a golf pro," she continued with a shrug, as if that would explain. "At least, he tries to be. He claims he can't make it on the tour without my support. I caught him sleeping with a cocktail waitress at one of the tournaments. I'm pretty sure she wasn't the first. Guess my support wasn't enough."

Or she wasn't enough. The silent fear that continually plagued her subconscious made its way to the forefront of her thoughts. She tried to laugh it off, but the noise came out more a squeaky sigh. "My own fault really. Like I told you yesterday, I'm a sucker for sad stories. But—" she raised the cup to her lips for another sip "—not anymore. From here on in, I ride solo. I won't get used again."

"Wise decision."

Says the man who swore off the world. "Thank you."

Spray from the waves splashed across her ankles, dampening her jeans. The sudden splatter of cold on her skin made her yelp. It took some getting used to the New England waters. Damn stuff didn't warm until July or August, if it warmed at all.

"What's this place like in the winter?" she asked Jake.

"Thinking of hiding here year-round?"

The idea had merit, this morning anyway. "Wondering, is all."

"Cold," he replied. "Raw. Most of the businesses close up except for the hardware store and a couple others. You can go days without seeing another person."

"Sounds…" She was about to say "lonely," but realized the isolation was what he wanted. The idea of him holed up alone all winter shouldn't upset her, but it did.

Knowing any commentary would be unwelcome, she went back to studying the tide pool. From her perch she could see the ripples left by small fish as they snacked on algae.

"Look," she said, catching sight of five spiny rays out of the corner of her eye, "a sea star. I've never seen one up close before. Not outside an aquarium."

"According to the fishermen, there's been an increase in numbers the last couple years. I gather they're not happy to see them around."

"They may not be, but I am. I'm going to get a closer look." Setting down her coffee, she slipped off her sandals and slid downward, searching with her toes until she found purchase. After a few tries, she finally found a small rock an inch or so above the water she could lower down onto. Unfortunately, her stepping stone could only accommodate one foot so she was forced to balance on one leg.

"This might be harder than I thought," she said.

"Been a while since my gymnastics days. My center of gravity's not what it used to be."

"Looks fine to me."

The blush that shot down from her head to her toes did not help her balance. Surely he didn't mean the comment *that* way. Glancing up in his direction, she saw no indication in his expression that would refute the thought.

To cover her reaction, she kept talking. "My specialty was tumbling. Coach said I had powerful legs. Which was a polite way of saying I couldn't keep still. Ants in my pants, my mother used to say."

Steadying herself with one hand, she slowly crouched down. "Will you look at this beauty?" she said, lifting the yellow-orange creature to get a better look at the suckers on its underside. "The summer we stayed here, my dad and I would go scavenging on the beach. I got very good at finding dismembered crab claws and empty skate cases."

"Priceless items to a little girl," Jake said from above.

"Exactly. I had a whole treasure chest filled with booty. Well, a shoebox full anyway. Those were fun times." She tried—and failed—to keep a note of melancholy from slipping into her voice.

"How old were you when you stopped coming?"

"Seven. My father got sick that winter. We only got to spend one summer." From then on, life became about staying out of the way and not being a burden. *Settle down, Zoe. You're not helping.*

"We didn't get to do a lot of things," she said in a low voice. A chill ran up her leg. She blamed the cold water.

"We didn't live near the beach, but our town had a pool. My brother and I would ride our bikes there every afternoon."

Zoe wasn't sure what surprised her more: that Jake shared a personal memory or that he had a family. For some reason, she'd assumed he was alone in the world. *Because that's the way he wanted it to be.* Knowing the truth, however, made his isolation even sadder.

"Where's your family now?" she asked.

"My dad's in Florida. I'm not sure where Steven is. New York, I think. We've…" He picked at the sand on the rock. "We've, uh, lost touch."

In other words, he cut ties with them. *Such a shame.*

"No, it's not."

She hadn't realized she'd spoken aloud. However now that the words were out, she saw no reason not to continue. "You don't think your family misses you?"

"My family's better off." The air stilled while he sipped from her coffee cup. Zoe's insides stilled as well. Did he really believe such a thing? That his family wouldn't want him around?

He must have sensed her question. "I'm not the same person they knew before. I don't have anything to offer them. Not anymore."

"You don't know—"

"Yes, I do."

Zoe bit her lip. She disagreed, but arguing would only close him off again, and she didn't want to spoil this tenuous whatever-you-want-to-call-it they'd formed.

Looking down, she realized, guiltily, she still held the starfish in her hand. "Sorry, little guy. Didn't mean to forget about you." *It's just that the man sitting on the rocks tends to make the rest of the world fade away.*

She set the creature back under water, on the rock she found him on. "Wonder what other critters we might find if we looked."

"Dismembered crab claws and smashed clams, most likely."

"You're no fun."

"Never said I was."

Bet he was once. Before the demons took hold. Suddenly, she was possessed by an idea. Frivolous, perhaps, but if she could get him to go for it, well... it might do him some good. "Want to come on a scavenger hunt with me?"

The minute she made the suggestion, Jake chuckled. A low throaty rumble that came from deep within his chest and made her long to hear a full-blown laugh. "You want me to help you look for broken seashells?"

"Don't forget skate cases. Finding the starfish has me feeling nostalgic. Plus, a walk on the beach is exactly what I need to clear my head."

"So take the tube of terror."

"Reynaldo would only try and eat my discoveries, and as good a companion as he is, sometimes it's nice to have a human being around to talk to." *Something you need to realize, too.* "What do you say? Will you keep me company?"

Jake shook his head. "I don't think so, Zoe."

"Bet I can find more sea glass than you."

Again, he gave a chuckle. God, but the sound was musical. "Are you always so persistent?"

"Yes." It was, as Paul used to say, one of her most annoying qualities. Not knowing when to quit. In this case, she probably should. Quit, that is. But she couldn't. Somehow in the last two minutes, her frivolous idea had become a challenge. This was the most open she'd seen Jake since they'd met. She couldn't shake the idea that if he allowed himself to relax, Jake might let down some of those walls he'd built around himself.

And okay, she wanted to keep this whatever-it-was going on a little longer. Given Jake's mercurial moods, who knew how long it might last?

"A half-hour walk. That's all I'm asking. Then I'll leave you alone for the rest of the day."

From the way he shook his head, she was ready for another refusal. It surprised her, therefore, when one didn't come. "One half hour. And then you'll leave me alone?"

Zoe smiled, thrilled with her victory. "Scout's honor."

What the hell was he doing? First, against all reason, he brought Zoe a cup of coffee. No, he didn't simply bring her coffee; he sat and listened to her problems. Now here he was beachcombing, for God's sake. He'd lost his freaking mind.

Actually, he could explain the coffee. From the moment she moved in, Zoe had this annoying sparkle about her, a kind of energy that made her impossible to ignore. When she saw the flowers, that sparkle dimmed. Her features fell and she lost all expression. It reminded him of the reflection he saw in the mirror every morning. Except, on Zoe, the melancholy and flat, mirthless eyes looked all wrong. So, when she threw away the roses and retreated to the beach, he felt compelled to check on her. To make sure the dimness was only temporary. Naushatucket didn't need two empty souls.

All right, maybe he was curious, too. The flower delivery bugged him for some reason. Who the hell sends flowers over on the damn ferry? He knew they were from the ex as soon as she tossed them, and he wanted to know what kind of man could snuff out Zoe's brightness.

Come to think of it, that brightness was to blame for this whole beachcombing craziness, too. Her whole damn face lit up finding that starfish; he was afraid to say no and watch it dim again.

Yeah, he didn't want to disappoint her. That was the reason he agreed.

It certainly wasn't because she looked sexy as hell standing ankle-deep in the tide pool.

Nor was that the reason he was still accompanying her long after the half-hour mark had passed.

The tide had come in. Formations that previously rose ten feet out of the water were now half-submerged, making exploration difficult, but Zoe didn't seem to care. She scrambled up and over the rocks, scouring the sand and tide pools. Her most exciting discovery so far was a sea slug—a sighting that had her wrinkling her nose and uttering a high-pitched "Eww!"

He himself wasn't doing too much searching. He found watching her way more entertaining. How she caught her lower lip between her teeth while she concentrated and how, when she thought she spied something, she would kneel down and bring her face close to the object she wanted to study. He simply walked along behind her, carrying both their shoes. Been a long time since he'd felt cool moist sand under between his toes.

"And once again, I've cornered the market on skate cases." Zoe tossed a four-pronged hollow tube at his feet. Jake laughed.

The sound sent guilt tearing through him. This wasn't right. Him, relaxing. Laughing. Enjoying himself.

Why couldn't he stop?

Meanwhile, Zoe had scrambled her way to the top of yet another rock formation and now appeared stuck. Jake knew why. The rocks on this section of the beach were particularly mossy, and when covered with water, hard to stand on.

"Need a hand?" he asked.

She shook her head. "I think I can make it. If I look where I'm going." Gingerly, she stepped down, her foot finding a moss-covered point.

Jake saw the impending calamity before it happened. The moss, soaked from waves, had become a blanket of slime that, when it met with Zoe's wet foot, became even more slippery. She immediately lost her balance and fell. The momentum propelled her forward, and she wound up half falling, half running down the remaining three rocks. Acting on instinct, Jake moved in to catch her, reaching the base in time for Zoe to land full-force onto him. Together they fell backward in a heap, Jake sprawled in the sand, Zoe sprawled across him.

As soon as they each caught their breath, Zoe said, matter-of-factly, "I slipped."

"No kidding," he replied.

"Did I hurt you?"

He shook his head. "My backside caught the brunt of the impact."

"That's good— Oh, your hip!" She pushed herself up from his chest. "I'm so sorry!"

"Don't be." The pain in his hip was nothing compared to the throbbing that flared elsewhere along his body when she shifted her weight. Heat, primal and instinctive, spread to every part of him. He'd felt every inch of her tiny frame, from her hips pressed against him, to her toes tickling the denim of his jeans.

During the fall, her glasses had fallen off, leaving him with an up-close, unobstructed view of her pale blue eyes. The most polished sea glass in the world couldn't come close to how gorgeous they looked. And her lips. He'd never noticed how plump and full they were.

"You've got sand in your hair," he murmured. Before he realized what he was doing, his hand reached up and combed the strands from her face. The dark locks were warm from the sun. And soft like silk. He twisted the strands between his fingers.

"We should get up before a wave lands on us." Though he said the words, he didn't feel any urgency. What he wanted was an excuse to touch her hair again. Dear God, when was the last time he'd felt something so soft?

Zoe smiled. "Afraid we'll wash out to sea?"

"You might." Taking care not to tip her off, he raised himself up onto his elbows. "I've seen sand fleas bigger than you."

"I'm not sure if I should be flattered or insulted."

"Ever see what a sand flea looks like? Definitely be flattered."

Her skin was already pink from the sun, and the blush covering her cheeks only deepened the color. It reminded him of pink frosting. If he ran a finger on her cheek, would it come away tasting sweet? His mouth watered with curiosity.

What on earth had her ex been thinking? He had to be insane, cheating on someone so beautiful and sweet. And sending flowers to apologize? The man should have come in person to beg on his knees for forgiveness. Kissing those perfectly plump lips 'til they were sighing with desire.

He couldn't help himself; he brushed some imaginary hair from her cheek. The softness under his fingers took his breath away. Her eyes had darkened, their paleness eclipsed by her widening pupils.

He felt pounding against his ribs. Took a moment, but he realized it was Zoe's heart beating in rhythm with his. She probably had no idea he could feel it.

God, but he bet those lips tasted amazing. He bet

every inch of her did. They were so close, too. All he needed to do was lift his head and they'd be his.

"Zoe?" His voice sounded raw and rough to his ears.

She raised her head, edging those lips closer. "Yes?"

It took all his resolve, but he found the right words. "You need to move first."

"I can't." The blush managed to deepen yet another shade. "I don't know where my glasses landed."

Oh, right. Her glasses. He'd been so mesmerized by her blush, he'd crazily mistaken it for arousal. Somewhere deep inside him, the truth brought a sense of relief. What else would it be?

Patting around the sand, he located the frames. She grabbed them from his hand like they were a life raft, and shoved them into place. "Thanks."

Her vision restored, she rolled off, leaving a cold empty sensation in her wake. The feeling was so sudden that his hand automatically began reaching out to pull her back. Fortunately he kept his head.

Or rather Zoe kept it for him. "I'm hungry," she announced.

Her pronouncement pulled him from his inner struggle. "Excuse me?" he asked as he struggled to his feet.

"I haven't had anything to eat since dawn, and I'm starved. Aren't you?"

"Hadn't thought about it." Eating had long ago

become something he did when he needed to do; he didn't give meals—or lack of them—much thought.

"Well, I have. It's late afternoon, in case you haven't noticed."

It was? How the hell did a whole afternoon pass by?

"Poor Reynaldo must be starving, too. He hates it when dinner is late."

"Then you better go feed the both of you."

"Hmm." She was looking at him, the sparkle all of a sudden reappearing in her eyes, brighter than before. Jake got a sinking sensation.

"Or…" She smiled. "I've got a better idea."

Better was a relative term.

"I still can't believe I agreed to this," he said.

"Why not?" Zoe tossed a piece of driftwood onto the campfire, sending sparks shooting into the sky. "I can't cook and you don't have any food. This is the perfect solution."

Jake shook his head. A campfire. His earlier assessment was right—he was out of his freaking mind. Actually, when Zoe first suggested the idea, he told her she was the one out of her mind. If only he hadn't slipped up and mentioned that his refrigerator was empty… She'd argued him into a corner at that point. "I'm going to build the fire anyway so you might as well join me. What else are you going to do? A man's got to eat, right?" She'd badgered him 'til he had to say yes, just to get her to stop.

Go ahead. His mind flashed back to them lying together on the beach. *Tell yourself you don't really want to be here.*

Meanwhile Zoe was busying herself with piercing a hot dog with a skewer. Soon as he acquiesced, she'd dashed across the street for supplies. After ordering him to gather wood, of course. She was, Jake was slowly learning, a bundle of enthusiasm. Once she made up her mind to pursue something, she wouldn't be deterred.

Or ignored, for that matter, he thought with an internal smile.

Hot dog in place, she handed him the skewer. "What I can't believe," she said, "is that you've never cooked over a campfire before."

"I didn't say that. I said I'd never roasted hot dogs over a fire."

"My mistake. What have you cooked?"

He thought of the chipmunks, snakes and other creatures scrounged during survival training. "You don't want to know."

"Something tells me you're right."

Reynaldo came trotting up looking for a snack. The dachshund, who'd returned with her, was happily covered with sand. Zoe reached into her sweatshirt pocket and pulled out a dog biscuit. "Here. This should tide you over." Rey took the treat and settled contentedly on a nearby towel.

"My dad loved campfires on the beach," she said. "We used to have them once a week. Hot dogs and S'mores. Inevitably he'd set the marshmallows on fire. Funny how some memories stick with you, isn't it?"

"Hmm." More than she'd realize.

"Then again, I suppose mine are tainted by child-hood nostalgia. I guess that's human nature for you. We tend to romanticize the past. Paint it better than it really was."

Jake didn't answer. *If only all memories worked like that.* But some could never be repainted. They were doomed to repeat themselves with perfect Technicolor accuracy. Zoe didn't need to hear that, though. She, like so many, was better off untouched by dark thoughts.

He looked over at his companion. She was perched on her knees, carefully holding her hot dogs over the flame. You'd think from the way she was turning the skewer—slowly, like a rotisserie—she was cooking a gourmet meal. Her skin was pink from the sun and heat. And her hair was pulled back in a haphazard ponytail. It wasn't hard to picture her as a young girl licking marshmallow from her fingers.

"It's going to burn," she said, jerking him from his thoughts. He realized she was looking at him.

"If you stick your hot dog in the flames like you're doing, you're going to burn it."

Turning to the fire, he saw that he'd absently stuck his skewer deeper into the flame. "I like them burned. The carbon adds flavor," he added when she quirked a brow above her frames.

"Right."

"You don't believe me?"

"What I believe is I've finally found something you're not good at." The way she cocked her head reminded him of Reynaldo, all eyes and cuteness. "Hard to imagine you not being good at everything."

The compliment hit him cold and he looked to the fire. "I'm far from perfect, Zoe."

"I never said you were perfect. Just capable. Extremely capable."

He had no business feeling pride from her compliment, but he did anyway. "I am a handyman."

"Good thing, too, for me," she replied with a grin that made his pride stand at attention. "Otherwise the bats and I would be roommates. However..." She leaned over and, taking his hand, adjusted the angle of his skewer. "That doesn't change the fact that you can't cook over a fire."

Jake's skin tingled where she touched him. He found himself contemplating lowering the skewer again so she'd repeat the action.

"You're in good company, by the way," she told

him. "When my father burned the marshmallows, he claimed the flame added flavor, too."

"See? Great minds think alike."

Jake fell silent. The beach was empty now, the locals having gone home for the evening. Only he, Zoe and the dachshund remained.

He looked at the fire. It felt strange, seeing flames without destruction. But here, watching the sparks rise and fade into the night, it was almost—*almost*—possible to imagine a more innocent time. Before everything turned dark and painful.

It was Zoe, he decided. Her enthusiasm and energy trumped everything around her. Odd, but what he'd first found incredibly annoying, tonight he found amazingly calming.

Looking over, he noticed she was lost in thought, she, too, focusing her attention on the fire. Shadows moved across her face like dancing clouds.

"Would you mind if I asked you a personal question?" she asked.

Jake's spine stiffened.

"Did you ever think that somewhere in life you took a wrong turn?"

Of all the questions she could ask, that wasn't one he expected. *Every damn day,* he wanted to say. "This is about the ex, isn't it?"

"Paul?" She shook her head. "No. Maybe a little. It's just that I can't help but wonder how I ended up where I am in life."

"You mean divorced?"

"My divorce, my career, everything. I mean, I like what I do, but lately…" She lifted her shoulders in a sad shrug as if the gesture alone was enough to fill in her thoughts. "It's like I'm out of step with the universe. Know what I mean? Like the universe is sending me signals and I'm missing the meaning."

"What kind of signals?"

"Beats the hell out of me. Don't fall for a needy golf pro?" She gave another hollow laugh. He hated the sound. It lodged heavily in his gut, like lead. He sought to change the subject, hoping at least one of them could shake the encroaching despair.

"How do you become an advice expert anyway?" he asked. It was something he'd wondered since she'd told him what she did.

"My college newspaper used to have a column and when the writer graduated, I volunteered for the position. I enjoyed it so much that after graduation I decided to see if I could keep it going. I started with a blog, and voilà, 'Ask Zoe' was born. All because I wanted to be useful."

"Useful?" Sounded like an odd word choice.

"Helpful," she corrected, brushing sand from her legs. Not, however, before he caught a flash of something in her eyes. "I like being helpful."

Making her the target for every sad story that came along.

"Anyway, I'm being maudlin." She broke off a

piece of hot dog and tossed it to Reynaldo. "That's the downside of being nostalgic. For every memory, you get a matching what-if."

And for every what-if, you got ten more. Then a hundred. Until eventually you have so many regrets and what-ifs you can hardly breathe from the weight. Jake heaved a sigh. The contentment he'd felt earlier, however slight, vanished, replaced by the familiar weight of guilt.

Did you really think you could escape yourself?

He stared into the flames. At the red-orange tongues. Just like Zoe warned, his hot dog had caught fire. The smell of burning meat met his nostrils. He watched as the flames turned the casing blistered and black.

Like a length of charred flesh.

Bile rising in his throat, he hurled the skewer into the fire. The force sent ashes scattering across the sand. A stray piece of wood flew up and landed on the back of his hand. Jake hissed from the contact.

"What the—?" Zoe was in front of him before he saw her move. "Are you all right? Did you burn yourself? Let me see."

He must have clasped his fist to his chest, because all of a sudden he could feel her soft touch as she pried open his fingers. "Doesn't look too bad," he heard her say. "We should wash off your hand with cold water, though."

Before he could protest, she slipped away. She was

back a moment later, a bottle of water and a paper towel in her hand. "This will have to do for now. When you get home, you can put some antibiotic ointment on."

He tried to shake off her attention. "It's just a burn. I've had worse." Far, far worse.

Although right now, his heart seemed to be slamming against his ribs more violently than it ever had under fire.

"Even a small burn can get infected," she retorted as she pressed the damp cloth to his skin. The lemon scent of her hair rose up to greet his nostrils and he inhaled deeply. More than grounding, it was the scent of clean and home and everything good he'd forgotten could exist. He breathed and breathed until his lungs were so full he feared they might burst. He wanted to lose himself in the aroma, in Zoe herself with her silky sweet skin and promised refuge. An ache, unfamiliar yet strong as steel, took hold in his chest.

Zoe looked up at him from beneath her lashes. "Better?"

Hell no. He was off balance and out of breath. And God, how he ached.

"Yes." It wasn't a complete lie. His hand didn't hurt anymore.

"Good." She smiled. Jake's insides spiraled into free fall. A groan rose in his throat. Just a slip of his arm around her waist. That's all it would take to pull her lemon-scented brightness tight.

Refuge. It called to him. *She* called to him.

Expectancy hung in the hair. Zoe felt it, too. There was no mistaking the desire dancing in her eyes.

He heard a dull thud as the water bottle fell to the ground. Free, her hand reached toward his face, her fingers shaking as they tracked the line of his jaw. Jake's breath caught. The feathery touch stoked the fire inside him. He wanted her. God, but he wanted her.

But then what? Did he kiss her senseless? Lose himself in the sanctuary of her arms for a night, taking what she so willingly offered without giving anything in return? Because what did he have to give but emptiness and darkness and cold?

What kind of man would that make him?

No, he couldn't—wouldn't—do that to her. She'd already been used by one man—he wouldn't add to the list. He might have precious little honor left, but he had enough.

Summoning up all his resolve, he broke away. "I'll take care of myself now," he told her.

For a second, Zoe didn't move except to sway in his direction. Damn if he didn't want to grab her up again. He had to stomp a few feet away to resist the temptation.

"I don't want— I don't need you to play nursemaid." The harshness of his words made him wince. Who was he trying to admonish, her or him?

"I didn't mean to presume otherwise," she replied in a soft voice. So soft it hit him square in the gut. He turned, ready to apologize, only to catch her staring sightlessly into the fire.

Earlier in the day he'd wondered what kind of man could kill her brightness. Now he knew.

How many more people were going to be hurt because of him?

CHAPTER SEVEN

"I CAN'T decide if I like the light grey or the dark."

"Zoe, they're roof shingles, not a work of art."

It was the first time they'd interacted in two days, and Zoe wasn't in a hurry for the conversation to end. Following his abrupt departure the other night, Jake had become a human ghost. He was at work on her roof before she could say hello and packed up before she could say goodbye. He even brought lunch, which he insisted on eating while working.

"I've got other customers to get to," he'd told her when she commented on his workaholism. "Your roof repairs can't take all summer." A perfectly valid reason, if...

If she didn't have the nagging feeling he was avoiding her.

"If I'm going to have this roof for twenty years, then I want to make sure I like what I end up with," she told him, picking up the samples for another look.

Behind the counter, Javier snickered. Jake rolled his eyes and leaned against a nearby shelf.

It wasn't that Jake hadn't been cordial. He'd waved when she had waved, spoken if she'd started a conversation. Once she caught him scratching Reynaldo under the collar. Despite all that, however, something between them was *off*.

She set the samples on the counter. "I'll take the light gray. They go best with the paint."

"You sure? There might be some samples in the back you haven't looked at," she heard Jake mutter.

"Very amusing. I'd like to see you pick something out from a three-inch square."

"I wouldn't have needed that big a sample."

Zoe shot him a smirk. The exchange was the most relaxed conversation they'd had all morning.

For the past two days, she'd felt as if they were both on guard, with each of them monitoring the other's actions. She knew why, too. That little slip of hers while standing at the campfire.

Who wouldn't be freaked out by their neighbor making goo-golly eyes at him? Lord knows what she'd been thinking by touching his cheek.

Check that. She knew exactly what she'd been thinking—or in this case, not thinking. She chalked it up to too much sun and the distracting way the campfire light danced across his features, drawing her in.

And what excuse do you have for the other times? a voice in the back of her head asked.

Javier promised to have the shingles delivered first thing the following morning. While he was writing up the order, Zoe noticed the young man stealing a glance in Jake's direction. He'd been doing so their entire visit.

She turned to give Jake a reassuring smile, pretty sure he'd seen the looks as well. The handyman stood with one hip propped against the shelf and his thumbs hooked in his pockets. To anyone who walked by, he looked like a man casually waiting on his companion. Unless, that is, you were like Zoe and noticed how stiffly he held his shoulders, or that his gaze remained frozen on a spot right behind Javier's left shoulder.

What was going through his mind? Coming back here had to be awkward after his abrupt exit last time. Yet he handled the clerk's surreptitious stares with aplomb. Zoe was impressed.

Then again, Jake continually impressed her. More so than he should, she worried.

She returned her attention to the clerk. "How are you doing?" After all, it had been his bad news that precipitated everything. "I'm sorry about your friend."

"*Obrigado.* I'm doing well. How are you, *senhor*?" he asked Jake. "Are you feeling better?"

The slight rise of color in his cheeks was the only

indication Jake found the question uncomfortable. "Better," he replied. To Zoe, he added, "I'm going to wait outside. Come find me when you're finished."

Behind the counter, Javier looked like a young boy who'd been reprimanded. "I ticked him off, didn't I?"

"Who? Jake?" She shook her head. "Not at all. He's only trying to speed me along."

"Still, I shouldn't have said anything. Ira told me Captain Meyers is touchy about things. I wasn't thinking."

Captain Meyers. She knew he'd been an officer.

She was surprised to hear the manager had shared the information after being so closemouthed with her. Then again, traipsing back and forth between the stores, Javier wasn't exactly an outsider the way she was. Would the young man have the same protective standards as Ira? Hoping to look casual, she twisted her credit card between her fingers. "Did Ira tell you anything else?"

"Only that he was injured in an attack. And that it was bad."

An understatement, to say the least. Zoe turned her gaze toward the front of the store and the tall shadowy figure on the other side of the glass.

"Yes," she replied softly. "I think it might have been very bad indeed."

* * *

Jake was waiting on the sidewalk when she emerged. "Sorry about in there," she said, joining him.

"You have nothing to apologize for."

Perhaps, but she felt like she should. "Javier's worried he ticked you off."

"He'll recover."

"And you?"

"What about me?"

"Well, it had to be awkward being back here. I mean after last time…"

He'd started down the sidewalk, slowly so Zoe could keep up. Now he paused. "That was almost a week ago. I'll recover, too."

Would he? She wasn't so certain. Though his eyes were masked by his sunglasses, she was pretty sure that, if visible, they'd belie his nonchalance. By now she'd learned he wasn't as indifferent as he pretended to be. Though she also knew if she challenged him, he'd deny the charge.

"I was wondering," she said, as they started up the pace again, "do you mind if we stop at the general store before heading back to the marina? I need to buy Reynaldo some dog chews."

"Wouldn't want the tube of terror going without, would we?"

"Trust me, we don't. Besides, I wouldn't mind getting some better coffee beans. The ones at the 'gourmet—'" she framed the word with her fingers "—store in Pitcher's Hole are more gour-maybe and—"

He cut her off. "I don't really have the time…."

There it was again, that *off* feeling.

"Look," she told him, "the shingles won't be delivered until tomorrow and by the time we get back home it's going to be too late to start a project for someone else, since you'd only have to stop and finish my roof. And if I don't run my errands now, I'll have to take the ferry back, and what with it being off-season and the boat not running every day…"

What Zoe didn't mention about the errands was that they were an excuse to spend more time together. Going home meant returning to their cordial stand-offishness, and she wasn't ready to go back to that quite yet. At least here on the island, Jake had to make conversation.

Why that mattered, she wasn't sure, but it did.

"Fine." Jake let out an exasperated sigh, though to Zoe it sounded a tad too loud and a tad too long to be serious. "We'll go run your errands. But—" he held up a finger "—if you dither half as long about coffee as you did about the shingles, I'm leaving you behind. I don't care if the ferry doesn't run again until July."

She reined in her victory smile. "Oh, don't worry. I'm very definitive when it comes to my coffee."

The general store was exactly as the name implied: a catchall tourist destination selling everything from souvenir T-shirts to whole bean coffee and imported cheese, with knickknacks and brassware thrown in. True to her word, Zoe selected her coffee in record time. Likewise, the sunscreen and fresh-baked biscuits. Ironically, it was Jake who ended up slowing their progress. He walked up and down every aisle of the store studying the contents.

"You mean in all the times you've come to this island, you've never been in this store?" Zoe asked him.

"Not once."

How sad. Granted, visiting some tourist shop wasn't a big deal. But she doubted Jake visited any kind of store, unless he absolutely had to. It was as if he did the bare minimum to exist: eat, sleep and work. With eating and sleeping being optional, she'd bet. No friends, no extraordinary experiences, no joy. Not much of a life.

At least he appeared to be enjoying this visit. "Look at this," he said. "All-natural, Himalayan dog chews made from reindeer antlers." He frowned. "Regular antlers aren't good enough?"

"Says the man who just slipped a package of Aunt Millie's Organic Canine Cookies in my basket."

"That's different. I want to see if dogs actually like those things."

"Right. And the fact it's shaped like a chipmunk is a coincidence." She laughed and gave his rib cage a nudge. "Face it, my dog's growing on you."

Jake looked down at her smile and their eyes

locked. Silence, heavy with unspoken thoughts, swept between them. Zoe was suspended in place, as if her moving hinged on what he was about to say. Jake's gaze dropped to her mouth, and a tremor ran down her spine. "Maybe it's not only the—"

"Jake? Jake Mcyers, is that you?"

A balding man in his sixties who was wearing a Black Dog Tavern T-shirt approached from the other end of the aisle. "Talk about a fortunate occurrence."

From the look on his face, Jake obviously didn't agree.

"You, Captain Meyers, are a very difficult man to reach. How many messages have I left? Three? Four?"

"The fact I didn't get back to you should have been a hint."

The man let out an indulgent-sounding laugh and rubbed a hand over his scalp. "So, are we going to see you at the ceremony? We'd like to get as many vets on the dais as possible."

"Ceremony? What ceremony?" Zoe's curiosity got the best of her and she spoke up. When the men looked in her direction, she offered a sheepish smile. "Sorry. Didn't mean to interrupt."

"Nonsense. A pretty lady is never an interruption. I'm Kent Mifflin, by the way," he greeted, holding out his left hand. That was when Zoe noticed his right hand had been replaced by a prosthetic hook.

"And the ceremony," he continued, after she'd introduced herself, "is the upcoming Flag Day dedication."

"You all celebrate Flag Day?" The June fourteenth holiday wasn't a largely recognized one, so she was surprised. Come to think of it, however, she had seen red, white and blue fliers in store windows around town.

"Normally, no, but one of our summer residents, Jenkin Carl—ever hear of him?"

"The artist?"

"That's him. He and I served together and I convinced him to make a statue to help honor the veterans from the Cape Cod islands."

"How wonderful." She looked to Jake, who looked away.

"Anyway Jenks can't get here until after Memorial Day, and since Fourth of July is always so crazy, we settled on Flag Day. We were hoping Captain Meyers—"

"Jake." The sound of his interruption startled them. "Just Jake," he repeated.

"Sorry, old habit," Kent said. "We were hoping Jake would join us."

"I can't," Jake replied.

Kent looked about to press, but Jake's expression stopped him. "That's too bad," he said, his voice slow and strangely understanding. The older man regarded him for another second or two, and then he pulled out his wallet. "If you find your schedule opens up, give me a call. I'll make sure they save you two seats at the post-dedication breakfast. It was a pleasure meeting you, Zoe."

"Same here."

Jake remained silent as stone. All the humor from earlier had vanished. His face was distant, his jaw clenched so tightly, she feared the bone might crack from the pressure. "You ready to go?" he asked when Kent was out of view.

Zoe nodded. Not until she reached the checkout did she notice that Kent had dropped his card in her basket. She slipped it into her pocket before Jake noticed.

To her credit, she managed to wait until they'd rung up their purchases and were almost to the dock before circling the conversation around to the encounter in the store. "So, your friend Kent seemed nice."

True to form, Jake looked straight ahead, his expression stony and unemotional. "He's not my friend."

Right, he didn't do friends. How could she have forgotten? "This ceremony he's organizing sounds like a pretty big deal. Too bad you can't attend."

"I have to work."

Again, Jake stared straight ahead as he spoke. A tiny flinch of his jaw muscle betrayed his tension... and told Zoe his answer was nothing more than an excuse. "I'm sure whoever your customer is, he or she would understand if you rescheduled, given the circumstances."

"I don't want to."

"Reschedule or attend?"

Finally he turned to her, and despite the sunglasses, Zoe could feel his glare. "Why do you care?"

Good question. Why did she care? What Jake did or didn't do should be of no matter to her. But it was. Watching him battling himself caused her professional instincts to kick in. She'd grown so used to people asking for advice, she'd begun dispensing guidance unsolicited.

Yes, she thought to herself, that had to be the reason. Habit. Her ingrained need to help. Any other reason would imply she was getting personally involved with Jake, and she wasn't. She wouldn't. She couldn't.

You almost kissed him by the campfire. If that's not getting involved, what is?

Quick as it came, she shoved the memory aside. What mattered right now was Jake.

"Would my caring be so awful?" she asked him.

"Your caring would be a waste of time. What I do—or don't do—is none of your concern."

He must have realized how hard his comment sounded, or perhaps he caught her stunned expression out of the corner of his eye, for his face softened. "I'm sorry, that was uncalled for. I know you mean well. But you're better off spending your energy on the people who want help."

Want. Can't. He threw those two words around a lot. He couldn't do this; he didn't want that. But what about what he *needed?*

Let me in, Jake, she implored silently. *Let me be there for you. Let me…*

She swallowed the first word choice that came to mind, replacing it with a phrase far less risky to her heart. *Let me care what happens to you.*

They cruised back to Naushatucket in silence. For once, Zoe refrained from filling the quiet with conversation. She was far too distracted figuring how to draw out Jake. Unfortunately, no solution came and when they pulled into her driveway, Jake was poised to depart immediately.

Zoe scrambled to think how she might keep him around. "Would you like to try some of the coffee I bought?" she asked. "Guarantee it'll convert you for life."

He shook his head. "No thanks. I'm coffee'd out."

"Then how about a cold drink? You've got to be hot and thirsty after all the walking we did. We could cool off by the tide pool."

"Not today. I've got paperwork I should catch up on."

"You at least have to come in and give Reynaldo the cookie you promised."

"Give him the cookie for me. I'll get those shingles first thing in the morning."

He was pulling away. Literally. The engine revved as he shifted into reverse, preparing to leave.

Zoe planted her hands on the open driver's window. "Jake, wait."

He sighed. "Look, Zoe, I told you, I've got paperwork to do."

Before that it was customers that needed his attention. And before that her roof. All sound reasons that might very well be true, but they were also excuses to avoid talking with her, and they both knew it.

Well, she could use excuses, too. "What about my bat house? You promised to hang it this week."

"Your bat house can wait until morning."

"Not really. Those poor bats have been displaced all week now, and they need a home. It's nesting season. You said so yourself."

Inwardly, she knew calling them the "poor bats" was laying it on a little thick, but she achieved her goal. With an irritated groan, Jake shoved his car back into park.

"Screw the bats. What is it you really want, Zoe?"

Sunglasses or not, his glare could ignite driftwood.

Folding her arms across her chest, Zoe matched his stare. "I want to know why you don't want to attend the ceremony."

There, she'd asked the million-dollar question. Now out, it hung between them waiting for a response.

She got one word. "Because."

"*Because* isn't an answer," she told him. "It's a brush-off. And don't tell me the real reason's none of my business, either," she added, holding up an index finger. "I know it's not my business. I still want to know. Because unfortunately, whether or not you think I'm wasting my time, I want to help you."

"Why?"

Zoe hadn't expected him to turn the tables on her. Nor was she expecting the fluttery ache that struck her chest when he asked. "Because," she began, using his own word against him, "I care."

She watched as the word settled over him, and wished that she could see his eyes. If for no other reason than to see if the yearning emanating from him was real or her imagination.

"I told you, I don't want friends," he said, his face turning toward the steering wheel.

"Too late. The damage is done."

Never had the shake of a head felt so hopeless. "Dammit, Zoe, why can't you leave things alone? You aren't responsible for solving every damn problem in the world. Besides—" his voice grew lower "—some things are so broken they can't be fixed."

He'd said the same thing the other day on the roof.

Dear God, was that how he saw himself? She hadn't realized...

"Nothing is irreparable," she said, echoing her answer from that day. *Not even you.*

"That's where you're wrong."

Slowly, he returned his gaze to hers and from the taut line of his jaw she knew he had to steel himself for what he was about to say. When he spoke, his voice was gruff and raw. "Do you really want to know why the hell I won't attend that ceremony? Because it's a ceremony for heroes, and I'm the last damn person that belongs there."

"You're not making sense." Didn't belong there? "Of course you belong there."

Jake's knuckles were white, he'd gripped the steering wheel so tightly. Zoe wondered if he were trying to snap the metal in two, since he couldn't snap himself. "Forget I said anything."

No. This time she wouldn't let him brush her off when she got close. This time she pushed back.

"What do you mean you don't belong at the ceremony?" And why did he fight so hard against the term hero? "Tell me, Jake. Talk to me. Please."

She watched as Jake turned her words over in his mind, holding her breath for his response. He was waging that internal battle he always battled, debating whether or not to let his barriers down. She hoped this time the results came out in her favor.

Let someone help you, Jake.

"You think it's so simple," he replied aloud, as if he heard her thoughts. "That if I talk, everything will magically fall into place, but you're wrong. I've talked, Zoe." He let out a hollow laugh. "I have talked 'til I'm blue in the face. You know what I learned? Talking doesn't change a damn thing. It doesn't change what happened. And it sure as hell won't bring back the dead," he added in a whisper.

No one should lose a friend. Zoe closed her eyes. She couldn't begin to imagine the horrors Jake had experienced; only a fool would try. But he needn't bear his burden alone, either.

"You're right. Talking won't bring back the dead." Gently, she cupped his cheek, conveying with a touch what her words were unable to say. "But that doesn't change the fact you're here. And that you're very much alive." Or could be, if he'd allow himself.

Jake leaned into her touch and her hopes rose that she'd finally broken through. The promise lasted but a second. No sooner did his shoulders begin to sag than he pulled away again, sitting up straight and pushing away her hand as though her touch burned him.

"That's just it. I shouldn't be here," he rasped, his voice contorted by restrained emotion. "I shouldn't be alive."

CHAPTER EIGHT

JAKE'S head hurt. Why the hell did he say anything? Now there'd be no escape. Zoe would press and press until she got the whole story.

Even now, she stood stock-still, waiting for him to explain. God, he missed her touch. So gentle, so comforting. He'd had to pull away. The words wouldn't have come otherwise.

Jake dragged a hand over his face. Funny how words he'd said so many times were still hard to get out.

"We were part of a convoy. The truck in front of us triggered an IED. They must have driven over the trip wire. Next thing I knew, we were taking fire. We never saw it coming."

You should have been on alert, expected the attack. The accusation came as it always did when he made the excuse.

"They had a grenade launcher. We could see the fire coming at us from the hills. I told my driver to blow through, figuring we could outdistance the attack, but then one of the grenades hit the front of our vehicle."

He closed his eyes and the memory played out before him. "It blew a hole right through. I must have... I must have gotten thrown because all of a sudden I woke up on the side of the road and the truck was on fire. My leg... I couldn't drag myself more than a few inches at a time."

The familiar burn started behind his eyelids. Cursing his weakness, he reached under his sunglasses to rub the wetness away.

"Ramirez, the driver—he was trapped. I—I don't know about the others. They were in the truck but..." He took a breath. "I could hear Ramirez screaming. He kept— He kept saying *'Ayúdame. Madre de Dios, ayúdame,'* over and over. I tried. God, I tried, but my leg...

"I couldn't get to them in time. I tried, but I couldn't get to them. The fire..."

Self-reproach rose like bile in his throat, choking him. "Ramirez had just had a baby boy. He'd freaking showed us the photo that morning. Kid was a month old. He never saw him."

"I'm sorry." Zoe's apology floated through the open window, her tender whisper offering absolution. Jake shook it away. He didn't deserve the gift.

"I was their CO. They trusted me to get them home, and I failed." His voice cracked. He tried to swallow, but his throat was too dry. A vice was squeezing the words out of him.

"That's why I won't go to Mifflin's ceremony. How the hell can I sit on the dais and be hailed a hero when I came home and my men didn't?"

He squeezed his eyes, fighting the shudders building inside him, and waited for the chill that told him Zoe had backed away. How could she not, now that she knew what he was, what he'd done?

Then, suddenly, there was a rush of air and he felt himself being enveloped by a cocoon of lemons and salt air.

"Shhh," Zoe was whispering in his ear. "Shhh." Quiet sounds promising peace and salvation. A shudder broke free, tearing through him. With a strangled cry, he collapsed into her, burying his face in the crook of her neck, inhaling that wonderful scent and briefly, ever so briefly allowing himself, for the first time since coming home, to rest.

"Shhh." Zoe couldn't think of anything else to say. She rocked back and forth, her heart crying for the broken man in her arms. His hair felt damp and she realized the moisture was coming from her cheeks.

"It'll be all right," she murmured. "It's going to be all right. I promise."

"No." She felt him shaking his head. "It won't be." Fingers dug into her shoulders as he broke from their embrace. "I can't do this. I don't deserve—"

"Stop." Cutting him off, Zoe pressed her fingers to his lips. "Don't say what I think you're about to say. It's not true."

"How can you say that?"

"Because I know." One look at the anguish in his eyes was enough. "You're a good man, Jake Meyers. A good, decent man."

She moved to touch him again, longing to reestablish the physical connection. To bring him close again.

Awareness flashed in his eyes, and she knew he'd read her thoughts. Seeing his need, the tightness in her chest shifted, changing form until it felt bigger than a simple need to give comfort. Shaking his head, he caught her wrist before she could make contact.

"The man you think I am doesn't exist, Zoe. I'm dead inside."

Zoe's eyes fell to her wrist. To the scarred thumb unconsciously rubbing circles on the inside hollow.

Jake must have followed her gaze because he dropped her hand. "I shouldn't have told you."

"Why? Because I might care?" Too late. That rule had been shattered.

"Because I've got no business getting involved with anyone. Not as a friend, not as a—"

While he was speaking, he'd been leaning in closer. Realizing at the last moment what he was doing, he drew back, closing the door between them instead.

"Not as anything," he said. "I'm sorry, Zoe, but like I told you, some things are too broken to be fixed."

You're wrong. The words died on her tongue. A piece of her broke as she watched Jake pull out of the driveway. The fragment stabbed at her heart, bringing a fresh batch of tears.

"You're wrong," she whispered, out loud this time as he pulled into his driveway and hobbled to the front door. Even though he couldn't hear her, she said the words anyway.

"You're wrong."

"It's called combat trauma, and it's far more common than you think," Kent Mifflin told her.

From behind her coffee cup, Zoe nodded. The two of them were having breakfast in Vineyard Haven. Following his confession, Jake had disappeared into himself. And this time she wasn't imagining the distance. Jake had barely said two words. The shingles arrived, and he buried himself in work. The roof was almost complete. Soon he'd be finished and off on another job. Knowing Jake, that meant she'd see little to nothing of him for as long as he could avoid her. Then she wouldn't see him at all, except at a distance or unless she could make up some kind of house project for him to work on. The idea of never seeing those green eyes again left an ache in the pit of her stomach. So, after another sleepless night where she found herself replaying Jake's story, she called Kent, hoping the understanding she'd heard in the older man's voice meant he knew what Jake was going through.

Her instinct had been correct.

"Problem is," Kent said, "soldiers think they should come home after serving, put the fighting behind them, and go back to regular life. Except it's not that easy. For most of them, the war is still going on. They might not be physically fighting, but they're fighting—" he tapped the side of his head "—in here. Slightest thing can send them back to the battlefield."

Zoe thought of what happened at the hardware store. "Flashbacks."

"They can be hell. For the person experiencing one, it's literally like being right back on the front line. The sounds, the smells, the whole shebang. It's one of the reasons we didn't hold the dedication ceremony on the Fourth of July."

"Because of the fireworks."

"You got it. While most of the crowd's busy oohing and aahing, these men and women are thinking tracer bullets and mortars. Jenkin and I want to honor these people, not make things worse."

Again, Zoe nodded. "When I called, I'd hoped you could give me some insight. I had no idea you were an expert."

"Not an expert—experienced." He brandished the

prosthetic. "Think I simply fell into this good nature of mine? 'Course, back then we didn't have a name for what guys like me were going through. All I knew was I was angry and empty."

Just then the waitress arrived with their orders. While Kent bantered with the waitress regarding the "doneness" of his eggs, Zoe thought about what he'd told her. Angry and empty certainly described Jake. She was certain the incident he'd described the other day, while the worst, was only one of many horrific things he'd witnessed. She'd give anything to erase those images from his head.

"Great gal," Kent said after the waitress left, "but doesn't understand the meaning of 'nonrunny' when it comes to eggs. One of these days I'm going to have to show her myself. Now, where were we?"

"You were telling me about how you learned about combat trauma."

"Oh, right." He bit off a piece of toast. "I was lucky. I had a good support system. My family could afford help. Therapists, rehab, stuff like that. And my grandfather was at Midway, so he had an idea what I was going through. Not everyone's so lucky though. Their families don't know how to help, or they pull away from their families for whatever reason so that they don't have a support system."

Like Jake.

"Can I ask you a question?" Kent asked. She

looked up from her coffee. "Does Jake know you're here talking with me?"

She shook her head. Part of her—a large part—felt enormously guilty for the betrayal. While she hadn't told Kent the exact details of what Jake endured, she'd said enough. Sometimes you have to cross a line when there's no other choice, she rationalized. She only hoped the blow back wouldn't be too harsh.

"Didn't think so," Kent replied.

"I hate going behind his back, but he seems so…" She didn't want to say *broken*, even though that was the best choice, so she shrugged, trying to hide the emotion burning her eyes. "I didn't know what else to do."

"I understand. It's not easy loving someone who's battling demons."

Love? Quickly Zoe held up her palm. "Oh, no, I'm not… I mean, Jake and I aren't…"

Sure, she cared about him. And okay, she was attracted to him. Who wouldn't be? But love? For goodness' sake, she barely knew the man. Besides, even if she were to fall in love again—which she wasn't anywhere near ready to do—people didn't do so in a couple of weeks.

"We're friends, is all," she told Kent. "Jake's my neighbor and handyman."

"Oh." The look on Kent's face made her feel like a kid caught cheating. She had to struggle not to squirm. "My mistake. When I saw the two of you in the store together, I would have sworn…"

He waved off the thought. "Never mind. Either way, he's lucky to have you on his side."

"Except I have no clue what to do to help him."

"You're doing it. Be his friend. Worse thing a guy like him can do is isolate himself. Gives him too much time to think, and believe me, thinking can be your worst enemy. Encourage him to get out and enjoy life."

"Easier said than done," she murmured.

"Hell, if it were easy, the world wouldn't need therapists. Just be patient. There's no overnight fix, I'll tell you that. I'm not sure if there is really a 'fix' at all. The memories never go away. Why do you think I can't stand runny eggs?"

He chuckled, bringing a small smile to Zoe's lips. "Best we can do is learn how to cope," he continued. "A good first step, by the way, would be to get your *friend* to attend the ceremony."

Was it her imagination or did he accentuate the word *friend*?

"Might help to see other vets, too, talk to people who know what he's going through."

"I'll try, but I'm not sure I'll have much luck. He's pretty stubborn, in case you didn't know."

"I know," Kent said with another chuckle. "He and I have crossed paths before. But something tells me if anyone on these islands can convince him, it's you."

"Me?" His confidence in her was astounding. As well as misplaced. "You overestimate my influence. Jake and I have known each other a little over a week."

"And yet he told his story." Kent sawed off a piece of fried egg with his fork and popped it in his mouth. "That's got to count for something."

It didn't surprise her to see Jake on the roof when she drove into her driveway later that day. At the sound of her tires meeting the gravel, he glanced upward, but nothing more. Zoe sighed. Still withdrawn. Her stomach sank when she saw that only a small patch of tar paper remained exposed. Her window of opportunity was closing faster than she thought, taking Jake along with it.

Since the chances of getting Jake to come down and speak with her were slim to none, she had no choice but to approach him. Squaring her shoulders, she marched into the house, grabbed a water bottle and headed back outside.

"Time to mount another rescue mission," she told Reynaldo, who she discovered sleeping on the back step next to a full water dish. "Wish me luck."

Kneeling at the far end of the roof, Jake was hammering away at the shingles with a fury. Drowning his thoughts with work? Or in a rush to be finished?

Because of the unusually hot day, he'd exchanged his T-shirt for a sleeveless tank top. His fully exposed biceps rippled and flexed with each stroke. Their sweaty definition was close to perfection, but it wasn't his physical good looks or his ever-present grace making her breath catch as she stood on top of the ladder. This time it was the lines marring his marbled skin. Lines she now recognized as shrapnel wounds. Her throat caught thinking of the burden being carried by those broad shoulders.

She waited until he'd reached for another nail, then cleared her throat. He turned to look at her straight on, and her heart skipped. Dear Lord, but those eyes… She waved the water bottle. "Hi."

"I'll be done in a couple hours."

"What is that supposed to mean? You'll wait until then for a drink? It's got be close to ninety degrees in the sun. Is it against your rules to have a cold drink?"

"I don't have any rules," he replied. "I'm simply trying to get this job finished."

So he could retreat further. Standing her ground, Zoe waved the bottle again. "Ice cold."

Those must have been the magic words because, giving a long sigh, Jake set down his hammer and made his way to her. While he drained half the bottle in one gulp, Zoe gave thanks to the heat gods and scrambled up the last couple rungs. She perched herself on the peak, making it clear she planned on sticking around.

"I found where the swallow came from," she announced brightly. "Actually Reynaldo did, but I refuse to feed his ego."

"Zoe…"

"He's got a nest on the corner of the shed. Can't believe I didn't notice before. But then…" She took off her glasses and cleaned them on her T-shirt. "Experience has proven I'm slow on the uptake."

"Slow or stubborn?"

"Take your pick." She grinned at him over her shoulder.

Across the street, white caps dotted the dark blue water, the only evidence a breeze existed on this hot day. As she watched the caps turn to waves and foam, Zoe stretched her arms and summoned her resolve. "So…" She swallowed the tremor in her voice. "I was thinking about that Flag Day ceremony."

Behind her, she heard the crackle of plastic, and imagined Jake squeezing the bottle in his fist. Gulping back another tremor, she plunged ahead. "I was thinking maybe you should reconsider attending."

Took less than half a beat for him to respond. "I've got to get back to work."

"Jake—"

"Zoe. I thought I made it clear the other day, there's no way in hell I'm going to that damn ceremony."

"But it might—"

"Might what? Help me find closure? That what you're going to say? Save the argument for one of your columns. I've heard it a thousand times. Standing around admiring some freaking piece of art isn't going to give me closure."

"Neither is shutting yourself off from the world."

"It's worked so far."

"Has it?" She scrambled to her feet, confronting him. "You had a flashback in a hardware store, for goodness' sake. You freaked out at a campfire. How may more times does that have to happen before you admit the truth?"

"I don't have to admit anything."

No, he'd much rather the emotions stayed tamped down so they could eat him alive. "You can only keep things bottled inside for so long before they explode."

Up to that point, Jake had remained stock-still, plastic bottle cracking in his fist as he stared at a point beyond her shoulder. Now he tossed the bottle over the edge and turned back to his work area.

Zoe's frustration boiled over. "You can't keep walking away from this," she snapped at him. "Sooner or later you're going to have to deal with what you're feeling."

"I have work to do, Zoe. I don't have time for this discussion."

"And when your work is finished? What then?"

Stepping toward him, she let her hand come to rest on his shoulder. The muscles beneath were tensed to the point of shaking. Concern twisted in the pit of her stomach. He couldn't keep fighting his own feelings.

"Why won't you let me help you, Jake?" she asked his back.

"I'm not some animal you can rescue, Zoe."

"No, you're a flesh-and-blood man who's been through way more than I can ever imagine."

The breath he let out sounded somewhere between anger and disgust. "I never should have told you."

"But you did, and if you expect me to take a page from your book and pretend it never happened, you're wrong. I can't sit on the sidelines knowing you're in pain. I can't. I care about you too much."

"Well, don't!" The cry echoed through the ocean air. Whirling around, he grabbed her by the shoulders with such ferocity Zoe gasped. His fingers dug into her flesh, holding her in place. Her own hands splayed against his broad chest. Beneath the cotton she could feel his heart racing, certain her own beat as violently.

"Don't," he repeated. His eyes glittered hard and brilliant.

Beneath the hardness, however, she saw his conflict. She saw caution and fear and, dare she say— longing? In that moment, her desperation to help him grew tenfold.

"You think you have to shoulder this burden your-self and you're wrong. You're not alone, Jake. You're not."

Taking a chance, she cupped his cheek, letting him feel the compassion she offered.

His eyes clouded and the grip on her arms soft-ened. "Why can't you leave me alone?"

His protest lacked conviction. "Because that's not my nature."

"Don't you mean you're a sucker for sob stories?"

"Yes, I am." But this time… This time didn't feel like her usual reaction. This time her insides swirled with a host of sensations that went far beyond sym-pathy. Hot, frantic sensations as if she were the one needing him and not the other way around.

Jake's breathing grew harsher. Or was that hers? When they were close like this it was hard to tell. If only she could prove to him how much she cared.

"You're not alone," she whispered again.

"Zoe."

His resolve was breaking. She could tell by the crack in his voice. She ran the back of her hand across his stubble.

"There are so many people out there who want to help you. Me. Kent—"

"Kent?" Big mistake. Jake shoved her aside. "You told Kent?" He looked her up and down, apparently noticing for the first time she'd scaled the ladder in a golf skirt and sleeveless blouse. "That's where you were this morning, isn't it?"

Crap. She knew going behind his back was a bad idea. "We had breakfast and you know what?" She rushed to fill the air before Jake could shut her out. "He had a lot of good information. He understands what you're going through. He's been there. If you would just talk to him—"

"You had no right," Jake spat at her. "No right at all."

"Maybe not, but someone had to start talking. I—"

"Get away." She tried reaching for him and he put his hands up, blocking her path. Erecting his barriers. "I knew it was a mistake to tell you anything. What happened over there is between me and my men."

"Your men are dead!"

She couldn't help herself. His words had kicked her in the stomach and she wanted to lash out. From the way he stumbled back, she couldn't have hit him harder if she physically struck him.

"Don't you think I know that?" he growled. "Not a day goes by that I don't regret the fact I'm here and they aren't."

"Really? Because it looks to me like you're trying to bury them all over again, only this time you're trying to forget they ever existed in the first place!"

Jake's shoulders flinched, and his eyes flashed so

that she feared she'd finally pushed too far. But with all his other feelings, the outburst she expected never came.

"I'll be done with your roof in a couple hours," he said. His voice was flat and controlled. "After that, I think you should look for another handyman. I'm sure your friend Javier can recommend someone."

Inside, a piece of Zoe crumpled. The barriers had slammed firmly in place, thicker than they'd ever been. She felt helpless, useless. Worst of all, she felt…alone. More alone than when she arrived on the island.

Anger welled up inside her. This was what she got for getting involved.

Jake heard the screams. *"Ayúdame! Ayúdame!"*

Flames surrounded him. Hot stickiness covered his legs. When had the ground turned red? He dragged himself forward, toward the truck. His body wouldn't move.

Why couldn't he move? Ignoring the pain, he dragged himself onward. Yet every time he looked up he was in the same damn place.

"Ayúdame!" Ramirez's cries rose above the gunfire. "Don't forget me!"

"Hang tight, Ramirez! I'm trying."

"Don't leave me, Captain!"

"I won't." But as he looked up, the truck was farther away than before. The fire rose, ready to engulf the vehicle. Inside, his men were screaming.

"Captain! Don't forget us, Captain!"

Breath tearing from his lungs, Jake sat up. What the hell?

He peeled off his sweat-soaked shirt and stumbled to the window. Next door, Zoe's bedroom light shone, its soft yellow glow the only brightness on the moonless night. A yearning—fierce and overwhelming—rose up inside him, forcing him to squeeze the windowsill.

No, he scolded himself. *You can't go there.*

Don't leave me. Ramirez's disembodied voice rang in his ears. *Don't forget us.* The helplessness and self-hatred he always felt following a dream engulfed him. God, but he wished things could be different. If he'd been a minute sooner, moved a foot faster, he might not have this emptiness. Instead of standing alone with his nightmares, he could be seeking solace in a pair of warm arms. A pair of lemon-scented arms.

But things weren't different, were they?

His pain pills were by the bed. Ramirez's cries still in his head, he stumbled to the night stand. As he reached for the bottle, his fingers brushed the photo propped against the lamp. There was no need to turn on the light for him to see it. Like so many others, the image was burned into his memory. Sergeant Bullard—Bulldog—had taken the shot with his cell phone a few days before. To remember their ugly faces, he said. Bullard had been lucky. He'd shipped home that afternoon. Some place in Arkansas.

Don't forget us. Like he ever could.

Ramirez's voice morphed into another. A soft gentle voice that promised comfort and light. "Don't bury them, too," the voice said. He wasn't.

Or was he? Was that what he was doing? Was he burying his men's memory?

He washed his hand across his face. "Dammit, guys," he whispered to the photo. "I'm so sorry."

CHAPTER NINE

"Ow, ow, ow! Crap!"

It was the second time Zoe had sworn in fifteen minutes. Her project wasn't going well.

Jake did his best to ignore her. Whatever she was doing, she could handle it herself. He focused on the account books in front of him.

"Arrrgh!"

Jake threw his pen down. Yesterday's nightmare, a repeat of the nightmare he'd been having for the past three days, had given him a headache, making concentrating difficult enough. The last thing he needed was the racket next door.

"Son of a—"

Oh, for crying out loud! Jake combed through his hair. Time was he could sit in the backyard and balance his receivables undisturbed. Then again, time was his backyard was quiet. B.Z. *Before Zoe.*

What on earth was she doing over there anyway? And since when did he start measuring his life in terms of Zoe's arrival? For that matter, since when did he start measuring his life, period? He was a day-to-day existence guy. And yet...

His eyes drifted toward the fence. A flash of orange caught his eye, causing his chest to constrict. He hated the sensation. For days now, the same damn feeling kept creeping up on him, catching him off guard. Bad enough he had Ramirez haunting him every night. He didn't need to spend his days riding some kind of emotional tidal wave where one minute he was fine, the next he couldn't catch his breath. The fact he'd been having these "incidents" since that night on the beach meant nothing. Nor did the fact that their frequency had increased since he'd finished Zoe's roof.

"Give me a break!"

The sound of a falling ladder crashed into his thoughts. Jake sighed. He was never going to get these books done.

He found her standing beneath the pine tree in her backyard wearing her bright orange T-shirt and a pair of blue gym shorts. Pine needles littered her hair.

"What the hell are you doing?" he asked, ignoring the way his heart lurched at the sight.

"I'm trying to hang the bat house," Zoe grumbled.

Of course. Ever the problem solver, wasn't she?

"Is it necessary to kill your ladder in the process?" Not to mention trampling all over his psyche.

"Stupid thing fell over when I was positioning the bat house."

Jake surveyed the ground. No wonder. Exposed roots burst through the grass-barren area.

Grabbing the ladder, he walked it outward to a flatter section of the ground. "Give me the bat house," he said, putting a foot on the bottom rung.

She refused. "I can hang the damn thing myself."

"Obviously not, based on the racket you're making. Now give me the house so I can get back to my work."

He waited while she contemplated his request. Finally she must have decided pride was less important than getting the job done, and she shoved the wooden box in his direction.

"Here," she muttered, refusing to look at him.

He should be glad she didn't. Her eyes would only churn up his already jumbled insides. But as he made his way to a spot fifteen feet up the trunk, he couldn't help feeling their absence.

He still felt the loss when he finished. Or maybe it was the chill in her voice that left him cold.

"Thanks," she said when he stepped off the ladder. "You can add the charge to my invoice."

"Zoe—"

In the process of walking away, she stopped. He'd been better off when she wasn't looking at him, Jake realized. There wasn't a speck of brightness in her eyes. *You did that,* he reminded himself.

Zoe folded her arms across her chest. "What?"

"I—" What indeed? Was he going to tell her he forgave her for speaking with Kent? Even if he did, saying so would only make her think they had some sort of relationship again. Which they didn't. Couldn't.

This was what he wanted. Distance. Lack of attachment. Best to leave things the way they were.

"No charge for the bat house," he told her.

The heavy feeling in his gut was not caused by the flash of disappointment he caught in her eyes. Nor was the emptiness in his chest because she walked away without a word.

This, he reminded himself, was what he wanted.

Dear Zoe,
I've screwed up. I think I might have fallen for my best friend's boyfriend. I wasn't planning to. It just happened. Now I can't stop thinking about him. What should I do?
In Love and Regretting It

Dear In Love,
First, are you sure you're in love? Because sometimes we convince ourselves of feelings that aren't real, simply because the person says they need you or they make your heart

race every time you see them. Second, nothing good ever comes from loving the wrong
person. Trust me. Walk away while you still
have the chance.

Zoe

Tossing her glasses on the kitchen table, she
rubbed her eyes. Beneath her feet, a low whine could
be heard. "Don't start, Rey. You know perfectly well
I'm right."

A knock on the front door interrupted their conversation. Instantly, Reynaldo emitted a low growl.
Zoe frowned. "What's with you this morning? You
mad because Jake didn't stick around and scratch
your ears? Get over it." Whatever "it" she and Jake
had had going on was over. If "it" had ever begun
in the first place. The sooner Reynaldo accepted the
fact, the better.

The knock sounded again. A little louder this time.
Whoever the person was, he or she had a heavy hand
on the brass door knocker. "Come on, Rey, we better
see who it is before they bang a hole in the wood."

Undoing the bolt, she opened it a crack and peered
out. A perfect tan and a set of perfect teeth smiled
down at her.

"Hey, babe."

CHAPTER TEN

UNBELIEVABLE. Her ex-husband sitting in her kitchen drinking coffee was the last thing she expected this morning.

Paul looked good; she'd give him that. Being outside three hundred days a year had given him a permanent golden tan, which his highlighted hair and pale blue golf shirt accentuated perfectly. In fact, everything about him was flawless, from his wardrobe to his features. There wasn't a mark or weathered line on him.

It made him look quite superficial, she realized.

"This is good," he was saying. "You always did have a knack for brewing a fine cup of coffee."

"Seeing how you spent more time in hotels than our apartment, I'm surprised you noticed."

He chuckled. "I've missed that sarcasm, too."

"Yes, it's always been one of my charms." She walked around him to lean against the kitchen counter. "Why are you here?"

"Did you get my flowers?"

"I got them." Memories of Jake bringing her coffee on the beach came to mind, bringing with them an ache in her chest. "You shouldn't have gone to so much expense."

Paul waved off the remark. "Nonsense. You're worth every penny. And I remembered how much you liked calla lilies," he added with a smile.

Actually she liked tiger lilies, but why argue the point? "You still haven't said why you're here."

"To see you, of course. Why else would I come to this godforsaken island?"

Zoe could think of a few reasons, most of them with dollar signs. "I told you on the phone I didn't want to see you."

"That was almost three weeks ago, Zo. You were still angry. I figured you had time to cool down since then."

Had it really been that long? She glanced at the calendar. Dear Lord, it had. She'd been too caught up with Jake to notice time passing. Automatically, her eyes went to the kitchen window, seeking a glimpse of the house next door. How would time pass now? she wondered.

Still at the table, Paul set down his coffee. "I'm assuming you have. Cooled down, that is."

Outside on his run, Reynaldo was barking, angry he'd been banished to the backyard at Paul's arrival. "If you mean do I still want to castrate you for cheating on me, the answer's no. It's not worth the anger."

His sigh of relief filled the room. "Good. I'm glad. I knew you'd realize what we had was too good to throw away, though I admit…"

She heard the sound of a chair, and suddenly Paul was behind her, hands on her hips. "I was willing to get down on my knees and beg if I had to. Still could, if you want." Perfect teeth nipped at her ear lobe.

"Oh, good Lord, stop." She pushed him away. "All I said was I wasn't angry anymore. What on earth makes you think we're getting back together?"

"But, babe, if you're not angry, what's holding you back?"

"How about the fact I don't want you?"

The expression on Paul's face made it seem like she'd spoken a foreign language. "Of course you want me," he said. "We're Team Brodsky. Don't you remember all our plans? Our dreams?"

"Yeah, I remember."

"Then how can you throw all that away? I came all the way here to get you. Surely that means something."

"It means your short game's gone to pot," she told him. "You gave it your best shot, Paul, but Team Brodsky's history. You'll have to find another way to fund your dreams."

"No, I don't believe you." He closed the distance between them. Grasping her shoulders, he forced her close. "I need you, babe," he whispered in his honeyed voice. "I need you too much."

Zoe looked into the brown eyes she'd once found so irresistible. They were really quite bland, she realized. Passionless even as he declared his desire for her. Dear Lord, Jake showed more emotion closed off than Paul did at his most effusive.

Jake. Just thinking his name made her heart catch. She thought of the hunger he tried to disguise when they were close. Of the way she could see down to his soul when she stared into their green depths. Those were the eyes she wanted to look into. Not these.

"You don't need me, Paul. You're just needy."

She moved to push him away, but Paul held fast. His voice grew a little rougher. "I'm not giving up that easily, babe. You're still upset—I get that. Soon as I show you how I need you, though, things will be different."

"No, Paul."

"Remember that time in the condo? You were making toast, and I came up behind you? You said you liked when I took charge." One hand snaked its way to her neck, cupping her jaw, forcing her face upward. His eyes glittered with determination. "That what you want now, babe? For me to take charge?"

Zoe couldn't breathe. Couldn't hear. Blood pounded in her eardrums, drowning everything but her fear. Paul had always been selfish, but he'd never been violent.

Then again, she'd never turned him down before, and he hated to lose.

"Let me go!" She shoved at his shoulders, but years of swinging a golf club left him with a power-ful grip. His knee slipped between her thighs. She felt the edge of the counter cutting into her back as he bent her backward.

"I believe the lady said stop."

Jake.

Zoe had never been so relieved to see a man in all her life. Everything would be okay, now. Jake was here.

Crossing the room in one giant step, he grabbed Paul by the collar and yanked the golf pro off her.

"Hey!" Paul hollered, breaking free of his grip. "Who the hell are you?"

"I'm her handyman."

No, thought Zoe, heart in her throat. *He was her hero.*

"Well, if you'll excuse me, Mr. Handyman, my wife and I were having a private discussion."

"Doesn't look like much of a conversation," Jake replied. "And last I checked, Zoe was divorced."

Jake leveled his green eyes like lasers straight at Paul, making it clear he was about to mount another attack. From the way his fingers flexed, she could tell this time he wouldn't be as gentle. Paul folded his arms. Zoe recognized the stance. He wasn't going quietly. That had been his problem as a golfer, too. He never could read the breaks in a green.

"And last time *I* checked," he said with more than a little bravado, "the *handyman* didn't call the shots in my house."

"*My* house." Both men looked at her as Zoe finally found her voice. "This is my house."

Paul nodded. "Sure, babe. Then tell this *handyman* to leave us alone so we can talk." His eyes raked her up and down, as if to silently add, "You know you want to."

The leer made her sick inside. Instinctively she moved toward the one thing that made her feel safe. Jake. "The only person leaving, Paul, is you," she said. "Get out."

Her ex-husband looked like he'd missed a two-inch putt. "You can't mean that."

"You heard the lady," Jake added. "Get out."

"And stay out," Zoe added. "I don't want anything to do with you."

At first Paul didn't budge, preferring to stare at the two of them, and making Zoe fear the altercation would escalate. Venom shone in his eyes. At last, she thought to herself. He's finally showing his true colors.

"You'll be hearing from my lawyers about this, Zoe," he said at last. "I won't stand for being assaulted."

"Neither will I," she replied. "I suggest you rethink that call."

Before he could say anything else, Jake escorted him to the front door, remaining in the open entrance until the golfer had climbed into his car and driven away. As soon as his car disappeared over the horizon, Zoe sagged against the wall. Shivers racked her body. What if…? She hugged her midsection, trying to hold herself together. Jake's large frame appeared before her. "Zoe?"

"What if…? He…" She took a sharp breath. Her lungs burned for the effort. "If you hadn't come by when…you…did…"

The smell of bay rum wrapped itself around her, along with a pair of strong, warm arms. Zoe buried herself in the embrace, letting the security of Jake's presence calm the storm inside her.

"It's okay," she heard him murmur. "Everything's going to be okay."

Zoe believed him. Inside, her heart opened, finally acknowledging the emotion she'd been dancing around for weeks. Everything would be all right. Jake was here.

Her fingers brushed the lip of Jake's breast pocket. Beneath them, she could feel his heart, the erratic beat mirroring her own.

"Zoe…" Jake's voice had deepened. Looking to his face, she saw his eyes had darkened, too, the pupils blown so wide, their green depths were nearly black.

"Do you have any idea how beautiful you are?" he whispered. "So bright. So sweet." His hand reached up and thumbed her cheek. "So tempting."

Her, tempting? She'd have looked away in embarrassment, but he had too tight a hold on her.

Meanwhile, Jake closed his eyes and took a deep breath. Her throat ran dry in anticipation. "You make me feel—" He shook his head. "Doesn't matter."

Yes, it did. "Why not?"

"Because." His smile was sad. "Nothing's changed, Zoe. I'm still as dead inside as I ever was. I could never give back to you what you deserve."

Nothing's changed. Red flashed in front of Zoe's eyes. "Damn you!" The events of the day had left her insides ragged. Hearing his rejection, the tenuous hold on her nerves snapped and she began beating her fists against his chest. "You son of a bitch. Who the hell gave you permission to walk out on life? Huh? Who decided you get to sit on the sidelines while the rest of us carry on?"

"Look, I know you—"

"No, you don't know anything." Hot, angry tears sprang to her eyes. She was sick of it. Sick of caring and not being cared for back. Sick of investing her heart and soul only to get hurt time and time again.

Stay out of the way, Zoe. Don't be a bother, Zoe. Help me, Zoe.

"Know what?" she asked, wiping her nose. "Paul might have used me, but at least he wasn't a coward."

Jake drew in a breath. "A what?"

"You heard me, a coward. At least he went after what he wanted. He didn't lock himself away, afraid to live life."

The ragged sound of his breathing told Zoe she was treading on thin ice, and she didn't care. It was worth the risk if she could get through to Jake. All this time everyone had been treating him with kid gloves, afraid of opening his wounds or making him lose control. Well, maybe it was time to take off the gloves and give him a strong dose of truth. Maybe losing control was exactly what he needed.

"You say you're barricading yourself from the rest of the world because you're dead inside. You're not dead. You're afraid. You're afraid to be happy. At least be that honest. Don't act all noble and pretend you're doing the 'right thing' when the truth is you're simply too scared to live."

"Don't." One word. One simple word of warning. Zoe ignored it.

"Worst thing of all is, you're too blind with guilt to see happiness when it's standing right in front of you, offering itself on a silver platter. Tell me, Jake. How long are you going to keep punishing yourself for coming home alive? What would your men say if they knew you were using them as an excuse to avoid the world?"

Jake slammed the front door behind him, leaving her standing alone in the foyer. Anger still coursing through her, Zoe watched until his blond head disappeared behind the fence, then buried her face in her hands. She didn't know whether to cry or throw something. Stupid blind fool.

The only bigger fool was her. Because now she knew Kent Mifflin was right.

She was in love with Jake.

Of all the insane ideas…

He was not afraid of living. He *wasn't*. He dragged his sorry self out of bed every morning, didn't he? If anything, he spent every freaking day painfully aware that he was alive.

Zoe was simply wrong. All the more reason he needed to back away from her. Despite all his explaining, she didn't understand he couldn't be the kind of man she deserved. Eventually she'd see the wisdom of his decision and thank him. She would.

Back in his house, he was halfway through grabbing a beer from the refrigerator, when he caught the date on the calendar. June thirteenth. The day before Flag Day. Terrific. Now he had two subjects to ruminate about when the nightmares woke him up. Zoe and Kent Mifflin's big "hero" celebration.

He grabbed a backup beer. Looked like it would be a long night.

The dream was the same as always. Flames surrounding him. The smell of blood and sulfur in his nostrils. Ramirez and the others crying out for him. *Ayúdame!* Don't forget us! *Ayúdame!*

Jake lay prone in the sand, his body sticky with blood. He was trying to crawl his way to the truck.

Ayúdame! Ayúdame!

A new voice joined the chorus. Soft and sweet, like a siren song. "Over here, Jake! Over here!"

Looking to the hills behind him, he saw Zoe hopping from rock to rock. She wore her orange T-shirt and denim cutoff shorts. Her messy ponytail bounced with each hop she took.

"Get down!" he hollered. "Take cover!"

But Zoe ignored him. "I'm not in danger," she told him. "It's perfectly safe here. Come and see."

He tried. Digging into the sand with his elbows, he pushed himself forward. But he went nowhere.

"Ayúdame!" Ramirez and the others chanted. "Captain! Captain!"

"Jake, come over here. It's safe here!"

"Don't forget us…."

"You'll be safe here."

Back and forth the two sides called to him. Jake

could hear them, but he couldn't move. Not in either direction. The sand had turned into a giant block of cement. He was stuck.

"Move, Jake. Move!" the voices began chanting.

"I can't," he told them. "I can't move."

"You have to move…"

Jake's eyes flew open. His clothes were cold and damp from sweat, but at least he could move his legs again. *He could move.* The realization hit him square in the gut. He. Could. Move.

Swinging his feet to the floor, he moved to stand, but not before glancing at the alarm clock to see how long he'd managed to sleep. Four-thirty, the display read.

Flag Day.

In the end, Zoe went to the celebration because someone should. She'd go and she'd pay tribute to the men Jake lost. Maybe doing so would help her say goodbye to her neighbor.

Nothing else had.

"May I have your attention please?"

Kent Mifflin's voice loomed over the loudspeaker, louder than the waves crashing the beach behind them.

"In 1916, President Woodrow Wilson declared June fourteenth as Flag Day, a day to honor the American flag and the ideals it represented. Therefore, we thought it only fitting that on this day, we honor those men and women who fought under that flag…"

As the speech went on, Zoe let her gaze flit over the crowd. Kent and his committee had to be proud. The turnout was outstanding. In addition to the VIPs and veterans joining Kent on the podium, a sizeable crowd had gathered in the park to watch the ceremony. Some were even in uniform, including several men old enough to be her grandfather. One particular gentleman, with a cane and wearing a brown infantry uniform, caught her eye and winked. She smiled in return.

Yes, sir, Kent managed to draw quite a crowd. Too bad not everyone he'd invited was in attendance.

Even though she knew Jake wouldn't be here, she hadn't expected his absence to feel so glaring.

"…men and women who wore their uniforms so others would not have to…"

She tried telling herself the empty feeling in her chest was guilt for telling him off yesterday, but her heart knew better. The emptiness was Jake himself. He belonged here, with those men and women on the platform.

With her.

"…who suffered and made sacrifices many cannot imagine…"

The sun broke through the clouds, heating the late morning air. Zoe slipped off the cardigan that covered her denim sundress. After three weeks, she'd finally smartened up about New England weather and worn layers. Now if she could only smarten up about other things. Like the fact she'd fallen in love with yet another man who didn't love her back.

She supposed she should be grateful Jake wasn't after her money, too. Though it would be easier if he were. But no, he was trying to protect her from being used and hurt. And hurting her ten times more in the process.

Boy, she sure could pick them, couldn't she? An ex-husband who needed everything, and a man so mired in guilt he was afraid to need anything.

Nothing good ever comes from loving the wrong man. Talk about not following her own advice.

"Therefore, we stand today in their—"

Kent's voice stuttered, catching her attention. Looking up, she saw the older man look to the crowd before continuing, "We stand today in their honor..."

She wasn't sure why—maybe it was his expression that compelled her—but Zoe suddenly turned to her right. A flash of blue toward the rear of the crowd caught her eye.

Dear Lord...

He stood at attention, resplendent in a navy blue uniform. Hair neatly trimmed, the black brim of his cap straight over his eyes. Blue-and-gold epaulets gleamed on his broad shoulders. A rainbow of ribbons hung over his heart.

Dear Lord but he was awe-inspiring in that uniform. It was as if all the confidence and command he carried inside himself had turned outward for the world to see.

Zoe's heart lurched. What made him change his mind about attending?

Sensing her, Jake turned in her direction. Quickly, Zoe looked away. Not before, however, she felt his hard stare. It reminded her of the day they'd met. When he'd wanted nothing to do with her.

On stage, Kent and Jenkin Carl prepared to unveil the statue. Jenkin was explaining something about vision and experience. Zoe didn't listen. Her attention was on the man across the crowd. Glancing back again, she saw Jake had returned his attention to the dais. He knew she was here, and yet he didn't move to join her. It looked like his change of heart was only regarding the ceremony. Tears sprang to her eyes.

"Ladies and gentlemen," Kent announced proudly. "We give you *Sacrifice!*"

The crowd broke into applause. Swallowing back her own emotions, Zoe joined them. Next to her, the old man in uniform snapped into a salute. She pictured Jake doing the same.

Oh, Jake.

As the ceremony drew to a close and the crowds thinned, Zoe saw Jake hanging back. Occasionally someone would walk over to him and say something. He would nod and shake their hand. A couple even saluted. Though the brim of his hat cast his face in shadow, Zoe could tell from his reaction that he was taken aback by the show of respect.

At least he was trying. Maybe she'd helped him a little after all. Too bad she had to break her heart in the process.

"I know you'd convince him," a voice said from behind her.

Kent's face was flushed with enthusiasm. "I couldn't believe my eyes when I saw Jake in the crowd. Your boy looks pretty damn impressive, doesn't he?"

He's not mine. Zoe forced a smile. "I didn't have anything to do with it. I didn't know he was coming, either."

"Once again, I think you sell yourself short."

Not likely. At least not this time. She stole a glance at the other side of the green. Jake stood thirty feet away, but it might as well have been a canyon.

"I'm going to head over and speak with him," Kent said. "You coming?"

Zoe shook her head. She was pretty sure she was the last person Jake wanted to see right now. "I think I'll take a closer look at that statue of yours, if you don't mind."

"Suit yourself. I'll catch you later at the breakfast." He gave her an indulgent pat on the shoulder. "Thanks for coming."

"Thank you," she replied, "for doing a really great thing."

Jenkin Carl's "statue" was really a mass of twisted metal. Black and harshly contrary to its setting, the work featured a trio of spires rising skyward from out of the tangle, as if rising above the chaos. Looking at the piece, Zoe's own insides twisted, too. You could feel the darkness reach inside and touch you.

She ran a hand along the gleaming black surface, thinking of what the statue represented. What men and women like Jake gave up.

Jake. Her insides crumpled. How was she going to spend the rest of the summer with him next door? She'd come to Naushatucket to fix a broken heart, only to find out what a real broken heart felt like.

Guess there was no reason to stay, was there? She sure as hell couldn't heal here now. At least Caroline would be happy.

"Looks like burnt-out wreckage," a familiar voice said.

Her pulse skipped. "I imagine that's what Carl wanted." She forced her voice to stay steady. An emotional scene wouldn't help anyone. "He's trying to evoke an image."

"There are a few images I could do without."

"I imagine so." She kept her eyes on the statue. "I was surprised to see you."

"I'm surprised to see me here, too. But as someone

I know pointed out, we need to remember the ones who didn't come back."

Zoe's vision blurred. She *had* helped. The notion gave her some solace. "I'm sure your men would have appreciated the gesture."

"I'd like to think so."

She could feel his eyes on her now, As always, when he looked in her direction, her skin came alive. This time, Zoe cursed the reaction. Yes, she thought. She had to leave Naushatucket.

"Did you want something?" she asked him.

"I've never seen you dressed up before. You look nice."

"What?" She looked at him to see his eyes had a sheen to them unlike ever before. A light in their depths that turned the green warm and open. Zoe didn't dare believe the expression meant anything. Because if it wasn't true...

She turned back to the statue. "Thank you. So do you."

"You mean this old thing?" It was a lame attempt at humor. Neither of them laughed.

She heard him clear his throat. "Look, Zoe, about yesterday. The things you said were pretty harsh."

Here it was. The part where he told her not to read too much into his change of heart. Zoe was glad she hadn't got her hopes up.

"I spoke my mind," she told him. "I'm sorry

if I was harsh, but I'm not sorry for the words themselves."

"You shouldn't be. You were right." His hand settled on the statue next to hers. "I have been hiding. I've been stuck in my anger and guilt, beating myself up for being alive. I probably would have stayed that way too if you hadn't given me a good harsh dose of reality."

Zoe didn't know what to say.

"It woke me up. Well, a lot of things woke me up. But in the end, I realized there was always one common thread. You. You burst into my world and you wouldn't give up. And you made me long for things I didn't believe I could have."

"And what do you believe now?"

"I don't know. Not fully anyway. But I know I have to start living life again. I need to for my men and I need to for myself."

He slid his hand closer, his little finger grazing hers. Zoe didn't want the hope that rose inside her, but it rose anyway.

"I still have a lot of demons to battle," he said. "And I can't promise I'll get all the way back. Hell, I'm not sure if I'm ready for this at all. But..." His voice caught. "If I'm going to try, I'd like to try with you."

The love in her heart grew a little stronger. She slipped her hand over his, thinking he was the bravest man she knew. "I'd like that, too."

Smiling, Jake raised their hands to his lips. "Good."

A tear dripped down Zoe's cheek. She reached to brush it away, but he beat her to it, his touch reverent and gentle. "I promise I'll do my best not to hurt you."

"I know," she told him. "Just be honest and the rest will fall into place." She touched his cheek. Her fingers grazed his scars, but she couldn't feel them. All she could feel was the warmth. Jake had taken the hardest step today. Looking into his eyes, shining and ripe with sincerity, she had faith he could win. Best of all, this time there wouldn't be some mythical "team" she'd created. It would be a partnership. A real, true partnership. She could feel it in her heart.

"Tell me, Captain," she said, rising on tiptoes, "this 'trying' of yours. It wouldn't involve starting with a kiss, would it?"

The corners of Jake's mouth lifted skyward. "Yeah, I think it can." With that, he leaned forward and pressed his lips to hers.

As kisses went, it wasn't deep or passionate. More like a feathery promise. But the promise was one of love and sincerity. And to Zoe, no kiss had ever been so perfect.

One year later

Jake woke to the smell of lemons and crackling firewood. His eyes scanned the room, searching for the woman who, only an hour before, had been wrapped around his body like a tiny human blanket.

He found her staring at the patio doorway. "You're not going to believe this," Zoe said. "He's back."

"Who?" He yawned and reached across the covers to scratch a dozing Reynaldo's head.

"The swallow. I swear this house is part of his migration pattern. I opened the door to look outside and in he swooped. Look! There he is!" Arm extended, she scrambled toward the sofa. "Did you see him?"

"Actually, no."

"Well then, pay attention. We have to shoo him out of here."

"I would if you weren't prancing around in nothing but my open work shirt." An idea came to him. "And how do you know it's a swallow? This time of evening, it could just as easily be a bat."

Zoe shrieked and dove back to their nest of blankets. Laughing, Jake pulled her close. "Don't you remember what I taught you? If you leave the creature alone, he'll fly to safety all on his own."

"Your advice won't do me any good if safety involves tangling in my hair."

"Don't worry, I'll protect you."

"My hero."

"You better believe it," he murmured, giving her neck a playful bite.

Life, he decided, was good. He still had his demons. He had flashbacks, and there were nights when the terrors struck hard and he woke up screaming. But there were also long stretches where the memories stayed buried and on the bad nights, he had Zoe to hold him. He had Zoe to help with a lot of things.

She'd decided to move to Naushatucket at the end of last summer, when they both realized they didn't want to spend winter apart. It was Zoe who insisted they stay. She'd fallen in love with the island. And Jake…

Jake had fallen in love with her. Looking back, he'd probably loved her all along, but the day he offered to move in with her was the day he finally admitted it. He hadn't stopped loving her since.

Yes, he thought, life was pretty good. Only one thing would make it better. He sat up and reached behind the kindling box.

Zoe was back to looking for her winged nemesis. "You know," she pointed out, "not every problem resolves itself. Sometimes a creature—or person—needs a little push."

"You mean like me?" he teased.

She smiled. "You, my love, needed a shove."

"How about a plunge?" He held out a small velvet box.

Instantly, Zoe's playfulness disappeared. Those gorgeous blue eyes of hers went as wide as saucers, and she sat up. "Are you sure?"

"Positive." To his surprise, his hands were shaking

as he opened it to reveal the diamond inside. "I told you once that I hoped to dream of the future again. Now I can't imagine a future without you in it. I love you, Zoe Hamilton. Will you marry me?"

She beamed, warming his insides like he once hadn't dreamed possible. "There's nothing I'd rather do."

Winged creature forgotten, she wrapped her arms around his neck and showed him exactly what their future would hold.

* * * * *

Coming Next Month

Available October 11, 2011

#4267 TALL, DARK, TEXAS RANGER
The Quilt Shop in Kerry Springs
Patricia Thayer

#4268 AUSTRALIA'S MAVERICK MILLIONAIRE
Margaret Way

#4269 BRIDESMAID SAYS, "I DO!"
Changing Grooms
Barbara Hannay

#4270 HOW A COWBOY STOLE HER HEART
Donna Alward

#4271 HER ITALIAN SOLDIER
Rebecca Winters

#4272 SURPRISE: OUTBACK PROPOSAL
Jennie Adams

You can find more information on upcoming
Harlequin® titles, free excerpts and more at
www.HarlequinInsideRomance.com.

REQUEST YOUR FREE BOOKS!
2 FREE NOVELS PLUS *2 FREE GIFTS!*

❖ Harlequin®

Romance

From the Heart, For the Heart

YES! Please send me 2 FREE Harlequin® Romance novels and my 2 FREE gifts (gifts are worth about $10). After receiving them, if I don't wish to receive any more books, I can return the shipping statement marked "cancel". If I don't cancel, I will receive 6 brand-new novels every month and be billed just $4.09 per book in the U.S. or $4.49 per book in Canada. That's a savings of at least 14% off the cover price! It's quite a bargain! Shipping and handling is just 50¢ per book in the U.S. and 75¢ per book in Canada.* I understand that accepting the 2 free books and gifts places me under no obligation to buy anything. I can always return a shipment and cancel at any time. Even if I never buy another book, the two free books and gifts are mine to keep forever.

116/316 HDN FESE

Name	(PLEASE PRINT)	
Address		Apt. #
City	State/Prov.	Zip/Postal Code

Signature (if under 18, a parent or guardian must sign)

Mail to the **Reader Service:**
IN U.S.A.: P.O. Box 1867, Buffalo, NY 14240-1867
IN CANADA: P.O. Box 609, Fort Erie, Ontario L2A 5X3

Not valid for current subscribers to Harlequin Romance books.

**Are you a subscriber to Harlequin Romance books
and want to receive the larger-print edition?
Call 1-800-873-8635 or visit www.ReaderService.com.**

* Terms and prices subject to change without notice. Prices do not include applicable taxes. Sales tax applicable in N.Y. Canadian residents will be charged applicable taxes. Offer not valid in Quebec. This offer is limited to one order per household. All orders subject to credit approval. Credit or debit balances in a customer's account(s) may be offset by any other outstanding balance owed by or to the customer. Please allow 4 to 6 weeks for delivery. Offer available while quantities last.

Your Privacy—The Reader Service is committed to protecting your privacy. Our Privacy Policy is available online at www.ReaderService.com or upon request from the Reader Service.

We make a portion of our mailing list available to reputable third parties that offer products we believe may interest you. If you prefer that we not exchange your name with third parties, or if you wish to clarify or modify your communication preferences, please visit us at www.ReaderService.com/consumerschoice or write to us at Reader Service Preference Service, P.O. Box 9062, Buffalo, NY 14269. Include your complete name and address.

HRIIB

*Harlequin Romantic Suspense presents the latest book
in the scorching new* KELLEY LEGACY *miniseries
from best-loved veteran series author Carla Cassidy*

*Scandal is the name of the game as the Kelley family fights
to preserve their legacy, their hearts...and their lives.*

Read on for an excerpt from the fourth title
RANCHER UNDER COVER

*Available October 2011
from Harlequin Romantic Suspense*

"**W**ould you like a drink?" Caitlin asked as she walked to the minibar in the corner of the room. She felt as if she needed to chug a beer or two for courage.

"No, thanks. I'm not much of a drinking man," he replied.

She raised an eyebrow and looked at him curiously as she poured herself a glass of wine. "A ranch hand who doesn't enjoy a drink? I think maybe that's a first."

He smiled easily. "There was a six-month period in my life when I drank too much. I pulled myself out of the bottom of a bottle a little over seven years ago and I've never looked back."

"That's admirable, to know you have a problem and then fix it."

Those broad shoulders of his moved up and down in an easy shrug. "I don't know how admirable it was, all I knew at the time was that I had a choice to make between living and dying and I decided living was definitely more appealing."

She wanted to ask him what had happened preceding that six-month period that had plunged him into the bottom of the bottle, but she didn't want to know too much about him. Personal information might produce a false sense of intimacy that she didn't need, didn't want in her life.

"Please, sit down," she said, and gestured him to the table. She had never felt so on edge, so awkward in her life.

"After you," he replied.

She was aware of his gaze intensely focused on her as she rounded the table and sat in the chair, and she wanted to tell him to stop looking at her as if she were a delectable dessert he intended to savor later.

Watch Caitlin and Rhett's sensual saga unfold amidst the shocking, ripped-from-the-headlines drama of the Kelley Legacy miniseries in

RANCHER UNDER COVER

Available October 2011 only from Harlequin Romantic Suspense, wherever books are sold.

SPECIAL EDITION

Life, Love and Family

Look for
NEW YORK TIMES AND *USA TODAY*
BESTSELLING AUTHOR

KATHLEEN EAGLE

in October!

Recently released and wounded war vet
Cal Cougar is determined to start his recovery—
inside and out. There's no better place than the
Double D Ranch to begin the journey.
Cal discovers firsthand how extraordinary the
ranch really is when he meets a struggling single
mom and her very special child.

ONE BRAVE COWBOY,
available September 27 wherever books are sold!

USA TODAY bestselling author

Carol Marinelli

brings you her new romance

HEART OF THE DESERT

One searing kiss is all it takes for Georgie to know
Sheikh Prince Ibrahim is trouble....

But, trapped in the swirling sands, Georgie finally
surrenders to the brooding rebel prince—yet the
law of his land decrees that she can never
really be his....

Available October 2011.

Available only from Harlequin Presents®.

HP13020

The pressure from his lips and arms increased, till she was being squeezed so mercilessly tight that breathing was difficult. Some nameless, amorphous thing mushroomed in her breasts, growing into her throat, till she felt weak, as though she would burst from the strain of containing it. Yet while it weakened her will, it imparted strength to her arms and lips. She was aware, at a hazy distance, that she was returning every pressure of the embrace, that she was not only enduring it but enjoying it. *I am being seduced—how lovely it is* was the last conscious thought she had. . . .

Other Fawcett Books
by Joan Smith:

Lady Madeline's Folly
Love Bade Me Welcome
Love's Way
Prelude to Love
The Blue Diamond
Lover's Vow
Reluctant Bride
Reprise
Valerie
Wiles of a Stranger

MIDNIGHT MASQUERADE

Joan Smith

FAWCETT CREST • NEW YORK

A Fawcett Crest Book
Published by Ballantine Books

Copyright © 1985 by Joan Smith

Library of Congress Catalog Card Number: 84-90947

ISBN 0-449-20501-0

Manufactured in the United States of America

First Edition: February 1985

To my Son, Patrick Healey

Chapter 1

❋❋❋

Deirdre Gower slid her dainty dancing slippers into a pair of galoshes and pulled a dusty greatcoat over her ball gown. She eased the attic window up and crawled out on to the flat roof that overlooked the countryside. From the vantage point of the roof of Beaulac, she should have had a good view of the private road up from the main road, but her vision was hampered by the swirling snow. Thick enough to show the pattern of the wind currents, the snow was like a moving curtain composed of discrete, glistening particles. Rather beautiful, really, but her mind was on another of nature's wonders at the moment—namely, her fiancé.

She inched closer to the edge of the roof and was rewarded by the sight of two bobbing moons of light from a carriage. As the rig came closer, she recognized through the snow the stylish lines of Baron Belami's curricle. It was just like him to be driving an open carriage in the teeth of a howling storm. He'd catch his

1

death of pneumonia and that would be the end of it. A respectable finish to the mismatch of the century. Her nose and fingers were cold, but her heart was colder.

For three days she had waited at Beaulac, her fiancé's home in the country, for his arrival to celebrate their betrothal, and to announce it publicly. It was to have been made at midnight, but there would be no announcement now. Such rough usage as she had endured at his hands required desperate measures. She must head him off before he reached the ballroom, and detain him. His arrival before the hour of midnight would ruin everything. She drew out her watch and squinted into the snow to read the hour. Ten minutes to twelve!

She must hurry back downstairs, but at least it was unlikely Belami could get dried out, dressed, and into the ballroom by midnight. She would remain on the alert near the door to divert him if he tried to enter. She hastened back through the window into the attic, removed the galoshes and greatcoat, and was back in the ballroom in time, nervously watching the door. She saw her chaperone, the Duchess of Charney, enter on Herr Bessler's arm.

The long-case clock in the corner heaved and moaned, indicating to bystanders it was gearing up to do its most strenuous duty of the day—emit twelve tinny chimes. This particular dozen tintinnabulations were of more than ordinary significance. They indicated the demise of A.D. 1816 and ushered in 1817. The party assembled in Lady Belami's ballroom stood in a wobbly circle, rather thinking they ought to join hands, or sing, or at least wish their partners a happy New Year. Lady Belami was not the sort of hostess who organized matters well. She stood frowning, muttering to her companion, "I suppose we ought to . . ." "If Dickie were here, I'm sure he would . . ." "I don't know why someone doesn't. . . ."

Her disjointed ramblings were interrupted by a high shriek. Like every other head in the room, hers spun to the source of the noise, which was a lady near the ballroom door. "A mouse! I know it is a mouse," Lady Belami moaned. "The larder is full of them. Nothing works—arsenic, traps. Wouldn't you *know* one of them would decide to attend my New Year's Ball and make a shambles of it."

The shriek, however, was not followed by a series of shrieks, as it would be had the mouse continued its way into the room. It was followed by a sudden buzz of excited exclamations, then a dead, ominous silence. Lady Belami was not quite five feet tall, she couldn't see a thing over Pronto Pilgrim's head. "What is it? What's happening?" she demanded.

Pronto, no reliable source of information at the best of times, though not usually reluctant to speak, was as quiet as the rest. Lady Belami had to bolt around the corner to see what was afoot. She wished she had not. In fact, she felt very much like fainting at the awful scene that greeted her bulging blue eyes. It was like something out of a vulgar melodrama. "I'll *kill* him," she muttered to herself. "If this is one of Dickie's pranks, I shall personally carve him with a hot knife and feed his entrails to the carrion crows."

It was impossible to *know* the form under the sheet was Dickie, her son, though it was the right size for him. The face was transmogrified in some manner. A silk stocking was pulled over the head, with two holes burned in it for eyes. My, what a grotesque, frightening effect it gave. Was he playing at being Knag, the family ghost? How he used to love to dress up and scare the servants. He hadn't covered his hands in those days, but tonight he had his hands covered in a large pair of ladies' kidskin gloves. In the left hand he held his handsome dueling pistol, with the nacre insets on the handle. As she watched, the pistol was played around in a circle, threatening all the helpless guests, till it reached the guest of honor, the Dowager Duchess of Charney. This was really too bad of Dickie. If he wanted to play off a joke, he ought to have chosen someone other than the demmed Duchess for the butt of it. He

3

was doing it to discourage the dame's notion of having him marry her niece, of course, but surely to God he might have discouraged them in a more civilized manner.

Lady Belami waited with bated breath to see what his next freakish start would be. The man's right hand went out to the duchess's wattled neck and grasped her ugly necklace. Without even asking her to unfasten it, he yanked. Just yanked, yanked, and yanked again, while poor Charney's gray head tumbled about like a rag doll's, till at last he had the necklace in his gloved hand. Then without a word he flashed the pistol all around at the guests again, and backed out of the room without saying a single word. How very wise of Dickie. His mellifluous voice would have been a dead giveaway. The double doors slammed violently. A key was turned in the lock, and the pandemonium broke out.

Lady Belami was blissfully unaware of it. She had keeled over in a dead faint, into the arms of Pronto Pilgrim. She later claimed it was all that saved her from dying of heart failure. The body had its own wisdom; it knew when the system could take no more. She often told Dickie so, when he tried to push his pills and potions down her throat. She missed the ensuing excitement, and was heartily glad of it. While the gentlemen recovered from shock and fear and rattled at the locked doors, she lay on the floor being vigorously fanned with Pronto's handkerchief, being told to just take it easy and by jove she'd be right as a trivet in jig-time. When this news did not revive her, Pronto looked around the milling throng for someone to aid him, but the clunches were more interested in gaping and yapping, like a bunch of untrained hunting dogs.

Happening to catch Deirdre's eye, he tossed his head to signal he wanted assistance, but she ignored him. Where did she get the reputation of being such a worthy girl? The minx was *smiling*!

Deirdre *did* feel one small pang of conscience when she ignored Pronto's tacit plea, but she had more press-

4

ing matters to attend to. She meant to be the first to find Belami, and ring a resounding peal over him. She would claim a belief that *he* was the thief, and demand in outraged accents how he *dared* to subject her to this infamous insult. Bad enough he had not *once* called on her in London, after she had accepted his stilted offer; worse that he had not bothered to come to the ball that was to announce their betrothal. But to turn thief and steal her aunt's necklace was really the outside of enough. In fact, it was dangerously indiscreet. But when had Belami ever behaved with even a modicum of discretion? she would ask haughtily. The only decent thing he'd ever done in his life was to offer for her after all but seducing her in her aunt's conservatory, and now he was turning that into ignominy and shame.

She would *not* be robbed of the pleasure of telling him she had no intention in the world of marrying him. The contemplation of that had consoled her through it all. She meant to inform him as well that she only ever agreed to marry him to escape the clutches of Lord Twombley. That would set him down a peg, to be found only marginally better than an aging drunkard with a face like a cod. But now the cod had found a lady so undemanding as to accept him, so she was safe, and could give Belami his congé without fear of reprisals from her Aunt Charney.

She remembered the little door at the end of the ballroom. She darted to it and, finding it open, ran through the adjoining card room to another door that gave access to the hall. By this time, three gentlemen were hot on her heels. The men went immediately to the ballroom door and unlocked it to free the captive guests, who had not the least desire to leave the scene of the crime, so the men went inside instead to receive congratulations for their daring.

Deirdre was alone in the hall, looking all around. There was no one in sight, but Snippe, the butler, soon came forward from his little room near the front door.

5

"Where did he go? Did you see which way he went?" she asked.

"Who are you looking for, ma'am?" he asked, peering over her shoulder to the ballroom, where he knew by the excited voices and liberal use of vinaigrettes that the New Year had been celebrated in some unusual manner.

"The thief! He ran out this door. Where is he?" she asked.

"Thief, ma'am?" Snippe asked, his forehead corrugated with lines of astonishment, his little snake eyes opened wide. "I haven't seen anyone. I was overseeing the preparation of the trays of champagne."

"Sampling them is more like it," she charged sharply. A lying, bibulous butler, exactly what one might expect of Belami. This was not the first aberration from propriety observed in the household.

As Snippe spoke, three liveried menservants advanced, each holding a tray of filled champagne glasses, balanced on one hand, just at the level of the ear. They passed into the ballroom and were soon distributing their cargo.

Deirdre thought a moment and concluded that the thief would not have gone out by the kitchen, where he would have met several servants. He would have gone out that front door, and Snippe, into the wine, had not seen him. She marched to the door and pulled it open. When she looked outside, she observed that the falling snow had covered the ground in an undisturbed blanket of white. There wasn't a single footprint to mar its smoothness. So he was still in the house then. She pelted up and down the hall, throwing open doors and running into chambers, some lit and warmed by a fire, others dark and cold, but all perfectly empty. He had vanished without a trace, with the fabulous Charney Diamond necklace.

She looked to the carved staircase leading to the bedchambers, thinking the thief might have gone upstairs, but in the end the number of possible hiding places de-

6

feated her. And where was Belami through all this? He had arrived some minutes ago. A pensive frown wrinkled her brow. Was it possible he really *was* the man under the sheet and mask? She returned, not too uneagerly, to the ballroom. She saw the groups of excited guests, gesturing, drinking the champagne, discussing the theft, and joined them. Before long, she met Pronto and another gentleman carrying Lady Belami out, and stood aside, but made no offer to attend the stricken dame. It was a wonder the duchess didn't faint, she thought, forgetting, in her excitement, the heroic nature of the octogenarian.

The Dowager Duchess was having a marvelous time, and would have for days to come. Nothing had a stronger appeal to her than to have such a prime piece of depravity to hold over her hostess's head. And the whole of society would know it. There wasn't a chance of Bertie's hushing up *this* scandal. Hah! The baron *must* marry Deirdre now, to repay them for this affront. Truth to tell, she was close to despairing of ever bringing Belami to the sticking point, especially when he had chosen not to attend the betrothal ball. Not much was beyond her notions of what a duchess might do, but announcing an engagement to a man who had quite possibly skipped the country did exceed the pale. *Just* like him, ramshackle fellow, but an excellent parti for all that. Good blood, good fortune, and a good brain. That he was also as handsome as a Greek statue was acceptable, though not very interesting. Marriage to a lady of strong virtue like Deirdre would tame him of those little vices of gaming, whoring, and using too much scent. It had not yet occurred to her that the baron might have been instrumental in the theft. She was cagey, but not very inventive in her scheming.

It had occurred to others. His mother, Bertie, knew perfectly well Dick had done it, and took a solemn vow to kill him when he came waltzing in grinning the next morning with some story of having gotten snowed in somewhere. She regularly vowed to commit sonicide, as

7

Dick called it, but had thus far neglected to execute her vows. It was no easy thing to be the mother of Baron Belami, the scapegrace darling of society. He was spoiled rotten. Handsome, rich, sought after—but really a very good son, she decided more leniently as a memory of his boyish face floated before her closed eyes.

When he was away from home, as he usually was, it was easy to think of him as still a boy. She had no mature portrait of him. What was propped on her dresser was a likeness taken on his fourteenth birthday. Since the summer when he had sat impatiently for Romney, his frame had stretched to six feet, his shoulders had grown broad and his body muscled. His nose and face had lost the last traces of childhood fullness, to reveal the perfect set of classical bones beneath. The lips, to be sure, had taken on a sardonic cast, but that was seldom in evidence when he was with his mama, whom he unceremoniously called Bertie, as though she were one of his chums. And really she was closer to a chum than a mother in her dealings with him. It seemed a father's job to chide a son for irregularities, and Dick hadn't had a father since that portrait was taken. His eyes hadn't changed much, she thought, looking at the portrait. They were still as dark as coffee, with lashes a yard long, which she knew Dickie hated. He had actually trimmed them once, which had the effect of making them grow even longer. He liked the haughty line of his eyebrows well enough, especially the one he had trained to lift an inch higher than the other when he wished to indicate displeasure, disagreement, a question, or even plain dislike. A very expressive set of eyebrows had Dickie.

And *where was he*? She had hoped he would have sneaked into her chamber by now, to explain with his laughing eyes why he had done it, how he had done it, what he had done with the curst necklace, and ultimately, of course, who he meant to blame it on and how he meant to return it. He was not a thief, certainly. That at least need not disturb her mind for an instant.

8

A perfectly rapscallion son, but *not* a thief. The only thing he ever stole was ladies' hearts, and really that was not so much theft as involuntary acquisition. The present involuntary acquisition, Deirdre Gower, was to be turned off by the charade of stealing Charney's necklace. That was what he was up to.

A sound at the door caused her to sit up, but it was only a maid asking if she would like some wine, or hartshorn, or laudanum.

"My son. I want Dickie," she said in a weak voice.

"We haven't found him yet, mum," the witless maid answered, and received a pillow on the side of her head for the insolence of suggesting Dick had anything to do with the night's imbroglio. It was one thing for a mother to know he had done it, it; she would not allow others to say so.

"Send him up the minute *he arrives from London*," she ordered in her most cutting voice.

The maid left without realizing she had been put in her place. Even Bertie's most cutting voice was not very sharp. Dick had gotten his mellifluous tone from her. His papa had barked like a dog.

Chapter 2

✳✳✳

At eleven o'clock on the night of December the thirty-first, Baron Belami disentangled himself from the warm arms of a compliant widow friend and said, "I should be shoving off, Bess, before Bertie's ball is over. I ought to put in an appearance, or the old girl will cut up stiff."

"You'll never make it," Bess answered, lounging back on the pillow and running her fingers through a cloud of black hair that had recently been likened to a Stygian snare. "It's eleven already."

"It's only ten miles. I'll make it for the midnight revels, with time to spare," he assured her, hopping out of bed. "Damme, it's *snowing*!" he exclaimed, looking out the window.

"Stay; maybe we'll be snowbound," she tempted, stretching like a cat.

He considered this appetizing suggestion, but in the

end shook his head and put on his clothes. "Pierre will get me through. He knows snow."

"Knows snow?" she asked in forgivable confusion.

"He is an expert on snow," he told her. "Pierre is from Lower Canada. He tells me that in the winter there he has often had to burrow his way from his cottage. He also possesses a pair of snowshoes that allow him to walk on deep snow drifts. I've been praying for a good snowfall to try them."

"It looks as if your prayer has been answered," Bess said lazily.

"That's a change. God usually ignores me."

"And *vice versa*," Bess answered with laughter in her voice.

"Saucy pedantic wretch," he said in his sweet, mellifluous voice, which belied any displeasure with her pertness. He leaned down and placed a kiss on her cheek while shoving a wad of bills into her reaching fingers. "Maybe I'll be able to drop in again on my way back to London. Are you free—say, a week Wednesday?"

"Try me," she invited, reaching for the flint box to count her take. She waited till Belami closed the door before lighting the taper. She smiled in satisfaction at the denomination of the bills, shoved them beneath her pillow, and went to sleep, dreaming of the scarlet gown she would order from her earnings.

Pierre Réal, Belami's French-Canadian groom, liked nothing better than to put his master firmly in the wrong. As soon as he saw the snow begin to fall, he had melord's grays hitched to his curricle and the rig drawn from the stable. When Belami came out the door, over an hour late, horses, carriage, and driver were all covered in an inch of snow.

"I hope you had a good time," Pierre said. He spoke with a heavy accent, but his actual words and syntax were taking on an English flavor, unless it had been decided between his lord and himself to speak French, which they frequently did. At times of excitement he might lapse into an admixture of the two languages,

11

but he was not excited now. He was happy. It put him metaphorically as well as literally in the driver's seat, to have been kept waiting an hour in the freezing snow while melord took his pleasure in a warm bed. Melord was missing his mother's ball, he was fornicating with a woman of pleasure, and he had kept Pierre and, more important to them both, the grays, standing in the cold, to look entirely pathetic as they waited patiently. Oh, yes, Pierre was in a prime mood.

"Go to hell," Belami growled, glaring at the exposed nags. Guilt and shame conspired to put him out of humor. "Don't you know any better than to leave these bloods out in the middle of a howling storm? Damme, it's cold. I wish I had brought my closed carriage."

"*I* suggested the closed carriage, me," Pierre reminded him, snapping the whip and urging the animals forward. "I know snow. I saw the snow forming in the clouds. 'The curricle,' you told me."

"Yes, yes, you're a bloody genius and I'm a fool. Spring 'em," Belami said, wrapping himself in the fur rug, which Pierre had had the foresight to include in the carriage. The groom shivered dramatically as Belami wrapped himself to the eyes in the rug. "Grab a corner if you like," he offered.

"I couldn't keep on the road with my arms wrapped up. She's slippery," Pierre said.

"I thought you were waiting for winter with great impatience," Belami reminded him.

"You call *this* winter? Hah, late summer, I'd call her. I've seen colder Augusts at home. I said slippery, not cold."

"Does slippery usually set you to shivering?" he asked, pulling a corner of the rug loose and throwing it over Pierre's knees.

Any pose of not being cold had to be abandoned. The groom changed the subject to the lateness of the hour instead. "We'll never make Beaulac in time for the ball," was his next cheerful speech. "She must have

12

been some frolic, the widow Barnes, to keep you three hours."

"We played chess," Belami said. "Wake me when we get to the home road." Then he pulled his curled beaver over his eyes and pretended to be asleep. He had deep scheming to do, to figure a way out of marrying Deirdre Gower. He was frequently in hot water with women, but not customarily with innocent debs. It was still half a mystery to him how he had bungled the affair so badly that he had actually stammered out a sort of offer.

The trouble was, Deirdre was such a flat she had no idea how men acted with women. It was her very lack of knowing how to flirt that had done him in. Chaperones ought to teach their charges how to flirt, for God's sake. He had mistaken her shyness for haughty indifference. Haughty indifference was irresistible to him. He had to prove to himself he could engage her interest. Well, he had. And it hadn't taken much work, either. Stood up with her three or four times, walked out with her once, then followed her to the conservatory at her aunt's ball. That was his undoing. She had looked damnably attractive in the shadowy moonlight, so he had kissed her. What else could one do when alone with a woman in the moonlight, surrounded by the exotic spice of flowers in bloom in December? She shouldn't have gone there alone; she knew he would follow her. If she hadn't been a flat she would have known he'd have to kiss her. And if *he* hadn't been a complete idiot, he might have suspected old Charney would be lurking at the window, to see the kiss, and insinuate what course was now necessary for a gentleman.

But Deirdre could still have saved them both, if she'd had the decency to refuse his offer. He was *obliged* to offer; she wasn't obliged to accept. It was a trick to nab him, and one trick deserved another, so he had stayed completely away from her while he was in London. Charney and Bertie between them had cooked up this curst ball and the announcement to be made at midnight. He trusted his late arrival would have convinced Deirdre of any lack of real affection on his part. If there was a gentlemanly bone in her ladylike body, she'd turn him off.

There were some few members of society one did not like to offend, and the Duchess of Charney was one of them. And really he didn't want to hurt Deirdre either. It was naivety as much as anything that ailed the girl. If only she'd call off the engagement, he was perfectly ready to find her unexceptionable, for anyone except himself.

Before leaving London, he had taken the precaution of worrying loud and long to a few friends, who were also intimates of the duchess, that some of his investments had gone sour. A diminution of fortune might discourage Charney, but on the other hand, he could hardly claim to have lost three rather large estates within the space of a few weeks. Setting up a high flyer as his mistress would not be sufficient to do the trick. He had had one under his protection at the time Charney put her niece forward. The risk of Bedlam discouraged him from claiming insanity in the family. Any pending major misalliance on Bertie's part would be bound to help, but then, one's own mother. . . . And Bertie was such a jingle brain she'd end up marrying whatever hedgebird he got for the part.

When they reached the home road, it was nearly midnight, and he still had no solution to his problem. "Wake up!" Pierre said, nudging him in the ribs with the butt of his whip.

Belami pulled out his watch and focused his eyes to read it in the moonless shadows. Ten minutes to twelve. He left it in his hand to watch for midnight, but looked around at the scene before him. Beaulac reared its handsome head and shoulders up into the whirling snow that swept through the black night on eddies of wind. Beaulac was too formal a building to entirely please this romantic young lord. He would have preferred a heap in the gothic style, with arched windows

14

that were so much more feminine than the mullioned rectangles of Beaulac. He was fond of flying butresses, and an occasional gargoyle would have pleased him; but on this night, with the darkness and snow concealing the severe geometry of Beaulac, he was satisfied with his home. The many lit windows lent a lively and haphazard air to the place. His gaze wandered off to the grounds, noticing the undisturbed snow. The last guest must have arrived several hours ago, he thought, but at least no one had *left* yet.

He happened to glance up to the roof, and thought he discerned a shadow moving there. He smiled, recalling the many times he had stood there himself, draped in a sheet, to scare the wits out of the gullible servants. What had he called that ghost he was supposed to be? Knag, that was it, with the *k* silent. Pity Beaulac didn't have a real ghost like Longleat's Green Lady, to rescue him from this unwanted entanglement. A bemused smile hovered about his lips as he sat, staring and thinking unholy thoughts.

The long hand was still several minutes away from twelve as they pulled into the stable, but Belami said, "*Bonne et Heureuse Année*, Pierre," anyway.

Pierre sneezed violently. "*La même pour vous*, melord."

"*Gezundheit.*"

"*Comment?*"

"Let another groom tend the grays and you look after yourself. I suggest a warm bath and a hot drink," Belami said.

"No hands but these take care of my grays," Pierre declared, holding out his hands.

"Those hands won't do any of us much good if they're attached to a corpse," Belami said, and hastened off.

He entered by the kitchen door, to slip up to his room by the back stairs and change his clothes. It was odd, but convenient, that there were no servants in the kitchen. They must have gone up to serve the midnight

15

dinner. The stable was full of carriages, so the ball was obviously in progress.

Belami had left his valet in London, as the man was in the throes of a torrid triangular love affair with Lord Norris's upstairs maid. Belami was a firm believer in true love, especially for people other than himself. He had given Uggams a handful of golden boys to help his suit along, and offered the woman a position in his own household as well, if she accepted his valet's offer. His generosity had left him with only Pierre to help with his dressing, and for the present, he must help himself. Naturally his grays came first.

He struggled out of his topboots, fawn trousers, and jacket alone, and scrambled into his pantaloons and black jacket. He brushed his hair and tied up his cravat with a careless disregard for the Waterfall and Oriental and such fashionable arrangements as prevailed amidst the ton. While his fingers performed these automatic functions, his mind reverted to Knag, and other more plausible means of egress from an unwanted engagement.

Belowstairs, the hands of the clock rapidly approached midnight.

It was some moments later when Belami hastened, head bent, along the upstairs hall. He took no notice of the female guest approaching till he had nearly capsized her.

"I beg your pardon, ma'am," he said, steadying the girl by placing a hand on either arm. How *cold* she was!

She wrenched herself from him with an unusual degree of violence. He blinked, and recognized the form of Deirdre Gower. His anger was not less than hers. *Naturally* the curst woman had to be the first person he encountered, before he had his alibi properly rehearsed. Her back was stiff, her neck stiffer, and her eyes on fire.

"Good evening, Deirdre. Happy New Year," he said with a cool civility that did not belong on a fiancé's lips. "Not at the ball?"

"You have the *temerity* to ask me that!" she exclaimed, preparing her accusations. "*Ac*-tually I came up looking for you."

Ac-tually! Deirdre Gower was the only woman in England who thought *actually* was two separate words, and that the *t* was not only pronounced, but given an awful stress. Many times he had winced under the word, as it usually preceded some pedantic lecture of which he did not stand in need. And to think, when he first heard it, he had found it a beguiling affectation.

"You're no doubt upset that I'm a trifle late," he said, knowing some apology must be uttered.

"No, I'm not upset that you're late. I wouldn't have cared a brass farthing if you hadn't come at all. In fact, I wish you hadn't come!" she told him, eyes flashing.

He stood bemused. *Ac*-tually, Deirdre was mildly attractive when shaken out of her customary lethargy. Was that why he had once found her worth investigating, because she had been angry about something? What could it have been? he wondered. His glance roamed from her great gray eyes, illuminated by unspeakable anger; to her nose, short, straight, well shaped; to the upper lip, short, and giving a kissable quality to her full lips. The hair, alas, was archaic. She wore it in a scraped-back style not noticeably different from her aunt's. The gown too, while passable, lacked any flare of distinction. It was a white gown, crepe, somewhat limp, its only embellishment a string of pearls, unless you could call that gray band around the bottom embellishment. What was it, anyway—wet, dirty? Her speech soon diverted his attention upwards again.

"Why didn't you stay away?" she asked.

"Sorry to disappoint you. I had a spot of trouble. We lost a wheel in the snow. Miserable traveling weather," he added blandly.

"If you had come three days ago when you were supposed to, you would have missed the vile weather. But then I suppose the story is to be that you arrived *after*

17

midnight tonight," she said, lifting her brow and looking at him with all the scorn of his banker when the account was overdrawn. She noticed his somewhat impetuous toilette, and thought he had taken enough time to make a tidier one.

Belami was noticing something else. There seemed to be some meaningful weight on the words *after midnight*. Was it a reference to the hour the announcement was to have been made? "I believe I arrived around twelve," he answered.

"Not around twelve, Belami. *Ac*-tually it was twelve on the dot. Very dramatic, very effective, but totally unnecessary, I assure you. You didn't have to add melodrama to the affair. I had already decided to jilt you. Yes, you are released from the burden of marrying me. And in case you're wondering *why*, let me enlighten you. It has nothing to do with tonight. Twombley is engaged to Lady Cecilia Carruthers. I only ever agreed to have you to escape him. Bad as you are, at least you're not as bad as Twombley. He was my aunt's first choice for me."

A blessed cloak of relief descended on his shoulders, like a mantle of peace. He felt like the Ancient Mariner when the albatross finally fell into the sea. For a fleeting instant, he loved Deirdre Gower, stiff neck, *ac*-tually, and all. "I have always heard comparisons are odious," he said, smiling broadly.

"Not as odious as *you* are!"

"Another comparison! Where does that leave me? Stranded above Twombley and below comparisons." He crossed his legs and leaned against the wall, smiling down at Deirdre.

"At least Twombley is not a *thief*!" she charged with an angry toss of her head.

"That, at least, is beneath him," he agreed. "Er, do I descry some intimation in your conversation that I *am* a thief?" he asked playfully. "What have I stolen? Let me guess."

18

"What did you do with it?" she asked, ignoring his playful attitude.

"Tell me first what I have purloined, and I can give you a better answer," he parried.

"It is *not* a joking matter, Belami. I know you take nothing seriously but your dissipations, but the duchess is speaking of calling in Bow Street. I know you only took it to break our engagement, but it wasn't necessary. You can sneak it back, and my aunt and I shall leave quietly."

A frown settled on his handsome face. His mobile brow was lifted to its full height, and though he did not give up leaning on the wall, there was a new air of alertness about him. His eyes looked black and dangerous. "But you still haven't told me what I took," he pointed out in a patient voice at odds with his eyes.

"The diamond necklace, of course. How *could* you, Belami?" she asked, her voice husky with emotion. Logic told him it was the missing necklace that upset her, and his sensitivities told him that she was much prettier when so agitated. Instinctively he stood up straight and put out an arm to comfort her.

Again she wrenched away from him, with a good semblance of revulsion. Alas, it was only a semblance. Blackguard that he was, she still felt a strong attraction to his physical presence. His soul and his character she despised heartily, but these invisible entities fell from her mind when she was with the physical specimen. It wasn't fair that a blackguard should be so attractive. He was often described by society as an Adonis, but the name didn't do him justice. It was too old and lifeless. Belami was more than a hero from antiquity. He was Romeo magically grown to a more mature manhood, and he was Byron's Corsair, for there was a beguiling hint of wickedness in those dark eyes that studied her.

As she watched, his first show of concern deepened to consternation. "Are you telling me someone stole the

19

Duchess of Charney's diamond necklace?" he asked, his voice high with disbelief, like a stage actor.

"As if you didn't know it!" she said, with a scathing eye. But still he looked on, nonplussed, causing her to run in her mind from stable to house, don the disguise, and descend to the ballroom in ten minutes. Then to get back upstairs and hide it and change again into pantaloons. It hardly seemed possible, but such was her opinion of Belami that for him, it seemed not only possible but very likely.

"Deirdre, how can you accuse me of common theft?" he demanded, offense writ large on his features. She watched as the offense turned to haughty disdain.

"There was nothing common about it. It was extremely bizarre, and everyone thinks it was you," she added righteously.

He looked up and down the hall, then turned around and opened a bedroom door and pulled her inside. "Don't be alarmed," he said with a mocking smile. "I have no designs on your virtue. I never cared for scaling mountains. I would just prefer to have this conversation without interruption. Now, suppose you tell me the whole story, from start to finish."

She told him in a simple, methodical way that required very few questions.

"That solves one of our problems at least," was his comment when she had finished. "Your aunt won't be likely to push this match forward now."

"No, and neither shall I," she answered sharply. "I hope I am too discreet to ask where you spent the hours preceding midnight, but I hope for your sake they were in company that can be brought forward without blushing. You might quite possibly require an alibi."

"Well, now, I promise you *I* shan't blush, and as for you ladies, you may do as you wish. You always do. Shall we go down now?"

"You should go to see your mother. She was taken to her room when she fainted."

"Ah, poor Bertie!" he said with the first show of genuine sorrow since his arrival.

Deirdre returned belowstairs to mingle and listen for what was being said, and Belami went to see his mother. She sat up when he entered, and directed a wild-eyed look at him, before bursting into tears. The wrinkles in her cherubic little face were concealed in shadows, giving her the look of a baby.

"We are ruined, Dickie! Utterly disgraced. The Duchess, of all people. How *could* you?"

"How *could* you?" Twice he had heard it within ten minutes. He had the sickening apprehension he would hear it many more times before this holiday was over. In three long strides, he was at her bedside, where she threw herself into his arms, all thoughts of hot knives and carving forgotten. He hugged her close against his chest, trying to soothe and comfort her.

"You know I didn't do it, Mama. What a thing to say to your own son," he replied in soft, injured tones that touched a responsive chord deep within her, but did not quite convince her.

"I know you got your freakish nature from me. There is no need to rub salt in the wound. Your papa would never do such things. Oh, why couldn't you have been like *him*?"

"Because I preferred to be like you. Tell me all about it, everything you remember," he urged, patting her shoulders gently.

"I didn't see much. Fortunately, I fainted. It is all that saved my life. Someone—one of us, I mean, ought to go below and hear what is being said. Or maybe it would be best if you ran away somewhere and hid for a few weeks. If you turn up now, Dick, they are bound to know it was you."

"It wasn't me!"

"Who all knows you are here?"

"No one but Deirdre," he answered.

"She will keep quiet. Very proud, all the Gowers. She

21

won't want it said her fiancé is a felon. Do you think—France, Dickie? You could be quite comfortable in Paris till it blows over."

"I can't run away."

"But if you stay, you know, you'll end up investigating into it yourself, as you love to do. Why don't you go to France instead?"

"Flight would be taken as a sign of guilt. I must stay and see if I can find out who did it, catch him, and get the necklace back to Charney."

"You had great luck in finding the little Everton girl who was kidnapped," Bertie said reluctantly.

"It was not luck!" he said, offended. "It was ingenuity, and hard work. Of course I can and shall do it. I must go now. Don't worry, Mama. I'm not a thief."

"I know that, love." She smiled a watery, sad smile that caused an ache in his heart. He kissed the top of her head, and left.

One might be forgiven for thinking his tread was slow, his shoulders sagging, his face set in gloom. It was no such a thing. The expression that took possession of his features was not quite delight, but it veered in that direction. The young baron's occasional brushes with mysteries provided variety in an otherwise self-indulgent and unchallenging life. He could not think, offhand, when he had been happier than the week he undertook to find Lord Everton's kidnapped daughter. The excitement of the chase, the challenge of outwitting a mind nearly as quick as his own, the satisfaction of bringing a lawless wretch to justice and restoring an innocent family to peace—why, it was more amusing than making love, or money, when you came down to it. There was an added spice in the dish this time, as it was himself he had to extricate.

By the time he bounced off the bottom step and met a distracted Snippe, he was not far from smiling. He rubbed his hands together in anticipation. "Happy New

Year, Snippe," he said. "It got off to a bang here, I understand."

Snippe compressed his lips and glared. "*Some people* might think it amusing to go dressing up like ghosts and stealing diamonds and throwing their mothers into pelters. *I* think they ought to be horsewhipped."

"*I* think their butlers ought to be turned off without a reference. Get me some champagne. Where's the Duchess now?"

"Gone to her room to gloat, and her niece with her. You'll be wanting the whole bottle of wine, then?" he added in an accusing way.

"We'll start with one. What's going on in there?" Belami asked, tossing his head towards the ballroom.

"Gossip and a deal of drinking."

"Serve 'em dinner, if it's ready."

"It's ready. Who is to sit at the head of the table? Her ladyship isn't up to it. I shouldn't think you will wish to show your face."

"What's wrong with my face?" he asked, lifting one of his mobile brows.

Snippe pinched his eyes into slits and left, to return in a moment with the bottle of champagne and a glass. "Here you go, then," he said, chucking them towards his master.

"Is Uncle Cottrell here?" Belami asked.

"Aye, His Lordship is here."

"Good, he'll be the host for dinner. Kindly tell him so. I have a spot of looking around to do. I'll duck into your lair while you herd the guests into the dining room. Send Pronto to me."

"I've only got two feet," Snippe pointed out.

"Use them. Go!" He shook his head at the bad habits Bertie had allowed his servants to slide into. But then it wouldn't be home if it were well run.

He poured a glass of champagne and sipped carefully as he walked along to the butler's private room, close to the door. The mask, gloves, sheet, and pistol the thief

23

used indicated that some preparation had gone into the job. As it was only Charney's necklace that had been stolen, this was apparently the thief's aim, to steal that one particular piece. The thief therefore knew she would be wearing it. This was helpful, as it eliminated the country neighbors. It had to be one of the guests from the city, then, and one close enough to Charney to know she had brought the diamond pendant with her. The next job would be to learn who had been in the ballroom when the thief entered. It was beginning to look like a case of eliminating suspects, and not finding one.

He heard the babble of voices and shuffle of footsteps as the guests went to dinner. Soon there was a tap at the door and Pronto Pilgrim entered.

"If you say 'How *could* you,' Pronto, I'll land you a facer," was Belami's greeting.

Pronto sniffed. "No such a thing. I *know* how you did it. Got it all figured out. Know why you did it too. Dashed havey-cavey business, Dick. Ought to give it back to her. Knag won't work."

"*Et tu*, Pronto?"

Pronto sniffed again and looked about for a wine glass. Finding none, he called Snippe and sent him off for one. "We're missing dinner," he warned Dick. "Don't know about you, but I'm ready for fork work."

"Have Snippe bring you a plate, if you dare incur his wrath."

"Don't know why you keep that ghoul in your service. No, I'd sooner go hungry than have to look at his eyes disappear into slits."

As he spoke, he sauntered to the murky mirror on the wall and ran a hand over his brown hair. It was luxuriant and waved. He was proud of it. It was the one good feature on an otherwise undistinguished body. Pronto was blessed with no impressive physique. He was shorter than the average, with narrow shoulders, eked out with much wadding. There was no tailor clever enough to conceal the protruding stomach and bowed legs. His face was not actually ugly, but the bewildered expression he generally wore did not enhance it. He had gray eyes, a nose crooked from having been broken in a brawl with a chairman, and a scar on his left cheek. He found this assortment dashing, and hoped the scar would not sink into insignificance with the passing of time. He spoke vaguely of a duel when quizzed as to its origin, but in fact he had tripped over his own feet and scraped it on a sharp dresser edge.

With a last admiring look in the mirror, he turned back to his friend. "So what's to do about this mess, Dick?"

"I've been working out my plan," Belami answered, and sat down with his feet on Snippe's desk, the glass in his hand, the chair tipped at a perilous angle, to explain his line of attack.

There was a sharp rap at the door, and without waiting for an answer, Deirdre stepped in. "My aunt is resting. Do you mind if I join you?" she asked.

"They're serving dinner," Pronto told her, hoping to be rid of her.

Belami had lowered his chair and arisen to his feet. She glared at him and said. "I'm involved too. I want to know what you're doing."

"But of course you do," Belami agreed, offering her his chair and removing Pronto's glass from his fingers. He filled it and handed it to Deirdre.

"That's *my* glass!" Pronto told him.

'Call Snippe for another. I won't let him hurt you."

With mutinous mutterings, Pronto waddled to the door and shouted to Snippe to bring a tray of glasses and a couple of bottles, as it seemed the party was transferring here. It struck him this was also an opportunity to order food, but Snippe's countenance made him change his mind.

Belami's impassive countenance gave no notion of the thought going on in his head, and his eagerness to get busy. He would give the two a little talk on criminal investigation and find a harmless job for them to do while he went on with the real work. Pronto he could have used, but Deirdre was definitely de trop.

Chapter 3

✳✳✳

While the guests ate and drank and discussed the startling theft, Belami introduced his colleagues into the intricacies of criminal investigation. He rather enjoyed giving this particular lecture. Motive, method, and opportunity were the three magical keys. Deduction was the power that fitted the keys to the proper locks. In a case of theft, one assumed the motive was financial gain. The method they had already learned, and it was the opportunity they must discover. He impressed upon them that no detail was too small to bring to his attention, in the unlikely case that he overlooked anything. While he spoke, Pronto sat regretting the dinner he was missing, and Deirdre admired his vocabulary, the delivery of the speech, and general physical appearance. At the lecture's end, they dispersed to begin searching for clues. Belami went abovestairs to go inch by inch over the guests' rooms, while their servants were busy below celebrating the New Year in the kitchen. Various clues were collected and put into blue envelopes for further perusal. This done, he darted to the stable to seek the help of Pierre. There he learned that no one had made any secret trip to his carriage, which loomed as a possible hiding place for the necklace. The grays had been rubbed down and blanketed for the night. At about two o'clock, Pierre decided he would just take a walk around the grounds on his snowshoes, to calm himself for a night's sleep. He enjoyed these balmy nights, with the wind howling and the snow swirling around his head.

"Pity the pond is frozen over, or you could have a swim," Belami told him.

"We often took an ax to the river at home, for a short swim," Pierre told him, his steely gaze daring a contradiction.

"Go to bed, you fool. You're shivering worse than I am."

Deirdre and Pronto examined the unoccupied rooms downstairs, not quite sure what they were looking for, but knowing that anything "unusual" was suspect. As they had no real idea what might be usual in another man's house, however, they were not hopeful of great success. But at least they realized that one window had been opened, as it had markings in the snow on the ledge outside.

More than an hour elapsed before dinner was over. Belami went to his mother's room. "You must brace yourself to see the guests out, Mama. I have decided not to appear tonight. If we don't get them blasted off soon, they'll be battened on us for days. The snow is still falling. By morning, they won't be able to move their carriages."

This alarming news was enough to get her up off her bed. She struggled manfully to her little feet, had her woman in to tidy her hair, and, with a pathetic effort at a smile, went downstairs. A few guests were loath to tackle the snow, already two inches and higher where the wind had drifted it, but she assured them blithely it was only a sprinkle. If they hastened, they'd make it home with no trouble. No trouble at all.

It took another half hour before the city guests had straggled upstairs to their rooms. Bertie claimed she was ready for the grave by the time the last of them finally went up. "And I look it," she said with an accusing stare at her son, who was back hiding in Snippe's room with Pronto and Deirdre.

"You'd best hit the tick too, Dick, and let poor Miss Gower get to her bed," she advised.

Deirdre had not the least wish to miss out on the excitement. Life was dull with Aunt Charney. Such venturesome goings-on as she was enjoying at Beaulac were a rare event in her life, but she worded her objection in a different light. "Who could possibly sleep with so much worry and confusion surrounding us?" she asked.

"There's nothing for you to worry about," Belami told her. "Mother is right. Why don't you go on up to bed?"

Her jaw squared, and a mutinous light entered her gray eyes. "There are a few points I'd like to discuss with you this evening, Belami, while they're fresh in my mind."

"Such as?"

"I had just returned to the ballroom. I can tell you who was present."

"She's right," Pronto agreed, "Women have sharper eyes than us. Besides, she'll only come down and listen at the keyhole. You might as well let her stay."

"Oh, very well," Dick agreed.

With this warm welcome, she sat on a very hard horsehair sofa and prepared to add her mite to the investigation.

"Your aunt will blame *me* in the morning if you have black circles under your eyes," Bertie said, but sleep was overtaking her. She was too tired to fight with youngsters. Where did they get such stores of energy?

They looked as fresh as squirrels in spring, every one of them.

"I have Mama's guest list here. Can you help me check off anyone who didn't come?" Belami said after Bertie had left.

Between Deirdre and Pronto, the list was soon shortened to possible suspects. After considerable dicussion, the possibles were further reduced to what Belami termed "likelies." "Let us see what cream—or scum— has risen to the top," he said, thinking aloud.

"There is old Bessler, the duchess's boyfriend," he began.

"My aunt's doctor," Deirdre corrected quickly, but already there was an asterisk by Bessler's name.

"An Austrian who came to London five years ago," Dick continued. "He once had a shingle hung on Harley Street and called himself Doctor, till the College of Surgeons paid him a visit and took away his gold-knobbed cane. He calls himself Herr Bessler now, as he likes to wear something that sounds like a title. You'd be surprised how many folks think it *is* one."

"It means 'gentleman' at least," Deirdre pointed out.

"And *is* he one?" Belami asked her archly. "It's not uncommon for immigrants to hop their social standing up a notch or two when they take up residence in a foreign land. I'm surprised he hasn't stuck a von in front of his name."

"My aunt considers Herr Bessler a gentleman," she insisted. "A professional man, but genteel. He lives very much in Aunt Charney's pocket. *Ac*-tually, he came in the carriage with us. He still treats my aunt, even if his license has been revoked. She had a session with him after she arrived. She had a megrim from the trip," she added.

"I expect it set in as soon as she learned I wasn't here," Belami said.

"Possibly. She said it was the garish red carpet in her room that aggravated it, but it didn't hurt *my* eyes."

"Waste of time," Pronto said, calling them back to

business. "Bessler was in the ballroom when the diamond was snitched."

"That's true," Deirdre corroborated. "He was near the door, with Auntie."

"Then next we come to Lady Lenore Belfoi," Belami said, wearing a little smile. "I notice by the list her husband didn't make it."

"Chamfreys is here," Pronto mentioned knowingly.

"Which explains the husband's absence," Dick said, quirking a brow. "I wouldn't put it past either of them. Did you happen to notice if this pair were present when the thief entered?"

"Lady Lenore—is she the woman who looks like an actress? Wears paint, too much scent, low-cut gowns?" Deirdre inquired with condescension.

"She has black hair, lovely green eyes, and a superb figure," Belami explained.

"And a wart on her chin?" Deirdre asked, bristling.

"A beauty mark to the left of her lips," Dick countered.

"If she is the woman whose bedroom is next to Chamfreys', I think I know who you mean," Deirdre said.

"That's that, then. Was she at the ball at midnight or not?" Pronto asked impatiently.

"I didn't see her," Deirdre said after a frowning pause. "I *do* remember seeing her roll her eyes at Chamfreys at about eleven-thirty, though. She slipped out immediately after and went upstairs, and he had a quick glass of wine with Bidwell, than he followed her up. I happened to be watching them."

"Only till they got to the top of the stairs, I hope?" Belami quizzed.

"Yes, I didn't see them come down," she said with a quelling stare. "They went in to dinner, so they must have been finished by then."

"Finished what?" Pronto asked. Belami rolled his eyes ceilingward and sighed.

"Whatever they were doing," Deirdre replied,

31

unfazed. "Sir Lawrence Bidwell went up as well, with Chamfreys."

"Was Bidwell in the ballroom at midnight?" Dick asked.

"No, I'm quite sure he wasn't. I was looking for him," Deirdre said. It was quite true she had been looking for a personable gentleman to stand up with so Belami wouldn't find her unpartnered. Bidwell had occurred to her as a possible partner.

"We'll give him two asterisks," Belami said with relish. "He is chronically dipped. Handsome, but ramshackle,"

"Bidwell dipped?" she asked, astonished. "He looks as fine as ninepence, and drives such a handsome carriage, with a team of four. He has lovely jackets and wears fine jewelry. I thought he must be a nabob."

"No, his uncle is a nabob," Pronto told her.

"He makes a grand appearance," she insisted.

"When a gentleman is at pains to make a grand appearance, you may suspect his bank balance," Belami decreed, annoyed with her praise of Bidwell.

Her eyes wandered over his well-tailored jacket, his immaculate white tie and diamond pin, the heavy emerald crested ring on his finger. "I'll bear that in mind," she said.

"Suspect," he repeated with emphasis. "It is not necessarily an indictment."

"It could indicate simple vanity," she agreed with an artless smile.

"She's got you dead to rights there, my lad," Pronto snorted.

"About Bidwell; he is the right size for our masked intruder. You said he was my own size, more or less, did you not, Deirdre?"

"Yes, but it could have been Chamfreys. It certainly wasn't Lady Lenore. How would either of them know my aunt was to wear her diamond, though?"

"Deduction," Pronto answered. "Whole world knows she owns it. She often sports it about here and there."

"Yes, but they couldn't be sure," Belami mentioned.

"Comes to that, the only ones who *knew* were Deirdre herself and Charney," Pronto pointed out with a sharp look at Deirdre.

"Lenore goes everywhere. She might have weaseled the fact out of the duchess in some manner," Belami thought aloud. "She's good at that sort of thing."

"Good at lots of things," Pronto added with a lascivious smile that earned a repressive frown from Belami.

After more talk, the list stood at Herr Bessler; Lady Lenore; her lover, Chamfreys; and Sir Lawrence Bidwell. Not all had a motive—Chamfreys, for instance, was well to grass. Not all were suited to the method—Lady Lenore was certainly not built like Belami. And Bessler was lacking the opportunity and suitable build for the method employed, but still they were on the list. They had to put someone on it, and there was no point thinking a man one step from being a bishop had done it, or a cabinet minister, or a very well-to-do marquis who owned a quarter of Surrey and diamonds bigger and better than the one stolen. It was mainly the fact that all of the suspects except Bessler had left the ballroom at eleven-thirty that accounted for their being under the cloud of suspicion. As to Bessler himself, he was a foreigner living on the fringes of society, and no Englishman really trusted foreigners.

"As for the results of our search, what did you find?" Belami asked, turning to Pronto.

"Didn't find your pistol. Was it missing from your room?"

"Yes, one of them is gone,"

"Didn't find the sheet or gloves or stocking with the holes burned in it either. Didn't find the necklace, of course. Didn't find anything, really, except a very decent bottle of brandy behind the books in the morning parlor. Wonder how that got there?"

"Probably been there since Papa's time," Belami said. "He used to drink brandy in the library and hide the bottle from Mama."

"You have forgotten what I discovered in the small room just west of the ballroom but on the other side of the hallway," Deirdre announced. "It was dark, and there was no fire. I took in a lamp and found one end of the curtain jammed into the window, as though it had been closed in a hurry. And the snow on the ledge outside had been all messed about by someone. The funny thing is, there were no footsteps outside on the ground. Do you think he could have thrown the necklace out in the snow, Belami? I didn't see any holes in the snow."

"I doubt it. Such a small thing is easily concealed and would be hard to recover from a snowbank. Let's have a look at the room."

They went along to the small parlor, brought in several lamps, and examined the guilty window ledge. It was just as Deirdre had said.

"It couldn't have been closed from the outside. That's certain," she pointed out, "but someone could have entered from outside and closed it hurriedly after him."

"No footprints," Pronto reminded her. "Would have had to swing down from the roof."

"Now, that's odd! I had an impression I saw someone on the roof when I arrived," Belami said, his interest quickening. "But that particular roof isn't on this side of the house. It's the kitchen roof, on the other side."

"Is there a window above this one?" Deirdre asked rather quickly, to divert interest from the roof. She would die sooner than admit she had crawled out on a roof in the storm at midnight. Dick would be extremely suspicious of anything so unusual.

There was a window above, but it did not issue from anyone's bedchamber. It was a hall window. When investigated, it was also seen to have had the snow on the ledge disturbed. To add to the incrimination, there were a few small puddles of water beneath it, which were assumed to have come from melted snow. The puddles were not obliging enough to lead to any room.

After some cogitation, Belami announced he had figured out how it was done. The criminal had let himself

34

out the window upstairs in the hall, after first opening the parlor window below. He had entered by the parlor window, stolen the diamond, after which two courses were open to him. Either he had returned above up the rope which he had left hanging, or he had changed his clothes in the dark parlor and rejoined the party.

"And if he did the latter," Deirdre said, "then the sheet and stocking and so on would be hidden in that small parlor."

Without another word, they all darted back to the parlor for a more thorough search. Stuffed down the back of a sofa, under the cushions, was hidden a length of rope with wet spots on it. Whether the disguise had been donned before or after coming down the rope was not seen as being terribly important. The fact was, he had not returned via the rope, or he would have pulled it in with him upstairs. And if he hadn't returned in secret via the rope, he must have left his outfit in this room. He wouldn't have roamed the halls and stairway in it.

"Rubbish!" Pronto jeered. "He couldn't have pulled the rope in from down here. How could he have untied it?"

"The rope wasn't knotted on to anything," Belami said. "It's a long piece."

"And you call yourself an expert!" Pronto chortled. "He would have fallen to the ground if he didn't have the rope attached to anything. A rope don't hold itself up straight."

"The windows are mullioned. There's a heavy piece of wood between the doors where they open and close. He could have looped it around the window divider, if he opened both windows. Then he only had to pull one end, and it would come free."

"Then the outfit should be in here," Deirdre said. "Where *could* it be?"

"Ain't here. Looked all over," Pronto insisted.

Belami stood, arms akimbo, going over the room with

35

his sharp, searching eyes, till he reached the fireplace. He paced forward and took up the poker.

"I'll call Snippe," Pronto offered. "Let him lay a fire, if you're cold. It *is* a mite chilly. We could move along to another room."

No one paid him any heed. Belami was on his hands and knees, asking for a lamp and poking at the chimney with the poker while Deirdre went forward and pushed the lamp into position to give him better light. There was a whoosh, a shower of soot, and a thump. When the dust had settled, Belami carefully lifted a dirty sheet on the end of the poker. The stocking with burned eye holes, the gloves, and the pistol tumbled out of it on the hearth.

"By the living jingo, this deduction business *works!*" Pronto exclaimed in surprise.

"The difficulty is to lower one's mind to the level of a common thief," Belami said grandly as he gingerly picked up the fallen objects and examined them. One sheet is very much like another. There was no saying whether it came from his own house, though a servant might recognize the stitching of the hem. The kid gloves might prove helpful. They were a lady's, not new, but they were large. The stocking too could help, if its mate were discovered. Belami folded these items into a bundle with his pistol and the rope for removal to his laboratory.

"We can't do much more tonight. We might as well get some sleep," he said.

"I'm dead on my feet," Pronto agreed. "Hungry as a horse too, by Jove."

"The servants should be questioned," Deirdre said. "Certain of your guests ought to have someone spying on them too."

"Neither servants nor guests will be going anywhere before morning. My groom is sleeping in the stable. If anyone prepares to leave, he'll call me. I'm a little worried about my grays. The idiot left them standing in the snow an hour while I—" He stopped as a pair of very inquisitive gray eyes grew larger in curiosity.

"Widow Barnes?" Pronto asked behind his hand but in a loudish voice.

"Yes, I stopped off to visit the Deacon's widow. Old Mrs. Barnes, with a donation for her—er . . ."

"Orphans?" Deirdre asked with a disbelieving eye.

"Just so. I spent longer than I planned with the children."

"Was that before or after you lost a wheel in the snow?"

"After."

"She must have a great many children, to have kept you so late. I hope she doesn't find herself blessed with another, come next autumn."

There was a garbled tittering from Pronto's direction. Belami turned a frustrated glare on him. "Will you please go to bed! One hesitates to take a poker to a female guest, but I see no reason to cavil at landing you a blow."

"He is lowering his mind to the commonest level, Pronto," Deirdre explained kindly. "You mentioned being hungry. Your host failed to feed you, but as he will not take a poker to me, I plan to go to the kitchen for a glass of warm milk. Why don't you come with me?"

"*Warm milk?*" Pronto asked, screwing up his face. "I'll starve, thankee kindly."

"Suit yourself." She curtsied prettily and scampered down to the kitchen.

"Warm milk!" Pronto repeated, shaking his head. "That woman belongs in Bedlam."

"So do you!" Belami charged, turning on him angrily. "Why did you have to blurt out the name of Widow Barnes?"

"Blurt it out? *I whispered.*"

"Loudly enough for her to hear. I don't want you talking broad in front of Miss Gower, Pronto."

"Hmph. Who mentioned an addition to the widow's

brood come autumn? Talking broad indeed. You'd have to go some to keep up with the chits nowadays. Even the nice ones, like Deirdre."

"I'm going to bed," Dick said and stalked from the room.

Before retiring, he took one last tour of the ballroom, looking for clues. As he came from it five minutes later, he met Deirdre in the hallway, wearing a very important look.

"I have found a clue," she told him.

"What is it?" he asked eagerly.

She unclenched her fist and showed him what she held. He was unimpressed by a short length of ornate gold chain. "Don't you see?" she asked. "It's the chain Auntie's diamond was hanging on."

"Are you sure?" he asked, taking it in his fingers. It was sticky, some residue clinging to it. "Where did you find it?"

"It was at the bottom of the syllabub bowl. The thief has disassembled the piece already, torn the diamond off, and discarded the chain. That will make the diamond easier to hide and smuggle out of the house."

"It might have been dropped into the bowl by anyone, while at dinner," he said, shaking the chain in his palm.

"Isn't it important?" she asked, deflated.

"Of course it is. Everything is important," he assured her. She smiled softly, basking in his approval. She was much prettier when she put off her bristly facade.

"I suppose none of the servants saw it being dropped in."

"No, unfortunately," she replied. "I expect it was concealed in the thief's hand and slid into the bowl, hidden by the spoon, as he helped himself to some syllabub. It doesn't help much to discover the thief, but at least I know now . . . That is—I mean, someone who wasn't at dinner couldn't have done it."

"But our suspects were all at dinner," he reminded her.

"*Mine* weren't," she answered with a little tilt of her chin up in the air.

"You still think *I* might have been involved!"

"Not now," she answered, and laughed.

"Who found it, you or the servants?"

"I did. I decided to have some syllabub instead of warm milk. I felt it sort of rustling against the spoon, and pulled it out. Meg was there with me."

"I see. May I keep it for the present?"

"Of course. Is it all right if I tell Auntie I found it?"

"Let's keep it quiet for the moment. It's better to keep all our investigations strictly confidential. No point giving anything away to our enemy, whoever he may be."

"Whatever you say," she agreed.

"Deirdre, did you *really* think I might have done it?" he asked, frowning.

"Yes," she answered blandly, "and it was very humiliating. To be so disliked you would sink to *stealing* to be rid of me—you can imagine how utterly depressing," she told him.

"No, I wasn't *that* eager to be rid of you," he said, trying to make light of it. But in fact he had humiliated her, and to a proud woman like Deirdre, it must have been painful. He felt ashamed of himself, and determined to make it up to her. "You're much too good for me, you know."

"I expect that's half the problem," she agreed readily. "You wouldn't care for a *good* woman, when there are so many of the other sort available."

"Do you take me for such a deep-dyed villain that I couldn't be comfortable with a good woman?"

"I'm not sure, but certainly a good woman wouldn't be comfortable with you," she told him earnestly. "*Actually*, I don't believe you're ready to settle down yet, Belami."

In two strokes she managed to activate all his lively dislike of her. A *good* woman couldn't stand him. *Actually*.

39

"Good night, Deirdre," he said stiffly.

He let her mount the stairs before he went up himself. It seemed like a good idea to get a few hours' rest. He'd have a rough day pacifying the duchess. Deirdre lay awake long in her canopied bed, reliving the evening. She had learned the story of Knag in the kitchen, and suspected the servants thought Belami was involved. The chain and the investigation he was executing belied it, but then he would have to *pretend* to investigate. All the world knew it was his hobby. And if it *was* Belami, how had he gotten the chain into the syllabub, when he hadn't been near the dining room or kitchen?

Chapter 4

Belami had various techniques for getting information from his victims. The lower orders reacted favorably to intimidation and threats—the vaguer the better. Ladies of higher birth found his interrogations palatable providing they were seasoned with outrageous flirtation. Gentlemen, being reasonable creatures by and large, were asked to "help." If the information from one man differed startlingly from the others, he was assumed to be lying, and further deductions were made. Belami knew none of these techniques would quite do for the Dowager Duchess of Charney. When bereft of an idea, he proceeded on sheer brass. He took the courageous decision to face her in her bedchamber before she sent for him. That would put at least the element of surprise on his side.

He intercepted the servant at her door and personally presented her breakfast tray to her. She sat propped amidst a battery of pillows, looking like a featherless bird in a snowbank. Her face was narrow and mean, her eyes close-set, standing guard over a beak of a nose. As her position in bed concealed her great height, she looked small. She wore a lace-edged cap tied under her chin. A gloating expression took possession of her features when she saw him enter.

"Ha!" was her morning greeting.

"Happy New Year, Your Grace," he had the poor idea of saying.

"Happy? *Happy?* I would have to be an *idiot* to be happy under the circumstances. Do you call me an idiot, sir?"

"Certainly not, madam," he said, setting the tray on the bed table and removing the silver cover from her gammon and eggs. The duchess was known to be a good trencherman. The steaming food brought an involuntary smile to her lips.

"So you finally got home, did you? I trust your mama, the widgeon, has informed you what goings-on occurred here last night?"

"I have had the story from more than one source, and want to express my very deepest chagrin. Naturally I shall repay you for the theft, if the gem is not recovered."

"*My* understanding was that you are already dipped, Belami. Several of your investments have gone sour, if rumor is to be believed. Not that you couldn't raise a mortgage on one of your estates. Whitehern, I believe, is not even entailed."

"That is correct," he said as she lifted the knife and fork to attach her victuals. "I am extremely upset about this dreadful affair. No stone will be left unturned to discover the perpetrator. It will be helpful if you could tell me who knew you were bringing the Charney Diamond with you. Do you customarily travel with it?"

"Sometimes I do; sometimes I don't. It is purely a matter of chance. I keep it in a vault in London. I go on home to Fernvale from here, not to return to the city till April for the wedding. I shall be wanting the diamond for my own country ball, which is why I brought it along. I frequently take it back and forth—the country for the winter, the city for the seasons. Anyone might know it, though I did not actually tell anyone, so far as I can remember. Owning a diamond of the first water is a responsibility."

"No one at all?"

"The men at the bank would know. My servants, of course, but such people did not attend your ball. Nor did *you*, I might add."

"I was regrettably detained. The storm—"

"The storm began at the same hour as the party, well after dinner, as a matter of fact. Never mind gammoning me you had any intention of attending. When did you blow in? This morning?"

"Late last night. I understand Herr Bessler accompanied you and your niece in your carriage."

"He did. One likes to have a man in the carriage for a trip. Bessler has no horses. He has a decent carriage, but uses job horses around town. I was happy to have his escort."

"He would know you were traveling with the diamond?"

"You're not suggesting Bessler had anything to do with it!" she gasped. "He was at my side when the thief entered."

"Where were you standing, exactly?"

"Very close to the doorway. We had been in the hall before, taking a walk, for of course I do not dance at my age. We went to the ballroom for the midnight festivities. Your mama, the peagoose, had nothing organized."

"Who suggested the walk?"

"I did. Bessler suggested we return to the ballroom for the striking of twelve. If you mean to infer that Bessler arranged the theft, he would not be likely to have reminded me it was nearly twelve, and time for us to return. The thief would have had easy work of robbing me

43

at a dark end of the hall, with no witnesses but Bessler."

"That's true."

"Of course it is true. I know your reputation of playing at solving crimes, my lad, and I do not approve. It is not work for a gentleman. Forget that nonsense, and let Bow Street handle it. You will send off for Townsend this morning, of course."

"Much as I should like to, the snow has continued all night, making it impossible."

"Bother. You mean we are snowed in?"

"Precisely, but we must not despair. It also means your diamond is snowed in. Whoever took it cannot leave the premises. We shall find it."

While he spoke, she ate greedily. When he stopped, she swallowed, said, "Hmph," and prepared to set him down a peg. "We" indeed, as though he were the king. "Finding it is all well and good. Repaying me its value if it is not found is, of course, the proper thing to do, and I shall not offend you by any reluctance to accept the full price—thirty thousand pounds. You must own, it still leaves an unpleasantness to the visit. However, I'm quite sure Deirdre will not allow me to continue long at odds with her husband," she finished with a sharp look to Belami.

He smiled, swallowing all his anger. When he spoke, his voice was as dulcet as ever. "How is Deirdre this morning?" he asked.

"What, you mean you haven't been to see her? Strange behavior from a suitor! Why, she'll take the notion you are setting up a flirtation with me!" She laughed merrily at this idea, revealing a full complement of yellow teeth.

"It's a temptation," he replied with a small but extremely winsome smile.

Breeding: there was nothing like it, she approved silently. Belami would be an unfaithful husband, but he would at least take the time and bother to conceal it from his wife. "My niece was dreadfully upset last night," she invented. "She is a sensitive girl, not the brassy sort of chit too often foisted upon a gentleman. She felt it, your not making a point of being here." She took a bite of egg and chewed carefully, for her molars were no longer so firmly anchored as they had once been. Even a piece of soft bread or egg could cause a bothersome wobble.

At least she did not say "How *could* you?" "Did you notice anything striking or unusual about the man who took your diamond?" he asked.

"He was about the size of you," she answered with no particular emphasis. "He moved lightly, quickly—certainly not an old man. His hair looked dark under the stocking. Every inch of his body was covered, even his hands. He wore black pantaloons and black patent slippers, as nearly everyone at the ball did. Actually, Herr Bessler wore silk stockings and breeches. He continues the old customs. The thief was a boor. He wrenched the thing from my neck, leaving a bruise as big as my fist. It's fortunate I wear high necks to my gowns. I don't know how the ladies can stand the winter winds across their necks and shoulders. I can tell you nothing more. I was too shocked."

"A most regrettable incident. Once more, I offer my sincere apologies. I must go now. I hope you will be able to join us belowstairs today."

"As to that," she said, lying back with a comfortable sigh, "I am not at all sure I shall. It has taken its toll on this wreck of a body, but you might send Bessler to me later, in about an hour. He will read to me. You are going to see Deirdre now?" she asked in an imperative way.

"I expect she will be at breakfast by now," he prevaricated, and left with a graceful bow, to descend to the breakfast room.

Deirdre was indeed at the table, though the empty plate before her indicated she had not bothered to order any breakfast. A fairly sleepless night had left its calling card on her face, in the form of half moons under her eyes, in a hazy opal shade of blue. Looking at her with this trace of dissipation, Belami was struck anew at how attractive the woman could be, if only she were not so full of rectitude.

Belami ignored Pronto, who was also at the table. He bowed and mumbled the absurdity of, "Good morning, ma'am. I hope you enjoyed a good night's sleep."

"Yes, a wonderful sleep," she answered ironically, suppressing a yawn behind her fingers. "All forty-five minutes of it. Quite delightful."

"I have been to see the duchess," he said, thinking this at least would please the woman. His thinking automatically shifted from girl to woman, when there were blue circles beneath a woman's eyes.

"That would account for the mood you are in."

"We had an interesting talk," he said, ignoring her taunt.

"That *is* good news. I trust she conveyed to you that any notion of an alliance between us is now over."

"That was not the tenor of our talk. I said *interesting*, not *satisfying*, not pleasing, not what you and I could wish for. No, she informed me that she would not abuse my sensitivities by refusing cash reimbursement for the stolen jewel, and that this regrettable incident in no way hampers her plan for our marriage. Neither, I might add, did she indicate you had shown any wish to call off."

"I could hardly discuss it with her when she was in a state of shock!"

"Eh?" Pronto asked, setting his cup in his saucer without quite smashing either vessel. His companions looked at him, then at each other, in surprise. Pronto's beady eyes were focused on the lady; they were brimming with the deepest suspicion. "Insured!" he declared.

"We hoped this might ensure an end to the engagement." Belami said.

"Hear, hear," Deirdre agreed heartily.

46

"Eh?" Pronto demanded again. "Not the deuced engagement. The necklace—*it* was insured."

"How *very* strange your aunt neglected to mention it," Belami said, his head turning to stare at Deirdre. The news so cheered him that he picked up a fork and ate a bite of gammon, without once removing his accusing eyes from the lady.

She was annoyed with herself for being unable to halt the flush that rose up from her neck to engulf her face. "It's true the necklace was insured," she admitted.

Pronto went on to pinpoint the transaction more closely. "Bidwell, it was, mentioned it last night."

"How would Bidwell know?" Belami asked.

"His uncle Carswell has the policy. I fancy Bidwell wasn't half sorry to see the thing nabbed, though he'd have thought better of it by now."

"Carswell, the Lloyd's agent?" Belami asked.

"The same," Pronto told him. Deirdre nodded her head in agreement.

"He's Bidwell's uncle, you say? It's Carswell who will have to pay it out of his own pocket. The Lloyd's agents are all independent dealers."

"Don't be ridiculous, Pronto," Deirdre said. "Bidwell is Carswell's heir. Carswell has no one else to leave his fortune to. Why should Bidwell be glad his uncle had the policy?"

"Just what I meant. Said he'd have thought better of it by now. He's the one will be out the thirty thousand in the long haul. Daresay he's in the sullens this morning. Chirping merry enough last night, but he'd be down to earth by now."

Belami listened, arranging and rearranging these facts to look for a meaningful pattern. "But Carswell isn't an *old* man. Bidwell couldn't look for anything in the way of an inheritance for a couple of decades."

"Very true," Pronto agreed, "but eventually . . ."

"Eventually he may not lose a sou," Deirdre announced blandly.

Belami looked surprised. "Why, thank you, ma'am. I

47

didn't realize you had such confidence in my powers of solving the case."

"That was not my meaning, Belami. The fact is, the insurance policy expired at midnight. It will be for the courts to decide whether Carswell is liable for it."

"Why did your aunt let it lapse?" he asked.

"It was prohibitively expensive."

"I see. Pockets to let, eh? Ten or so pounds a year was too steep for her. Well, well, this puts a new light on the matter." There was some insinuation in his tone that Pronto could not fathom. Whatever it meant, Deirdre had pokered up like a ramrod. Her eyes were shooting sparks at Belami. Soon she arose from her seat and stood rigid, staring at him.

"Are you *daring* to suggest that my aunt acted in collusion with someone to have her necklace stolen?" she demanded.

"What a shocking thing for you to say, my dear," Belami replied, rising languidly to his feet. He had some strange admixture of courtesy and bad manners that permitted him to say or imply the most monstrous things, but do it with all outward show of politeness. When a lady stood, he would not retain his seat, even if he was calling her a scoundrel. "Really, that is a most dangerous notion for you to be bruiting about. We did not hear the lady, Pronto."

"*I* heard her. Ain't deaf," Pronto countered. "Her aunt colluded to pinch the glass herself, for the insurance money, then tried to weasel payment out of you as well. Dashed clever scheme. Old Charney is up to all the rigs, but we still don't know who was wrapped up in the sheet and stocking. Wasn't Knag, and that I do know. You never wore gloves when you was scaring the servants."

"Why don't we sit down and finish our breakfast?" Belami suggested pleasantly. How obliging of Pronto to say all those things civility prevented him from saying himself.

Deirdre thumped angrily back into her chair, while

48

Belami resumed his in a more graceful fashion, gliding gently into it, as though wafted by a zephyr.

"This is utterly ridiculous. Preposterous!" Deirdre declared, her white hand thumping the table to reinforce her position. "My aunt would not wait till the very last minute to have done it, if it were her intention to claim insurance money. And why would she have arranged it to occur at a ball? To have it burgled from the London house, or while traveling in the carriage, or from her bedroom here would be much easier."

"I see you have canvased the options open to her," Belami mentioned casually. "I expect the insurance companies are reluctant to insure jewels—so easy to lose or have stolen, in any of the ways you mentioned. I have heard of their refusing to honor claims, due to those suspicious circumstances. A jewel stolen, and seen to have been stolen by a roomful of witnesses, of course, is quite a different matter. It would be impossible to renege, I should think, without being hauled into court."

"It would not be reneging if the policy had lapsed," Deirdre fired back. "And it very likely had. The clock was striking twelve at the precise moment, the ugly old long-case clock in the hallway. It may have been a few minutes slow."

"You mean fast, surely. And can you *possibly* be referring to my exquisite green lacquered clock with the painted panels, by Edward Moore, of Norwich?" Belami inquired, amazed at her description of this priceless objet d'art.

"I mean that *ugly* piece of merchandise with the balls and fins on top of it, like a Chinese pagoda!" she snapped back.

"The Edward Moore! She actually calls my Moore an ugly piece of merchandise," he told Pronto, who sniffled and poured another cup of coffee.

"Was never fond if it myself," Pronto admitted.

"You never claimed to have any taste. I expected better of Miss Gower. It keeps perfect time, by the by. I tend to the regulation of it myself, the balancing of the pendula—there are more than one—the oiling, and so on. It is a very precise clock. If it was chiming, then it was past midnight."

"In that case you can hardly claim my aunt arranged the theft to profit from the insurance."

"But I didn't suggest it, my dear. It was you who first cast such a wicked aspersion on Her Grace. Downright ungrateful, I call it, after all she has done for you. And will do still upon her demise. You are her heiress, *n'est-ce pas*?"

"Now you're saying *I* did it!"

"Not in the least. How you do jump about, from accusation to accusation, with no basis. I am merely pointing out that Her Grace would not live to enjoy much of the thirty thousand pounds, whereas you will have the benefit of it. You did not care for the necklace, if memory serves. A gaudy lump, I seem to remember hearing you call it."

"*Ac*-tually I was in the ballroom when it was stolen," she reminded him.

"I did not mean to suggest you worked alone. An accomplice of more or less my own size and height was required. You don't suppose folks will take the notion we contrived it together, do you?" he asked, smiling at this whimsical idea. "No, impossible. No one would think *me* foolish enough to steal it when the policy had elapsed."

"I doubt very much it would occur to anyone but you that *I* was involved," she said. "It is known well enough, however, that *you* have suffered severe losses recently at the gaming tables.

"True. Very true."

Pronto snorted into his collar. "Rubbish. Won a monkey at Whites t'other night. Never lost a guinea. Luckiest gambler I ever saw. Only put about he lost to sour old Char—Heh, heh." He subsided into silence as he became aware he was being glared at.

"Pronto, dear boy," Belami said, "would you be so terribly kind as to—ah, see if Mama is, ah, up yet?"

"Yes, Pronto, *do* see if Lady Belami is up yet, before you blurt out that His Lordship only pretended he was dipped, to prevent my aunt from forcing me to marry him," Deirdre said, directing her speech over Pronto's head to Belami.

"Well, I will see if Bertie's up yet if you like," Pronto answered amiably, "but it ain't likely she is. Never does get up before noon." He picked up a piece of toast and wandered from the room, muttering to himself. "Believe I put my foot in it. Didn't mean any harm."

As soon as he was gone, Belami directed a fierce, white-lipped look at Deirdre. "What do you mean, *forcing* you to marry me!"

As there had been nothing but persuasions brought to bear on her, she twitched guiltily. "You know perfectly well what I mean."

"I'm afraid I do not."

"How could I refuse when—when I . . ."

"When you are well over twenty, and no one else offered, you mean?" he goaded.

"That's not true! I had plenty of offers my first season."

"But that was many seasons ago."

"Plenty since too! Twombley offered last season. And never mind saying he's an old man, Belami. He's only ten years older than you."

"Yes, dear heart, but I already am ten years your senior, nearly."

"Seven years."

"Seven and a half. *Did* you have anything to do with this curst robbery? Did you arrange it to embarrass me because I didn't come to the party?"

"Certainly not! I was delighted you stayed away."

"I would have been here if I'd had the least suspicion of this robbery."

"Of course you would. The least aroma of crime or any indecent behavior will always draw you like a fly to carrion, where as common courtesy to your fiancée and your family are neglected. Birds of a feather roost together," she finished, flouncing her shoulders.

Belami listened punctiliously, his face showing no emotion but boredom. When she finished, he asked, "Why does Bidwell dislike his uncle Carswell, do you happen to know?"

"I have no idea."

"The relationship, if I recall aright, is on Lady Carswell's side. Lady Carswell used to be a Bidwell. She's dead, of course. Why would Bidwell think he is to get Carswell's money? Only an in-law sort of relationship."

"Pronto knows more about it than I do. Why don't you ask him? When he's finished verifying that your mother is still sound asleep, I mean."

"You don't want to marry me, Deirdre, and I don't want to marry you. That is why I put about the story I was dipped, to call Charney off."

"Then why did you offer for me?"

"Why did you accept?"

"I claim temporary insanity," she said. "I have no objection to your sharing the excuse. We are both sane now, however."

"You've had three weeks of studious neglect. It was enough reason to return you to sanity before now."

"I couldn't jilt you. It would look horrid."

"No, it would not much tarnish the glow of rectitude that enshrouds you. Your reputation would benefit from a suggestion of levity, my dear, whereas a gentleman can less easily call off."

"Yes, especially when he already has a string of jiltees to his discredit."

"I never jilted anyone. A misunderstanding arose between me and Miss Mersey."

"The misunderstanding being that she thought a fiancé would call upon her occasionally, and *not* call on quite so many other ladies."

"I *meant* to be here before midnight last night," he said in a mildly apologetic tone.

"Midnight? You knew we arrived three days ago! You should have been waiting for us, as you did not see fit to offer us your escort."

"I offered to accompany *you.*"

"You knew my aunt wouldn't let me come alone in a curricle with you. That's the only reason you offered."

"If I am such a dangerous fellow that I couldn't control my base impulses for a half day in an open carriage, why did she encourage me to dangle after you?"

"Because she thought a good wife would cure you of your . . . *ways.*"

"I am touched by this solicitude on Her Grace's part, and on your own, as I am left to assume you shared her views. It is misguided solicitude. I have no intention of changing my ways. A 'good wife' rarely drives a man to anything but distraction, but I suppose one must appear to accept that you actually believed that bit of impertinent nonsense. I wonder if your concern would have been as great if the sinner did not come with a fortune and title."

"Believe what you like—it is immaterial to me—but I tell you now that despite the fortune and the title, I will not marry you. My turning you off at this moment is impossible. It is tantamount to saying I accuse you of stealing my aunt's diamond. I don't know whether you had anything to do with it or not, but after the affair is settled, our engagement will be terminated as noiselessly as possible."

"And I will thank you, as quietly or as noisily as you wish."

"You are entirely welcome, I promise you."

"And we are *still* left with the riddle of how we ever got engaged in the first place," he said wearily.

"The sooner we can solve this case, the sooner we can become unengaged. I mean to speak to Bidwell and see if I can learn anything from him. He and Chamfreys were out of the room at midnight."

"Good enough. I'll speak to Lenore."

"I thought you would," she answered with a sardonic grimace which he mistook for a smile.

She arose and strode briskly from the room. Belami arose with her, then sat down again, looking after her. The item that caught his interest was her walk. Deirdre didn't walk like a prude, as one would expect her to. She undulated, her hips weaving from side to side like a real woman. So far as he could tell, the only feminine bones in her body were in her hips.

Ah, well, it would soon be over. He'd be rid of her, once and for all. Bidwell or some man-milliner like him would marry her. They could undulate together. Bidwell walked like a woman too. Odd that she chose to go and talk to Bidwell. What was there to learn from *him*? They already knew he was Carswell's nephew and heir. This was just an excuse for putting herself in his way, now that she had jilted himself. She certainly wasn't wasting a minute. *That* at least she shared with other women. She could have waited till they had announced the termination of the engagement.

With an injured air, he went abovestairs to accost Lady Lenore. Such an errand would normally put him in humor, but there was a scowl on his brow as he bolted up the stairs, two at a time.

Chapter 5

✳✳✳

Deirdre ran Bidwell to ground in the hallway in front of the ballroom door. He was called handsome by society, though there was an effeminate air in him that made the word hard for her to accept. Pretty came closer to describing him. He had brown hair, waved and worn rather long in the poetic style. His eyes were blue, with long lashes. He was dandified in appearance, wearing a jacket that carried more wadding than really suited his narrow waist and thin legs. His build was not much like Belami's, but she supposed that with a sheet over the jacket, he would look larger than he was.

"Good morning, Bidwell. Investigating the scene of the crime, are you?" she asked, approaching him with a friendly smile.

"Just so, Miss Gower, just so," he answered with his sweet smile. He had lips like a girl, she noticed. Or was it that the more masculine lips of Belami were still in her mind? "I missed all the excitement last night."

"That's too bad. You retired early, did you?"

"I went abovestairs for a rest before midnight, but came back down in time to join the search. How is Her Grace holding up under the strain?"

"Nobly, as we all expected she would," she told him.

"A pity about her insurance lapsing. I little thought when Carswell mentioned it to me a fortnight ago how dire the consequences would be."

"Ah, yes, your uncle was her agent. Well, my aunt's loss may prove your gain."

"There is no saying. We don't jog along so well as we ought. We never did hit it off."

"Why was that, I wonder?" she asked. They walked along the hall as they spoke.

"He's no blood kin to me. I was living with my aunt, old Miriam Bidwell, at the time of the marriage. I was only a lad. I'd been raised by Aunt Miriam. I felt resentful at his usurping my place with the old girl. She was like a mother to me."

"Carswell failed to fill the role of father?" she inquired, displaying a casual commiseration.

"Hardly! I was packed straight off to school. I went to them for holidays regularly till Aunt Miriam died. I haven't been back since. That was two years ago."

"But you and Carswell meet from time to time?"

"Not by arrangement, but only by chance."

She wondered what he lived on. He didn't work. His own father had presumably left him something. "Perhaps you and Carswell would go on more smoothly if you had joined him in his business," she suggested.

"He would have been richer in any case. A shocking bad manager."

"The insurance business is risky."

"So it is. But enough gloomy talk. I see Belami has arrived."

"Yes, he's at breakfast."

"What time did he arrive?"

"Late last night," she said vaguely.

"I daresay he is taking the affair in hand. Our thief is

intrepid, to pull off his stunt under Belami's roof. He'll get caught certainly. Don't you think?"

"I hope so."

"Has Belami made any startling discoveries?" he asked. The question struck her as significant, as dangling for information, yet it was also a perfectly natural question under the circumstances.

"I don't believe so. Not yet."

"I will be perfectly happy to help him in any way possible. I shall tell him so as soon as I see him."

"He'll appreciate that."

"Oh, I am eager to find your aunt's diamond, even if my uncle doesn't have to stand buff."

They finished their tour in front of the doorway to the room where the sheet and stocking had been discovered.

"I must go and see my aunt. She'll be eager to learn if there is any news."

He bowed and stood waiting while she left. After a minute, her head peeped around the corner of the stairway to see where he went. He was gone. She didn't think he had time to go anywhere but into the small study where the thief's things had been hidden, but this didn't tell her much. If he had been seen coming out with them in his hands, *that* would have been meaningful, but Belami, the genius, had made that impossible.

With nothing more interesting to do, Deirdre decided to go to the library till lunchtime. She scampered quickly around the corner in case Bidwell should come out and catch her in a lie. Much of her time was spent in libraries of one sort or another. They were better company than her aunt and her friends. She pulled a book from the shelves and sat at an armchair by a window, with the book open on her knee in case Belami or anyone should glance in, but she was not reading. She couldn't have told you what book she held. No, she was cogitating on life.

The aspect of her own private life that most preoccupied her was Lord Belami, though she would sooner have lost the last tooth in her head than admit it. She told herself firmly that she despised him. He had insulted her, publicly insulted her by his lack of attention both here and in London. She had been humiliated in front of her friends, and he had done it on purpose so that she would break off their engagement. Furthermore, he had told her so. There was clearly no hope of going through with it after this. It would be back to her aunt's library and the dull round of nothings on Belvedere Square till another Twombley came along to rescue her. It was madness to have thought she could live with Belami. She should never have accepted him. She knew that when he asked he was under some duress. There had been no warmth, no enthusiasm in his words. Well, she had been under duress too. If the threat of Twombley wasn't duress, what was? Belami may have been unreliable, unstable—in short, a womanizer. But at least he wasn't personally repulsive. The necessary intimate side of marriage with him would have been possible. Indeed, she had looked forward to it with lively curiosity. She would learn at last those secrets known to the Widow Barneses and Lady Lenores of the world.

Soon her mind had wandered off to the bedroom upstairs, where Belami was this instant with Lenore Belfoi. Deirdre had spoken disparagingly of that dasher, but in fact she admired her with all her heart. Such charm, such easy manners and grace, such beauty, and such skills in making the most of it with batting eyes, insinuating voice, and fluttering fan. She would forget that Belami was this minute in her bedroom, holding Lenore in his arms, kissing her. She felt a tingling sensation on her own lips, such a tingling as she had never felt before Dick kissed her, that evening in her aunt's conservatory. Her head was still reeling a quarter of an hour later, when he had proposed with those stilted phrases, so different from the impassioned words used earlier. And she, a confirmed ninnyhammer, had accepted. People thought she was a cold girl, but she knew that beneath the ice there was a fire. If she let the ice be chipped away, it would roar out of control and consume her, so she continued to be the prim and proper Deirdre Gower. "Hidden passions," Dick had said that night in the conservatory. But he had ferreted out her secret, had opened a chink in the icy door, and she had taken many a peek inside the door since.

While she sat with her book and her thoughts, Dick prepared his most ingratiating smile, and went tapping at the door of Lady Lenore Belfoi, who was *aux anges* to receive a bedroom call from her handsome host. She had arranged a carefully tousled coiffure and put on her prettiest lace bedjacket in preparation for Chamfreys' visit, but was not tardy in ordering a servant off to delay him once she laid her lovely eyes on Belami.

"Good morning, Lennie," he said, lounging in with no discomfort at being in a lady's boudoir. He looked for a chair, but she patted the side of the bed invitingly, and he was not slow to proceed to it.

"I didn't steal it, darling, if that's what brings you calling at this farouche hour," she said, by way of greeting, in her husky voice. Lady Lenore had a voice like a foghorn—low and misty. He adored it.

"Farouche? No, it is nearly nine-thirty. Nine is farouche; nine-thirty is only inconsiderate. Anything before nine we shan't even discuss. It is too barbaric."

"Are you here to play Bow Street, Belami, or . . . something else?" she asked with a sultry peek at him from beneath her lowered lashes.

He reached forward and kissed the tip of her nose. "Bow Street," she decided aloud at this tame token of affection. "If that's all you came for, you won't mind if I have my coffee while it's still tepid?"

He handed her the cup that rested on the table beside her bed. Then he sat and watched while she sipped daintily. He was intrigued why a husband should display so little interest in a wife of Lenore's obvious charms. Black hair and green eyes were a stunning combination. She had a heart-shaped face, a perfect nose, perfect teeth, which sparkled behind a set of perfect rosebud lips. Her body was similarly flawless. And with all this, she was neither ill-natured nor stupid. She was one of the few women in the country a man ought to be able to find happiness with, yet to the best of his knowledge, Lennie and Belfoi never spent so much as a week together from head to toe of the year.

"Don't frown, luv," she said, setting the cup aside. "It makes me think I have grown a wrinkle, or got a dirty face."

"I was pondering the riddle of the age. How does it come Belfoi ever lets you out of his sight? If I had the good fortune to be your husband, I'd have you manacled to me."

"Extraordinarily uncomfortable, I should think. But perhaps if *you* were my husband, I shouldn't mind. Belfoi and I go on very well together. We don't meet often, but when we do, it is always on the best of terms. We were at Badminton together only last autumn. I thought we might meet at Christmas, but we got our plans mixed up somehow. We both hold the belief that variety is the spice of life. We have that in common with you, I believe."

"I too am Latin in my taste. I like life highly spiced."

"How do you find the dash of bitters this house party has added to the dish?" she asked archly.

"I never flinch to try a new flavor. It must have been quite a show, the rape of the duchess's diamond. I wish I had been there."

"Weren't you?" she asked blandly.

"No, I wasn't, Lennie. There's no truth to the rumor I did the deed. I didn't happen to think of it," he added lightly. "They say the fellow was my size, more or less. You are a good judge of a man's physique. What's your opinion?"

"Don't play games with me, luv. We're not children. I'm sure the cats have been telling you I wasn't there. I was judging a different man's physique at the time, right here in bed."

"Chamfreys or Bidwell?"

"Bidwell agreed to play guard for us. I was afraid Belfoi, dear Harvey, might take into his head to join the party after all, since I missed him at Christmas. I sent him word I would be here, and if memory serves, he's not far away. At Boltons', just ten miles west of here."

It popped into Belami's head that Belfoi was more or less the same size as himself and the thief. "It's hard to believe he wouldn't travel on ten miles to meet you."

"If I'd had any idea he was so close, I wouldn't have told him. I only got his note telling me he would be at Boltons' after I wrote him of my plans. Well, I shouldn't think he's quite alone at Boltons'. There's that pretty Bolton niece who has been known to throw her cap at semi-available gentlemen like Harvey."

"You chose an unlikely hour for your romp— midnight. Couldn't you have waited half an hour, for convention's sake?"

"Dinner, darling! Your sweet Bertie serves such wonderful dinners, we wanted to be done in time to partake. It was marvelous, too. We had some good intention of being downstairs at the stroke of twelve, but we got . . . carried away. Bidwell was supposed to let us know by a discreet tap on the door when it was five to twelve. But he got carried away too, with the champagne he had for company. The first we realized the new year was upon us was the crash of Bidwell's glass against the hearth. He had welcomed it in with a drink, and decided to break the glass, as people will often do when it is not their own glass they hold. By the time we all got downstairs, the fun was over. I'd have given a monkey to see the duchess's face when it happened."

"Why did you choose Bidwell as sentry? He's no particular friend of yours or Chamfreys', is he?"

"Not at all. He'd been drinking a bit and mentioned he was going to have a lie down before the midnight jollity. I'd been dancing with him just before I left. I told him to go upstairs with Chamfreys to dilute suspicion in case anyone was watching us. People *do* gossip at these country do's. I wouldn't want anyone telling Harvey I had just gone upstairs with Chamfreys, if he happened to pop in unexpectedly. So Chamfreys and Bidwell had a drink, then followed me up."

"It was a last-minute thing?"

She nodded. "But Harvey wouldn't be likely to make a scene, would he? Or do I misunderstand the nature of your marriage?"

"We allow each other freedom. There is no denying, however, that he resents to have to see it. Rather flattering, really," she added with a self-indulgent smile. "He speaks of making a fortune and keeping me all to himself. Thus far he has been careful not to notice when I appear in a new fur or diamond that my allowance would obviously not cover."

"How does he propose to make this fortune?"

"The same way he lost it, darling. Upon 'Change. He was well to grass when we married. We had a conventional marriage for nearly a year, he playing Darby to my Joan, then his investments went sour, and we had to scrimp and save, and in the end, we became utterly bored. That's when we began going our separate ways. I can impose on gentlemen, and he on ladies, without having to repay hospitality tit for tat. Much cheaper. If I had married a really wealthy man, I might have made him a good wife. In any case, Harvey does get a bit jealous if he actually sees me in another man's arms, and that is why it seemed a good idea to have Bidwell stand guard for us."

"But Belfoi didn't come after all?"

"No, he didn't. The storm."

The storm had not kept Belami away, however. There was the sound of a man's voice in the drawing room. "Does Chamfreys get jealous too?" Belami asked with a quizzing smile.

"I *told* that idiot servant to stall him. Shall we find out if he gets jealous?" she asked, putting her arms around his neck and pulling him down on top of her. A miasma of musky, heady scent emanated from her white arms and the bedsheets, almost overpowering in its strength. That was the trouble with Lennie. She was too much of a good thing. Halfway through a leisurely embrace, he felt a surprising wish to withdraw. It would be too rude to push her away, but really he felt suffocated by her clinging arms. It was purely emotional. Sense told him this embrace meant no more to her than to him. If there was a woman who was *not* a clinger, it was Lennie Belfoi, but still he wasn't enjoying this little flirtation. He felt—damme, he felt *guilty*! It was the image of Deirdre Gower, pokering up and saying a *good* woman couldn't stand him, that was causing this unlikely aversion to the most gorgeous woman in the county.

After a few minutes, she withdrew and smiled at him. That little mole at the corner of her lips—adorable, but all he wanted to do was get out of the room. "Where do you go from here, Belami?" she asked, her eyes suggesting she would not be loath to accompany him anywhere.

He willed down the urge to read her a lecture, to warn her against being a cat that anyone might pick up and stroke. Coming from him, it would be ridiculous. And besides, he would have further questions for her. "I haven't been to Paris in an age," he said leadingly.

"Oh, goodie! Neither have I!"

"We'll speak about it later," he said, kissing her ear, then he left by the nearest door, to avoid meeting Chamfreys in the drawing room.

He went back to his own room and took from his jewelry box a small watch fob found in Lennie's bed the night of his quick search of the rooms. Her bed had been still unmade when he searched it. Her scent was on the sheets, and the small golden acorn fallen off amidst the tangled welter of bedclothes. There was no reason to think Lennie had been doing anything but what she intimated. It was in character for her, and therefore unsuspect, but whether Chamfreys had been her partner was still to be determined.

At the luncheon table some hours later, Belami produced the golden trifle. "One of the servants found this in the ballroom," he said, showing it to the group assembled at the table. "Did any of you drop it?"

The innocent location of its discovery caused Chamfreys to claim it with no hesitation. "By gadrey, I'm glad to get it back. It's a bit of good-luck piece," he said as the acorn was passed along to him. This confirmed that Chamfreys had been in her bed, though the exact minutes could not be known. Had he worn his waistcoat and watch? Or had the fob come loose as he undressed? Belami envisaged a hasty ripping off of garments, which would have been necessary if they planned to be back in the ballroom by midnight. All this envisaged evidence supported their tale.

Of more interest to him was the state of the room where Bidwell had stood guard against Belfoi. He had not been surprised to see a hand of solitaire laid out on the table. The broken glass had been found on the hearth too, to bolster the story of smashing it at midnight.

When lunch was over, Belami gave a meaningful look to Pronto, which Deirdre observed. When the two men strolled nonchalantly towards Snippe's room, she was not far behind them. Snippe had something to say about being kicked out of his room, but Belami was ready for him.

"Get some servants out shoveling a path to the road," he ordered, to be rid of him.

" A mile and a half?" Snippe asked, blinking in disbelief at such slavish labor.

"Speak to my groom. He's rigging up some contraption to make it easier. Some sort of plow, drawn by the horses."

"I do not go to the *stables*, milord," Snippe answered, on his high ropes.

"Then request the stables to come to you, Snippe. Use

your wits, man. What am I paying you for? Send for Réal."

"I'll have him come here, to *my* room," Snippe answered.

"No, Snippe, you will meet him in the kitchen. Go!" As this command was accompanied by a shove, Snippe went, but with a glare over his shoulder that would freeze fire. He also left the door standing open.

Deirdre closed it and slid onto the hard sofa. "The sheet used last night was yours. Greta recognized it," she said, to divert him from suggesting she leave. "Did you learn anything from Lenore?"

"She confirmed that Bidwell was with her and Chamfreys—in the next room, I mean."

"He said the same thing to me—that is, he said he had gone abovestairs, but did not give the reason," Deirdre corroborated.

"There were cards on the table by the grate in the drawing room that adjoins Lennie's room, and the broken glass on the hearth," Belami mentioned. "Lennie confirmed hearing him smash the glass at midnight, or thereabouts. I shouldn't think she looked at her watch to confirm the precise moment."

"I'll bet a pony he don't smash glasses at his own house," Pronto mentioned. "Though I must say, it is enjoyable. Makes me feel like an unruly boy."

"He not only broke it; he ground it to bits," Belami added.

"A bit unusual, ain't it?" Pronto asked suspiciously. "Mean to say, anything unusual, however small. . . ."

"I found it unusual enough that I collected the ground glass and particles of the glass into envelopes for checking in my laboratory," Belami told him.

"Why?" Deirdre asked, frowning. "What do you hope to learn from examining glass splinters?"

"Whether one glass was smashed, or two. The quantity of debris suggest two, and that suggests Bidwell was not alone."

There was a stir of interest at this notion. Belami went for the blue envelopes holding the remains of the glasses, Pronto got two footed glasses from the sideboard, and the three met in Belami's bedchamber, which had been chosen as a private site for their experiment.

Deirdre looked around his chamber with keen interest. She was not surprised that it should be elegant, with massive furnishings in the old style of Kent, and silk brocade draperies. What did surprise her was the tumble of books at his bedside table, and the brace of candles arranged for comfortable reading. The desk too was littered with books, some of them open, some closed with a paper marking his spot. A quick perusal of the titles showed her Belami's tastes ranged from poetry to science, history, philosophy, novels, and gardening. Others bore titles in foreign languages, indicating the catholicity of his education. She was also happily surprised to see nothing that could shock a lady—no lewd writings, at least not in English. Her host noticed what she was about, and cocked a questioning brow at her.

"You approve?" he asked.

"You have catholic tastes," she commented.

Pronto scowled at her. "Ain't Popish, if that's what you mean."

"Deirdre means broad tastes, catholic in the nonreligious sense."

"Oh, aye. Very catholic tastes, for a Protestant," he agreed.

Meanwhile Belami paced toward the fireplace, with the glasses in his hands. "The card table was about here," he said, stepping back. "He might have stood up. So he drinks"—he took an imaginary sip from the glass—"and then he throws the empty goblet." He threw the glass against the hearth. It shattered in a dozen pieces, bits of glass flying for a few feet. Deirdre and Pronto watched, the former lamenting the waste of a fine crystal goblet, and the latter scratching his ear.

66

The procedure was repeated from a seated position, with much the same result. Thrown with less force, only one piece was broken from the glass. Both pieces remained on the hearth. Belami arose and ground them into the stone apron with his heel. "That's demmed odd," he said, frowning at the powdered glass.

"Don't see why. What did you think was going to happen, heaving good glasses at a stone fireplace?" Pronto asked in a huff. "Bound to break. Even *I* know that."

Deirdre, suspecting some deeper meaning, went to stare at the mess. "What is it? What are you thinking?" she asked him.

"The quantity isn't right. He didn't break two glasses and grind up one."

"Demmed unnecessary to break even one," Pronto told him.

"Maybe he ground a part of the one broken glass into powder," Deirdre suggested. "The stem, perhaps."

"Could be he broke a smaller glass than that you just smashed," Pronto contributed.

"That's a possibility. I must get to my laboratory now and do some weighing and testing—see what residue, if any, remains with the powdered glass. There were wine dregs on the other; some pieces were large enough to hold droplets," Belami said. He stood gazing at the two separate piles of glass remains, rubbing his chin.

"I'll sweep it up, shall I?" Deirdre offered, reaching for the broom on the hearth.

"No! No, it must be done carefully. I want to keep the two glasses entirely separate, as I did in Lenore's room."

"If there were two people in that room at midnight, then who do you think the other was?" Deirdre asked. There was no doubt in her own mind. She wanted so much for Lady Lenore to be guilty that she easily convinced herself it was so.

"Whoever was on the roof when I arrived," Belami said. "I believe Bidwell *was* upstairs, as he claims, and he let his henchman down via the attic stairs, to execute the robbery, while he stood guard above, opening and closing windows and so on. That window in the upper hall—it would have remained open had Bidwell himself gone out it and returned through the downstairs parlor. No one, none of the servants, has mentioned finding it open. Bidwell arranged to gather up the necessary disguise and gun, and left them in the parlor for his friend."

"For that matter, Lady Lenore could have arranged the whole," Deirdre pointed out. She could hardly tell him the person on the roof was innocent. "She could have left the attic door open in advance," she added, to give an air of accepting that fiction. "And the parlor window below as well."

"Basing all this on a bit of broken glass. Foolishness," Pronto said, kicking at the glass powder with his foot, while Belami howled his dismay. "Still don't tell us why the deuce he did it in such a public way, either. Hardest place to rob anyone. Demmed near impossible when you come down to it."

Such statements always caused Deirdre to narrow her eyes at Belami. Had he done it himself? With a cohort to slide the golden chain into the syllabub, he could have done it. Lady Lenore popped into her mind as the likeliest cohort.

"I'm taking these glass remains to my laboratory now," Belami said. "Deirdre, why don't you question the servants to learn if the upper hall window was found open by any of them?"

"Very well."

"How about me? What can I do?" Pronto asked.

"You can help me in the laboratory," Belami said, to keep his friend from mischief. He was curious why this should cause Deirdre to sulk, as he had no idea she would have preferred to be with him.

He found no residue of wine on the glass that had been ground to powder. As it was not the weight of a glass and had not been used to hold wine, who was to say it had been a glass at all? it might have been some other smallish object made of lead crystal, like a chandelier pendant, except that none were missing from Beaulac.

Chapter 6

✳✳✳

The kitchen seemed the likeliest place to find a collection of servants. It was Meg, the same girl who had been with Deirdre when she found the necklace chain in the syllabub, who had closed the window.

"It was about fifteen after midnight when I took a run upstairs to give Lady Belami her vinaigrette. I saw the curtains blowing like a pair of sails, and locked the window. I thought one of the guests had had too much wine and took a breath of air to sober hisself up," she said. "I should've told His Lordship, shouldn't I? 'Every little thing, however small and unimportant it may seem.' That's what he asked us, and I, nodcock that I am, didn't think a drunken guest could matter one way or t'other."

"Has anyone else anything to add?" Deirdre asked.

Meg was still twitching nervously. "Oh, mum, don't tell him. I locked the attic door as well. It was hanging open a inch too. But you and Her Ladyship was upstairs

70

that same afternoon getting the tin pot for making the ice, and I was sure it was you what left it ajar."

"As a matter of fact, I did, Meg, so that is all right. You need not mention that to Lord Belami," Deirdre said nervously.

"Thank God," Meg sighed.

Such trivial details—yet they were important after all, and Deirdre had a nauseating sensation that before the case was solved, her secret would come out. Belami would pry and question, deduce and measure and weigh and analyze, till he learned she had gone up to the roof in the howling storm to search for him. How utterly degrading.

Belami's skills were being employed in a different direction when he was finished in his laboratory. He happened to encounter Bessler on his way into the billiards room, and decided it was time to give the old boy a quizzing. He was a tall, burly man, wearing an antiquated blue jacket, shiny at the elbows, with not a suggestion of nap anywhere on it. The footmen at Beaulac were better outfitted. But with all his inelegance, there was some distinction about the man. He held his head proudly. The monocle stuck in his eye lent him a faintly menacing air, but his booming voice was friendly enough.

"A bad business," Bessler said, shaking his grizzled head. "The duchess is done up with it. She's lying down now, trying to get a bit of rest, pour soul."

"You were with her when it happened. Can you tell me anything about the thief? Other than that he was the size and shape of me," he added as Bessler ran his eyes over his host in an assessing manner.

"As to that, my attention was on Her Grace. It was a ruthless business, all done more harshly than was necessary. He might have asked her to unclasp it, instead of wrenching it from her neck. You are looking for a brutal man, sir."

"Yes, I realize I am not looking for a timid woman," Belami said haughtily. "Can you be more specific? We

71

all possess five senses. Did no one employ any of them except sight? Was there anything in the way of sound, scent. . . . You are a medical man, I hear. You must be accustomed to minute observation. Was there nothing?"

"No scent. I did not touch him, or taste him. He made no sound; didn't say a word. One assumes he was reluctant to speak, and that is why he pulled the thing off her neck."

"Yes, a man's voice can betray him," Belami agreed, thinking that Bessler's own accent, for instance, would be a dead giveaway. "An accent, for example."

"There were no other foreign guests besides me. Your groom has a French accent, has he not?" Bessler inquired. "Not that I mean to imply . . ."

"Réal was with me at the time and therefore cannot have had anything to do with it. He is also quite small, not more than five and a half feet."

"Milord, you protest too much for a man whose *bona fides* were never in doubt! I have assured Her Grace on that point," Bessler said, removing his monocle and polishing it on a bedraggled wisp of handkerchief.

"How very kind of you," Belami said, sneering. He was not accustomed to being patronized by foreigners of unknown pedigree.

Bessler hunched his shoulders and picked up a cue. "Will you give me a game, sir?"

"I would prefer a few moments of your undivided attention, if you will be so kind," Belami replied. "You are the duchess's closest friend, were with her when she got her jewel from the vault, accompanied her here, and were with her when it was stolen. Do *you* have any idea who could have learned she was bringing it, and stolen it from her?"

"I have been asking myself that question," Bessler replied in a meditative way, his eye behind his monocle looking troubled. Strange how that affectation drew attention to itself, robbing the onlooker of other facial expressions. "Her Grace has no enemies, and yet has no

72

really close friends either. It must be a case of some-one's requiring money and not being particular about how he gets it."

"I think not," Belami said bluntly. "A man in desperate need of money steals money. He does not steal a jewel that must be disposed of with some difficulty, for a small fraction of its worth. Neither does he do it in the most public way possible, at a ball. You knew, of course, that the jewel was insured."

"For thirty thousand pounds. Yes, I knew it. Alas, if our thief hoped to sell it back to Lloyd's, he is out in his luck. The policy was allowed to lapse. I should have urged Her Grace to renew it when she told me her plan."

"*You* knew it, Herr Bessler, but I don't believe this was generally known. I confess nothing else makes sense to me. Why else was it stolen at my ball?"

"I cannot answer that. *You* are the clever one who indulges in crime solving. The Everton case—very well done indeed. We wait for you to explain these obscure matters to us." Bessler leaned over the table and began arranging the balls. Then he looked over his shoulder and added, "About the lapsed policy, Bidwell knew it also. His uncle is—or *was*—the duchess's agent."

"He made a point of telling you that, did he?" Belami asked.

"No, the duchess told me. Sure I can't tempt you to a game?"

"Another time, Herr Bessler," he answered, and strode from the room, chewing on that last-minute decision to tell him Bidwell was aware the policy had lapsed. A pity the snow prevented him from checking on all these details. Detail was the crux of the matter, but at least he could check that Bessler had known of the lapsed policy.

He darted upstairs to inquire into this matter. "Well, well, still malingering, are we?" he asked Her Grace in a joking way.

As she had no large vocabulary, she ignored the ques-

73

tion. "That mutton that was sent up for lunch has given me indigestion, Belami. When you reach my age, you like softer foods. I'll have ragout for dinner, if you please."

"Thy will will be done," he said with a mock-humble bow.

"What brings you to call, sir? Things must be dull below if you prefer my company to your own entertainments."

"The entertainment today is solving the crime," he said.

"No work for a gentleman, but I'll help, as it is my jewel that is gone missing. What can I tell you?"

After some preliminary questions to throw her off the track, he broached the subject of the insurance policy. "Good gracious, I've no idea whether I mentioned it to Herr Bessler or not. We are together three hours a day. I speak quite freely to him of all my little problems. Very likely I told him, if he said so. Yes, I remember very well lamenting it last night, and he showed no shock, so obviously he knew."

"But you *did* mention it last night? At what time?"

"When he accompanied me upstairs to give me a session after the robbery. He is magic, you know. *Any* ache or pain is removed after a session with him. In fact, you can send him up now, to relieve me of this bellyache. Demmed tough mutton. Ragout, mind!"

It was a good excuse to escape. Belami sent Snippe to request Bessler to step upstairs, while he went looking for his helpers. He found Deirdre waiting for him in the saloon, which gave a view of the hall.

"Meg closed the upper hallway window," she told him, as though it was nothing but crime business that interested her. "Shortly after midnight."

"Really? That doesn't lie well with my theory of two men working in tandem. I made sure one of 'em hung about upstairs to close windows and cover any other traces."

"Have you learned anything?"

"I've just been quizzing Bessler. He's gone up to see your aunt now."

"He's so very good with her. I don't know what she would do without him," she said.

"What sort of treatment is it he gives? A powder, laudanum . . ." There drifted into his head a picture of Bessler quacking the old dame with laudanum, lifting the diamond from her neck while she dozed, but he knew this didn't coincide with the actual method.

"Oh, no, not *medicine*! Auntie won't take anything of that sort. She claims it is all poison. Even coffee is slow poison in her view. He soothes her, talks, uses his fingers to manipulate the nerves in her temples. He is wonderfully effective in that way. He studied animal magnetism with Mesmer on the continent years ago."

"Ah, yes, that old quack Mesmer," Belami replied, his suspicions fading. Mesmer, he knew, had been revealed as a fool, been investigated by a government commission of physicians and scientists, and fallen into disrepute. It was small wonder Bessler did not widely bruit about his training. "It actually seems to help, does it?"

"Very much. Aunt Charney is always calmed and relaxed after Herr Bessler treats her."

This sounded like a means of a lonely old lady getting attention from a dependent. It was exactly how one would expect Charney to go on, using her friends and associates. "I'm afraid this is a visit that will require many treatments by Herr Bessler. Perhaps I should sic him on Bertie. She's not feeling too chipper either."

"I would be happy to visit her and cheer her up, if you think it would help," she offered.

Looking at the stiff-necked, proper young lady, Dick did not think she would do anything but add to Bertie's troubles. He also thought she only offered from a sense of duty. Say that for the girl, she had been very properly reared. "It might be best for me to go to her myself," he said.

He knew Bertie's favorite hiding place when she had

75

company she wished to avoid. It was a small study with a large grate and a soft sofa pulled close to it. She was there, eating away her worries. A box of her favorite bonbons was on the table beside her.

"There is nothing like a box of sweets when you are miserable," she said wearily as he stood before her, shaking his head in disapproval.

"Tch, tch, you'll require a tentmaker to fashion your gowns, if this self-indulgence continues." He put the lid on the box and removed it beyond her reach.

"Don't bother tch-ing me. I had enough of that when your Papa was alive, God rest his soul. The only thing the modiste will be fashioning me is a shroud," she replied dolefully, and switched from bonbons to a glass of very sweet Madeira. "Have you made any headway with the investigation, Dickie love?"

He sat beside her and took her hand in his. "It's confusing, and frustrating that I cannot check any of the details. I think the necklace was stolen to dupe the insurance company, but the policy ran out at midnight last night."

"The robber didn't know it, you mean?"

"The robber *did* know it. At least my suspects *claim* they knew it, and I can't prove otherwise."

"And who have you settled on as suspects?" she asked.

"Bessler maneuvered her into a good public spot, handy to the door too. Bidwell, Chamfreys, and Lennie Belfoi were available upstairs; one of them might have helped him, or it might have been a third party, whom he had hidden on the roof. Lennie's husband was only ten miles away. But then where could he have gone after?"

"Oh, Dickie, why must you make everthing so confusing? Stealing a diamond for insurance when it was not insured, and men hiding on the roof? I shouldn't have put it past old Charney to have arranged it herself. And not for insurance either, but to make you marry her niece, or at least have to give her thirty thousand for the diamond. It was *she* who maneuvered herself to the doorway at the proper moment. You notice how she hasn't had the nerve to leave her room all day, thank God. She has that grenadier of a dresser with her. Now, *her* hands are huge, and you said the ladies' gloves were big. Anyone might put on a man's suit of clothing, and you remember the thief didn't speak. That is why; because the man was a woman, and didn't want to use her voice and give the show away."

"I've thought of that, but where would she have gotten the man's suit? And the grenadier-dresser is at least sixty. Well past clambering down ropes, I think. Besides, Bidwell's shoes were wet. I had the servants examine all the shoes sent down for polishing this morning. His still had traces of damp around the edges."

"He might have stepped out for a moment."

"No, he didn't. The snow—Pierre is keeping an eye on it; he knows every blot in the snow, and who made it. It must have been Bidwell. Yet he too claims to have known the policy lapsed. And if he didn't know it, it seems he would only be robbing himself as he is Carswell's heir. Carswell is the insuring agent."

"Then he didn't steal it for insurance, but to sell," she pointed out.

"Yes, but why that particular jewel and no other? And if it was only to sell, and not claim insurance, why do it in the middle of a crowded room? A pretty tangle, is it not?"

"I wonder he didn't rob *me*. *I* was wearing the rubies your Uncle Digsworth stole from that maharaja fellow in India, worth more than the diamond, and so much prettier."

"There must have been hundreds of thousands in jewels there."

"Millions! Lady Shandy wore that whopping ugly emerald her first husband gave her. It is worth a fortune. He would certainly have known she would be wearing it. She always does, wears it everywhere. It is the only decent stone she has to her name. And she would have been easy work, as she is old and feeble."

"I am convinced it was the Charney Diamond and nothing else the thief had in mind to steal. It had to do with insurance. There is a matter of three days' grace in paying policies, but that is to cover an oversight on the part of the insurer, and Charney had told Carswell that she meant to discontinue the policy, so I doubt he'll be stuck to pay for it."

Bertie shook her head in bewilderment and sipped her Madeira. "It almost begins to look as though it was pure mischief-making. Which brings us back to *you*, Dickie," she said regretfully. Which offended Dickie so severely that he left her.

She sipped and frowned, and decided, midway through her glass, that Dick would never be so ungallant as to bruise the duchess's neck. It couldn't have been Dick. But then he could not speak, so perhaps he *had* to pull it off. All his earnest investigations counted for naught. Naturally he would have to make it look innocent. He was much too thoughtful to worry her by acting guilty, whatever he had done.

Chapter 7

❋❋❋

It preyed on Belami's mind that he used Deirdre badly, and would add a further injury when he got her to jilt him. With some notion of being nice to her, he set about looking for her. He found her sitting alone in the saloon, again in a position that allowed her to see the comings and goings in the hallway. She was leafing through a magazine, looking forlorn and bored. In fact, she was not so much bored as unhappy. Such lovely gowns as were illustrated in the magazine, all of them so very different from what her aunt allowed her to wear. She looked up when Belami appeared in the doorway, gazing at her. His every appearance caused a tightening in her chest, to see him so handsome, so very unavailable to her, who was his fiancée. Some traces of the regret she felt were on her face.

"I'm showing you a very flat holiday," he apologized, stepping into the room.

"Flat?" she asked, astonished. "Oh, no, I never had

such fun in my life! It's very exciting, helping you with the case. What are we to do next?" she asked eagerly.

"We can't ride or drive or even walk in this weather," he pointed out.

"I meant what do we do to solve the case?" she answered. "Naturally your work must take precedence over mere entertainment."

"Your aunt is less understanding. She tells me it is not a fit occupation for a gentleman."

"She is old-fashioned. I think it is edifying that you go to so much trouble, and remarkable that you do it so well."

His chest swelled a little at these unexpected compliments, and from the last source he would have imagined. "It helps to pass the time."

"Pray don't feel you have to waste a moment amusing me, Belami, but if there is anything I can do to help, I should enjoy it. What will you do next?"

"I'd like to find the mate to the stocking our thief wore."

Her neck stiffened perceptibly. "You are going to see Lady Lenore, in other words?"

"You offered to help. Why don't you see her? It would come more naturally from another woman. You could ask to borrow a pair from her."

"My aunt . . ." she said, hesitating, knowing too close contact with Lady Lenore would be frowned upon.

"Yes, I understand. I'll go to her myself," he said, with no reluctance.

"No! That is, it's business, after all. It's not as though I were seeking her friendship," she said quickly. "I'll go up now, and be back here in a minute. Will you wait for me?"

"It's the least I can do. You waited three days for me."

"No, three weeks," she answered with a pert little smile as she turned and fled the room.

Belami pondered his heart as he waited in the saloon. The stocking was an excellent excuse to go to Lenore's room for a bit of a frolic, yet he had been relieved at Deirdre's agreeing to go for him. There was the business of Paris hanging in the air between Lennie and him now, and he had no wish to finalize it. He mused on, wondering if he would go. In his mind's eye, it was not Lennie who was with him on the ship crossing the Channel, but Deirdre Gower. She'd be easy to entertain, at least. Never had such fun as this dull holiday! The girl must have been raised in cotton wool. A pity, really—there was some fire and spirit there, but all suffocated with the cotton wool. But only pull at the wool and you found yourself engaged to her, for all of mortal eternity. Bound for life to a woman who expected you to behave yourself, do the proper thing. At least she didn't cavil at his playing Bow Street. Then too, while she would expect a man to behave, she would certainly not act up herself, in the manner of a Lady Lenore. Belami knew his nature was not of the sort that could tolerate a philandering wife. He supposed, in a vague way, that the time would eventually come when he was ready to settle down, and it was a bit of a pity he hadn't met Deirdre later in his life.

While he mused along these lines, Deirdre went tapping at Lady Lenore's door, feeling as daring as though she were entering a house of ill repute. Lenore was alone in her chamber, which was a relief, making a toilette. She sat in front of a mirror, brushing out her raven hair. She had a woman who performed this chore for her at home, but the monetary exigencies of travel made it preferable to hitch a ride with someone else, and bringing servants along limited the number of carriages one could squeeze into.

"It's Miss Gower, isn't it?" Lenore said, looking in the mirror at the reflection of the bright-eyed girl behind her. She could hardly have been more startled if the old duchess herself had come to call.

"Yes, we haven't had much chance to become acquainted."

Oh, my God, Lennie thought with a silent laugh.

She's come to warn me away from Dickie. "I have regretted the wasted opportunity, Miss Gower. Do have a seat. I hear tantalizing whispers that you have landed Belami. If it is true, I offer my heartiest congratulations. You've pulled off quite a coup."

"Thank you, *Ac*-tually, I have come to ask a favor, Lady Lenore."

"Ask away," Lenore invited with a swallowed smile as she tried to decide whether to play the outraged matron or woman of the world when the Bath Miss told her to keep away from Belami.

"Yes, the thing is, I have got a ladder in my last good pair of stockings."

"What?"

"I want to borrow a pair of stockings, if you would be so kind. Would you happen to have a spare pair?"

"Oh, is *that* all?" Lenore asked, finally letting a laugh escape her pretty lips. She arose and went to decide what gown she would wear to dinner. "Help yourself, my dear. They're in the top left drawer," she called over her shoulder, "but don't take the blue ones. I shall be wearing them myself."

It was better luck than Deirdre hoped for, to have the run of the drawer. She was amazed to see a dozen pairs of stockings packed for a brief visit. They came in beautiful shades—blue, and red, and green. But soon she spotted what she was really looking for: one lone stocking of a flesh tone, surely the mate to that which Dick had pulled from the flue. She bunched it into a ball in her fingers, thence into a pocket, while she selected the red stockings.

"Can you spare these?" she asked. "I'll wash them and get them back to you tomorrow. It's just for tonight. I haven't a thing to wear."

"Will your auntie like you to wear red stockings?" Lenore asked with a teasing smile. "Never mind, I'm sure Belami will approve."

Deirdre's eyes next strayed to the dresser top, to the array of beauty aids spread before her eyes. Powder and rouge and scent and creams, all in the most beautiful chased silver traveling case she had ever seen. It was sybaritic, almost decadent, and wildly interesting. There were even bits of someone else's hair there— curls, in the same shade as Lady Lenore's own hair. She lifted one and hung it before her ear.

"Give me a hand with this, will you?" Lenore asked as she pulled off her robe and lifted a blue gown from the clothes press. "It fastens up the back."

Deirdre dropped the silk stockings and went to do as she was bid. Though she was astounded that Lady Lenore should strip herself to her underwear before a virtual stranger, her interest was soon diverted to the underwear itself. It was lace trimmed, *inches* of Belgian lace so beautiful it was a shame to cover it. It was as carefully designed as one's outer garments, with little tucks and frills everywhere. Obviously, it was made to be seen. There was a little difficulty getting the dress to do up, as Lenore wore them tight, but by pulling it was done.

"Now for my face," Lenore said when she was dressed, and walked to the dresser to resume her seat. Deirdre stood transfixed, to learn the secret of applying the contents of those pots. Her eyes rounded to see that a black grease pencil was the first item lifted. It was not applied to the brows, but to the mole, to accentuate it.

"Thank you, dear. You can go now," Lenore said. "You won't forget to bring the stockings back, will you?"

"No, I won't," Deirdre told her. Had it not been for this reminder, she might have forgotten to take them with her, but she reached down for them. As she did so, her eye was caught by a glimmer of something metallic on the hearth. It was at the inner edge of the hearth stone; it shone gold in the rays from the window. A quick peep at Lenore told her the woman was busy at her mirror, blending some combination of rouge and cream into the palm of her hand. In a twinkling, Deirdre reached down and garnered up the bit of sparkling metal. She could not take a good look at it till she was safely out of the room, but when she was able to do so, she saw very clearly that it was the metallic clip that had held the diamond on to the chain. There was miniature gadrooning around its edge, which made it unmistakable. There was a loop on top, which had been pulled or pried open. She pelted down the stairs as fast as her legs could carry her, still holding the red stockings in her other hand.

Her heart was hammering when she tore into the saloon. "Belami, another clue! I've solved the case! It was Lenore for certain, and I have got proof."

"That's not all you have got. Red silk stockings. Very daring," he replied , smiling at her enthusiasm.

She pulled the flesh-colored one from her pocket. "The red stockings were a red herring. She only had one of these," she said, handing him the other. "Compare it with the other, the one with eye holes in it."

"I don't have to, but I shall, for confirmation. Only the one, you say?"

"Yes, and furthermore—*voilà*!" She opened her closed hand to reveal the gold trinket. "On the hearth, stuck off in a corner where we missed seeing it. It is certainly from my aunt's necklace. I should recognize it anywhere."

He took it up and examined it carefully. "I wonder why I didn't see it when I swept up the glass."

"If the sun hadn't struck it at the proper angle, I'd have missed it myself," she said forgivingly.

"We knew he had pulled the diamond from the chain, but why remove the end piece from the diamond? It's so small, it doesn't make the stone any easier to hide."

Pronto came strolling in to ask what was afoot, and have the situation outlined. After some confusing brangling that red stockings had nothing to do with it—it was a flesh one the thief wore—it was finally explained to his satisfaction.

"But actually it is this little golden clasp that we're more interested in," Belami said, and outlined its importance. He looked to the others for their ideas. He did not frequently look beyond the walls of his own body for an opinion. Insensibly, he was coming to place some trust in Deirdre's ability as a helper.

"Would he have recut the stone, to try to pretend it was just a number of small diamonds and not the one large one?" she asked, although feeling it was unlikely. "I have heard that thieves will do that sometimes."

"Not just anyone can cut a diamond. It must be done by an expert, and under very special conditions. It's not a matter of giving it a tap with a hammer."

"Fell off," Pronto told them. "Loose, from being yanked so hard from old Charney's neck."

"That's possible," Belami agreed.

"At least we know for certain the diamond was in that room," Deirdre reminded them. "We also know Lenore's stocking was used. Now that absolutely puts her in on it, in my opinion."

"Opinions are not absolute, but only tentative," Belami decreed. "And we do not know for certain the diamond was in that room. We only know that you think your aunt's clasp from the necklace was there."

"It *is* the clasp, Belami. If we're not to trust our eyes, what are we to trust?" she demanded.

"I accept it is the clasp, but there is no diamond with it, and we don't *know* that the diamond ever was in that room."

"If it were someone other than Lenore, I think we would know it," she shot back quickly.

"Give me credit for more professionalism than overlooking evidence because I happen to like the person it incriminates," he replied, becoming hot.

"What more do you want?" she asked scornfully. "She is without funds, without morals, the diamond was in her room, her stocking was used. She did everything but climb down that rope herself. She got either Bidwell or Chamfreys to do that for her, or both of them acting together, while they all stick together like thieves, giving each other alibis. It is plain as the nose

85

on your face. *I* think you must go to her and demand my aunt's diamond back."

"It *does* look black for her," Pronto agreed, much impressed with this tirade.

"No," he said softly, but very firmly. "This doesn't jibe. It is out of character. Lenore has easier, less dangerous means of procuring diamonds. I don't say she wasn't involved—it looks very much as if she were, but I don't believe she is behind it all. I want to catch the instigator. In the first place, she wouldn't have used her own stocking if she were involved. She's too clever for that, and she wouldn't have left the other for you to find if she had. Whoever did it made free of the house—took my pistol from my room, the sheet from the cupboard. Why then take her own stocking?"

"Still don't see why they bothered to pull the diamond from the chain," Pronto said in an important way. "Way *I* see it, after a deal of deducing, either the clasp thing or the chain might have gotten pulled off, but not both of 'em. You want to solve the case, Dick, that's the line to take. Why yank 'em off the diamond?"

"Let's think about it a little," Dick said. "What did they plan to do with the diamond? Either sell it or strike a deal with Lloyd's"

"Good lord, do you mean to say you think Lloyd's is in on it?" Pronto gasped.

"Possibly, but in no illegal way," Belami told him. "Now, if they meant to sell it back to Lloyd's, I think they would have kept it intact. Don't you agree, Deirdre?"

"I suppose so," she agreed reluctantly, still angry that he refused to accept Lenore's obvious guilt and do something about it. "In either case, he'd have to go to London. He'll want to get it out of here very soon."

"It won't be hard to hide till he *can* get away," Pronto pointed out. "Ten million places to hide it, a thing that size. Can't hardly go searching your guests either."

"No, but he must be on coals worrying all the same," Dick said, with a thoughtful smile. "He knows I'm on his tail. He might fear I *will* search my guests. Where would you hide it, if it were you, Pronto?"

"Toe of my boot," he answered promptly. "They're a size too big."

"You, Deirdre?" he continued, glancing to her and making it an excuse to examine her thoroughly, from head to toe. "Coiled up in that bun you wear on the back of your head?"

This weak attempt at humor was scorned. If the jewel were hers to hide, she would deposit it somewhere in her underclothes, but this was not a thing that could be even intimated to gentlemen. "In my clothing," she said vaguely.

"I wouldn't keep a stolen jewel on me for all the money in the Bank of England," he said. "Once it is discovered on your person, you'd have uphill work convincing anyone you were innocent. Why do it, with so many other places to hide it for a few days?"

"You'd hide it in your room," Deirdre said.

"No, I'd hide it in any room other than my own," he told her. "To be found in one's room is nearly as damning as to be found on one's person. I'd hide it in some room that isn't much used—say, in winter, the summer room. Hmmm," he finished, tapping his lean cheek with his finger. "Shall we just fan up the coals a little? Make a noisy display of searching unoccupied rooms, and see who comes peeping over our shoulders? If you two will be kind enough to carry out that exercise, there is something else I must investigate."

Till nearly dinnertime, the two helpers searched every unoccupied room in the large house. From cellar to attic they went, very methodically, going through cupboards and into pots and vases and making no effort to conceal their movements, as half their aim was to fan the coals and turn the thief into a quivering mass of jelly.

They concluded between them that they were dealing with an extremely hardened criminal, when none of their suspects showed any stronger emotion than mild curiosity. Bessler was annoyed to have his billiards game interrupted, which sent Pronto delving into side pockets, cue rack, and potted plants, all without a bit of luck. Lady Lenore stopped Deirdre in the hallway upstairs and asked her if she had by any chance happened to pick up a pair of flesh-colored stockings while she was borrowing the red ones. She was sure she had brought them with her, but couldn't find them. She could only surmise, by the pink face of Miss Gower, that the chit had pocketed them on the sly. Imagine, the duchess's niece!

Deirdre went looking for Belami to tell him of this incident. She did not think to look in the attic, where his investigation had taken him. He sat at the window ledge in a dilapidated wicker chair dragged from another room, looking at the prints on the roof, surveying his clues. Method and motives did not run in harmony.

Method—so public, so pointedly stealing the Charney Diamond and ignoring equally valuable stones—indicated an insurance fraud. This had taken firm possession of his mind. Yet to disassemble it made identification for insurance purposes less certain. Something had arisen between the theft and the disassembling to make the insurance deal no longer feasible. The thief had not known the insurance had lapsed; he had discovered it later. But Bidwell and Bessler claimed to have known. One or both of them had lied. On the other hand, Deirdre had assembled a rather strong case against Lady Lenore. He himself was tiring quickly of the woman. Had her other lovers been similarly tired, and less than generous in their rewards?

When at last Deirdre noticed the open attic door and went running up to find him, he narrowed his eyes. What he had discovered in the attic had thrown a new suspect into his orbit. The unlikeliest one that had come along yet. "Come and have a look at this, Deirdre," he said, observing her closely.

She walked most reluctantly to the window, seeing

the greatcoat and galoshes she had worn were still on the floor beneath the window, and the traces of her footprints on the roof. "Someone has been on the roof," she said quietly with a stain of pink spreading forward from her ears to her cheeks.

"What do you make of this?" he asked dispassionately. "There's nothing in the pockets of the coat, nothing to indicate who wore them. They belong to my late father, were left up here to perish. Now, why would anyone have gone out on the roof just a few minutes before the robbery? The tracks lead to the west side, giving a view of the road. Someone was playing lookout up here. Waiting for someone to arrive, probably by horseback. It's my belief some signal or message was to have been relayed. Or possibly it was just a quick check to see if the other person had arrived, through the snow."

"That's possible," she agreed in a small voice, while her face turned a delicate shade of rose.

As Belami observed her reaction, he reviewed the facts in his head. Last night, Deirdre's arms had been cold as ice when he touched her, and her skirt was all bedraggled with water around the hem. "You have nothing more to tell me?" he asked gently.

"No. That is, Lady Lenore asked me just now if I had seen her silk stockings, the ones used to make the mask. Do you think she would have mentioned them if she were guilty? I told her I hadn't seen them; I don't think she believed me."

"That's interesting, but do you have anything to tell me about these footprints?"

His dark eyes gazed into hers. It was completely silent in the airless attic. A bright shaft of sunlight turned the motes of dust in the air a pretty gold and green. Her eyes met his. Unaware that she did it, she grabbed her lower lip between her teeth, then her eyes dropped.

"No, nothing," she said, in a guilt-ridden voice. How could she tell him it was her? She couldn't.

"I see," was all he said.

She ventured a peep, and discovered a very compassionate face looking down on her. The agitated surprise was controlled within Belami's breast. He felt he was looking at a women he had never seen before, so great was his shock to learn that Deirdre Gower was dashing enough to be involved in a robbery. Who would have thought it—that tower of rectitude! What other surprises might such a woman have in store?

To complete the charm of her, she was sorry for what she had done. She was worried, guilty, and sooner or later, she would throw herself on his chest and confess all. Why she had done it was the next question to ponder. Any behavior so deviant from the norm must have an excellent, a compelling reason, and he feared that he was it.

He quickly decided that the way to handle this particular suspect was with kind sympathy, generously tinged with flirtation. She had taken pretty well to flirtation in her aunt's conservatory. He allowed a sleepy smile to settle on his lips. With a playful gesture, he reached out and touched her hair. It was soft and fine, but so closely bound up in pins that he couldn't loosen one hair as he hoped to do.

"Why do you wear your lovely hair in this knob?" He asked.

The unexpectedness of the question threw her into a tizzy, but a grateful tizzy, since he abandoned the thorny subject of footprints on the roof. "It's tidy," she said.

His fingers fell from her hair to her neck, where they felt warm, and shockingly intimate, stroking her with caressing movements. A heat formed inside her and spread outward in a glow that brought to mind the sun on a summer's day. "Will you wear it down tonight, for *me*?" he asked in a quiet, meaningful tone.

"It looks horrid," she told him.

He continued in this playful vein, pulling out a few pins, till her curls toppled about her ears. "No, it looks

90

enchanting," he said softly. Then he lowered his head and placed a chaste kiss on her ear.

"I must go," she said in breathless accents. "My aunt will be looking for me."

"At the moment we're still officially engaged," he pointed out. "Even your aunt would not be so gothic as to find anything amiss in our spending a moment alone together."

"Yes," she answered, quite at random. With a soft swish of her skirts, she turned and sped down the stairs, while Belami shook the two hairpins in his hand, looking after her.

Deirdre hardly knew what to make of the meeting. All thoughts of the footprints on the roof dropped from her mind as she went to her room alone, to relive the magic of Belami's fingers on her neck, the touch of his lips on her ear. Was it possible he loved her after all? It looked remarkably like it.

In the attic, Belami turned to the coat, to examine it thoroughly. From the collar, he extracted two black hairs. He removed from the hairpins a hair that was wound around them, and placed the three on his palm. They looked identical. The galoshes too were small enough that few men could get into them. Almost certainly it was a lady who had put them over her slippers, and equally certainly, that lady was Deirdre Gower.

So who was her partner? Not Chamfreys, a married man. Bidwell? She had run after him with an unexpected haste that morning. She had also used the word *forced* in connection with her marriage to himself. If the duchess were indeed forcing her into the marriage, it might be enough to turn her into a criminal. And if Bidwell had been making advances to her, she might have confessed her dilemma to him. He was sure the idea for the robbery had come from Bidwell. It would also account for the fact that only the duchess's diamond had been taken. It was to be Deirdre's one day in any case, and of course she knew it was to be worn at the ball.

He sank onto the wicker chair, stunned by his conclusions. He thought he knew something about human nature, but it could always surprise him. That was its fascination, really, but he wasn't fascinated now. He was aware of a strong feeling of injury. He had come home determined to be free of the wretched girl, but now that she was in tune with his desires, he felt piqued. How could she prefer that man-milliner to him? The rotter had been making up to her on the sly, that was it. Everyone had a weak point, and Deirdre's was a susceptibility to flirtation. He had known there were hidden passions beneath her frosty exterior. She kept her fire well banked, but it was there, glowing beneath the frost.

He went to his laboratory and put the three hairs under the microscope. There was no doubt in his mind that all came from the same head. They were the same size, the same color, all three with a twist that denoted naturally curled hair. Such a vital new clue should have cheered him. It opened vast horizons for deduction, yet he felt a sense of loss. An idol had been shattered. Deirdre Gower was made of mortal clay after all, and not marble, as became a goddess. It did not occur to him just yet how little he really cared for marble statues, and how much for mortal clay, when modeled in the feminine form.

Chapter 8

✳✳✳

Pronto Pilgrim came puffing up the staircase as Belami was running down.

"Clue!" Pronto told him, eyes wide with importance.

They went to Snippe's study and sat down. "Well, what is it?" Belami asked impatiently.

"Bidwell's been asking how the road to London is. Asked Snippe. Seemed mighty anxious to get away too. Said 'Oh, damme' when he learned it was blocked solid with snow."

"To London?" Belami asked. "I made sure it was the Great North Road he'd be interested in."

"No, he lives in London. Why would he want to be rushing north in the middle of winter? Nothing there but Scotland."

"There is Gretna Green," Dick answered with a mysterious smile.

"What of it? Bidwell don't have a ladybird, not that I ever heard of."

"True, and he wouldn't be likely to marry her if he had, though I expect his abstention from the muslin company stood him in good stead in certain quarters."

"Wouldn't matter a tinker's curse to old Carswell, if that's your meaning. He's got his light o' love tucked away right and tight."

"No, that was not my meaning."

"What *did* you mean, then?"

"Prepare yourself for a shock, Pronto. I have made a startling discovery."

"Knew it. Can always tell when you get to smirking like a jackdaw that you've been deducing to good purpose. Well, out with it. Who stole the diamond?"

"This is in the strictest confidence, you understand. The fact is, Deirdre is involved in it with Bidwell."

Pronto stared at his friend a long moment, blew air out through his lips, then finally spoke. "You're sick, my lad. Sick as a dog. Sicker. In fact, you're crazy. Bidwell and Deirdre, when the duchess has managed to get the rope around your ankle. Not bloody likely!"

"The duchess has nothing to do with it." Belami went on to outline his findings to Pronto, who maintained throughout the recital that his friend was insane, that Deirdre and Bidwell had never been seen together in London, that Bidwell liked dashers, by Jove, and so did Deirdre, and neither of them was a dasher, so there. No amount of persuasion budged him an iota from his conviction that Dick was crazy, which he euphemistically termed sick, when he remembered.

"Oh, another thing I forgot to tell you. Bessler's going back to town with Bidwell. Came with the duchess, you know," Pronto said.

"I am no longer interested in Bessler. This has become a different sort of problem, hardly a robbery at all, in fact. It is more like a retaliation of wrong for wrong. The diamond will be Deirdre's one day; she has taken possession of it early. And as to Bidwell, even he isn't your common garden-variety thief. He is Carswell's heir—if, in fact, insurance is involved at all. I expect that was his rationalization to Deirdre at least."

"Whose rationalization?" Pronto demanded sharply. "Seems to me you're the one doing the rationalizing. It's plain and simple thievery, my friend, and I hope you mean to unmask them. Only it wasn't them at all, because they never had a thing to do with each other."

"You can't deny the diamond was stolen," Dick mentioned.

"I ain't trying to . Deirdre has proved Lenore is half the act. Oh, I know she was supposed to be with Chamfreys. Who's to say he didn't fall asleep? There's that old Latin saying, *omnes vires* . . . something or other. Means men fall asleep after doing the featherbed jig. Lennie would wear a man out more than most. Yessir, Chamfreys was sawing logs while Bidwell scampered down that rope, and Lennie stood up above to help him."

"And forgot to close the window after him? Not Lennie. And how do you account for Deirdre's being on that roof?"

"Taking a breath of air," Pronto thought. His next suggestion was equally foolish. "If you think it was her, why don't you ask her?"

"Because it is ungentlemanly to call a lady a liar. Much better to simply prove it."

"You ain't having much luck proving anything so far. I begin to wonder just how you stumbled on the Everton girl's hiding place last year. Your deducing has gone downhill sadly since then."

"That was a particularly brilliant piece of deduction. It will be difficult to match it," Belami agreed, "but I have every confidence in myself."

He strolled out of the room with not a single new premise on which to perform his deductions, but with no doubts that he would solve this seemingly baffling case and add another bit of luster to his reputation. Something was bound to break, and if it didn't, he had some ideas for fanning coals that had nothing to do with deductions.

Belami encountered his mother passing through the front hall as he left Snippe's room. She was scuttling along like a little bird, her head darting forward at every step, her feet scarcely touching the floor. On her head she wore a cap, a very pretty lace-edged cap, but as she usually wore none, her son wondered why she had it on. He also disliked it. It reminded him that she was no longer young.

"Why are you rigged up like a quiz, Bertie?" he asked.

"Do I look perfectly wretched? I know I do, but I am going up to see Her Grace, and must appear respectable. She has *sent* for me, Dickie, in my own home! Very brazen of her, don't you think? Oh dear, I hope she isn't going to scold me. I don't suppose you've found her old diamond, so I can give it back to her and have done with this visit."

"It hasn't turned up yet," he admitted, "but I can save you this unpleasant chore at least. I'll go to Charney."

"She sent for *me*."

"She will get *me*. And would you be so kind as to go to your room and remove that lid you are wearing, luv. It doesn't become you. For dinner, I want you to don your most festive and outrageous gown, all the jewelry your body can hold, serve jeroboams of champagne. *Sparkle*, Bertie. We're not in mourning. This is a party we have invited our friends to. It's unfortunate the duchess lost her diamond, but it's not our fault. All this sackcloth-and-ashes business is unnecessary."

"We can't celebrate, Dick. It would look too inconsiderate."

"I haven't seen Charney go a step out of her way to show consideration to *you*. You would not have spent the day in bed complaining if it were your emeralds that were lifted from her house."

"That's true," she said with a sharp nod of her head.

"She wouldn't have offered to pay for them either, as you have done. You don't think it was a bit precipitous of you, Dick? I mean, if you don't find the diamond . . ."

"I'll find it," he said simply. "I have a plan."

"I am happy to hear it," she said, and heaved a sigh of relief. "I hope it doesn't involve *me*."

"It doesn't. Why don't you round up some guests and play cards till dinner?" he suggested, to cheer her up.

"I was playing with Uncle Cottrell and some other saints when she summoned me. So boring, not even any good gossip, but only prosing on about politics. You must tell me what politics is all about some day. Now I shall read my novel."

"Fine, you do that," he said.

She frowned as he left. Was that why he said he hadn't *stolen* the diamond? Because he meant to pay Charney in cash?

Belami straightened his shoulders, put a politely indifferent smile on his face, and strode up to Her Grace's chamber. The duchess sat up in bed, pillows piled around her like a sultan.

"Oh, it's you, Belami. I sent for your mama," she told him, lifting her chin to show she had taken umbrage.

"Unfortunately, Mama is indisposed."

"Small wonder, with this miserable business on her hands," Her Grace replied with relish.

"New Year's is always a trifle trying, is it not? I expect she had more champagne than was good for her. Was there something you wanted, Duchess?"

"Yes, I wanted to talk to your mama. Why do you think I sent for her?"

"I shall be happy to relay any message for you."

"Hmph. You can tell her for me this is a demmed lumpy mattress she has given me."

"Would you like to have it exchanged? Another room, perhaps?"

"No, no, I just got settled in here."

"Any other messages to add?" he asked with a satirical glint in his eyes. "Damp sheets, smoky flue, draughty windows . . ."

"He heh, you're a caution, Belami. I like a lad with spirit. Sit down. Sit down, boy, and talk to me. I'm bored to flinders with no company but my own. I believe I shall go down to dinner. That was really what I wished to tell your mama."

"She will be delighted to hear it," he said with a slight inclination of his head.

"Yes, since the betrothal is on, it is high time we make the announcement formally. We'll do it at dinner this evening, which is why I must be there. Your Uncle Cottrell will do the pretty. Tell him so."

He leveled a black stare at her. "It will be best to wait till the storm is over and it can be announced simultaneously in the London papers," he parried.

"That was never the plan. Planning to shear off on us?" she asked with a narrow-eyed glare in his direction.

"One never knows how an incident such as the loss of your diamond will affect a relationship."

"It hasn't affected us. Deirdre and I. Nothing has been said about calling off. Speak to Cottrell. Have it announced," she ordered.

He gave a barely perceptible nod of his head in grim acquiescence to her command. He did not wish to annoy her at this time, as he had some fairly impertinent questions to put to her. He began with vague queries as to where she usually kept the diamond. Insurance was not involved in the theory currently favored that Deirdre was involved. And as this was so, why had the theft been done so publicly and dangerously?

"When we picked it up at the bank, we drove directly to my home—Herr Bessler and myself, I refer to. We had a glass of sherry, and he left. Here is where it has rested, from the minute I got it from the vault." She slapped her bony breast. "I had it on under my gown during the trip here and all the time I was here. What has that to do with anything? We know when and where it was stolen."

"I like a clear picture of all that led up to it. Did Bidwell happen to call on you during the latter part of December?"

"Certainly not! I don't encourage such seven-day beaux as that to dangle after Deirdre. Especially when she was already engaged."

He saw that it would have been impossible to steal the diamond without assaulting the duchess, as she wore the thing on her. That could account for doing it in public perhaps. "It is dangerous traveling with jewels. Did you never consider having paste replicas made, as so many do?"

"Duchesses do not wear paste," she decreed grandly. Then she relented, slapped her knee, and cackled like a hen. "By God, I wish I had! What clever thoughts have been going through my mind as I lie here alone. If I had a copy, and *it* had been stolen before the claim ran out, I could have claimed my reward and still have kept my jewel. Not that I could have worn it in public again. No, there was no copy. Never mind thinking what you are thinking, my lad. Duchesses don't *lie* either."

"They *do* read minds, do they?" he asked with a flashing smile to which even an aging duchess was not entirely immune.

"By Jove, I can't quite read yours. Why are you asking these questions? What are you after, eh?"

He hardly knew, but he plodded on, picking up such details as had occurred to him during the day. "Are Bidwell and Bessler on terms?" he asked. If Bidwell hadn't called in person, then he must have had a go-between.

"Nodding acquaintances, no more, until they turned up here together. I believe they frequent the same club. Not one of the grander ones, of course. Do you think that rattle of a Bidwell is involved?"

"I'm still open-minded on the matter. If you have no further messages for my mother, I shall leave you now, Your Grace."

"Send someone up to amuse me."

"Herr Bessler?"

"I'm bored with him too. Send Cottrell. I'll give him a quizzing about politics. His monologues are better than Bessler's for closing my eyes. He could put Macbeth to sleep."

"I believe he is at cards."

"Bother! Send *someone*. Send Pronto Pilgrim."

Belami felt that was a meeting he would not mind auditing, but as he had more pressing matters to attend to, he found Pronto and sent him up.

"Me? What does she want to see *me* for?"

"She's lonesome," Dick told him.

"If she wasn't such a nag she wouldn't *be* lonesome. Nobody goes near her if they can help it. Dashed harpy. I'll take cards. That'll keep her quiet."

Chapter 9

✳✳✳

There was a music room at Beaulac in the west wing.
As Bertie did not play any instrument, nor much like to
listen to music, it was not a well-used chamber, but
when Belami reached the bottom of the stairs, he heard
the ghostly, distant sound of a piano badly out of tune.
Curious, he walked along the corridor to see who was
brave enough to tackle it. Lady Lenore, he thought,
judging from the sprightly waltz, which grew louder as
he approached the door. He was greatly surprised to see
Deirdre Gower at the keyboard, her hands flying over
the ivories and her whole body swaying in time to the
music. He had never credited her with much sense of
rhythm. Dancing with her on the few occasions when
he had done so was much like dancing with an articula-
ted doll. The limbs moved, but jerkily. He should have
suspected from her undulating walk that she had
rhythm.

She finished the tune and sat still, her head drooping

forward. A deep sigh escaped her, followed by a word that sounded like "damn."

Belami lightly clapped his hands and walked forward. "Bravo, Deirdre. One of Méhul's waltzes, wasn't it?"

Her head whipped around to stare at him. "Your piano is out of tune," she said, and immediately got up from the bench.

"You seem a little off-key yourself. Till you join my family, we have no one who plays."

"I'm not joining your family," she said firmly.

"I wish you would tell your aunt so. She has just ordered me to make the announcement this evening."

"No! You mustn't, Belami," she pleaded.

"It will come as a shock to a few people," he said, looking to see what reaction this got.

"What do you mean?"

"I was thinking of Bidwell," he told her.

"Bidwell? What has it to do with him?" she asked, her face a mask of incomprehension. It was enough to make him doubt his convictions in that regard. Was it possible he was wrong about Bidwell?

He gave his enigmatic Mona Lisa smile, designed to confuse his victims. "I'm not marrying you," she said, and made to brush past him. Quick as a lizard's blink, his hand flew out and grabbed her arm. She was jerked to a stop, and looked up at him. There was hardly six inches between them. His eyes held hers, then he slid his gaze down to her lips. She had the strongest sensation he was going to kiss her. Something in her chest began growing and expanded till she felt suffocated. Her breaths came in quick, light sounds.

"You had best tell your aunt so," he said, and with a little laugh he released her arm.

"Don't worry, I will," she shot back, and marched from the room. Even when she was angry her hips swayed. He stood watching her retreat, with an appreciative smile on his face.

Her Grace was playing piquet with Pronto when

Deirdre burst in on them. "I must speak to you at once, Auntie," Deirdre said.

"Be happy to leave," Pronto offered with the greatest alacrity. Demmed duchess was *cheating*. She'd dealt herself a pair of face cards from the bottom of the deck, or her nightgown sleeve, or under her coverlet. Wasn't even a good cheat. The two cards she'd discarded peeped up from under the blankets. She'd won a golden boy from him too, by Jove. Dick had to hear about this. A woman who'd cheat at cards would cheat at diamonds too.

"Very well. Run along, Pronto," the duchess said.

"I don't want you to announce the betrothal this evening," Deirdre said as soon as they were alone.

"I wish we had announced it in London the day he offered. He wished to tell his mama first in person, he said. It was a put-off, Widgeon. If you cannot get him to the altar now, when he is in such deep disgrace with us over my diamond, you'll never accomplish it. Strike while the iron is hot, my girl. It'll cool down soon enough," the duchess advised her.

"I don't wish to take advantage of the situation. It isn't fair," Deirdre replied with a noble toss of her head.

"All is fair in love and war," her aunt pointed out.

"But this is not love."

"No, ninny, it is *war*. You're fighting for a husband. I've done the reconnaissance for you. I've worked him into a corner and spiked his guns. Ha, he'll have you now. See if he don't."

"But I don't want to marry him."

"Enough of your *but's*," the duchess said peremptorily. "You didn't want to marry Lord Twombley either, a perfectly respectable earl, with ten thousand a year. What *do* you want? I am not a hard woman, Deirdre, but I am not quite a fool either. I'm eighty years old, and if I see eighty-one I shall count myself blessed. I have a fortune to leave you. I mean to see a decent gentleman in charge of it and you before I go. Belami is well to grass. He ain't overlooking my money, but he ain't marrying you for it either. He has plenty of his own. What's amiss with the fellow? I swear I could take a tumble for him myself, if I were half a century younger. He's got a flashing eye in his head that could melt a milestone."

"Well, it doesn't melt *me*," Deirdre said mulishly.

"I said a milestone, not an iceburg. Have you been trotting after that nipper of a Bidwell?" the duchess asked, wearing a sharp, questioning look.

"Certainly not. Where does everyone get that idea?"

"Belami seemed to think so. I took the notion he was very jealous."

"Really?" Deirdre asked with a little smile turning up the corners of her lips.

"Why, he asked a million questions about him and you," the aunt exaggerated wildly. She was indeed no fool. She knew a girl didn't smile at a charge of jealousy on her lover's part if it didn't please her. And why should it please her, if she was as indifferent as she claimed regarding Belami? "If you want to hold off a little on the announcement, it is quite all right with me. You may tell him I said so," the duchess added, to ensure another meeting between the brangling lovers.

"Thank you. I shall," Deirdre replied. With a pretty curtsy, she turned and darted from the room to seek out Belami, and if she had any opportunity to flirt with Bidwell in front of him, she'd do that as well.

She went to Snippe's door and rapped. Pronto opened the door an inch to squelch any caller. "We're busy," he told her.

"I wish to speak to Belami. It won't take a moment," she told him, and pushed her way in.

"Matter of fact, I want to speak to *you*," Pronto decided, and shut the door. "That aunt of yours— a regular Captain Sharp. 'Pon my word, she yanked a pair of kings from her sleeve and fleeced me with them."

"She only cheats when she knows she's playing with a Johnnie Raw," Deirdre said, then turned to Belami. "I spoke to Auntie. You are not to announce the engagement this evening after all," she told him, with a vastly superior smile. "*Ac*-tually, I doubt that you'll ever be announcing it at all."

"I am much obliged to you, ma'am," he replied with a stiff bow.

"The pleasure is all mine."

"One hesitates to disagree with a lady, but I must insist the pleasure is mutual."

"Then you should have been firmer with Her Grace," Deirdre answered, trying to control her rage at his arrogant sneer.

"I am but a reed in the wind, vis-à-vis the ladies. They command, and I am honored to obey." A little bow accompanied this satirical utterance.

"I must go and speak to Bidwell now," she retaliated. "You wouldn't know where he is, Pronto?" she asked, never looking within a right angle of Belami but noticing from the corner of her eye the sudden jerk of his head toward her.

"Billiards room, all alone and smoking a cigar. Place is blue with smoke."

"Thank you." She left the room, slamming the door behind her.

It was opened much more quietly than it had been closed, to allow Belami to watch her route. She did not go toward the billiards room, but returned upstairs to begin her toilette for dinner.

"Bidwell. Looks black," Pronto said wisely.

"She didn't go to him," Belami pointed out.

"Mentioned him. Going to tell him she don't have to marry you. Pleased as punch about it. Quite a facer for you, Dick, being jilted."

"It's better than being shackled to her. *Ac*-tually, I'd sooner fry in hades than be that woman's husband."

"Expect you'll get your wish," Pronto told him with a hateful smirk.

Deirdre made a careful toilette, to appear in best form to frirt with Bidwell and make Belami jealous. She had not previously indulged in the primeval pastime of flirtation and had therefore little idea how to set about it. Her aunt was right. This was war. In her mind there was a vague intention of bringing Belami to his knees before her. He was a toplofty, haughty, spoiled rake who deserved a lesson.

She chose a white crepe gown with spider gauze overskirt. She had to arrange her own hair, as the duchess monopolized the woman who, in theory, was dresser to them both. As she brushed out her dark curls, she remembered Belami's request that she wear it loose, for him. Why had he said that if he was so happy to be free of her? She would wear it loose and be sure to mention to Dick that Bidwell preferred it this way. It looked rather nice, she thought as she brushed back a wave, which fell forward again in a provocative curl at her temple. She usually wore simple pearl earrings, but for this occasion she borrowed a much finer pair of her aunt's dangling diamond drops, which bounced against her cheeks when she turned her head. The scent bottle was used to anoint her wrists, the back of her ears, the hollow between her bosoms, as she had seen Lady Lenore do. Why would she put perfume *there?* In her innocence, she supposed the perfume wafted up, to enchant a lady's partner.

When she was finished, she pirouetted in front of the mirror feeling strangely reckless, with the heady perfume around her, the earrings bobbing against her cheeks, and her hair untrammeled and abandoned, now that it was free of its pins. She smiled at the image in the mirror and found the smile unsatisfactory. It looked cold, unenchanting. She remembered watching Lady Lenore the night before. A strange, lazy smile she had, with her eyelids half closed, while she peered up through them at her admirers, with her head tilted. Deirdre tried this trick, and was satisfied that it added warmth to her manner. She played with her fan, covering her lips with it and batting her lashes, then slowly sliding it aside from her lips. It was really quite simple, once you got the hang of it.

When she descended with her aunt to the saloon for a glass of sherry before dinner, she was careful to take up a chair beside Bidwell.

"How have you managed to get in this long day, Bidwell?" She pitched her voice low, to lend it an intimate sound.

He turned and cast a surprised smile on her. "I have been desperately lonesome, ma'am. Where did you choose to hide yourself?"

This uninspired reply brought forth a throaty laugh that sent Belami's head turning to observe her. Throwing herself at Bidwell to the top of her bent, the hussy!

"Here and there," she said, plying the fan. "Mostly in the music room. Just me and one very much out-of-tune piano."

"Lucky piano! Had I been there, I could have accompanied you. I sing out-of-tune quite naturally. We shall have plenty of time for duets. I fear we're here for a few days, since the road hasn't been cleared."

"You'll know where to find me next time," she told him.

The innocent flirtation continued. Once Belami had established in his mind what was afoot, he didn't pass another glance in that direction, but went to Lady Lenore to engage her in some more advanced carrying on.

"I see Charney has recovered sufficiently to come downstairs," Lenore mentioned.

"I'm the one who deserves to be in bed. I must stand buff if her jewel isn't recovered."

"Poor Dickie," she cooed. "Lucky we have Paris to look forward to. When will be convenient for you?"

"Tonight would be convenient for me," he answered daringly.

She laughed and tapped his wrist with her fan. "Naughty boy! Chamfreys wouldn't like that. Be patient. I can get away the third week of January. Is that date good for you?"

Panic rose in him. He didn't want to become heavily enmeshed with Lenore, but to make an excuse would put her out of sorts, and cut off any help she might give him in solving the case. "The sooner, the better," he said with a good semblance of eagerness.

"You'll have to advance me some blunt, dear boy. I'm as poor as a church mouse."

"What of Chamfreys?" While he spoke, his mind was busy with deductions. So she *was* having trouble getting monies from her escorts!

"He pays in *things*," she explained. "A lovely diamond bracelet this trip. I have half a dozen of them. I was hoping for a necklace, but it seems my price is a bracelet. I shouldn't have told you so, should I?"

"Very unwise."

"Are we to hear an interesting announcement this evening, Belami? An odd time you chose for a liaison in Paris, when your betrothal is about to be made in public. Can't say I blame you," she added with a look across the room to Deirdre, who had returned to respectable behavior when she noticed that Belami wasn't looking at her.

Belami's hands clenched into fists, involuntarily. He hardly knew why, but he knew he was angry at the slur on Deirdre's attractiveness. He took a hasty glance across the room and was struck at how well she looked this evening. Her cheeks wore the soft pink flush of a sea shell. Her eyes glowed with the gleam of youth, and on top of it, she looked elegantly respectable. In comparison, Lennie looked like a well-worn and slightly gaudy silk rose. "There will be no announcement," he said with bored indifference.

"*I* see! I'm catching you on the rebound, am I? Did she turn you off, or was it *la duchesse*?"

"We agreed to disagree."

"Pity. It would have been an interesting match, to see whether you debauched the child or she reformed you. I think you would have won. See, she's already learned how to flirt. A vast improvement, if I may say so."

Looking toward the corner, Belami watched as Deirdre resumed her flirtation. She hit Bidwell's hand with her fan, in a good imitation of Lenore. Anger surged through him again, causing him to ignore Lenore's question. She spoke on again.

"How does the case go on?"

"Superbly. I shall be announcing the solution shortly."

"Then we'll see her casting her wiles in earnest, I think," she said with a speculative look at Bidwell.

"You know about her and Bidwell, then?" he ventured, and listened sharply for her answer.

"I surmised. Truth to tell, I didn't suspect it before this visit. Does the duchess approve?"

"She won't, after I have solved the case," he said, to gauge how she reacted to hints of knavery on Bidwell's part.

"Oho, so that's the culprit! I can't say I'm surprised. Who else could it be, when all's said and done? I'll tell you this, Dick: he was silent as a mouse all the time Chamfreys and I were—were in the next room," she said with a nervous look around her. "And when he called us, I noticed a few droplets of water on his hair. Melted snow, it must have been. I didn't mention it to him."

"Nor to me either, Lennie. Are you sure?"

"Positive."

"Was anyone with him in the next room?"

"I don't believe so. Why do you ask?"

"Because two glasses were broken."

"No, there was only one smashing sound," she said, surprised. "You must be mistaken."

"You were preoccupied. You might have missed one."

"Chamfreys is not all that distracting. The noise alerted me that it was time to scramble into my gown and return downstairs. And by the by, it was discreet of you to have found Chamfrey's watch fob in the ballroom, and not in my bed, where he lost it. I noticed he wore it when we went upstairs. When did you retrieve it?"

"That same night, while you were at dinner."

"I'm glad you did. I feared Bidwell had pocketed it. He was in my room when we came out. He'd been down and heard about the robbery, and came darting up to tell us. It occurred to me Chamfreys might have dropped it in my dressing room. It means a great deal to him. We'd been on our hands and knees searching the floor for it."

Deirdre's flirtation across the room was not observed. Belami had gotten new nuggets of information and was busy gnawing at them. If only one glass was smashed, what was the other bit of glass ground into the grate? Lennie was awake on all suits; he didn't think she was mistaken about that. Or about Bidwell's wet hair either. And why had Bidwell returned to her room to tell them of the robbery? Wouldn't it be more natural to remain below, where excitement and gossip must have been rampant? So why had he really returned? Had he smashed the other glass then? Lennie denied this at once. No, no, they had all run down together at once. His musings were interrupted by Snippe's appearance at the doorway to announce, in injured accents, that dinner was served. Belami's chore, as host, was to lend the duchess his arm. On his way to her side he said softly to Pronto, "I'm going to make an announcement after dinner. When I do, I want you to regard Deirdre and Bidwell. Note their expressions closely."

"Eh? What announcement?"

"You'll soon know. Just do as I ask. I've seated you beside Deirdre and across from Bidwell."

Lady Belami usually followed her son's advice for the simple reason that it saved her thinking for herself. He had ordered her to throw a lavish dinner and dress up grandly, and she had done it. Her cook had been instructed to prepare an elaborate dinner of two courses and two removes, with champagne served throughout the meal. The turbot in lobster sauce was perhaps not so tasty as her Philippe usually made it, but the champagne did much to cover Philippe's lapse. *Le jambon à la broche* was a fine success. The troublesome duchess didn't even try it, but ate a deal of the ragout, which was kinder to her loose teeth. The fowl, too, she managed to masticate without unhinging any of her perilously anchored molars. *Le charlotte à l'americain* was a hit with all the ladies.

When the meal was finally finished, Belami caught Pronto's eye, nodded, and rose to his feet. He instructed the footmen to refill the glasses and said simply, "I have an announcement to make. It is brief and will, I am sure, make everyone at the table happy." He looked at Deirdre, whose eyes were wide with interest. He was going to announce the betrothal after all, she thought. Her first spontaneous reaction was of surprised, confused delight, but she soon realized she had to be incensed at this cavalier flouting of her wishes. She glared at her aunt, who had obviously conspired with Belami in the matter, but the only expression that showed on her aunt's face was rampant curiosity. Deirdre was too excited to notice Pronto sitting with his arms folded, his protruding eyes narrowed to slits, darting from herself to Bidwell like the pendulum of a metronome, while a frown of the most severe concentration creased his brow.

Pronto stared away as he had been told, but all he saw was that Deirdre had turned a shade paler. When the first babble of excitement had settled down, Belami lifted his glass.

"I would ask you all to join me in drinking a toast to the recovery of the duchess's diamond." As he finished speaking, his darts flickered from the duchess to Deirdre, then rapidly to Bidwell. He lifted his glass and drank, still observing the effect of his announcement on his guests. He was thrown into confusion by what he saw. Firstly and most importantly, Bidwell's lips split wide in a grin. Deirdre looked only surprised, and the duchess was in a state of agitated irritation. All these reactions were wrong, but he had very little time to consider any of them. Within seconds, his mother emitted a veritable squeal of delight, and hopped up from the table to express her rapture.

"Dickie, you're wonderful! You've done it again. Now you won't have to marr— Oh, isn't it wonderful, Your Grace?"

The duchess glared, but only Bertie observed this killing glance. The rest of the table had their attention directed to Herr Bessler, whose glass had clattered to the table, throwing champagne in all directions. Looking toward him, Deirdre noticed his quick, worried look to Bidwell, whose smile had spread even wider.

"That *is* good news!" Bidwell exclaimed. "I'll drink to that." He took a deep quaff of his wine, and those who had recovered their wits at all did likewise.

There was a clamorous demand for Belami to produce the necklace. He explained that it had been dismantled, and produced only the chain and hook.

"But where is my diamond? I want to see my diamond," the duchess insisted, still angry.

"It is in my vault, Your Grace. I could not risk having it stolen again," Belami explained. "I'll return it to you this evening or, if you prefer, keep it in my safe till you are prepared to leave."

"I'll see it at least, if you please," she told him, pushing herself up from her chair, using her arms for levers, in a way that jiggled her whole side of the table. She read the reluctance on Belami's face and thought she had deciphered his reason. He was afraid someone would follow them, and it was unwise to announce publicly the location of his safe. Very cautious of him.

"A little later perhaps, Your Grace?" he asked.

"Very well," she agreed, and plopped back into her chair to finish her champagne.

There were many requests to hear the story of the discovery, and of course to learn the identity of the perpetrator, all of which Belami modestly declined to discuss "at this time," as he expressed it. The inventive among them took it for civility in allowing the criminal the luxury of a private accusation, but in truth there was nothing to tell. Dick had no idea where the diamond was, and only suspicions as to who had stolen it.

He hoped his announcement would reveal the thief. There should have been a shocked, trembling, white-faced, wild-eyed man in that room, and that man should have been Bidwell. And what did he see? Bidwell grinning like a monkey. Deirdre's eyes should have flown to Bidwell in horror. The demmed duchess should have been delighted, though he soon deduced it was a simple preference for his thirty thousand pounds over her poorly cut diamond that accounted for her chagrin. Bessler should not have dropped his glass in amazement, and Bertie should not have blurted out that now he wouldn't have to marry Deirdre. Nothing had gone as planned, and he was left looking a complete idiot, with a deal of explaining to do to Charney.

The ladies soon left the gentlemen to their port, and Belami remained behind to see what he could learn from the men. He learned that Bidwell was in a state of high amusement, that Bessler had overcome whatever shock he had initially experienced, and that was about all he discovered. To distract attention from his imaginary recovery of the diamond, he regaled his guests with the tale of finding the outfit and pistol up the flue, and the rope trick used to descend from the floor above.

"The diamond is in good shape, is it?" Chamfreys asked. "It didn't get marred in the dismantling?" When Belami assured him it was in perfect condition, he said, "By Jove, you *are* clever, Belami. As clever as people say."

"Hear, hear," Bidwell agreed boisterously. "In perfect condition, you say? That *is* good news, is it not, Herr Bessler?"

"A diamond would not easily become marred," Bessler pointed out. "It is of an extremely hard consistency."

"As a matter of fact, a diamond is more easily destroyed than people often think," Belami said, eager to discuss anything other than how he had solved the crime. "A good stone is often destroyed in the cutting. It can even be demolished by accident after it is cut, if something heavy should fall on it. They're not indestructible by any means."

Chamfreys was at his elbow, trying to get him aside for a private word. With high hopes, Belami went with him, but he was disappointed.

"I'll tell you who could use a bit of your help, my lad, is Prinney. He's in the devil of a bind. It happened just before we left town. I've only heard rumors, mind, but Devonshire told me in the strictest confidence that he's being blackmailed. Don't know what it's all about, but you could do yourself some good if you'd straighten it out for him. There'd be an earlship in it for you, maybe even a jump up to a marquis. Shouldn't think he'd go as high as a dukedom. The timing won't suit you, with Paris in the offing, but Lennie is reasonable. She'd postpone the tryst."

In the midst of his annoyance with Lenore for having already boasted to Chamfreys of her new conquest, Belami felt some interest in the story of Prinney's problem. It was not the lure of a higher title that interested him, nor even the wish to help his Prince, but purely the intellectual curiosity, to get at another case.

"I'll look into it as soon as we can get out of here," he told Chamfreys.

Bidwell, who had been loitering nearby with his ears pricked, came forward in time to hear his last remark. "When do you think that will be, old chap? Any news on the condition of the roads?"

"Why, you make me fear I'm doing a poor job of entertaining you, Bidwell. What's the rush?" Belami asked with a bold stare.

"I'm promised to accompany Cookson's daughter to a skating party day after tomorrow. I wouldn't want to disappoint the lady," he replied.

"Especially when her papa is the king of brewers," Belami replied, and felt ashamed of himself. It was illbred to cast aspersions on one's invited guests. Just why Bertie had seen fit to invite the hedgebird was beside the point. Probably had known his mama. Bertie knew everyone's mama.

He was so engrossed in pondering Bidwell's smile that he didn't take into account the real gist of Bidwell's statement for forty seconds. If it were true he was dangling after Cookson's well-dowered daughter, then he and Deirdre were nothing to each other. All his conversations had confirmed the lack of interest. Such a uniformity of opinion caused him to deduce he had been mistaken. It was a blow to his powers of reasoning, but one that caused him more relief than pain.

Chapter 10

✳✳✳

When *it* was polite to get away from the taking of port, Belami and Pronto joined the ladies. Dick looked about for the duchess, dreading to confess his stunt, and was pleasantly surprised to learn that she had gone upstairs. Deirdre caught his eye, and beckoned him with a glance.

"My aunt has retired," she said. "She asked me to thank you for finding her diamond. Can you tell me about it?"

"No," he answered baldly.

"Why not? Surely you're not planning to keep it a secret. It must be reported to Bow Street as soon as possible."

"Not yet," he parried.

"Will you tell me who it was at least?" she asked with curiosity—*genuine* curiosity—lending a sparkle to her eyes.

"Have you no idea at all?" he asked in a playful manner.

"None in the least. Of course, I saw Bessler drop his glass, but we know it wasn't he. Ac-tually I was wondering if you did not suspect Bidwell, since Pronto was staring so hard at him. On your orders, I assume."

"Assumptions are dangerous things, I can tell you. I've made a few erroneous ones in my time."

"Oh, don't be so provoking, Belami!" she said sharply. "I'm as closely involved in this business as you are."

Her curiosity was certainly genuine. Belami was bereft of a new clue, and to enlarge his store of knowledge, he decided to bargain with her. "All right, I'll tell you, but we shall require privacy for the telling."

"Where?" she asked.

"Music room?" he suggested, picking an isolated spot.

"Very well, but first I must ask Herr Bessler to go up to Aunt Charney. She knows she'll have trouble sleeping, and wants him to waft her off to dreamland."

"That boring a conversationalist, is he?"

"Oh, no, that isn't his trick. Mesmerism—you recall we spoke of it."

"Does he actually put her to sleep?" he asked, interested in any novel nonsense, particularly of a scientific nature.

"Indeed he does. She makes sure she has on her nightgown before he does it. He usually mesmerizes her after she is in bed. Her woman sits with them, of course, for propriety's sake." A slow smile crept across Belami's face at the unlikely picture of the duchess indulging in the slightest impropriety.

"Of course," he agreed, his lips unsteady.

"He began it when he was a doctor, and it didn't seem improper," she pointed out, misunderstanding that smile.

"How very interesting."

"Yes, she didn't have him do it for ages after the College of Physicians revoked his license, because she didn't want to have a man who was not a doctor in her bedroom. Bessler said he could probably put her into a trance that would enable her to go to bed and undress herself after he left, but she didn't have him do it. Aunt Charney wouldn't want to be under anyone's control. There is Bessler now. I'll ask him to go up to her before we leave, if you'll excuse me."

Wild imaginings were flitting through Belami's ingenious mind. New rays of light were shining on the many-faceted problem that confronted him. Bessler was beyond his hearing, but he saw him nod his head as Deirdre spoke, then he turned and left the room, and Belami went with Deirdre to the music room.

He took along a branch of tapers from the hall and closed the door behind him before setting the candelabra on the piano. "Have a seat," he offered, nodding to the piano bench. She sat down on the edge of it, and Belami leaned toward her, resting one arm on the piano. Shadows hovered close by, as the two sat bathed in a puddle of light from the candles.

"Well, tell me all about it," she urged.

"I'll strike a bargain with you," he parried. "You tell me what you were doing on the roof last night, and I'll tell you the tale of the diamond. You were there, weren't you, Deirdre?"

"How did you know—what makes you think that?" she asked, hastily amending her question, but she knew she had not fooled him.

He reached out and stroked her hair. "Thank you for wearing it loose, as I asked. It looks lovely."

It occurred to her to say Bidwell liked it, but with the thief about to be announced, quite possibly Bidwell, she held her tongue.

"You didn't wear it loose for the ball," Belami continued, "But a few hairs came off on the coat collar all the same. Your gown was also damp along the bottom when I first arrived. Why were you there?"

She was very much averse to lying, but more averse

118

to revealing the truth. "Yes, I was there. It was hot and noisy belowstairs. I suddenly wanted to feel the fresh, cold air. I knew I couldn't walk out the front door, so I decided to go up and have a look out on the roof. I had seen it earlier, and the window leading to it, when I went to the attic with your mama to retrieve a large tin pot she wished to use for making ices."

"You could have opened the French doors in the library," he mentioned.

"Well, I didn't. I went up to the attic. I wanted to be close to the stars," she added with a face that challenged him to deny this unlikely claim.

"There were no stars out last night."

"I didn't know that till I got there. I couldn't see the sky from the ballroom," she said, becoming irritated. "I often skip away from a ball for a few dances, to a conservatory, or . . ."

"I remember," he said softly, smiling at her. "Why did you tread so dangerously close to the edge of the roof? Did you think to discover stars hiding below?"

"Of course not. I just went for a little stroll while I was out."

"That doesn't sound like sensible Deirdre Gower, but I suppose I must accept it. Now comes the more difficult question for you. Why did you bother hiding it from me this afternoon, as it is so innocent?"

She racked her brain for any excuse, however foolish, and said, "You were having so much fun playing at Bow Street that I decided to confuse you. Just dragging a red herring across the trail, to confuse the scent."

"That's a lamentable excuse. You were working with me, not against me. You were alone?"

"All alone, just me and the snow. Now it's time for your catechism, milord. Where did you find the diamond, and who took it?"

"I didn't find it, and I don't know who took it," he answered simply.

"You don't know! Belami, you cheat! After I confessed going up to the roof to look for you. To see if you were coming, I mean," she added quickly. "Naturally, while I was there I took a look down the road. Your mama was very much afraid you had had an accident, you know. She fretted about it all day long."

"That contingency did not occur to you, I take it."

"Certainly not. I'm not that foolish. And never mind talking about *me*. You mean to tell you don't have the diamond?"

"I haven't seen hide nor hair of it. It was all a hoax. I hoped the culprit might give himself away. He should, by rights, have been extremely worried. We're pretty sure it isn't hidden in the house. We've looked everywhere."

"You haven't searched your guests," she reminded him.

"It's too gothic. I haven't the gall to do it. I can't ask the likes of Cottrell to strip, and to pick out the select few suspects—well, it's hardly the thing, is it? I believe I'd sooner pay the money than do it. If the thief had it on him, though, he would have let a hand fly to his pocket to check, and thus give away its whereabouts. Someone ought to have been a little concerned at least. No one was. Your aunt wasn't any too pleased either," he added frowning.

"No, she thought she had you snug in her pocket with the loss of the diamond to keep you in line. Well, what a take-in this is. The great Belami, investigator extraordinaire, has no more idea than the rest of us who took it. I believe I must get busy and find it myself. Are you going to go on with the ruse of having found it?"

He shrugged his elegant shoulders. "For the time being, I shall. Confusion is good for criminals."

"A pity it's not the criminals who are confused, instead of you."

"It is a result of people telling me lies. Perfectly unexceptionable ladies, whose characters ought to be able to be depended on," he told her with a bold stare.

"I've told you everything now."

"There's one matter that still intrigues me. How did

you talk Charney into canceling the announcement of our betrothal?" he asked with an air of indifference.

"I pleaded on bended knee that she not condemn me to a life of waiting on rooftops for my husband to return."

"I suppose the truth of the matter is you have some other fellow in your eye," he suggested. "I'm not talking about Bidwell. Who is he?"

"Since everyone is telling me how madly I am in love with Bidwell, I have begun to discover qualities in him."

"Which qualities are those you refer to? Stupidity, foolishness, vanity . . ."

"Hush, I may marry him after all," she said with a smile that told him she was not serious.

"Are you prepared to do battle with the brewer's daughter he is currently courting?"

"If I decide he's worth it, I shall."

"Now that surprises me, Deirdre. I should have thought you much too proud to fight for a man you loved."

"Oh, no, not for one I *loved*," she answered sweetly. Then she lifted her fan, gave it a shake below her eyes, and turned to undulate from the room, perfectly aware that his black eyes were following her. She was aware too that there was an inference that she had not bothered to fight for Belami. And she hadn't. She was unsure whether she loved or hated him at that moment, but she had loved him at first, and she hadn't gone an inch out of her way to lure him when he didn't call on her. She had sat home for two weeks, pretending she had a cold, so she wouldn't have the ignominy of watching him flirt with other girls. If she had been wise, she would have gone out herself and flirted her head off with other men. How could you win the love of a man who never saw you? At the doorway, she turned around, smiled like Lenore, and dropped a graceful curtsy.

She had the unexpected joy of hearing his footfalls

hurry after her. "Deirdre, wait!" he said, and she stopped just outside the door.

His eyes, when he joined her, were kindled with a new, brighter light. They flickered quickly over her hair and face, with frequent darts to her lips—almost as though he were seeing her for the first time.

"Yes, what is it, Dickie?" she asked nonchalantly, using his Christian name for the first time, though she occasionally called him that in her private thoughts. Lenore often called him it as well.

"Dickie, what a stupid name! Call me Richard, if you want to please me."

"But I don't, particularly. Especially not after your wicked trick in letting on you'd found the diamond, Dickie." She tapped his arm with her fan as she said this, and smiled flirtatiously.

She watched, bemused, as he moistened his lips, his eyes kindling still brighter. Why, there was nothing to this flirting business. It worked like a very charm, too.

"Well, what is it?" she asked, feigning impatience.

He placed his hand on her arm and began walking down the hall toward the front of the house. "I am greatly intrigued by this business of Bessler treating your aunt. Have you seen him do it?" he asked.

She was aware of a stab of disappointment. Her answer was stiff, very much in her old mode. "*Ac*-tually, I haven't. My aunt's companion usually attends them. You can speak to her if you want to learn how it is done without quizzing Auntie."

"He was going to give her a treatment this evening, was he not?"

"Yes. It doesn't take long. He says Auntie is an excellent subject."

"Let us go up and see if he's finished," Belami urged.

"She wouldn't like our going to watch," she demurred.

"I meant to watch from the next room, through the keyhole," he admitted shamelessly.

"Belami! How horrid!"

122

"Isn't it though? I'm really a wretched fellow when you come down to it. You're sure we're too late?"

"Positive."

"Pity, let us return to the saloon, then,"

"Very well."

"Or better, come with me to my laboratory. I don't believe you've ever had a tour of it. It's fascinating. An intelligent woman like you will be interested to see what experiments I carry on there."

"I'd like to see it," she agreed, flattered at his unwonted attentions.

"It's upstairs, just beside my bedroom."

"Oh, I can't go there, Belami."

"You can call me Dickie. I'll lock the bedroom door, if it will make you feel more secure."

"And leave the door to the hallway open," she added carefully.

He sighed. "Would you like to find a chaperone, to ensure that I don't ravage you among the test tubes and scales? I don't know why you women always have your minds on lovemaking," he added, to annoy her.

"*You're* the one."

"I?" he asked, his brows lifting to his hairline. "*I* invited you to view my laboratory, madam. If you're only interested in flirtation, I suggest you remain belowstairs with Bidwell."

"I am not interested in Bidwell," she said, exasperated at his sophistry.

"Good, then come on up to my laboratory and flirt with me instead. I do it much better."

With a conning laugh, he turned to the stairs and they mounted together, the lady feeling almost sinful and Belami enjoying seeing the composed Miss Gower in an unnatural state of confusion. She hadn't said *actually* for two minutes. If she said it again, he'd tease her out of the annoying habit.

As if reading his mind, she said, "*Ac*-tually, I am very much interested in science."

"Good. Excellent. *Ac*-tually, I have a rather fine

123

setup. It's been a hobby of mine since I left Cambridge, where I read Science. I have in mind to perform a little experiment based on the work of a certain Friedrich Mohs, a German mineralogist, who worked out a table to determine the hardness of various materials a few years ago. Brilliant chap. *Ac*-tually, Miss Gower, I would be interested to test your hardness, but unfortunately Mohs' scale only applies to minerals. You wouldn't happen to be made of alabaster marble, by any chance?"

"No, of human clay, like everyone else. What is it you mean to test?"

"One of your fine diamond earrings *ac*-tually, if you will permit, and another substance I have got there."

"*Ac*-tually," she added with a laughing peep at him from the corner of her eye. "I know I say it too much. It's an irritating habit. Thank you for pointing it out to me."

He stopped and frowned down at her. "Are you trying to make me feel like two pennies, being so nice about my boorish behavior?" he asked.

"No, like one, actually."

"Do you know, till this moment I never suspected you had a sense of humor," he said in a complimentary tone as he resumed the climb.

"Now you *are* being nasty," she objected. "No sense of humor indeed, when I agreed to marry *you*. I'm sure society will find it a famous joke when you're jilted. Not that anyone outside of this party would have any cause to suspect we were ever engaged. You didn't exactly live in my pocket all month."

"I heard a rumor around town you were ill," he mentioned vaguely.

"Yes, I died, in fact, of boredom. Did the rumor not get about?"

"Not a whisper. You should not have dwelt on the tedium of a future with me. I expect that was the cause. *Were* you ill?" he asked at the end, with a guilty start.

"Do you care?" she countered.

"Of course I do!"

"Good, then there's another case for you to solve when you finish this one."

"I have a much more interesting one. Sorry. I'll bite my tongue."

"Another case? But how did you hear of it?"

"Chamfreys mentioned something about a case of blackmail in high places."

"Which high place?" she asked with interest.

"The highest."

"Mount Himalaya? What mischief can the sheep be getting into up there? Ah, you mean . . . Carlton House, or the palace?"

"I should not speak of it, but offhand, which would you consider the more likely?" he asked with a wink.

"Prinney, of course."

"There, you're deducing already. Nothing to it."

He opened the door of the laboratory and lit the lamps, while Deirdre felt uncurling in her breast an unpleasant emotion that she soon deduced to be envy. How exciting, to be investigating a case at Carlton House! And she would be dying of boredom again at Belvedere Square with her aunt.

Once the lights were lit, Belami went, with great ceremony, and opened wide the door adjoining his bedroom, then closed it and locked it. "You may hold the key," he told her, offering it to her.

She shook her head, indicating that this was unnecessary. She looked about the room at tables, two desks, and a few chairs. On the tables rested an assortment of scientific equipment. There was a microscope, surrounded by various small glass dishes, slides, and jars. Shelves above the table held bottles of various chemicals. A kerosene burner was set up on a stand to allow him to heat his materials, if the experiment called for it. Books were strewn all around, some open, some marked with sheets of paper.

"The work I want to do is over here," he said, pointing to a different table. On it rested a wooden tablet with some slabs of what looked like stones of various colors set into the wood.

"Mohs' Scale," he said. "The first material is talc—the softest of the lot. The last is diamond, the hardest. Those between are arranged in order of hardness. When I find a piece of material and want to determine what it is, I try to scratch these tablets with it. This, for instance," he said, picking up a jagged stone, "is quartz. Number seven on Mohs' Scale, you see. It will scratch feldspar, number six, but not topaz, number eight. In fact, the scratch you see here on the quartz stone was made by Mama's topaz ring. Now, may I have one of your earrings, please?"

She reached to unfasten it, but Belami bent forward and did it for her. She felt her blood quicken as his fingers brushed her cheek. With his attention on unfastening the earring, she was free to look at him, the clean cut of his jaw, the haughty sweep of his nose, the long lashes. She regretted her caution in keeping the hallway door ajar. She resented too that he proceeded directly to business.

He drew out from a drawer two blue papers, containing the remnants of broken glass collected from Lady Lenore's grate. Lifting one largish piece of the glass, he applied it to the talc tablet, which it scratched easily, but it made no mark on the topaz.

"Lead crystal varies in hardness. This piece is about six, I think. Now for a sliver large enough to hold from the glass Bidwell ground up with his heel. Here's one," he said, extracting it with some difficulty. It performed as the other piece had, scratching the low numbers on Mohs' Scale, but not the topaz. Then he took her earring, and with it, scratched the sliver, managing to draw a few drops of blood from his finger in the process.

"What have you proven?" she asked.

"That I am but flesh and blood," he told her.

"Had you reason to doubt it?"

"Yes, sometimes I think I'm an invention of my own imagination, like the theory I just disproved."

"What theory was that?" she asked with interest.

"That only one glass was smashed in the grate on New Year's Eve. I thought the second object was something else. The quantity wasn't right, you see. I weighed the two piles of debris, and I weighed the glass I broke in my room. The powdered stuff is much lighter, I have a very accurate scale. It would even weigh, say, a small lock of your hair, or a piece of paper. What must have happened is that some piece of the glass flew off into the room, and we didn't pick it up. Definitely the thing is lead crystal," he added with a frown of concentration between his brows.

"Is it possible Bidwell ground just a piece of the one glass he broke?" she asked.

"No, I tried that. The broken glass plus the powder weighs too much. He stepped on something, twisted it into the stone hearth with his heel, possibly to conceal its original shape."

"What do you think it was?"

"I *did* think it was your aunt's diamond. Don't laugh. It was only a theory, and diamonds *do* crush up fairly easily. It helps to follow Wordsworth's advice with regard to fiction, when working on a case. Suspend your disbelief, let the imagination soar, and see what possibilities take flight." As he spoke, he flung his splayed hands in the air. "We have assumed, for instance, that our suspects are both sane. Just suppose one of them is mad. That he went to the trouble of stealing the diamond for the sole purpose of destroying it. Bidwell *could* conceivably have done it in spite, to cost his uncle Carswell anguish. We don't know he is Carwell's heir. We only think so, but can't prove it here, isolated in the country."

"After you suspend your disbelief, you begin to recapture it, to bring the mad theory to earth and attach it to facts," she said, smiling at him.

"Oh, yes, it isn't just an intellectual exercise."

"But Bidwell knew the stone wasn't insured."

"He says he knew. I have no trouble suspending my

disbelief that he's lying. However, my disbelief balks at accepting that the diamond changed to lead crystal after he broke it, so that supposition is ruled out."

"Do you have any other suppositions?" she asked.

"Well, the diamond might have been paste, but your aunt tells me duchesses do not wear paste, and there was no copy. Dare we suspend our disbelief on that point?"

"I know she fiddles the cards a little, but there was never any copy that I knew of. And why should she perpetrate such a cruel hoax on you, Belami? She likes you."

"That's the wildest theory I've heard yet!" he laughed. "I don't suppose she would tell you if she had a copy made. And the fact of discontinuing the insurance . . . If they wanted to reexamine the stone, for instance, and it had magically turned to paste—you can see why she'd have to discontinue it."

"They wouldn't reexamine it if she'd just renewed the policy. It's been insured for years, but only examined when she first took out the policy."

"What other nonsense can we consider?" he asked, rubbing his chin.

"I wish I could think the whole thing had never happened."

"I wish I had been here when it did happen. In fact, I wish I had been here three days sooner, " he added. "Unconscionable behavior on my part. I don't believe I ever properly apologized. I *am* sorry, Deirdre."

"I don't blame you. I knew you never wanted to marry me. Why did you offer, Dick?"

"Because you looked beautiful in the moonlight, and I was overcome with a whim to kiss you. Great oafs from little acorns grow. Your aunt saw us—I don't know whether she ever told you so. She had me on the carpet; I implied my intentions were honorable. She gave me permission to marry you, and that was that. You could have knocked me over with a feather when you accepted. I thought you would scotch the plan. I was angry with you and decided to make it impossible for you to go through with it. My overweening pride whispered your supposed illness was a ruse to bring me to heel. A gentleman cannot call off, but if he is selfish and brutish, he can force a lady to do so. I am quite ready to go through with the wedding, if you wish."

"I don't want just a wedding, Belami. I want a marriage and a husband who comes home nights," she told him sadly. She didn't add that she wanted him to be that husband. She was new at suspending her disbelief.

"Naturally I meant marriage, and all that implies," he added stiffly.

"Yes, but it implies different things to me than it does to you. I got Auntie to postpone the announcement, and if you are only a little patient, I shall talk her into forgetting all about your unwise offer and my foolish acceptance."

"And it was only to escape Twombley that you accepted?" he asked, regarding her closely.

He had been taken advantage of once; she wouldn't do it again. "Yes, that's the only reason," she said in a dull voice.

"Most couples have a period of courting before they make up their minds," he said. "Why don't you allow me to court you, and see what happens? Who knows? We may suit better than either of us thinks"

"Why not? We're snowed in for the time being. We must see each other. *You* must have a flirt by all means, and I . . ."

He looked expectantly, curious to hear what she had to say of herself. " Do go on. You were just reaching the more interesting part."

"Well then, I shall. *I* have taken a New Year's resolution. I have resolved to enjoy myself, like other women. Like Lady Lenore."

"Not quite so much as Lenore, I hope!"

"You know what I mean," she said.

"I think I do. If your performance before dinner is an

example of how far you mean to go, I approve. Providing it is I you bludgeon with your fan, and not Bidwell."

They returned belowstairs in harmony. Deirdre was happier with their relationship than she had ever been. She had no real hope of reforming Belami, but who knew? Nearly impossible things could happen. They had already happened to her. Belami had apologized, and he had sounded sincere. She had forgiven him for his inattention, and that too seemed extremely unlikely twenty-four hours ago. She even felt comfortable enough to ask a question that had been puzzling her.

"Now that you know I saw you arrive from my perch on the roof, perhaps you'll answer me a question. What took you such an uncommonly long time to make a very careless toilette?" she asked.

"My conscience," he answered simply. "I dressed in less than a minute, and sat perched on the end of my bed, debating with myself how I should behave when I joined the party."

"Whether you should beg off, you mean?" she asked frankly.

"Yes."

"What did you decide?"

"I flipped a coin eventually, and Fate decided we were meant for each other," he answered. "You soon disabused me of the idea, but there's no arguing with Fate, you know," he told her with an intimate, devastating smile.

Chapter 11

✳✳✳

When Bessler returned to the saloon after wafting the duchess off to dreamland, Belami was at pains to engage him in converstion. Belami sat with Deirdre, looking at a new scientific journal that had recently arrived and explaining to her the principles behind the hot air balloon which he planned to have constructed. He thought it might be fun to make it himself. He was amazed that a lady would sit still for his highly scientific discourse on the molecular weights of various gases.

"Hydrogen is always used, as its weight is lightest, but it is highly flammable, of course. Helium is what I should like to try, but it is more difficult to come by, and expensive."

"Where would you get it?" she asked.

He didn't reply. His sharp eyes had spotted Bessler returning to the saloon. "Shall we ask Herr Bessler to join us?" he asked. This struck Deirdre as a disappointing notion, but she was too eager to foster the fragile friendship between Dick and herself to object.

"A glass of brandy, sir?" Belami offered, arising to accost Bessler as he passed their sofa.

"Very kind of you, Belami. I shall accept. Your aunt is in the land of nod," he told Deirdre with a smile.

Belami poured Bessler a tumbler of brandy and made room for him on the sofa. "Miss Gower and I have just been discussing hot air balloons, Doctor," Belami said, sliding in the "Doctor" to please the old man and disarm him. "As a scientific gentleman, perhaps you have some ideas on what gas other than hydrogen would be suitable."

"I haven't looked into the matter, to tell the truth," Bessler replied.

"Of course, your own field is not physics, but medicine," Belami said, willing to switch to what he really wanted to discuss in the first place. "I understand you worked with Mesmer in Austria."

"No, sir, in Paris. Animal magnetism; it is a pity the world has taken it in derision. He was a great man, Mesmer. He passed away a few years ago. I am carrying on with his work in a small way."

"Could you explain to me a little how it works?" Belami asked very courteously. "I take a keen interest in all medical matters. Truth to tell, I should have liked to be a doctor myself."

"It has been an interesting career," Bessler allowed. "Mesmer's theory—well, he proved it. It is more than a theory, whatever they say. He believed that the stars affect the human body by means of vapors, invisible vapors. What do we know of the human body, after all? Do we know what drives the pump of the heart, or what bellows make our lungs exhale and inhale breath? Invisible, it is all invisible. Your microscope will not reveal nature's secrets to you, my friend. These magical vapors are exuded through the body's skin, into the fingers. I have seeen Mesmer, by the simple placing of his hands on hysterical patients, reduce them to placidity. I have some of that same power myself, if I am not immodest to say so. Miss Gower will vouch for the therapeutic value of my work with her aunt. She suffers from the most wretched migraines, poor lady."

"I have that ailment myself," Belami said at once, all interest and sympathy. "How exactly do you go about easing her pain, Doctor? I should like to give it a try."

"It would be impossible to treat yourself. The vapors' magnetic powers would be all jumbled up if the ailing body tried to heal itself. You must have someone else do it. I place my hands on her forehead and her temples, just so," he went on, giving Belami a demonstration. He placed the pads of his thumbs on Belami's temples and pulled his fingers across his forehead, using considerable but not painful force. He repeated the strokes in a rhythmical way five or six times.

"You begin to feel the calming influence?" Bessler asked. "You feel the little electrical charges all line themselves up like soldiers, parading out from the middle of your head to the temples and marching down my thumbs? I can feel the tingling in my own thumbs as they march off, left, right, left, right. Away they go, leaving blessed peace."

Belami was amazed to realize that he felt remarkably relaxed. The doctor's voice was low pitched, slow, his fingers indeed possessed of some near-miraculous power. Another two minutes, and he felt he could have slipped into slumber himself.

Bessler stopped and sat back, looking at him through his monocle. "You see? It is not a fraud, animal magnetism, whatever the non-believers may choose to say."

"It's amazing! I never felt anything like it. It's got laudanum beat all hollow," Belami exclaimed, shaking himself back to alertness. "And what other magic can this animal magnetism perform, Doctor?"

"Do not use the word *magic,* if you please. That was the tool used to discredit poor Mesmer, that he dealt in magic. It is human nature, that's all."

"It would be a marvelous tool for relieving the

chronic pain of, say, gout. But then, of course, the patient would be asleep and couldn't perform his normal functions. It wouldn't be possible to move your limbs, when in such a deep sleep as animal magnetism would induce. As you said, it's not magic," Belami said.

"No, it's not magic, but there are more things in this world than men have dreamed of. Of course a person could not go through life in a deep sleep. What would be the point of living, unaware of what went on? But that is not to say the limbs are actually incapable of moving when under the induced sleep."

"I find that hard to swallow," Belami said in a doubtful way. "Have you ever performed this miracle?"

"I do not have Mesmer's incredible power. I have never achieved that, but then it is only a stunt. I can ease the pain of migraine or other chronic pain without putting my patient to sleep. And I can put my patients to sleep too, if that is what they wish. That's miracle enough for me."

"It's marvelous," Belami said simply, allowing an expression of awe to invade his features. Looking at him, Deirdre feared he was doing it too strong, but Bessler did not perceive it.

"Yes, I am a good doctor," Bessler admitted. "It was jealousy that caused the College of Physicians to move against me. Jealousy and the greed of the chemists. Who would buy their laudanum and hartshorn if all doctors were curing with their hands? Ha, no one, that's who."

"It's a disgrace," Belami declared. "Tell me where you keep shop in London, and I'll send a dozen patients to you."

"I am not permitted to hang a shingle. I have rooms on Glasshouse Street, just at the corner by Great Windmill. A brown brick apartment house, the upper story, but I doubt that your great friends would be willing to travel out of their way."

"Nonsense. *I'd* be happy to do it when one of my curst

migraines comes on, and so would any of my friends. I'll be sure to recommend you."

"That is obliging of you, sir. If you could put in a word with the College of Physicians to get my license back, it would be even better."

"I'll mention it to Halford," Belami said.

Bidwell chose that moment to join them. "The doctor has just been giving us a lesson in animal magnetism," Belami said, looking with apparent disinterest to Bidwell. "Why don't you join us, Bidwell?"

"Animal magnetism? What the deuce is that?" Bidwell asked.

"Mesmer's theory," Bessler replied, ready to go into it again.

"It sounds fascinating. What do you do, Bessler? Rub two cats together and see if they can't be pulled apart?" He gave a sardonic laugh and changed the subject. "Lady Belami has suggested a few tables of cards. We need another player. Can I recruit anyone here? You, Herr Bessler?"

"I would be happy to oblige Lady Belami. Thank you for the brandy, milord."

"You're entirely welcome. Thank you for the lesson, Doctor."

The old man arose and went off tho the card parlor with Bidwell.

"You laid the enthusiasm on a bit thick," Deirdre told him.

"Devil a bit of it. As another doctor, Johnson to be exact, said, a man with a bit of unusual knowledge is like a lady with a new petticoat. He's not happy till he's had an opportunity to display it. Did you not tell me Bessler offered to put your aunt to sleep in her saloon and send her to her bed afterward in some sort of a trance?"

"Yes, when his license was revoked he offered. He never actually did it."

"Hmm, but he told her he could do it, and he told *me* he couldn't do it. There's more to this mesmerism than I thought. I could have gone to sleep in two seconds, if I'd let myself."

"You have to cooperate. He insists it is a mutual job, not one working against the other," Deirdre told him.

Belami sat silent and pensive a moment, then spoke. "I once saw a man eat a fly," he said.

"Really! How revolting! Why did he do that?"

"He didn't know he was doing it. It was at a tent at Bartholomew Fair. An Indian fellow put three of the audience into a trance and told them to do ridiculous things. One man ate a fly; another took off his jacket and put it on backwards. The third danced a jig. The Indian chose a fat, dignified old gent for that. I thought at the time that they were his helpers, pretending to be members of the audience, but I later heard the fat man's wife give him a rare Bear Garden jaw for making such a cake of himself. I doubt that the Indian ever heard of Mesmer, but he was practicing a similar sort of magic. He didn't use his hands at all, just his eyes. He stared into his victims' eyes and sent them into a deep sleep, during which they did exactly as he directed. Afterward, they had no memory of it. It's a strange world, isn't it?"

"Very strange," she agreed. "Do you actually plan to visit him in London?"

"What for? I've never had a migraine in my life. I've *given* more than my share of them."

"But you'll send your friends to him?"

"I wouldn't let him treat my dog, let alone my friends. Did you notice that Bidwell made a point of interrupting us when we fell into a longish talk with Bessler?"

"Yes, I noticed. I also noticed you made a point of getting Bessler's address. Why bother, if you don't plan to use it?"

"I like to amass all the facts I can. I have a strong intuition this particular fact may prove vital."

"Dick, you're *deducing*! Please tell me what it is."

"No, I could be wrong again, and you already know

me for a jackass. Why confirm it? We were discussing Bidwell's running to carry off Bessler when I was quizzing the old boy."

"Do you suppose Bertie is in on it? It was she who sent Bidwell to round up another player."

He looked around the room. "There are several groups of people he might have approached. I doubt that Mama suggested he get Bessler. And she knows I don't like cards above half. Not for the chicken stakes we play for here."

"Have you considered *I* might have been the object of his solicitation?" she suggested with a sly smile. "He is at the same table himself. Is that too far beyond credulity to consider?"

"Digging for compliments, Deirdre? What a slow top I am, to make such digging and delving necessary. He *did* put the question directly to Bessler, however. A good way to keep an eye on him and to keep the conversation off such topics as mesmerism."

"You're obsessed with it. The only person Bessler could have mesmerized is Aunt Charney, and she is not the thief. She was perfectly wide awake and aware she was robbed. Unless he mesmerized Bidwell into doing it. Is that what you think?" she asked, feeling clever at this new idea.

"It hadn't occurred to me, to tell the truth. No, that's not what I've been thinking at all. But I *do* think Bidwell has more idea of animal magnetism than to suggest rubbing two cats together."

"You think Bidwell knows how to perform these trance things? That he went to Bartholomew Fair and talked to the Indian?"

"Good God, I thought *my* theories were bizarre till I heard yours. Still, there could be something in it," he added thoughtfully.

She observed the planes of his face, quiet now in contemplation, with only the eyes revealing the activity below the skull, while his fingers beat a tattoo on his knees. In a moment that mobile brow would lift, lending a satirical edge to his expression. She admired his visage in all its guises. "You really enjoy this, don't you?" she asked.

"Very much. It's like a breath of fresh air, to have something intriguing to puzzle over. I'm like a dog with a bone, unable to let it go. It's good for the brain, keeping it active. It's like armed combat in a way, pitting yourself against another man, only doing it mentally. The mind is really man's better half. What difference what manner of flesh carries it? I would be happy to have Voltaire's unlovely body, if only I could have his mind to go with it."

"I never thought you would be interested in—in objective, purely intellectual matters like this."

"This time it's not purely objective. I take a subjective interest, as the crime was executed at my own house. I see it as a challenge, as though I'd been slapped in the face, but I do like the disinterested challenge nearly as well."

"Your laboratory too, and your scientific work—I didn't know you were keen on science."

"What did you think interested me, other than horses and women?" he asked, and looked with interest to hear her answer.

"Jackets, haircuts, waistcoats."

"You mistook me for a *dandy*?" he asked, staring. "You might at least have said Corinthian."

"Oh, no, not a dandy. I knew your greater interest was in women," she told him, lifting her fan.

"It used to be," he answered lazily. "I am restricting myself now."

"To solving crimes?"

"No, to one woman was my meaning, *ac*-tually," he answered with an intimate smile. He reached out for the fan and took it from her. Leaning forward, he unfurled it to its full size, placed it to shield their profiles from the rest of the room, and placed one quick, electrifying kiss on her lips. Then he folded the fan and returned it.

"We wouldn't want to expose the company to the rare spectacle of Belami making a jackass of himself," he explained, resuming his former position.

"Rare spectacle?" she asked with an impish smile. "I hear these spectacles occur with monotonous regularity."

"I am deeply offended . . . that you choose to use the word *monotonous*," he parried.

She silently agreed it was the wrong word. Monotony did not cause so delicious a churning inside.

Chapter 12

✻✻✻

The morning dawned bright and crisp and very cold. Long wisps of tattered clouds hung in the azure sky, reminding Belami of Switzerland, and Deirdre of Mechlin lace. They both arose early, though not by prearrangement, and met in the breakfast parlor. The only other person there was Pronto, who was plodding his way through a large plate of Irish potatoes, laced with eggs, and a stack of gammon.

"That looks good. I'll have the same," Belami said to the servant.

"Just toast and coffee for me," Deirdre added.

"No, you must take more than that," Belami told her. "You are going to have an active morning. Take something to sustain yourself. Eggs and gammon for Miss Gower."

"And toast," she said, planning to eat only what she had asked for herself. "What activity have you got planned, Belami?" she asked. With Pronto present, she was reluctant to call him Dick.

Belami gave her a piercing glance at this reversion to the more formal name. It softened to a smile as he observed that shyness was the cause.

"I have a marvelous groom," was his oblique answer. "He has a way with snow. He has plowed off the pond for us to skate. He also has some snowshoes he's going to allow us to try. Great, unwieldy things that look like battledore racquets. In fact, one of us must use make-shift shoes that are battledore racquets. The youngsters of our party—we and perhaps Bidwell—shall spend a healthy day in the great outdoors."

"Hate snow," Pronto told him. "Ain't going to spend no day out freezing my toes off. Neither will Bidwell, I can tell you. Foolishness. Don't do it, Deirdre."

"Pay no heed to the slug," Belami remarked. "Pronto prefers to hibernate like a bear at the first flake of snow."

"Something to be said for it," Pronto replied.

"What about the necklace? Are you abandoning the search for it?" she asked, surprised.

"Not at all. There's nothing more I can do till after dinner."

While they talked, Deirdre forgot her intention of fasting and ate up the whole breakfast, and still no one else had come down.

After breakfast, Belami and Deirdre bundled up in warm coats and boots and went to the stable, where Pierre Réal was busy polishing the curricle.

"How are we to return to London?" was his greeting to his employer. "A foot of snow, an open carriage. I *told* him 'the closed carriage,' " he added, turning to Deirdre with accents of abuse. "But he—"

"*Tais-toi*," his master ordered. "Where are the snowshoes, Pierre?"

"I'll get them."

"You did as I asked last night?"

"*Certainement.* I strolled over to Boltons' and spoke with *monsieur.*"

"Boltons'! Dick, that's quite far away," Deirdre exclaimed.

"*Non,* ten miles, and in this balmy weather, the little walk is good for a man," Réal said casually. "Everything, she is all set," he added aside to Belami.

The snowshoes and battledore racquets were brought forth. The groom first lashed the snowshoes to his own boots and strolled into the yard to instruct them in the proper placement of the feet for this mode of ambulation.

"Well apart, you see," he said severely, straddling his legs and shuffling at a rapid gait. "Don't try to lift the shoes. Slide them softly forward, one at a time. By lifting the feet, you sink into the snow. If you could call this little dusting a snow," he added, to mitigate the impression that *he* considered twelve inches anything to be reckoned with. "This is not transportation for a lady," he added with another injured glance at his employer.

Turning to Deirdre, he continued his complaints. "I tell him so this morning, when he comes to see me. The skirt, she will impede the progress. It will be best to walk behind the stables away from the wind, for you *anglais.*"

"What do you say, *anglaise,* shall we show him what stern stuff we're made of?" Belami asked her.

They struck out for the main road as soon as they were accoutered in the uncomfortable aids to walking in snow. Progress was slow and cumbersome at first, but after a few false starts, they got the rhythm of shuffling glide that gave the best progress with the least effort.

"You're not too cold?" Dick asked solicitously.

"I'm roasting to death. It's hard work," she said, breathing heavily.

"We shan't go too far. This is straining muscles I

didn't even know I had. Can you make it to the road, or will you wait here while I go on down?"

"I'll go with you."

They completed the trek to the main road, to see drifts of snow as high as their waists in some places, with as yet no effort to clear the track. Dick thought a mounted rider could get through and pointed out that at spots the road was blown clear completely, and even the drifting was toward the banks of the road. A carriage would have trouble, but his own Diablo, he insisted, could make it.

"I'd say we've got a few days before our suspects can run off on us in their carriages," he concluded.

"Is that why we came?" she asked.

"And here you thought I had taken the day off, didn't you?"

"Guilty as charged. You really are like a bulldog with this investigating business."

"I can be tenacious as a barnacle when I decide to do something. You'll see what I mean," he added with a flirtatious smile that told her he had ceased speaking of the case.

They plodded back to the stable, to see Bidwell in the doorway speaking to Réal. "He *is* eager to get away," Belami mentioned.

Gliding forward, he greeted Bidwell. "The road is still blocked," he said cheerfully. "Have you come to try the famous snowshoes, Bidwell?"

"Your groom has been extolling their virtue. He tells me he once walked forty miles in them, in the teeth of a wild storm too. Amazing."

"*Oui*, in Canada, where we get real snow. Many times I have had to tunnel out from my front door," Réal told them.

"I doubt you or I could go a tenth of that distance," Belami said, rubbing his cramped muscles. "Do you want to try them?" he repeated.

"I think not. It's chilly. I'm not dressed for this weather. I'll go back inside and have breakfast." He turned aside and spoke to Deirdre before leaving. "I expect your aunt is chirping merry this morning, with her diamond back in place."

"I haven't seen her this morning, but she was in alt last night," Deirdre replied.

Belami noted his sly smile and was on thorns to learn its cause. He noticed Bidwell's eagerness to discover a way out of Beaulac, but didn't think he'd tackle a forty-mile trek to London on snowshoe. Already he was shivering and darting back into the house.

Dick turned to his groom and said, "I want you to tramp down to the inn and disappear for a few days."

"What I am to do at the inn?" Pierre asked.

"Enjoy yourself. Play in the snow. Take your snow-shoes with you, if you like. They will provide and excellent introduction to the serving girls. Thanks for the loan of the shoes. I'll redesign them for you. A narrower and longer shoe would buoy the weight up as well, and not require such an ungainly gait. Some sort of cane or walking stick would be a help too."

"The shoe, he is perfect, made for me by an Indian guide from Montréal."

"Fine, then I'll design one for *me*, and race you." Réal gave him a withering look and strolled back into the stables, while Dick and Deirdre returned to the house to warm up and rest from their exertions.

This was done in his mother's dressing room, where Bertie sat with a pot of cocoa and plate of toast fingers. Deirdre noticed the elegant dressing gown her hostess wore, all embroidered in roses down the front. Her gray curls were carefully dressed in a basket style, and her cheeks, if Deirdre guessed right, were tinted with rouge. How different from her Aunt Charney, who was ascetic in her private moments, and whose habits Deirdre followed to a large extent. She sat imagining herself in such a fashionable outfit as Bertie wore. In her mind, Dick sat with her, taking cocoa, being every bit as gallant and loving to her as he was with his mama.

This too surprised her. She would not have thought him a man to admire and love his mother.

"Can we rob you of some of that cocoa, Mama?" he asked cheerfully after he had wished her a good morning, kissed her cheek noisily, and found a seat. "I'll ring for another pot and some cups," he added when he lifted the lid and discovered the pot to be empty. He stuck his head into the hallway and asked the upstairs maid to attend to it.

"Well, old girl, how are you bearing up under the strain of this damnable party?" was his next question.

Bertie gave a quick, guilty glance at Deirdre and said, "Really, Dickie, I don't think you should . . ."

"Deirdre is becoming accustomed to my plain speaking. She, of all people, must agree with us that it *is* a damnable, boring party. It isn't even possible to call in the neighbors, or hire decent musicians, or ride or hunt or anything."

"It is a pity it has fallen so flat," Bertie had to agree. "Snippe can fiddle better than you might think, and someone must be able to play the piano. All the young ladies hammer away at it nowadays till your head is throbbing. Couldn't we get up a dancing party at least?"

"I hammer a little," Deirdre confessed.

"You hammer divinely," Belami objected. To his mama's utter amazement, he reached out and grasped Deirdre's hand. She stared, unable to conceal her astonishment, but at least she got a rein on her tongue.

"I didn't mean you, Miss Gower. I'm sure you don't hammer in the least," she said. "Oh, dear, why can I never open my mouth without putting my foot in it?"

"A family failing," Belami told her. "Have you seen the duchess yet this morning?"

"No, she sleeps late, thank God. Oh, dear—I didn't mean that, Miss Gower. It is only that I am a late sleeper myself, and . . ."

"I understand," Deirdre said, unoffended. "I've often thanked God for my aunt's late sleeping myself, ma'am. What a charming room you have," she added, glancing around at the flower-covered walls, the dressing table with dainty crystal pots ranged over the top.

"Life is too short to be miserable. I try to make my house attractive. I don't know why any lady who doesn't *have* to decks herself out in gray gowns and . . . They suit the duchess admirably. I didn't mean *her!* Yours is lovely too, my dear. Such a pretty shade of dove gray. I've done it again. Terribly sorry, Dickie. I wished the demmed cocoa would come." After this hapless speech, Bertie drew a deep, resigned sigh and looked impatiently to the door.

"Eager to be rid of us, are you?" Dick asked unconcernedly.

"Not *you,* dear. Oh, and certainly not *you,* Miss Gower. That was not my meaning."

"She refers to all these other invisible guests, you see," Dick explained to Deirdre. "You and I are perfectly welcome." He turned to his mother and said, "Why don't you call Miss Gower Deirdre? It makes conversation easier."

"She didn't ask me to."

"Please do," Deirdre said at once. "Perhaps I ought to go, Dick."

"Stay," he told her, squeezing her fingers. "Bertie will soon get over her nervousness. Won't you, luv?"

"I'm sure I'm not nervous in the least," Bertie objected. "How silly. As though I should be nervous about a young chit. Oh, dear!" Her fingers flew to her lips.

"That's your other foot you should be sticking into your craw, Mama," Dick advised, smiling.

"I *really* didn't mean . . ." She looked helplessly at Deirdre.

"Of course you didn't mean *me,*" Deirdre said, trying to control her lips.

"Of course I did. There's no other young chit here," the hostess admitted frankly.

"Bertie would refuse a lifeline if she were drowning," Dick explained.

"Oh, you were trying to help me cover up my blunder. How kind of you," Bertie said, smiling at the girl. "I would not have expected it from you. I—"

"I confess my first reaction was to leave in a huff," Deirdre said blandly.

"How nice. I had no notion you could take a joke either, Deirdre. However did you learn to do it, living all these years with that vinegar—with the duchess?"

"Born with a silver foot in her mouth," Dick said with a rueful shake of his head.

"I shan't say another word this visit," Bertie said, and promptly ran on with another bushel of nonsense. "It is only that Dick rang such a terrific peal over my asking you, Miss Gower. I mean Deirdre. And naturally I have been a little nervous ever since, wondering how we were to get out of the engagement. But as the two of you have very obviously worked it out between you without becoming mortal foes, I can just relax and enjoy myself, as soon as you leave. Have you told Charney?" she asked Dick, giving up all pretense of politeness.

"There's nothing to tell," Dick said. "We haven't worked anything out. We're working on it, but nothing is definite yet."

"But are you engaged or not?" she demanded, more confused than ever. "Why are you holding hands if you're not engaged? And why are you smiling if they've truly nabbed you?"

"She has grown three feet," Deirdre said, shaking her head ruefully.

"What we have here is a sixty-year-old centipede," Dick replied.

"Fifty-four!" Bertie snapped. "It's bad enough, without your making it worse. And don't you *dare* tell a soul I am fifty-four, either. I haven't publicly reached fifty yet. I was so very ancient when you were born, Dick, that I can easily let on I am still in my forties. I wish that demmed cocoa would come."

"I'll run down to the kitchen and hurry the servants along," he offered.

"No, don't leave me alone with her. I'm sorry, Deirdre, but I don't know how to talk to clever girls. I never had the knack of it. I can get along very well with clever gentlemen, but you clever gals always want to talk about books and things that are too boring for words."

"Here's the cocoa now," Deirdre said. "Isn't that lucky? Now you won't have to be alone with me, ma'am. A pity, really. I was all set to bore you with my notions on Gibbons' great, thumping, dull books of history. It will have to wait for another time."

"The worst thing about history is that it just goes on and on," Bertie said, nodding her head. "You think you've learned all you have to know, and someone goes and writes up another volume. Now they're doing them on Wellington's campaigns. I wish history would stop."

"They should have a moratorium on it at least," Deirdre agreed. "Besides, I'm sure history is half lies."

Bertie narrowed her eyes at her guest, wondering if she had heard her correctly. "You speak very much like Dick," she said, staring. "Satirical. That's what you are being. How clever. I wish I could learn to do it."

"It's really very simple," Dick told her. "You just say the opposite from what you mean, as if you meant it."

"It wouldn't be very clever of me to say 'no cocoa for me' when I really want another cup. People—stupid people, I mean—might misunderstand, and I should be cheated of my cocoa. Fill me up, Dick. I'm not being satirical. I need another cup of cocoa."

Dick poured three cups and they sat around the table, sipping nervously. "There has to be more to it than that," Bertie decided, after deep thought. "More than saying the opposite from what you mean. You should write up an extract on the subject. It would be a great hit with all the stupid ladies like me who want to be smart."

"You don't have to be clever, Bertie. May I call you Bertie?" Deirdre asked daringly.

"You may as well, even if it does sound fast coming from a chit. Why don't I have to be clever?"

"Because you are charming, and that's much better than clever."

"Is she being satirical?" Bertie asked her son, who shook his head. "I don't know how you can say so. I'm a perfect widgeon. The duchess herself told me so, not that I didn't know it already."

They talked on, discussing the walk on snowshoes, the condition of the roads, and their intention of skating on the pond that afternoon. Bertie accidentally insulted both her guests a dozen times, and her guests were good-natured enough to take it for satire. When she finished her cocoa, Deirdre arose and said she would go to see if her aunt was up yet.

"Oh, you're leaving now. Good," Lady Belami said with great feeling. "If your aunt is sleeping, pray don't awaken her. Let her sleep as long as she likes. Longer."

Dick covered his mouth with his hand and looked out the window. "I'll see you downstairs shortly," he said to Deirdre.

"What a strange girl," Bertie said when they were alone. "What on earth is going on with you and her? Why did you bring her to visit *me*? I've never done you any harm, except to drop you once when you were a very infant. I didn't think you even remembered it. You were only three months old at the time. You should learn to let bygones be bygones, dear. It's not nice to hold a grudge."

"Then why don't you drop your grudge against Deirdre? She can't help it if her aunt is a Tartar."

"Very true. No one can do anything with Charney. Deirdre is more conversable than I had hoped. And she don't poker up as I feared she would at any little thing that slips out."

"I'd like us both to know her better."

"It's not necessary now. You have found the diamond. You can wiggle out of the engagement if you are very sly about it."

"I was never sly, Mama."

"Pooh. The slyest man in the parish, always up to anything."

"The girl has qualities," he said, in a ruminative mood.

"Being satirical would not wear well in marriage. It's good enough for a brief conversation, but as a steady diet, it would be extremely tiresome."

"That was not the quality I referred to, though I like it too. She's . . . different. You don't get to know her in a day, like most of 'em. Get used to her, Bertie. All it takes is a little familiarity."

"She has countenance, intelligence—all those things I lack. But a trifle *cold*, don't you think?"

"A bit, but there are ways of warming up a lady, if a man has any ingenuity at all. I shall keep you informed of my progress."

"Walking in the ice and snow is a poor way to warm the poor girl up. Freeze her to death is more like it."

"Cold hands, warm heart," he said unscientifically, and poured himself another cup of cocoa.

Chapter 13

✳✳✳

Lord Belami was behaving as a fiancé ought to behave, the old duchess decided with a grimace which she
supposed to be a smile. She doubted he would do so if he
had indeed found her diamond, which he had not yet
brought for her examination. Just what freakish start
that false announcement was about she had no clear
idea, nor did she care much. One way or the other, she
would get her thirty thousand pounds, but she suspected Deirdre would only get Belami if the diamond
remained lost. She must mingle with the guests of the
house and hear what was being said about all this. To
this end, she had herself outfitted in her best day gown,
a hideous puce outfit, chosen for its ability to conceal
the ravages of gravy and wine. Such a nice, practical
color, puce. Her thin hair was stuffed up under a matching turban, adorned with a single feather. The absence
of any jewels would be her oblique reminder to the hostess of what happened to a lady's jewels at Beaulac. She

might praise the courage of any dame who appeared more finely bedecked. That would set Bertie down a peg.

Deirdre was at considerable pains to appear pretty. After skating all afternoon with Dick and enjoying a greater degree of intimacy than hitherto, even in the duchess's conservatory, she needed no cosmetic aids to enliven her face. Her cheeks were pink from the outing, her eyes gleamed, and her hair was arranged as he liked it, in loose curls. An elegant toilette could not be constructed from nothing, but she had borrowed a set of ribbons from Lenore to enliven her plain white gown and, by shivering judiciously in front of Bertie, had achieved the loan of a lovely paisley shawl.

Dick was appreciative of her efforts. He greeted her warmly when she and the duchess entered the saloon before dinner. His praise was equally directed at them both, but she was coming to know him well enough to see the compliment was intended for her. It was Pronto who noticed her livelier style first.

"By jingo, Deirdre, you're looking all the crack tonight," he told her, his eyes roaming from coiffure to ribbons to sparkling eyes. 'You've brightened right up, hasn't she, Dick?"

"Ravishing, as usual," Dick agreed.

"Eh? What are you talking about?" Pronto asked angrily. "She ain't ravishing now, and she was even plainer before. 'All the crack' was what I said. She's got a spot of color is all I meant."

"*You* should have spent the day outdoors as well," the duchess told him. "You look like a garden slug, Mr. Pilgrim. It is the Pilgrim constitution. Your papa too had always that faded complexion. His walk too just like you own, at the pace of a constipated turtle. An excess of wine was thought to be the cause, but I believe it is constitutional."

Pronto glared and stalked off, muttering into his collar, "Ain't constipated, by jingo. Ain't going to take the blue pill."

Bertie came hopping over to greet her troublesome guest. "How lovely, Duchess. Turbans are so becoming to old—elderly—they, my, I *do* like your turban. And a little old feather in it too. How stylish. I shall try one myself."

"Don't be a ninny, Lady Belami," the duchess said scornfully. "A turban would not suit you in the least. You haven't the countenance for one, though it's high time you were in caps. Wearing your rubies, I see. You are brave, I must say. I made sure your son would have them safely tucked away in the family safe. Old Cottrell has his emerald stud in place as well. Brave souls! I have been meaning to ask you to put my jewelry box away in your vault, Belami, just in case."

"Remiss of me not to have offered," Belami returned, unfazed.

They got to the table without further sparring. The duchess was more easily seduced into humor by a good dinner that by any other means. Bertie, to do her justice, did set a fine table. Her son was also amusing company. Beaulac was convenient to London too, whereas her own ancestral heap was in the wilderness. Tallying up these advantages, she determined she must not let Belami slip through their fingers. She had turned quite mellow by the time the ladies left the gentlemen to their port.

She disliked that Deirdre was again sitting with Lady Lenore. She'd hint her out of that increasing intimacy before the night was done. Her mottled teeth were revealed in a broad smile of approval when Belami pranced smartly to Deirdre as soon as the gentlemen joined the female party. He very properly exchanged a few social nothings with Lady Lenore, before taking up his seat beside her niece. Lenore, the hussy, hadn't the common decency to leave the young lovers alone, but stuck like a burr, trying her fading charms on Belami. Herr Bessler ran to her own side, and for the next ten minutes she failed to notice what was afoot across the room.

Deirdre Gower could not fail to notice that Belami was blatantly ignoring her in favor of Lenore.

"My poor head feels as if it is splitting wide open," she overheard Lenore say in pitiful accents.

"I am sorry to hear it. Can I get something for you?" Dick offered at once.

"Nothing helps," Lenore replied in a strange, choking voice. Peering around Belami's shoulder at the woman, Deirdre saw a coy smile stretching her lips wide. "Nothing except going to bed. Laudanum only makes it worse."

"Then you must go to bed," Belami dictated, also in a strange, strangled voice. It was some game they were playing, some act they had worked out in advance. She was immediately suspicious of their motives.

When the voices fell low enough to make overhearing impossible, Deirdre arose and strode majestically to another sofa, where she sat alone, in high dudgeon, and higher hopes that she would be joined by Dick. For several minutes she watched them flirting outrageously, with never so much as a glance at her. At the end of that time, Dick arose and went to speak to Bessler. Her aunt joined in the conversation with enough relish to make Deirdre wonder. Auntie had no use for Lady Lenore.

A disruption of the seating arrangements occurred when Cottrell insisted on leading two tables off to the card room. The duchess was among them, but Lenore and Belami remained behind with Bessler. Before long, Belami arose and went to Deirdre.

"You decided to study Lenore's tricks from afar tonight, did you?" he asked, having no idea he was out of favor.

She bristled at the very mention of the lady's name. "I shan't bother studing her further. How should that impress anyone, when the original is here to outdo me?"

"Lenore has a headache," he said.

"I wonder why she doesn't go to bed, then. It's

154

strange she should sit around complaining when she has a bed she could retire to. She *does* know beds are also for sleeping, I suppose?"

"You won't find her deficient in the wits department. She's going up soon. Bessler has agreed to give her a session, at your aunt's recommendation."

Deirdre's humor returned with celerity when Lenore and Bessler arose and went toward a small parlor where, presumably, he was to give her the treatment. "Are there enough of us to get up a small dancing party?" she asked, remembering they had spoken of it that morning.

"Later," Belami answered in a distracted way, as though not listening closely. "Perhaps Lenore and Chamfreys will like to join in," he added. "There are so few of us, we could hardly get up a set without them."

"Are we to dance in Lenore's bed? You said she was retiring."

"If she feels well enough to return, I mean."

They chatted for a few moments, at which time Pronto appeared at the doorway and beckoned to Dick, who excused himself and left with Pronto. There were other non-card players at the party. Deirdre fell into conversation with some of them but kept an eye on the hallway, to see when Dick and Pronto returned. Ten minutes passed, and the only person she saw going upstairs was Lenore, with a female servant. She held her hand to her head, indicating the headache persisted. A few moments later, Bessler followed her up.

She interpreted this to mean Lenore was going to bed, and when she was installed therein with propriety, Bessler would go to her and put her to sleep. This was entirely acceptable to Deirdre, even if it meant too few couples to dance. She was more interested to know what had become of Dick. Before long, she decided to go to Snippe's room, to see if he and Pronto were having a meeting.

Only Pronto was there, paring his nails with a pocket knife while glancing frequently at his pocket watch, propped on the table before him. "Oh, there you are," he said, as though he had been wondering where she was. "I was about to go after you, if you didn't come here. Belami said you'd come. Deduced it."

"Where is he?" she asked looking around.

"Gone deducing somewhere else."

"Where?"

"He can do it anywhere. Does it right in church, or at the table, or walking along the street. No saying where he went to do it this time," he said vaguely. "He'll be back. He said to wait here, and if you didn't come here, I was to go after you in fifteen minutes to make sure you wasn't . . . lonesome," he finished, with a satisfied smile that he had conned her. "And to keep you busy. Sit down, Deirdre. Care for a glass of wine?" He had taken several himself and was on the way to being foxed.

"No, thank you. You have no idea where he is?"

"Can't say."

"Can't, or won't?" she asked, suspicion mounting higher by the moment.

Gentlemen did not lie to ladies, and he was a gentleman, Deirdre definitely a lady. "Do have a glass of wine, m'dear," was his answer.

"I said I don't want any, thank you."

"A famous brew. One Belami decocts especially for his mama. He adds sugar to a perfectly good burgundy, you see. He says it destroys the bloom, but between you and me and the bedpost, it's dandy. Actually, it's—no offense, ma'am. I didn't mean *ac*-tually, just actually. Anyway, it's syrup he adds, not raw sugar. Two or three glasses of this and you won't care a tinker's curse *where* he is. Not to say he's anywhere he shouldn't be. And even if he is. it's not what you think. Nothing of the sort, I promise you."

She was not deceived by this jumble of clues. Dick was doing something he shouldn't do, but Lenore was in bed having a session with Bessler, so the something was not of a sort to disgust her. He was following up a

156

clue having to do with the diamond, that was all. Her face wore a slight frown of concentration as these thoughts flitted through her mind.

Pronto misread the frown, and continued dissuading her as to any wrongdoing on Dick's part. What was a friend for, if not to help a chap? "They ain't making plans for Paris, if that's what you think," he told her severely." 'Pon my word, it seems to me if a girl can't trust her fiancé to have a few private words with another lady, she should break the engagement. Either fish or cut bait is my own feelings on the matter."

"What lady?" Deirdre asked sharply. Lenore was the choice of the ladies in the house, but she was by no means the only possibility. "Who is going to Paris?"

"I didn't say Dick and Lennie was planning to go to Paris in a couple of weeks. Damme, Deirdre, I wish you will quit putting words in my mouth. Dick will kill me," he said, mounting his high horse and glaring at her. To his amazement, she split in two. The left side of her weaved left, and the right half to the right. He shook his head till she reassembled herself, then took another sip of the wine to clear his head, which felt strangely muddled.

"So *that's* what it was all about!" she exclaimed, remembering those choked, laughing voices when the great headache scene was being enacted. He was with Lenore now, this very minute, while Pronto bungled his orders to keep her busy. Bessler, the scoundrel, was in on the ruse as well.

"Pull yourself together," Pronto ordered as she began splitting apart again.

"I'm not upset, and I have figured out what is going on, so don't bother with any more lies."

"I never told one! Well, not what you'd call a real lie. It's not my fault if you've deduced it. Dick should never have taught you the trick. You've gotten hold of it now. There'll be no stopping you."

She bolted from the room, to see Bessler sitting at his ease in the saloon, having a glass of brandy. As he was the first encountered, he received her first angry outburst.

"Did you manage to get rid of Lady Lenore's headache, Herr Bessler?" she asked, her voice heavy with sarcasm.

"She is resting comfortably," he replied.

"I hope you didn't put her to sleep. Lord Belami would be very much disappointed if you did."

"I expect she will doze off soon. What has it to do with Belami? It was your aunt who suggested it," he told her.

"Did Belami not go along to observe the session? He has become so very interested in your cure, I was sure he would be there," she replied.

"No, there was a servant with us, but the silly female kept interrupting, so that we had to ask her to leave in the end. There were just the two of us."

"I see." There was some hasty revising to do on her thoughts. She chatted to Bessler for a minute, then went upstairs.

Her admitted excuse was to inquire how Lenore felt, though she was also highly curious to ascertain that Dick wasn't with her. She tapped softly at the door, waited a moment, and received no reply. She would just peek in and see if Lenore was sleeping. There would be nothing wrong in that. If she was asleep, she wouldn't awaken her. She opened the door, saw a low light gleaming, and stepped in. She noticed immediately that Lenore was not in bed; the covers were disturbed, but she had gotten up. She must be in her dressing room next door. She took a step toward the adjoining door and stopped dead in her tracks. There, cowering in the shadows of the dresser, stood Lenore, in Dick's arms, both of them looking as guilty as a pair of foxes caught in the chicken coop.

Lenore wore a salacious night dress that hovered beguilingly at half-mast over her bosoms. There was a wisp of some diaphanous material over it that nominally suggested a dressing gown, but of a sort never seen in a house of good repute. Although Dick was dressed, there was enough disruption of his usually precise toilette to indicate unwonted activity. His hair was tousled, his tie askew, and, most damning of all, he was without shoes. Why did a man take off his shoes, but to get into bed? All these convicting details were observed in a second, while a half of Deirdre's mind struggled with some cutting remark to make. It must be of a sort that made them perfectly aware that she knew what was going on, that they were trying to hide it from her, and most importantly of all, that she didn't care a groat. Dick's arms fell from Lenore's and went out toward Deirdre, while his jaw dropped in astonishment.

No clever words occurred to Deirdre. She was too overcome to be satirical. "Is your headache all better, Lady Lenore?" she asked in a tight voice.

Both Dick and Lenore began gabbing at once, in a contradictory way that only further condemned them. "Much better, thank you" collided head-on with "No, it's worse. That's why . . ." And Deirdre continued looking from one to the other. They tried again, still at odds. "Why don't you join us?" from Lenore was only half out when Dick suggested meeting her belowstairs in a moment.

"Don't hurry on my account," she said, glaring at Dick. "I can see I have come at an inopportune moment. *Ac*-tually I just dropped in to see if you are feeling more comfortable, Lady Lenore. I can see you're fine. Right in your usual spirits. I shan't disturb you further. I'm sure you have a great deal to discuss. Paris—in two weeks, isn't it?"

"That demned Pronto!" Belami said, and walked forward, grabbing Deirdre's arm to hasten her out of the room. He slammed Lenore's door and glared at Deirdre.

"Was this embarrassment really necessary?" he asked in a rather loud voice.

"Not only unnecessary but extremely ill-advised," she answered coolly. "I'll find my own way to my room. You can go back to her."

"I've finished what I had to do with her."

"Already? You *are* fast! Here I thought it was just beginning."

"We were *talking*."

"Criminal conversation I believe is the term for that particular sort of talk with a married lady. But then you're an expert at it; you made sure her husband was nowhere around."

"You're quick to judge."

"I'm not blind. I can see you have your shoes off, and your hair all mussed."

"The reason I look like this is because I was hiding in her closet."

"Oh, stop it, Dick! Stop your stupid lies. I'm not a child. I know what you were doing, and I doubt that even you, with all your imagination, found the clothes closet the place to do it."

On this stiff speech she pulled free of his hands and ran to her room, where she slammed the door and leaned against it, breathing hard. Before she had drawn three breaths, the door was forced open, without any warning knock, or even footsteps, due to the lack of shoes on the invader's feet. Dick plunged in and faced her, arms akimbo, with a black scowl on his face.

"I was watching Bessler," he said loudly, angrily.

"With a telescope, perhaps? Bessler is in your saloon, having a glass of brandy," she retaliated.

"He was with Lennie. She let on to have a headache, to give me a chance to watch his performance. I hid in her clothespress, with the door open a crack. She told him she habitually drinks too much wine, had become worried about it, and he said he could cure her of it. He put her off into a kind of trance, and told her she would not drink wine again. She would develop a strong aversion to it, and the damndest thing is, she *has*. After he left, I poured her a glass, and she pushed it away as though it were vinegar. And Dierdre, she doesn't remember anything about it! About what he did or said when she was in the trance. She just remembers look-

160

ing at the light play on his monocle. Isn't that amazing?"

"A lucky thing you were there in the closet, col-
lecting evidence, as Lenore will be no help in explaining it," she said, still angry.

"It wasn't luck; I arranged it."

"What has all this got to do with anything?" she
asked. "You had your arms around her, and she had
practically nothing on."

"She was properly dressed for bed, in my opinion.
Don't try to bearlead me, Deirdre. I'm not a child
either," he warned in an implacable tone. "I don't plan
to be petticoated by a wife or anyone else. I needed evidence, and did what I had to do to get it."

"You could have asked *me* to help you!"

"Could I? You wouldn't even sneak me into your
aunt's room to watch Bessler work on her. It didn't
seem likely you'd participate more actively in it. I
haven't done anything wrong, and I'm not going to
apologize."

"I'm not asking you to. Nature can't be changed; I
know that. Birds will fly and fish will swim; pigs will
wallow in mire, and Belami will carry on with any
indiscrimating woman who will have him, But he won't
drag me into the mire with him, thank you very much,"
she said, turning her back on him and marching to the
other side of the room.

He paced quickly after her. "Oh, it must be nice to be
above reproach," he said scornfully.

"It is. You should try it sometime," she returned with
an airy toss of her head.

"Are you jealous? Is that why you came pelting up to
Lennie's room?"

"Jealous of *you*?" A silver laugh tinkled on the air.
"I'd as soon be jealous of Bessler."

"Then why did you come spying on us?"

"I wasn't spying. I went to see if Lenore was comfortable. A pity I bothered. She was a good deal more comfortable before my untimely intrusion."

"You quizzed Pronto and came checking up on me," he charged. "I call that spying. I was about to leave when you arrived."

"Yes, I know. You had already finished what you went to do, but then it's understandable. You had such a fast partner."

"When I am innocent, I follow the motto 'Never explain; never apologize.' I have already bent it by explaining. I shan't apologize. You may believe me or not. That is entirely up to you."

"You've chosen your motto poorly, for a man whose behavior requires an unending series of apologies."

"It's not necessary to apologize for being human. Only one who fancies herself a saint would think so. My only regret is that you chose to interfere at that precise moment."

"Two minutes earlier would have shown me a more interesting scene. I'm sorry I chose the wrong moment too."

"Are you now?" he asked with a dangerous lift of his infamous brow, and a flashing smile. "That's a telling statement. You wished to see Lennie in action, did you? Why settle for watching the great debauch when you could be a part of it?" he asked suggestively, coming closer, leaning his head toward hers and gazing into her eyes. "That's what you've just blurted out without thinking, you know, that you would like to have seen me making love to Lennie. More observation to learn the lady's tricks, I expect." Deirdre backed away from the twin onyx eyes that held her mesmerized.

"Get out! Get out of my room," she said, her voice low, quavering with sudden fright.

"Would you prefer the clothespress?" he asked with a teasing laugh. "Cramped quarters, but we shan't mind that," he said, following forward as she retreated.

"If you don't leave at once, I'll scream," she threatened, her voice shaking.

"No, you won't. It would raise too much conjecture. As to why the irrepproachable Miss Gower has a gentleman in her chamber, for example. No smoke without fire, you know. If she truly wished to stop him, why did she let him in in the first place? A man of Belami's stamp too, the blackest sheep ever weaned," he said with gusto as his arms went around her.

"Dick, don't you *dare*!" she said in a breathless whisper as he tightened his arms around her.

"But you want to see how it is done, Deirdre. You're playing your role perfectly. A token show of maidenly resistance is to be expected. The villian in the case, *videlicet* Lord Belami, being the black-hearted knave intent on seduction, pays no heed to milady's token chagrin. He proceeds to *ravish* her," he said with dramatic emphasis, and placed his lips on hers while his arms squeezed her relentlessly against his chest.

The details of the situation conspired to betray her. Her mind was already on lovemaking from her suspicions of Lenore and Belami. It quickened her blood and filled her head with images never dared before. Soon her eyes were drawn into the betrayal. There in the shadowy reflection from her mirror she saw herself in his arms, his head leaning over hers. She saw in the mirror when he lifted a hand and began to stroke the back of her neck, gently, with warm fingers. It had the exciting effect on her of watching clandestinely while someone other than herself was embraced. His fingers cupped her neck, sending shivers of emotion tingling down her spine, scuttling along her arms, till the hairs stood up straight. Momentarily distracted, she did not hear the footsteps in the hallway. A pang of alarm sent her fingers clutching at Dick's waistcoat when a sharp knock was heard at the door.

She looked up into his eyes and said, "It *can't* be Auntie. She's playing cards. Oh, I *know* it's her!"

"She wouldn't knock," he said. "Ask who it is." While this was going on, he didn't loosen his hold on her, but only raised his head.

"Who—who is it?" she called, her voice barely audible.

"It's me, Huldie, milady. Are you in your room for the night? I'll bring up your cocoa now if you like."

"Later, thank you, Huldie," she called back, relief washing over her at the unimportance of the interloper.

"Very well, mum," the servant answered, and departed.

"Now, where were we?" Belami went on, as calmly as though there had been no interruption.

"You were about to leave," she told him, attempting a stiff tone. Even her voice betrayed her. It sounded soft, breathless, inviting. Her ears picked up the unusual tone, and Belami's light, answering laugh.

"You're in a hurry for me to get on with the lesson," was the interpretation he chose to put on her words.

"I am not!"

"Excellent, then we can take our time and do the thing properly. I have made my unsavory intentions clear and you have encouraged me with faint protests. Being a gentlemen, I naturally ignore them and . . . kiss you," he said, closing his eyes and lowering his lips to hers. Her will was suspended, an involuntary collaborator in the scene. She too closed her eyes, and gave herself up to the novel sensation of being vigorously embraced by the most dashing rogue who ever broke a lady's heart.

His lips felt warm, soft, yet demanding. She yielded to them, but her arms hung loose at her sides. She felt them rise to go around him, as though they had taken on a life of their own, but she retained enough sense to will them down. Belami reached for one arm and pulled it into place around his waist, without interrupting the kiss. The other arm she allowed to do as it wished. It went to his neck, where the fingers played in his hair. This trifling encouragement increased his ardor.

The pressure from his lips and arms increased, till she was being squeezed so mercilessly tight that breathing was difficult. Some nameless, amorphous thing mushroomed in her breast, growing into her throat, till she felt weak, as though she would burst

164

from the strain of containing it. Yet while it weakened her will, it imparted strength to her arms and lips. She was aware, at a hazy distance, that she was returning every pressure of the embrace, that she was not only enduring it, but enjoying it. *I am being seduced—how lovely it is* was the last conscious thought she had before yielding completely to those physical sensations. The perimeters of her own body were erased. She became a part of Belami, who was a part of her, the two of them a part of something beyond mere physical bodies.

When he finally released her, a sigh hung on the air. She hoped it was Belami who had emitted it, but thought it was she herself.

Opening her eyes, she saw Belami frowning at her. It was unexpected, like a dash of cold shower on a beautiful, sunny day.

"What's the matter?" she asked.

"Nothing. I knew you had—rhythm, but I didn't know you were such a good dancer." He dropped his arms and stepped back, examining her, still with traces of that unexpected frown. "I must go now. I have a million things to do," was all he said.

"Don't let me detain you," she said with chilly hauteur.

A fleeting smile lightened his face. He lifted her hand and placed one quick kiss in its palm, then closed her fingers over it. "Save it for later," he said, and he was gone, with no apology, and no explanation.

She stood alone for several minutes gazing at the door, with her fingers tightly holding that unexpected kiss. She slowly opened her fingers and smiled at it. There was nothing to see, but her palm tingled beautifully.

It was not till she emerged from the ephemeral cloud surrounding her that she remembered his cavalier refusal to explain or apologize. An unlikely tale of hiding in Lenore's closet did not constitute a real explanation of his presence there and did not even begin to explain the planned trip to Paris. She could find no satisfactory

165

reason why he should frown after embracing her, either. Was she that poor at being seduced? She doubted he frowned after being with Lenore.

Soon shame had added its mite to her worsening mood. Between vexation, curiosity, and shame, she was in little better mood than when she first climbed the stairs. She remained in her room for the rest of the evening and by morning had decided that the only proper position for such a wronged damsel as she was astride a very high horse.

Belami, being an impetuous optimist, had reached a quite different decision. The proper position for a man in love was within the bonds of matrimony. And he was in love with Dierdre Gower. That little touch of resistance made her more desirable. She had been properly reared—a real lady, but without any stiffness, once you got to know her. How strange that he had grown to love her after all, and stranger still that she should care for such a ramshackle fellow as he. All that would end, of course.

He fell asleep amidst plans of his reformation.

Chapter 14

✳✳✳

Deirdre dreaded to be alone with Belami again, yet looked forward to it with hardly another thought for company. Her first relief at seeing Herr Bessler at the breakfast table the next morning quickly turned to annoyance. For once, Pronto had slept in. She might have had Belami to herself were it nor for Bessler, polishing his monocle and smiling his greeting. The gentlemen arose punctiliously as she entered, but soon their conversation turned to general matters as they ignored her.

They finished eating before her but remained at table. Belami took up a newspaper from the chair beside him and glanced at it, occasionally reading an item aloud.

"That would be stale news from before the New Year," Bessler remarked, between sips of coffee.

"No, it is yesterday's paper," Belami told him. "My groom walked to Luton and brought it back with him."

"Are the roads open, then?" Bessler asked eagerly.

"Unfortunately this strip here in front of Beaulac is the worst of the lot. If you could get through the mile or so that has drifted here, it would be easy sailing. Réal walked the ten miles on snowshoe, however. Marvelous contaptions. Miss Gower and I have given them a try." He arose and went to the fireplace, where a fire burned sluggishly. He kicked a log with his boot and sent a shower of sparks falling into the grate.

He stood with his back to the fire, still looking at his paper. "Here's some shocking news," he siad.

Bessler sat nibbling his under lip. Deirdre asked what the shocking news was that he referred to.

"A bad fire in London during our absence. Half a block burned down—no one killed, thank goodness. At Glasshouse Street, by Great Windmill. I wish we had some of the blaze here. This fire is going out." On the last speech, he reached forward and poked the fire with his newspaper, then threw the sheets into the fire, where they were soon blazing up the chimney.

Bessler's head turned slowly, reluctantly toward him. "Did you say Glasshouse Steet, at Great Windmill?"

"Damme, I've forgotten already. Why do you ask?"

"I live there!" Bessler said, his eyes staring wildly, helplessly.

"Yes, that's the address he said," Deirdre told them.

"And like a fool I've burned the paper," Belami said. "I should be beaten. There was a fair-size article about it too—must have been something of particular interest, though I can't imagine what it would be. Does someone important live there, Doctor?"

"No, no, it is not a highly social spot. Have you any idea what the article referred to?" he asked rather fearfully.

"I hardly glanced at it. I believe I saw the words Bow Street. Must have been arson, I suppose. I'll send Réal over to Luton for another copy."

"No!" Bessler said, arising. "I would not dream of inconveniencing you, milord. Excuse me. I must go at once." He arose from the table, his hands trembling noticeably and his legs unsteady as he lurched toward the door.

"Poor man!" Deirdre exclaimed, and got up to follow him.

Belami stepped forward and placed his hand on her shoulder gently pushing her back into her chair. "I'll do it," he said, and followed Bessler from the room. She noticed that he did not walk quickly enough to catch the old man. He followed some yards behind and waited at the bottom of the stairs while Bessler pulled himself up, using his hand on the bannister for support.

Deirdre sat wondering whether this news was momentous enough to awaken her aunt, and decided against it. Within five minutes, Bidwell was in the breakfast parlor, his toilette indicating a hasty dressing.

"You heard the distressing news about Herr Bessler's apartment burning down?" he asked Deirdre.

"I was here when Belami told him. So unfortunate. I wonder where he will go," she said, fingering the handle of her cup in her dismay.

"I've no idea. Where is the paper? I'd like to have a look at it."

"Belami used it to stoke up the fire. It's gone."

"Jackass!" Bidwell said angrily, and went to the grate to see for himself the charred remains.

"He didn't realize it was Bessler's apartment building."

"He might have thought the rest of us would like to have a look at a new newspaper. Just coffee for me," he told the servant, and sat back in agitation.

"Belami's groom got through to Luton, I hear?" he asked.

"Yes, the worst of the snow is right here, at Beaulac. It looks to me as though the snow is melting rapidly. I think we'll be able to get through today."

"I think you're right," Bidwell said, jumping up to

walk to the window. A row of icicles dripped in the sun. There was a space of six inches between the walls of the house and the snow beyond, where heat from the house had melted the blanket.

"Do you know, I believe I'll tackle it," Bidwell said. "I have prime goers hitched to my rig."

Belami reentered the parlor. "Have you heard the dreadful news?" he asked Bidwell.

"If you refer to Bessler's apartment, I've heard. He was to return to London with me. He stopped in to see if there was any chance of getting back today. What do you think, Belami? Would there be any point on tackling it?"

"I'll speak to my groom. Réal knows snow intimately," he replied blandly, and walked off.

After a stretch of silence, Deirdre said, "I don't suppose another day would make much difference. If the apartment is totally ruined, then there is nothing to be done, and if it is not, there will be someone guarding it against loooting."

"I doubt very much that you would sit twiddling your thumbs if your home had burned to the ground," Bidwell remarked irritably.

"I suppose not. If it is possible to get through, Belami will arrange it."

"Belami!" he said scornfully. "He hasn't arranged the recovery of your aunt's diamond very well, has he, Miss Gower?"

She sat a moment in angry silence, finding him insufferably rude, before she began to wonder how he knew the recovery of the diamond was a ruse. Belami must have told Bertie, who would certainly let it out to the first person she spoke with. She had just opened her mouth to ask Bidwell how he knrew when she noticed that Belami had returned. He stood in the doorway behind Bidwell's back, unseen by him. He was staring at that back with a peculiar little smile on his lips and a noticeable glow in his eyes. He immedialtely walked on in, rubbing his hands.

"Réal tells me he is raring to tackle it. He will ride into London and check out Herr Bessler's apartment."

"*Ride?* You mean drive, surely," Bidwell said, turning around to look at Belami.

"No, I mean ride. The cold won't bother Réal. He will do what can be done in the way of safeguarding anything that remains unburned. I've ordered him to have a good look around. Bessler will have to give him a letter stating he is acting on his behalf and empowering him to remove any valuable papers or personal effects."

"Is getting a carriage through quite out of the question?" Bidwell asked, staring hard at Belami, who smiled softly in return.

"I'm sure *my* team could make it; whether yours is up to it, only you would know. A couple of carriages have been through."

"I believe I'll tackle it," Bidwell decided.

"I wouldn't expose my nags to such inclement conditions if I were you," Belami said. "The legs in particular are susceptible to the wet and cold. An inflammation . . ."

"Bessler is more important than a nag, Dick," Deirdre exclaimed, disappointed in him. She had thought him dashing enough to undertake the expedition himself.

"Ah, is it for *Bessler* that you go to such great lengths? That is philanthropic of you, Bidwell," Belami smiled.

"I'm anxious to get back in any case. You know I'm particularly eager to return as I mentioned earlier."

"I'll tell you what, then, I shall accompany you," Belami told him, "but in your carriage, of course, and with your team."

"No!" Bidwell said quickly. "No, there can be no need for you to leave your own party. I am promised to Miss Cookson this very night. I'll drop Bessler off first and see what I can do for him, then go about my business. Kind of you to offer."

"The least I could do was to offer," Belami said, not

pressing the offer at all. "I shall consult with Réal again, as to the best route." He disappeared and Bidwell went upstairs to make his own preparations, while Deirdre returned once more to her cold breakfast.

She was not pleased with Dick. He had very thoughtlessly annonced to Bessler the burning down of his apartment. He knew where Bessler lived—had asked him that question rather pointedly. Had he forgotten the address? Somehow, she did not think so. Bidwell was more thoughful. Had there been no question of a trip to Paris in the offing, she might have judged less harshly, but it was always there, nagging at the back of her mind.

And for all Belami's reputation as a keen solver of crimes, what had he actually done to recover the diamond? He had deduced, but to no good purpose. He had found the sheet and stocking and pistol. She had found the chain in the syllabub, and the clasp on Lenore's hearth.

As she pondered this, she came to the conclusion that the reason no solution was forthcoming was that he knew very well Lenore had done it—along with an accomplice, of course—and he was protecting her. All this business of broken glasses and scratching stones was a bluff, a show of doing something, to assuage Aunt Charney and Deirdre herself.

There was a commotion in the hallway of Bessler and Bidwell leaving, with messages from the former to be passed along to her aunt. As soon as they had left, Belami opened the door of Snippe's parlor and came out. She noticed the air of excitement about him, the sparkling eyes, the little lift of the lips, the general air of distraction. She also noticed he had not gone to check with Réal for the best route.

"You might have said good-bye to your guests," she charged.

"I waved from the window. They didn't see me, as they were in such an almighty rush."

"No wonder. Bessler is very concerned about his fire."

"A pity, but I don't suppose his apartment is furnished with rare, priceless objects, after all. What has he to lose, when it comes down to it?"

"Whatever he has means as much to him as your own rare and priceless items mean to you," she retorted, angry with his callousness.

He ignored her taunt. "You noticed what Bidwell let slip?" he asked with a knowing look.

"What, that Bessler went to him as soon as he learned about the fire? He was urging Bidwell to take him home, as *you* didn't offer to do it."

"No, I don't mean that, though Bidwell's sudden attack of philanthrophy is also highly suspicious. I mean that he knew I hadn't recovered your aunt's diamond. Did you tell him it was a hoax?"

"Of course not. You asked me to keep it a secret. It was more likely Bertie who let it slip," she answered.

"You don't think me foolish enough to have told *her*! No, no one told him, but still he knew, and with good reason."

"How could he have known? Do you think he got into your vault and saw the diamond wasn't there?"

"Not a chance. The vault is so well hidden I have trouble finding it myself. I'm sure they were looking. Bessler had been into my laboratory uninvited. He was aware I had a microscope—remember he mentioned it?"

"He might have guessed a laboratory would have a microscope. What a visit it has been! First the theft, then Bessler's fire."

"And before either of those, Belami's late appearance, to set the mood of jollity. Cheer up; it will soon be over."

Bad as it had been, its termination did not put her in a good mood. "You're looking forward to getting on to Paris, I expect?" she asked with a toss of her head designed to show her indifference.

"Are we going to Paris? I had thought a warmer clime. Italy perhaps, for the treacle moon."

"I have said often enough I'm not marrying you."

"Too often. Repetition becomes boring. You ought to vary your conversation a little. I deserve at least a maybe, after the way you have led me on. Shocking behavior, luring me into your bedroom, where you might have known I would behave with total indiscretion. I come to see you are not nearly as nice as you pretend. And it's a great relief, I can tell you." A dangerously attractive smile descended on his lips, while his dark eyes caressed her.

She felt a flush start at her collar and rise up to stain her cheeks. "I did not lure you into my room," she said stiffly.

"I insist I was lured by your charms, but acquit you of doing it consciously. At least admit you didn't try to put me out."

"I told you to leave!"

"You didn't mean it, did you, darling?" he asked. "But I shall obey your command, however tardily. I *am* leaving very soon. Another secret. Don't breathe a word. If anyone should ask for me, invent a credible lie."

"I don't lie!" she charged.

"No, and duchesses don't wear paste either. You were less than truthful about your trek to my roof, and caused me to waste a good deal of time. If invention fails you, you can say Belami told you he was going over to Boltons' to see how they are weathering the storm."

"But that's ten miles away."

"How did you know that?" he asked.

"Because Réal mentioned going there. Belami, what is going on at Boltons'?"

"Didn't you know Lennie's husband is there?"

"Lenore's husband! I knew this had to do with pulling Lenore's chestnuts out of the fire!"

"What on earth are you talking about?" he asked, frowning, but not very convincingly.

"You know perfectly well she stole my aunt's diamond, and are arranging some trick to cover it up."

He shook his head slowly. "How did you ever manage to convince the world you're intelligent?" he asked sadly. "Every bit as muddle-headed as Bertie. It is Belami's chestnuts I am retrieving from the fire—on Glasshouse Street, you know. I hope you liked roasted chestnuts."

"I despise them," she said firmly.

"Then I'll eat 'em all myself. I must take my leave of Bertie. Keep an eye on her for me, will you? You might as well begin learning you inherit a sixty- . . . sorry, fifty-four-year-old child with this marriage, darling."

"As reptitions bore you, I shan't repeat myself. You might as well go. I'm not trying to stop you."

"You don't have to try to wind me around your finger. So long as you stay there gazing at me with those great, stormy eyes, I am transfixed to the spot. Close your eyes, like a good girl, and let me go."

When she only opened them more wildey and blinked, he lifted his open hand and gently placed it over her eyes. She felt a brushing kiss on her lips, and when she opened her eyes, she saw his back disappearing down the corridor. He was gone, and she was in as much confusion as ever, though the surface of her mind did not dwell on it.

She stood remembering that even from the back, he was irresistible. Such a jaunty step.

Chapter 15

※※※

The temperature had risen to forty-nine degrees. The melting snow was troublesome underfoot, but not so bad for mounted riders as for carriages. Diablo and Marabel made it to London without much trouble, particularly with Pierre Réal mounted on the latter, with all his snow lore to aid them.

"What if you're wrong in your deductions?" Réal asked.

"I can't be wrong. Nothing else works. This theory takes in all the troublesome details."

"Can't be wrong? We shall see. Your theory, he don't account for—"

"Shut up, Pierre. I'm thinking."

"About the diamond; where he is?"

"No, about Italy," he answered with a soft smile. He enjoyed the warm sun on his shoulders; it gave a hint of the warmer climate soon to be enjoyed. As a few doubts still lingered with regard to the diamond's whereabouts, however, he drew his mind back to business. He anticipated with considerable relish the melodrama that would be enacted, with himself as one of of the principal players, when finally Bessler and Bidwell made it to Glasshouse Street. He sent Réal off to Bow Street, while he continued to Bessler's apartment.

Arriving an hour before the other players, he had plenty of time to conduct a thorough search of Bessler's premises. He was not disappointed when the diamond was not found under the doctor's pillow or mattress, or hidden in the pocket of any of his jackets, or the toe of his boots. He expected better than that from the man ingenious enough to have set up and executed this elaborate hoax. He continued in an unflustered manner to go over the premises systematically. Consisting of only three rooms, the place was soon examined. There was an office, a bedroom, and one jack-of-all-uses room, which had a stove, a cupboard, a table and two chairs, running water, a sink, a mirror with shaving equipment and washing materials nearby.

A man liked to keep precious possesions near him. It was in the study that Bessler worked most of the day, and it was searched first. The desk revealed a thick stack of unpaid bills and IOUs amounting to approximately four thousand pounds. These were scooped into a bag for evidence. After a fruitless search of drawers, bookshelves, vases, and medical equipment, he decided it was the bedroom where Bessler spent a third of his time. He would want it there, for safekeeping during the night. But the bedroom too proved innocent of the diamond. Time was pressing hard at his back now. He and Réal had made a faster trip, but they had left later and taken a slightly circuitous route to avoid passing the others.

The jack-of-all-uses room took the longest time. After a lengthy, careful search, it failed to turn up the diamond. He paced through the apartment, bringing a chair to the windows to feel along the tops of the draperies, then got on his hand and knees to feel the hems, still with no luck. Where could it be? He deduced wildly as he went from room to room with a frown creasing his brow. Was he wrong after all? Did Bidwell have the gem? But certainly Bessler had taken it and been in a frenzy to get back here when told of the imaginary fire.

He hastened to the bedroom, his wary eyes darting hither and thither, in search of any nook or cranny he had overlooked. His eyes fell on a covered decanter of water on the bedside table. He had already looked in it. It was empty, but a glass beside it was half full. The frown faded, and a fiendish smile replaced it. He lifted the glass, emptied the water carefully into the decanter, and shook the Charney Diamond out into his hand, with a sigh of satisfaction. A diamond of the first water, invisible in water. Yes, that was fairly clever of Bessler, he granted. He liked competing with a worthy opponent.

With a mischievous smile, he poured the water back into the glass and went to the window. In four minutes and fifteen seconds, Bidwell's carriage rattled up to the door, and the two men scrambled down. Their footsteps were soon heard clattering up the steps. Belami locked the door, to allow them a few more seconds of hope. He could not distinguish their words as Bessler put his key in the lock, but he recognized the tone as being extremely agitated.

"Good afternoon, Doctor," he said with a graceful bow when Bessler plunged in.

"Belami, what are *you* doing here?" he asked.

"My migraine—you remember I told you I would come. Bidwell, did those old jades of yours have any trouble making it through the snow?"

"Not a bit, thank you."

"I have no time for a session now," Bessler said.

"No? But your place hasn't burned down after all. That must save you any amount of bother."

"There's been no fire in all of the West End," Bessler said. "Why did you send us off on this wild goose chase?"

"Wild goose chase? No, you have misunderstood me. There was a very good reason. I wished to remove the venue of the crime from Beaulac, you see. Tell me, Doctor, why did you choose my domicile for the scene of your vulgar melodrama?"

"I don't know what you're talking about," Bessler said gruffly, and walked into the bedroom. He looked at the glass of water by the bed, and was aware of a great wave of relief. He smiled at Bidwell, who also relaxed into a better mood.

"Whatever stunt you're up to, Belami, it's gone awry. You might as well run along. You're bowled for a duck here," Bidwell said.

"What is it you were looking for?" Bessler asked, but his face was benign. He still coveted the patronage of the aristocracy.

"This," Belami answered, and tossed the diamond into the air, to catch it again. He displayed it on his open palm for a fraction of a second before pocketing it.

Bessler's mouth fell open. He took an involuntary step forward but was beyond speech. It was Bidwell who spoke, trying to caution Bessler, in case of another hoax.

"What's that, Belami? Found the duchess's diamond again, have you? Or is it paste, something made up to—"

"To shock you into a confession, you mean?" Belami finished for him. "No, this one is the genuine article," he told them, and watched from the corner of his eye as Bessler edged his way to the bedside table, picked up the glass of water, and drank it.

When the glass was empty, Belami turned to him. "Surprised, Doctor? Did you think the good fairies might have deposited a diamond in it for you? Too bad. We'll talk now," he declared, walking toward the door.

Bidwell moved sideways to block him. "I'll take the diamond, Belami." he said while his hand moved to a bulge in his jacket to withdraw his pistol.

Belami raised his two splayed hands and stopped

walking. "I abhor violence," he said meekly. As he spoke, one hand doubled into a fist and shot out like quicksilver. Bidwell sank to the floor, clutching his stomach. "Unfortunately, there are times when it can't be avoided. I really don't want to hurt an old man," he went on, with a warning glance to Bessler. "My groom has gone to Bow Street and will be arriving any moment with a Runner. Your best bet will be to come peacefully."

Bidwell stirred to life and got himself up on one knee. "What, have you grown the giblets to have at me again?" Belami asked, and rolled him over on his back with the toe of his boot. He leaned over and extracted the pistol from his pocket. "Glad to see you're using your own this time. You took it with you to Beaulac, no doubt, but decided to borrow mine instead, to incriminate me. You will regret that, jackanapes. How did you ever pair up with this creature?" he asked Bessler.

"Don't talk," Bidwell gasped, sitting up and rubbing his stomach. "He can't prove anything."

"He's got the diamond," Bessler pointed out, defeated.

"He can't *prove* anything," Bidwell insisted.

"Some things prove themselves," Belami remarked idly. "Possession of stolen goods is taken as *prima facie* evidence of theft, or complicity in theft. The duchess's diamond didn't hop into the glass of water by itself."

"It's true. I took it," Bessler admitted. "I mesmerized the duchess the day she removed it from the bank, and had her give it to me, substituting a copy I had made in advance. I never meant to involve you, milord, or have anything untoward happen at your house. I meant simply to sell it and return to Austria. It was Bidwell who convinced me to change my plan."

"How did Bidwell know you had made the substitution?" Belami asked.

"It happened over a couple of drinks the night before we left. We had both lost money at cards and were feeling miserable. He came back here and we drank brandy. I was indiscreet, mentioned a plan to pull myself out of my troubles. Another glass or two, and I had given him the kernel of my plan. He *improved* on it, as he said."

"Shut up, you bloody fool!" Bidwell said angrily. "Lies. All lies. I was never here before in my life."

"Pray continue, Doctor," Belami invited.

"Bidwell told me I wouldn't realize a quarter of the stone's worth. I'd be lucky to get five thousand for it at a fencing ken. He said the insurance company would buy it for three times that. He knew a fellow who acted as a go-between in these transactions. I told him the duchess would not know the thing had been stolen, the copy was so good, and if she *did* discover the replacement, *I* would be the first one suspected. He said we must steal the copy, very publicly, and let it pass for the original. I told him it could not be done, but he put himself in charge of it all, for half the profit realized. He was eager to get on with it, and chose the first public appearance of the diamond, at your ball. We didn't know the policy had lapsed. She didn't breathe a word of it, till after the theft that night when I was with her upstairs. Then she told me; I was ready to cry for grief. So much work and worry for naught."

Belami nodded with quiet satisfaction to hear his deductions all neatly confirmed. "Quite a facer for you, Bidwell," he remarked. Strangely, it was the younger man he despised more in the matter, though, of course, Bessler too was contemptible. Age, he supposed, had something to do with it. One felt pity for the aged and disinherited.

"It was just like my damnable uncle to fool me," Bidwell charged. "I wanted to get that money from *him*. I didn't mean you any harm, Belami. It's the only way I'll ever see a sou of it. Why must I wait till he's in the grave to have what's rightfully mine?"

"Rightfully yours?" Belami asked, staring. "You've already had and wasted what was rightfully yours in your father's inheritance. Where did you get the notion

Carswell owed you anything, only because he married your aunt?"

"He's got no one else to leave it to."

"I have a strong feeling he'll find someone else now."

"If only the duchess had renewed the policy," was Bidwell's next regret. He was ready to blame everyone but himself. That, Belami decided, was what was particularly revolting about the man.

"We decided we must pretend we had known of the lapsed policy all along, to keep suspicion from ourselves. That is why I made a point to mention it to you, Lord Belami," Bessler said humbly. "Bidwell had destroyed the copy; there was no way to prove we had stolen it. I had the original here. I planned to sell it for what I could get, and we would still split the profit. We are both in urgent need of funds," he added with a worried frown at his desk, where he had secreted his bills.

"Then the storm came along and confined us all to Beaulac," Belami urged him on.

"That delay was not too troublesome. It was your announcement that my aparment had burned down that worried me. I envisaged someone's finding the diamond in the ashes. Disgrace, a trial, possibly hanging . . ." His face mirrored these horrors.

"Quite possibly," Belami agreed calmly.

"Not for me!" Bidwell announced triumphantly. "All *I* took was a chunk of glass. I knew it was glass when I took it. They won't hang a fellow for that."

"Assaulting a duchess, causing her grievous bodily harm—the bruise on her neck, dreadful! To say nothing of collusion with Herr Bessler," Belami pointed out. "Then there is conspiring to defraud your uncle Carswell of a fortune. You may escape the gibbet, but I'd say you're looking at twenty or thirty years in prison."

"How did you come to suspect our scheme?" Bessler asked with waning interest.

"Simple deduction," Belami told him. "Bidwell had the opportunity. He was not in the ballroom when it happened. Neither was there any way of proving he was in Lady Lenore's dressing room, as he claimed. It was crushing the paste diamond on the hearth that really gave it away. The splinter's weight told me it was not another wine glass, nor a part of the one you broke at midnight—or was it actually a minute before or after that you called Chamfreys and Lenore? I have not been able to deduce the timing to the second. No matter," he said when Bidwell proved uncooperative. "Either before or after you lunged down the rope to steal the diamond, you had a drink and broke one of my crystal goblets. When Deirdre discovered the hook that held the diamond to the chain, I took the fantastical notion you had actually stolen the diamond and crushed it, though I couldn't believe you hated Carswell enough to play such a pointless trick on him."

"I do, if you want the truth," Bidwell interpolated.

"Oh, I already have the truth. If we had more time, I would tell you about Mohs' Scale, which proved that the crushed item was not the diamond. The little clasp kept niggling at my mind. A substitution suggested itself—don't ask how. I get inspired at times. Bessler, with his mesmerism, was the logical person to have done that. If you could convince Lady Lenore she don't like wine, you could convince the duchess to hand over her diamond. One trembles to think of that unchained power walking the world. Just as well it will soon be locked up."

He walked to the window to look for signs of Bow Street and saw Réal and a Runner trotting quickly toward the building. He hastened his speech then. "Once I had the idea of you two working in tandem, the rest was fairly simple. Bidwell was so palpably certain I had not found the diamond when I announced I had that I realized it was not at Beaulac. Where else could it be but in the house of the man who stole it? My story of a fire here confirmed it. I never witnesses such panic, outside of a *real* fire. It remained only to beat you here by a few moments and find it. And by the by, Doctor, I approve of your hiding place. I didn't look there first, I promise you. I know that if *I* were the thief, I would appreciate a compliment from an expert like me."

"It was clever, was it not?" Bessler asked, allowing himself a wan, sad smile. "The phrase 'a diamond of the first water' suggested the hiding place to me. The duchess herself used the expression. A flawless diamond will disappear entirely in water."

"True. It is the very expression that caused me to look for it in the glass of water," Belami told him with a mischievous twinkle in his black eyes.

They were interrupted by the sounds of Réal and the Bow Street Runner coming up the stairs.

"Pierre Réal will show you where are the premises," the groom was heard to say beyond the door. "*Voilà*," he exclaimed, throwing the door wide open.

Bidwell made one last futile attempt to escape. He bolted for the open door but was stopped by Réal's outstretched foot. He went sprawling, to be hoisted up by his collar by the Runner.

"What have we got here, then?" the swarthy man asked.

"Foolish, Bidwell. Flight is always taken for confirmation of guilt," Belami told him, shaking his head, "Your best bet is to go to your uncle and sue for mercy. I shall accompany you gentlemen to Bow Street to explain the nature of this crime. Rather complicated, I'm afraid, but I'll give you every assistance in explaining its intricacies."

"I, Pierre Réal, will come to hold a pistol at their heads. You will need assistance to get through the streets. There's a bit of snow—only a foot or two most places, but to the *anglais*, even a drop such as that present the problem. Come."

"That's true. We had a powerful bad time getting here," the Runner said to Belami. "The main streets is shoveled out clean as a whistle, but here in the hinterlands there's bad drifting yet."

"Lead on, Réal," Belami said. "Follow the leader," he

added aside to the others, and brought up the rear himself.

When all the explaining and charging were done, Belami sent his groom home to his London residence, to inform his servants he would dine there and sleep overnight. There was still sufficient daylight to allow a walk along the main thoroughfares and meet a few friends. He spotted a traveling agent's office, and went in to begin arrangements for his honeymoon. He also arranged for a passage to Paris for two, toward the end of January. In a benevolent mood after the successful completion of the case, he was feeling generous.

"The very best rooms, at the very best hotel that has anything available," he told the agent.

"What name would that be for?" the agent asked, writing down the order.

"Lady Lenore Belfoi, and, er, Mr. Harvey Belfoi."

"This here check says Belami, not Belfoi," the agent pointed out when he was accepting the advance.

"Yes, I'm arranging the holiday for friends."

The lady waiting behind him perked up her ears at the name of Belami. This would be the dandy old Charney's niece was said to have nabbed, then. Quite a fine dasher, taking a pre-wedding jaunt with Lady Lenore Belfoi, the fastest woman in London. This would be interesting news for Her Grace, if only she were in town.

Belami went straight home and spent a quiet evening alone, with only Réal for company. His valet had succeeded with his wench and was off to her parents' home to arrange the wedding.

"That's two of us. You'll be next, Pierre," Belami said as he leafed through some travel books of Italy. "Maybe you'll find yourself a wife in Italy. I hope you mean to accompany us. You won't care for the climate. No snow. You will not be accustomed to such heat as we'll get there."

"I, Pierre Réal, not accustomed to heat?" the groom asked, staring in amazement. "You think you get heat here, and in Italy? I have fried eggs on rocks at home in

Canada. You think we get only snow and winds and ice? Bah, in July we are hotter than the tropics. A hundred degrees: a fine, balmy day. One hundred ten is getting warm. I'll fry you an egg on a rock when we go to Canada."

"We're not planning to go to Canada. And I don't like my eggs fried. either. I take 'em boiled."

"You can do that too, in the ponds," Réal told him, his beady black eyes daring him to contradict this foolishness.

"Those extremes of temperature have either fried or frozen your brain, my friend. Have a glass of wine to celebrate with me. Not so potent as you are accustomed to in Canada, I expect, but it will have to do."

Réal drank it up while considering other imagined marvels with which to impress his employer, who thought he knew everything. Not accustomed to heat indeed!

Chapter 16

✻✻✻

At Beaulac, the Duchess of Charney did not descend
to breakfast that morning. Comfortably ensconced in
her bed and looking through the window to an endless
vista of snow, she could see no reason to. She would loll
against the pillows instead and summon guests to
amuse her. The first guest summoned was her hostess,
Lady Belami. With no son on hand to rescue her, Bertie
went trotting to the room, already on the fidget.

"Nasty, inclement weather," the duchess said in an
accusing tone.

Peering into the dim shadows beneath the canopy,
Bertie had the strange feeling she was being addressed
by a skeleton in a cap. "Why, the sun is shining, and the
snow melting wonderfully well," she objected brightly.
"The road is quite open now, Duchess. Several guests
have left—such a relief. You can get on home to
Fernvale and take Deirdre with you. I'm sure you must
be eager to get home."

"Without my diamond?" the duchess asked, her gray brows jumping to meet her gray fringe.

"But my son found it. Everyone knows that. Don't tell me you've lost it again!" Bertie exclaimed, deeply chagrined.

"What a bubble head you are, to be sure. Of course he hasn't found it. It was all a conning trick. Where is Belami? I'll speak to him and find out what progress he is making."

"Dickie is not here. He's scooted back to London. Oh, dear! I wasn't supposed to say so. He's—he's indisposed. Yes, that's it. Or was that to be this afternoon? No, he's gone over to see how the neighbors go on after the storm, and this afternoon he will be indisposed."

"Gone back to London, you say?" Charney asked, feeling the delightful shadow of offense descend on her. "Gone back to London without so much as a farewell, after being three days late for his own party? Were we invited here for the express purpose of being insulted, Lady Belami?"

"Indeed you were not! You weren't invited at all. You wrote and said you would be happy to come, and you came. Of course I didn't mean to insult you. I hope I never insult anyone accidentally. Dickie says it is vulgar to do so. You must only give offense intentionally."

"Widgeon! Why has he gone to London? And more importantly, when does he plan to return?"

"Since you know he is gone, there is no point denying it. He said he would return soon. Between you and me and the bedpost, Your Grace, I expect he is giving you and Deirdre a chance to get away to Fernvale, *then* he will come dancing home fast enough."

"Are you telling me he has shagged off on my niece?" Charney asked. As her head darted forth from the shadows she ceased to resemble a skull and looked instead like an angry mare, with her ears pulled back and her nose wearing a strained, snorting look.

"It has nothing to do with me. He did not speak to me

about it, though he *did* say Deirdre had qualities. I was dreadfully afraid he might actually marry her. But no—he admitted she is cold. That would never do for Dick."

"What does he hope to accomplish in London?" the duchess persisted.

"I've no idea. Perhaps Lady Lenore could tell us. Oh, don't worry that she plans to meet him. *She* is going east to Dover; I heard her tell Chamfreys so."

"Rubbish. You have certainly gotten it wrong. No one goes to Dover," Charney replied.

"They do when they plan to go to Paris," Bertie retaliated. "I always go to Dover when I go to Paris. It is where the ship stops to take you across, you see."

"Aha! That explains it. The trollop is going to meet some man in Paris. That will be a relief to her husband, to have her carry on outside the country for a change. Can't imagine why you asked the woman here at this time."

"We had already invited her before you said you would come. One can't very well ask a guest to stay away, Your Grace. I knew her mama—Cora Eversley before marriage. The world was amazed when she got Lord Pitticombe to marry her, though she was a very nice girl. One can only wonder how Lenore turned out so. Not that she isn't pretty. Dickie says she looked like a French angel. It's supposed to be a joke, I believe—or perhaps he said it was a paradox. I wonder if it is Dickie she is meeting in Paris. Surely not!" she exclaimed, frowning.

"Now it is beginning to make some sense," Her Grace said. She had more than enough insults to keep her happy. "Leave me, and send my niece up at once," she commanded.

"Delighted, my dear duchess. If there is anything you require to be comfortable here in your room, don't hesitate to ask for it. I will be very happy to supply whatever you need to keep you up here. Where you are better off, I mean! The weather is dreadful downstairs, cold and drafty. I'll send Deirdre right up to you. Would you care for a book as well? We have lovely books, in all colors. French novels and poetry—oh, and plenty of dull sermons too, if you prefer. Of course you would prefer a sermon. Doctor Donne, the very thing, as dull as ditch water. So very elevating." She chattered her way out of the room, happy to know she had done as Dick would like her to do, being polite to the duchess. Only it was a pity she had let slip about London.

Within a very few minutes, Deirdre was mounting the stairs with all the enthusiasm of a victim on her way to the tooth drawer. She knew as soon as she opened her aunt's door and saw the sharp, wizened face of her aunt, the eyes alight with schemes, that something had offended the dame.

"You sent for me, Auntie?" she asked, going into the room.

"Oh, is it you, Deirdre? I hardly recognized you, with your hair streaming over your shoulders like a street walker, and half a dozen ribbons stuck in it. What are you about, eh? Trying to impress Belami, are you? You'll catch cold at that, my girl. You ain't his style. His mama was just telling me so. He has gone off to make arrangements to take Lady Lenore to Paris."

"Did Bertie say so?" Deirdre asked.

"She let it slip out, though Belami had instructed her to hide it. And by the by, you will not address your elders by their first names. I have been overly hasty in urging you to accept Belami's suit, Deirdre. You're hard up, to be sure, but you ain't quite desperate. We shall return to London tomorrow and set about finding you another parti. Pity we let Twombley get away."

"He will be back tomorrow," Deirdre said. "I'm sure his mother has it wrong. Let us wait and see,"

"It takes longer than one day to arrange a trip to Paris, my girl. But in case he does come back for Lady Lenore, we shan't be here. We shall leave today. I must be in London to arrange the payment for my diamond from his man of business." This at least brought a smile to her hagged face.

"But I really don't wish to leave just yet, Auntie," Deirdre claimed, her chin jutting forth in unaccustomed opposition.

"I don't recall asking what *you* wished, Deirdre. I shall do what is best. Well, I ain't a complete tyrant. No doubt Belami will call on us in London. I'll see he knows we are there."

"I'll tell the servants to start packing," Deirdre said happily.

She was upset that Bertie thought Dick was going to Paris with Lady Lenore, but he would have a chance to explain it.

"Excellent. And Deirdre, perhaps you would just step into the corridor and see if Lady Lenore is up yet. If she is, tell her to drop in to see me."

"Lady Lenore?" she asked, astonished that this blue-blooded lightskirt would be allowed to darken the duchess's door, let alone receive an invitation.

"That's what I said, isn't it?"

"Yes, ma'am."

Deirdre tapped on Lenore's bedroom door and was asked in. The lady sat in bed, surrounded by a sea of pillows, with a breakfast tray before her. Even in the morning before her major toilette, she looked quite lovely. This is how Dick would see her in Paris, with her eyelids heavy from sleep, drooping languorously over her green eyes, with her hair just brushed from her face, to puff in an ebony cloud of waves.

"Good morning, Miss Gower. To what do I owe the honor of this call?" Leonore asked with a sardonic little smile.

"My aunt wished to see you, if you were up and dressed. As you are not, I'll tell her."

"What on earth can she want with *me*?" Lenore asked bluntly.

"I—I have no idea," Deirdre said, conscious of the lie but unable to even hint at the truth.

"This is worth getting up for!" Lenore exclaimed, and popped out of bed. She threw a pink silk dressing gown over her shoulders, tucked a pin in its front to cover her bosoms, and went pattering down the hall, with Deirdre following fast at her heels.

"You may leave us, Deirdre," the duchess said, her tone regal, her eyes flashing, her lips pinched into their most condemning scowl at the untidy spectacle before her. "Kind of you to come, Lady Lenore. Have a seat. I wish to speak with you. Run along, Deirdre," she repeated when Deirdre showed a tendency to dawdle.

The meeting was brief. Within three minutes, Lenore opened the door and wiggled back to her room, tossing her head in amusement. What a Turk the old lady was, to be sure. But there was no need to truckle to her. She had not corroborated the charge that she was going to Paris, but she wouldn't satisfy her to deny it either. If they thought to keep Belami on that tight a rein, they were sunk before they were launched.

"What did she say?" Deirdre asked, running into her aunt's room as soon as she heard Lenore's door close.

"Brazen hussy! She said she saw no reason to discuss her private plans with me. She said if I wished to learn Lord Belami's plans, I should ask *him*. She would have denied the charge if it were untrue. She's going with him certainly. I cannot tolerate this degree of dissolution in our family, Deirdre. Send Lady Belami to me at once."

Bertie didn't know whether she was angry or delighted when she fled the door ten minutes later, with her ears burning. But she knew it would be a wonderful relief to see the last of Her Grace's strawberry-leafed carriage. She was happy to hear the engagement was terminated, but the manner of it would not please Dick. He was a bit touchy about being called a rake and a

knave, and as to the charge of not being a gentleman—
well, she would not tell him that one for a few months
yet. It wouldn't do for him to punch a duchess in the
eye, especially not this particular duchess. She ought to
have done it herself, though.

She took her revenge by not appearing to take leave
of the duchess and Miss Gower. She left word with
Snippe to tend to their wants, whatever they may be,
but Her Ladyship was lying down and did not wish to be
disturbed. She had her view of the departing carriage
with very little disturbance, as her window looked on
the drive down to the main road. There was a bad moment when it seemed the carriage was bogged down,
but Bertie implored the Almighty, and her prayer was
answered. The grooms got out and pulled the carriage
over the rough spot.

Bertie's attention span was not long. Within ten minutes there were other occurrences to distract her from
the broken engagement and the duchess's huffy departure. There was Uncle Cottrell and a few of the other
guests deciding to leave too, in case the storm blew up
again. There were cooks and housekeepers and other
servants to consult with, for the remaining guests still
had to be fed and entertained, even if the duchess had
gone pelting off in a great pucker.

Pronto Pilgrim had taken the decision he would be
jogging along to London, if the party was over. Neither
guest nor hostess found anything ridiculous in his telling her he had had a wonderful time, the best party
he'd been to in years, by Jove. Chamfreys was stomping
around in an ugly mood, and Lady Lenore was pes-
tering her for a timetable for the mail coaches east to
Dover. Through all her turmoil she was visited, from
time to time, by the sad-eyed image of Deirdre Gower,
who sat twisting her fingers silently in the background
while old Charney ripped up at her. And just at the end,
Deirdre had accompanied her to the door and said ever
so softly, "I'm sorry, Bertie." That was thoughtful of

her. Perhaps that was the quality Dick had seen in her. He had said she was cold, but he had begun warming her up.

Chapter 17

✳✳✳

The duchess's diamond was returned to her by Lord Belami, accompanied by a Bow Street Runner. By a quick stop at the *Morning Observer* before ordering her carriage to Belvedere Square, Her Grace had ensured that the announcement of her return to London appeared in the next morning's paper, where Dick had read it with considerable surprise. Mrs. Morton also read it with surprise, but with more glee than anything else. She immediately called her carriage and had it slog through the streets, to relay her findings at the traveling agent's office.

The only course open to a proud duchess in defeat was ennui.

"So kind of you to call, Mrs. Morton, but it is stale news to me. It is precisely the reason I have decided to terminate my niece's bethrothal to him. A sad rattle of a fellow. Even his own mother can do nothing with him.

There is half the problem, to tell the truth. Lady Belami is not fit to run a house."

It was a keen disappointment to Mrs. Morton, but she assuaged it by a quick call on half a dozen other friends, who were not so well informed.

When Belami entered half an hour later, he found Her Grace pouring over Debrett's *Peerage of England, Scotland, and Ireland* in search of fresh quarry.

He sat at ease in Her Grace's mustard-colored saloon, on a puce—her favorite color—sofa. "I was having my bags packed to return to Beaulac when I read of your arrival. Why did you not send me a message?" he asked, all unaware that he had sunk to new depths of disgrace. He directed his remark to Deirdre, but it was her aunt who replied.

"I have explained all that to your mama," she said in her stiffest tone. "We have terminated the engagement, Belami. Thank you for returning my diamond. I shall take it to Love and Wirgman's to make sure it is genuine. I never caught on the other was glass; I shan't be so credulous again."

"Terminated the engagement?" he asked, dumbfounded. So dumbfounded that he did not recognize even a trace of infamy in her decision to have the diamond authenticated. She had intended a prime slur in that remark, intimating that he had stolen it and replaced it with more glass.

"Deirdre, what is the meaning of this?" he asked, staring across the room to Miss Gower, who had seated herself in the shadows—no difficult place to find in that gloomy chamber.

"You heard my aunt," she said in a small voice devoid of expression.

"But why?" he demanded, wheeling to stare at the duchess. "What caused this turnabout? You were eager enough to have me a day ago."

"Eager?" the dame asked. "It comes as news to me that accepting an offer constitutes eagerness. I was most reluctant to give my consent and only did it conditional upon your behaving yourself. I may not have said so explicitly, but any man of sense knows that he must be on his best behavior during the period of betrothal."

"But I *have* been on my best behavior."

"That's what I was afraid of," the lady said tersely. "When your *best* behavior includes what yours has included, Lord Belami, there is no point in thinking you will make a fit husband for a Gower. One trembles to think what your worst might encompass."

"I had nothing to do with stealing the diamond. I got it back for you. I have apologized for being late for the party. Deirdre accepted my apology," he said, looking to her for some verbal reinforcement. But she only sat pleating the skirt of her gown into neat folds with her fingers. She didn't even raise her head to look at him.

"There are other things not necessary to be mentioned before young ladies," the duchess said, and arose to see him out.

"May I see Deirdre alone?" Belami asked.

"No, sir, you may not. I do not run the loose sort of establishment your mama runs at Beaulac."

"Deirdre!" Again he turned to her. She looked at him this time, but her cool glance gave him no pleasure, and no hope.

"I'm sure you have arrangements to make, for Paris," she said, and rising up, strode past him into the hall.

"I'm not planning to go to Paris," he called into the hallway.

She ignored him. She climbed the stairway sedately, with her head high and her hand trailing along the bannister, as though she were only going up for a shawl or a book. Her lack of undulation might have given him a hint she was holding herself in, but he was too upset to notice it.

"What lies have you told her?" he demanded, turning a black eye on the duchess.

"Are you daring to call me a *liar*, sir?" Charney gasped.

"Yes, madam, I am. A liar and a cheat, and a damned ungrateful guest, to cast slurs on my mother's house."

"I am not casting *slurs*. I tell you to your bold face you are a blackguard, and your mama a peagoose, to have that licentious woman under the same roof as innocent girls. You have wanted out of this betrothal from the moment it was contracted, and you have gotten your wish. Now go, and don't darken this door again."

"By God, I wouldn't come back if you paid me!" he shouted.

He turned sharply on his heel, grabbed his coat and hat from the butler's outstretched arms, and stalked out, without waiting to put either of them on. The quantity of heat radiating from his collar made them quite unnecessary.

Alone in his closed carriage he argued with the squabs, saying all the nasty, clever, satirical things he regretted not having said to the duchess, till he had cooled down. When he was halfway to his own home, he pulled the check string and told the driver to return to Belvedere Square, but not to draw up the door. He was to stop the carriage half a block away from the house.

The duchess was so enthralled with the visit that she sat smiling to herself, instead of going abovestairs to pester Deirdre with the details. This left the niece alone with her bitter reflections. Her aunt was right. Dick was a confirmed liar. He would never do for her. Oh, but neither would anyone else, after having been in love with him. Very well, then, she would be a spinster. She was gazing with unseeing eyes at a book in her lap, with her mind far away, occupied with what might have been, when a smiling maid came tapping at the door.

"A billet-doux, miss," she tittered. "He's ever so handsome, your fellow."

With a wildly beating heart, Deirdre twisted the knot of paper open and read Dick's scrawl, not noticing it was written on the back of a betting sheet from Tattersall's. "I'll be at the circulating library at four this afternoon. If you still love me, be there. If not, please send a note to assure me this jilting is of your doing, and not your aunt's. Sincerely, Dick."

She promptly sat down and wrote a bleak note assuring him that it was entirely her own doing, then tossed the note into the blazing grate and went to tell her aunt she would be going to the circulating library that afternoon, if there was anything she could pick up for her.

The duchess nodded with satisfaction. Deirdre was behaving very properly, going about her business as usual. The heretical thought flitted through her mind that a *little* fit of vapors would not be out of place upon losing such a fiancé as Belami, but she could not condemn her niece for behaving as a lady ought to. The duchess, however, was busy with other matters: sending off for a jeweler to come and authenticate her stone, and reattach it to its chain. It must be returned to the vault, and before any of this, it must be reinsured immediately, before Carswell heard of the theft and increased his rate.

At three-thirty, Deirdre climbed into the carriage with the strawberry leaves and was trundled to the circulating library, where she arrived at three minutes before four, to see Dick pacing up and down in front of the door, looking out for her carriage.

Her heart flipped in her chest to see him, so tall and handsome, so dashing in his curled beaver and many-collared great coat. He hurried to the carriage and helped her to descend.

"You came!" was all he said, but the way he said it made up for the stilted words. His dark eyes glowed brightly and his head inclined involuntarily toward hers, till she feared she was to be kissed in the middle of the street.

"Yes. I—I wanted to hear what you had to say."

"What I have to say is, what's going on? What put this bee in your aunt's bonnet that I'm suddenly beneath contempt?"

"Let us go into the library," she suggested as a few heads turned to look at them.

"The carriage will be more private," he countered, and opened the door to enter with her. "It has to do with Lennie's going to Paris, I know. That was a ruse to get her to open up and tell me what she knew. I'm not going with her, Deirdre. Surely you knew that."

"You bought two tickets. Don't lie, Dick. A friend overheard you, and she heard you give Lady Lenore's name for one of them too. 'The very best rooms at the very best hotel,' " she charged, verbatim.

"Did she not hear me give Belfoi's name as the other occupant? He's staying at Boltons', near Beaulac. My groom spoke to him and arranged the whole. Lennie's not particular. She'll be happy to go off with anyone, even her husband. She'll take it as a famous joke, once she finds him there."

"Dick, you *didn't*! What a trick to play."

"Of course I did. I'm all in favor of marital fidelity, now that I am about to be leg-shackled myself. Darling, we *must* talk the old lady over. Or rather, *you* must. My vile frame is not to darken her door. Can you explain it to her?"

"She'd think it was monstrous, what you've done. She's so very dogged when she takes a notion into her head. Besides, she'll think you only made up the story about Belfoi going to con her. She's very suspicious."

"Hmm," he said, tapping his fingers on his knees. "I can't really count on Bertie to help me either, as she's dead set—that is—she's not completely convinced . . ."

"Keep on. There's room for another toe or two in your mouth. I know she doesn't like me, and even less after my aunt was through with her."

"I don't want to hear what she said. One problem at a time. Do you think it will put her in a better mood, having her diamond back?"

"It doesn't seem to have. Ripping up at Bessler might help."

"Good God, don't tell me she's going down to Newgate to see him?"

"No, she's having him brought to the house, to revile him there. If he's sufficiently self-abasing, she might plead for leniency. He was always so obsequious to her that she rather likes him. Bidwell hasn't a hope of her clemency. She isn't even having him hauled to the house for a scold," she said, slipping her hand through the crook of his arm.

He smiled down at her, patting her fingers. "Bessler, eh? Too bad we couldn't have him . . . Why not?" he asked, and a beatific smile took possesion of his features.

"When is he going to see her?" he asked.

"Tomorrow morning. Why?"

"Good, then I'll nip down and visit him now. Pronto has landed in town. I'll have him call on your aunt and you. What time is Bessler arriving?"

"Eleven, but what—"

"Right, eleven. If Pronto behaves even more foolishly than usual. just go along with him. Do whatever he suggests, outside of suicide."

"I wish you will tell me what you're planning."

"I am planning to marry you, dear heart. What strange capers love leads us into. Go home and have your summer gowns aired. It will be warm in Italy."

"Dick, she won't agree, and I cannot like to run off the Gretna Green, to be married over the anvil, like a runaway seamstress."

"They prefer a Fleet wedding," he answered, and pulled the check string. When the carriage stopped, he placed a quick kiss on the side of her mouth and opened the door.

Before he got out, he turned to her with a quizzical smile. "Whoever thought it would end like this? Going to Newgate, a little tinkering with the spirit, if not the letter, of the law, clandestine meetings—I had no notion you were so ramshackle, Miss Gower, or I would have married you sooner. Does it bother you much?"

"Oh, Dick, you're not going to do anything *horrid*, are you?" she asked fearfully.

"Don't ask. Do you want to go back to the library?"

"I suppose so, but what—"

"Don't start any long books. You won't have much time for reading after tomorrow. I love you."

He was gone, running after a hackney cab. He was going to see Bessler in prison, but for what purpose, she had not figured out. Did he plan to smuggle him out of prison? And if so, what good would that do? She was baffled, but confident that Dick would think of something to bring her aunt around his thumb. He always did.

In her turmoil, she forgot to pick up a pair of kidskin gloves for her aunt's dresser. Hers had mysteriously vanished at Beaulac. Deirdre suspected they were in Dick's laboratory, liberally grimed with soot from the flue.

Chapter 18

❋❋❋

Pronto frowned heavily at Lord Belami, and shook his head.

"Include me out," he said. "I'll be demmed if I'll go visiting the duchess when I don't have to."

"You won't have to spend two minutes with her. I want you to get Deirdre and the prison guard out of the room, so that Bessler has a few minutes alone with her. Just a few minutes, that's all I'm asking."

"And you'll give me the first foal Diablo sires for free if I do?"

"Absolutely gratis."

"You said *free*."

"That too. I'll even let you use my Marabel as the mare. It'll be a perfect match, Pronto. He's a long-legged, deep-chested goer, and she's big and sweet-tempered. A nick of the right bloodlines."

"Who's to say the foal won't get his hot temper and

her ungainly size? A wild big brute is what I've already got. Took a bite out of me last night."

"Then we'll match them again, till it comes out right. Or you can use him for stud with one of your own mares. Now, after you leave the duchess's place, come directly to me and tell me how it went."

"I don't like it. Demmed if I do. Daresay it's illegal, if the truth was to be told."

"It won't be—ever."

"You won't get Bessler off scot free, to send him off to Austria, if that's what you're thinking. He'll do time right enough. Bidwell as well."

"Bidwell can hang for all I care. He's the cause of half my woes."

"No, *you're* the cause, Dick. Of more than half. Might go so far as to say Bidwell is the cause of a quarter. So you mean to settle down with Deirdre Gower after all, then, do you?"

"No, I mean to go on exactly as I always have, but with Deirdre beside me."

"Hmph, I wonder how she'll like your Widow Barnes."

"Naturally that part of my life will have to be curtailed."

"Curtailed? It'll be abandoned, my boy."

"That's what I meant, naturally."

"Won't be natural to *you*. Then there's your gambling. Can't stay out for two or three days and nights handrunning, with a wife at home waiting for you. Squalling kids, bills . . ." He shook his head in dismay.

"I'm sick to death of gambling, if you want the truth. I'll be happy for an excuse to decline such offers."

"*Decline* them? They was always your own idea!"

"Well, I have better things to be doing now. It's time I settled down. I feel ready for it, Pronto. There comes a time in a man's life when he's fed up with squandering his time and money, and wants a more settled life."

"Aye, it'll be settled all right and tight. You and Deirdre and Charney."

"She won't be living with us."

"Then there's the investigating that'll have to go as well. Deirdre won't care for that."

"Yes, she will. She won't mind that," he said with a soft smile. "She's not the sort of girl you think she is at all, Pronto. She's very easy to get along with. Has a good sense of humor, and such pretty eyes—did you ever see such long lashes? The way she walks, too."

"Believe I'll be toddling along now. When you start on the eyes and the undulating, it's time to go. Eleven tomorrow morning at the duchess's place. Draw off Deirdre and the guard. See what I can do."

"Come directly back here after. I want to know how it goes before I barge in on them. Remember, now, you tell her Lord Belami is very upset with the broken engagement, and note carefully what she has to say. Have you got that all straight?"

"I ain't a jughead. Of course I have it straight. You've told me a dozen times already."

"I'm depending on you. Don't fail me."

"Have I ever?" Pronto asked, offended.

"Yes, always," Dick replied with a desperately worried look. But there was no one else to do this unusual job for him.

"I won't fail you. Diablo and Marabel," he muttered, sauntering toward the door. "Ain't sure I wouldn't prefer my own Snow White mare. Other hand, could set her up with Jenkins' Arabian. Black and white—wonder how it would come out. Wouldn't want a zebra. Look a dashed quiz."

Chapter 19

✳✳✳

To ensure gaining admission to the duchess's saloon, Pronto Pilgrim arrived ten minutes before Bessler and the guard from Newgate. He feared that if he came after them, he would be put to wait in another room. Those ten minutes were the ten longest of his life. It seemed an eternity that he sat looking at the wizened, glaring little face of that angry aristocrat. Nothing he said could bring her into humor, and all because she had fingered him as Belami's friend.

"Dandy little saloon you have got here, Your Grace," he essayed, gazing at the mustard walls, the puce sofa, the age-dimmed pictures that formed dark blurs on the wall.

"Little?" she asked sharply. "I have one of the largest saloons in London. What brings you to call on us, Mr. Pilgrim? Not bearing any message from your friend, I trust."

"Eh? Nothing of the sort. He didn't put me up to it, did he, Deirdre?"

"Oh, no. I'm sure he did not, " she assured her aunt with every semblance of truth.

"How would my niece know whether he did or not, idiot?" Charney asked.

But the greater part of her mind was on the tirade she would roll over Bessler. She had honed and polished her insulting epigrams till they gleamed. Such trite phrases as "adding insult to injury," "*not* a gentleman," and "not what I would have expected from one I deigned to call my friend" rolled around in her head. That would set him groveling. If it went off well, she might write the whole up in a letter to a newspaper editor, or at least to her sister in Scotland, to keep for posterity.

Pronto was surprised to hear her say, after a longish pause, "Actually, Mr. Pilgrim, I am very happy you are here. It will be best to have a gentleman in the room when I meet Bessler. One cannot call a guard from Newgate a gentleman. Odd that I did not think of it myself, but we have been very much at sixes and sevens, with this business of turning off young Belami, and of course finding a replacement."

He disliked the sharp, appraising gleam in her eye as she said the last. By the living jingo, the harpy was sizing him up! This was a difficulty never in his wildest fears foreseen.

"Don't look at me!" he warned her.

But it was Deirdre's spontaneous giggle that relieved his mind. A glass of watered wine was served, to wile away the remaining eight minutes. This was considered even a worse cheat than stuffing a pair of kings up your sleeve, but he drank it anyway, and held his glass out for a refill. You didn't have to try to talk when you were drinking. At last the long-awaited knock at the door sounded.

Pronto's job now was to remove Deirdre and the guard from the room, but how was this to be accomplished when the duchess had just said she was happy to have him present? Why should she fear Bessler, when he'd run tame in her house any time these two years?

The duchess did not arise from her seat. She sat like a queen, pointing with one finger to the chair Bessler was to occupy, directly facing her. When he was seated, she pointed the finger to the door, and nodded her head to the guard, who took up his spot there.

"I little thought, when I invited you into my home, and made a friend of you, that we should one day meet under such circumstances," she began.

There was a good deal more to come. After the "insult to injury" passage of her rant, Pronto began to feel she wouldn't notice if he sheared off. On the other hand, she was supposed to notice it, wasn't she? Or was it only Bessler who had to notice?

"Believe I'll just be toddling along now," Pronto said softly, and arose form his chair, tossing his head wildly to Deirdre to follow him.

She took her cue and began to tiptoe from the room. "Deirdre, sit!" her aunt called without ever removing her accusing stare from Bessler.

"I—I'm getting water for Mr. Pilgrim, Auntie," Deirdre replied, looking to see if this excuse passed muster.

Bessler, cagier than the others, went into his performance to distract the old lady. "Duchess, what can I say in my own defense? Nothing. My conduct is inexcusable," he began humbly, his head falling on his chest.

"I must agree with you, sir," Charney agreed, loud and clear, and completely forgot her fleeing niece and Pronto.

The next obstacle in their path was to lure the guard from the door. When Deirdre was informed of this by Pronto, she took over the project. "It will be best to allow my aunt a moment's privacy with Herr Bessler. There is no escape from the saloon. Why don't you have a glass of wine while you wait, sir?" she asked politely.

"Watered," Pronto warned him from the corner of his mouth.

"If she's watered, I expect I could handle a drop without losing the use of me wits," the guard said happily, and trailed into the hallway. He was seated at a table with a glass and a decanter.

"Why are we here?" Deirdre asked Pronto. "Dick didn't tell me."

"No secret to it. At least he didn't say so. Old Bessler's agreed to mesmerize your aunt, and make her agree to Belami and you getting shackled."

"No!" she gasped.

"Are you against it?" Pronto asked. "By jingo, I've failed again. It was *you* I was supposed to get mesmerized. Maybe I could do it myself. I must have a touch of animal magnetism like the rest of them. Got something to do with putting your thumbs in the person's eyes—or is it the temples?"

Deirdre was not listening. She was not laughing out loud, but there was such a gleeful smile on her face that Pronto, for the first time in his life, found her not only pretty, but demmed pretty.

"Listen," he said suavely, "what I said in there about not angling for me after turning Belami off—well, if you really think we could make a go of it, wouldn't mind giving it a shot."

She was not quite listening. Another difficulty had occurred to her. "Pronto, what if Bessler mesmerizes Auntie into not pressing charges against him? He might, you know."

"We know it. Dick says it's just a chance he has to take. He'll go along with whatever old Charney decides to do on that score."

Within seven minutes, they knew what she had decided to do. She came to the door with a smiling Bessler. "I'll do what I can for you, Doctor," she promised, "but you were naughty to steal my diamond. You can't expect to get off scot free." That he was again "Doctor," as before being discredited, was a good omen for him. Doctor Bessler had been a greater pet even than Herr Bessler.

"You are too kind. An angel," Bessler said daringly, and lifted her age-speckled hand to his lips. As his head arose, he winked broadly to Deirdre and Pronto.

The guard hopped up to put his hand on Bessler's elbow and usher him to the waiting carriage. "Back to the cell for you, mate," he said cheerily.

Pronto, referring to a slip of paper he carried in his pocket, rehearsed his next line. "Lord Belami is upset with the broken engagement," he said, then read it again and added, "*most* upset, actually. Sorry, Deirdre. Easy to fall into the habit. See how it happened to you."

"Good-bye, Doctor. Or perhaps it is only *au revoi revoir*," the duchess said with unaccustomed benignity. "What's that you say, Mr. Pilgrim? Belami upset over the broken engagement? He is not the only one. Truth to tell, we are all upset. I believe I shall give that young man another chance. I shall drop him a note, and tell him he may call on us. Say, four this afternoon, Deirdre, if that suits you?"

"Noon would be better," Deirdre said quickly. She was not sure how long the mesmerizing would last.

"I'll tell him. It happens I'll be seeing him the minute I leave here," Pronto told them. "I'll nip along to his place right now," he said, peering at his note. "Yes, that's right. *Go directly to my place*," he read. "Well," he said. wiping his brow, "seems I did something right for once. Dick will never believe it. Er—what are you going to do about Bessler, Duchess?"

"I shall not press charges against him. The law will demand some payment, but without my urging, retribution will not be so severe as it might have been. Perhaps I shall recommend he be returned to Austria. Each country must handle its own wrongdoers."

"It'll be for England to handle Bidwell, then," Pronto said with satisfaction. Then he rammed his curled beaver on his head, smoothed his jacket, and headed for the door. "And if it don't work out with you and Dick, Deirdre, remember what I said." With a theatrical bow, only slightly marred by bumping his head against the door, he was off.

It was still only ten minutes before twelve when Belami was admitted to the mustard saloon. "Your Grace," he said with a wary smile as he was shown in. "So kind of you to permit me to come and make my apologies."

"Faith, hope, and charity—the three virtues, and the greatest of these is charity. I seem to hear those words running through my mind like an echo. You would not have heard, Belami; I have decided not to press charges against Doctor Bessler. Of course, a report has been filed, and once the law has gotten hold of him, he cannot expect to get off free. I have decided to deal charitably with you as well, my lad. Do you still want this niece of mine?"

"Very much, ma'am," he said with a glowing glance to Deirdre.

"Very well, then, here is the bargain we shall strike. No more women, no more gambling—beyond what is gentlemanly, I mean—and no more investigating. Is it agreed?"

"Auntie, you didn't say anything about the investigating!" Deirdre exclaimed, casting an apologetic look to her reinstated fiancé.

"It has a low touch to it that is undesirable, dealing with all manner of person," Her Grace insisted.

Deirdre looked to Belami, who smiled innocently, then turned his charms on the duchess. "You are absolutely right, as usual. I shall send a note off to the Prince of Wales this minute, telling him I will be unable to find time to handle his case."

"The Prince of Wales! You never mean it! What is he up to that he requires your services, the rogue?" Charney asked, eyes alight.

"It is extremely confidential, as you may imagine. I don't know what will become of him, poor man." He shook his head sadly and looked up through his long lashes to see how this was taken. The whole town knew Charney doted on Prinney.

"No, no! Naturally you must help the Prince. That is another matter entirely."

"Why, Your Grace, I do not place his case higher than your own," Belami told her.

Seeing he was laying it on with a trowel, Deirdre spoke up. "When you stop to think of it, it was Lord Everton's daughter that Belami first helped. It is really shocking how so many respectable people are requiring assistance."

"Very true," Her Grace said sadly. "And there will be no objection to your lending a hand to our own sort, Belami."

"I had no intention of hanging up a shingle," he assured her.

"I expect you youngsters would like a few moments alone now, to make up. Five minutes, that is all I can allow," she said severely. But as she hobbled beyond their view, a genuine smile lit her face.

"One of her virtues is slipping," Belami said when they were alone. "She doesn't place much faith in my behavior."

"Dick, tell me all about it," Deirdre said, going to join him on the sofa.

"There's nothing to tell. When I learned the duchess was through with me, I had the notion of using Bessler's mesmerism."

"Not *that*! I mean about Prinney being in trouble. I wager it is over a woman."

"But don't you want to hear how I struck the bargain with Bessler, to help him if he would help me?"

"I heard all that from Pronto long ago. Is it his wife, Princess Caroline?"

"I didn't say it was a woman."

"What else could it be?"

"Miss Gower, we have five minutes to be alone together. You've already wasted one."

"I suppose you want to make plans for the wedding."

"No, *ac*-tually, I wanted to do *this*," he said, pulling her into his arms.

Beyond the door, the duchess sent the butler off for champagne, before bending down to peek in at the keyhole. She revised her minutes to three when she saw how little Belami had reformed his libertine character.